Praise for *Between Wild* … *and Ruin* Trilogy:

"This first installment in Jennifer G. Edelson's Wild and Ruin series offers brisk, crisp, entertaining scenes of romance, and builds to a surprising, satisfying twist . . . Line to line, *Between Wild and Ruin* is crisp, brisk, and appealing. Edelson pairs superb descriptions of nature and her characters with sharp, memorable dialogue. The exchanges between protagonist Ruby and her aunt Lydia have a pleasurable warmth and verve; Ruby's many scenes of flirtation with her three romantic candidates, meanwhile, are tense and tender . . ." —The Booklife Prize

"What could be a corny premise turns into an exhilarating, fun ride in Edelson's adept hands. Her characters are smartly drawn, and readers will easily identify with Ruby, a strong yet insecure young artist on the verge of adulthood, who is still recovering from her tragic past . . .Fans of *Twilight* and modern fairy tales will fall in love with Ruby and root for her eventual romance."—Blue Ink Review (Starred Review)

"*Between Wild and Ruin* is a stunning story of legends, romance, and destiny with themes of starting over, small towns, beauty, and community . . . Edelson perfectly breathes new life in mythology by honoring the oral tradition of a small community and the ruins that bring to life Ruby's destiny." —Manhattan Book Review

"Highly recommended to mature teens through new adult and adult audiences, this is a story that lingers in the mind long after its final revelation." —Midwest Book Review

"Author Jennifer Edelson's on-point dialogue, multicultural characters, and atmospheric setting, keenly conveys New Mexico's rich cultural roots and narratives, weaving a story that incorporates both folklore and romance into an engrossing, unforgettable YA story." —Ryan Sprague, Author and Host of 'Somewhere In the Skies' book and podcast, co-host of the The CW's 'Mysteries Decoded.'

"Descriptions of the New Mexico landscape are rich and atmospheric, arousing the senses with references to the scent of smoke and juniper, the predatory roar of mountain lions, and the brilliant dazzle of stars in the desert sky . . . The writing conveys a sense of timelessness, making it easy to believe Ruby's sense that the land is spirit-haunted and that Leo, the handsome young man she encounters near the ruins, is somehow connected to it all." —Clarion Forward

"An intriguing historical tale and an over-the-top lovequadrangle romance." —Kirkus Reviews

"The paranormal aspects of the tale are credible and richly steeped in traditional lore, and the plot is finely crafted . . . *Between Wild and Ruin* is most highly recommended." —Reader's Favorite (5-Star Review)

WILD OPEN FACES

JENNIFER G. EDELSON

Wild Open Faces

Published and distributed by Bad Apple Books
Santa Fe, NM 87506

For information regarding bulk buys, or educational, promotional, or business inquiries, please contact BadAppleBooksinfo@gmail.com

Publisher's Cataloging-in-Publication data

Names: Edelson, Jennifer G., author.
Title: Wild open faces / by Jennifer G. Edelson.
Description: Between wild and ruin trilogy, book two. First trade paperback original edition. | Santa Fe [New Mexico] : Bad Apple Books, 2021. | Also published as an ebook.
Identifiers: ISBN 978-1-7335140-1-9
Subjects: CYAC: Romance fiction. | Paranormal Fiction. | New Mexico—Fiction. | LCSH: Paranormal romance.
BISAC: YOUNG ADULT FICTION / Romance / Paranormal.
Classification: LCC PN3448.L67 | DDC 813.6–dc22

Cover design by Estella Vukovic
Interior design by Allusion Publishing

To my Mom and Dad, for giving me the gift of love and curiosity. But especially to my Mom. If not for her, I'd still be tripping through the wilds trying to pull this all together.

CHAPTER ONE

PLATITUDES

LIDDY HOLDS HER HAND OUT ceremoniously. She introduces Mr. Tezca, briefly ticking off his accomplishments like she just brought Einstein home for dinner while we stand in the foyer. As she tells us about Mr. Tezca's work at various excavations throughout Mexico, Torrance scowls, surprised, I think, by Liddy's enthusiasm.

Liddy isn't one to gush. And Torrance isn't the only one who's uncomfortable with her overblown introduction. Equally unimpressed, Ezra looks a little like Liddy just introduced him to Stalin. Still, he manages to keep it in check when he says 'hello' to our guest, frowning at me somewhat more discreetly than Torrance, who is outright scowling at Liddy.

Mr. Tezca T. Lipoca, former star graduate student at the Universidad de las Américas, in Puebla, Mexico, current new star professor in the University of New Mexico's Anthropology Department, holds out a hand, waiting for me to take it.

Smiling, I shake his hand, startling at the tiny rush that moves up my arm when our palms connect. "It's nice to meet you," I say congenially, trying to ignore Ezra's sour expression.

"Liddy tells me you'll be a freshman with the Anthropology Department next fall," Mr. Tezca says.

"Right." I tug my hand back, tucking it into my jeans pocket. "Focusing on archeology."

"Wonderful. You can intern full time at the Holy Ghost excavation after you graduate. Until then, you can intern on weekends."

Briefly, I glance at Ezra. His expression is priceless; he looks a lot like he just swallowed a jug of turpentine. "I . . . I didn't even know there was an opening. Thank you," I stutter. "I mean, holy cats, I'm not even sure I'm qualified."

Ezra mouths *holy cats* at me. When I shoot him my curtest *cut-it* look, he presses a hand to his mouth and shakes his head.

Mr. Tezca sizes me up. "You say it as though you have some limitation."

I swallow, thrown by his answer. From Ezra's mouth, I'd shrug the comment off or smack him in the head. But Mr. Tezca's face is as straight as it was when Liddy sang his praises. If I had to guess, I'd say the man never cracked a smile in his life. Which is too bad. Because he's handsome enough, even when he frowns.

"It depends on how you define limitation," I admit. "I've never seen a real dig in progress, much less participated in one."

Mr. Tezca raises his top lip just enough to look cocky. It reminds me a little bit of Ezra. "Liddy's told me much about you. I don't doubt you're fit for the job."

I sigh, unclamping my teeth. "Thank you, Mr. Tezca. I appreciate the opportunity." Spending the summer working with the University on an archeological dig at the Holy Ghost site sounds infinitely better than working at a big box store in Santa Fe.

"Call me Lee."

"Lee?"

He nods, and his suddenly glorious smile makes him infinitely more accessible. "It's easier. *Tezca* . . . Americans always make it sounds so dull."

Torrance snorts. He looks perturbed, but instead of commenting, he cocks his head at Liddy and pretends to bang it against the wall—not very subtle at all.

"Come on." Liddy holds her hand out, motioning everyone toward the kitchen. "Let's eat. I made paella."

Sticking close to my side, Lee follows me to the dining table, moving like a rivulet of water. He doesn't walk so much as flow. At the table, he pulls out a chair, holding it while he motions for Liddy to sit down. Liddy blushes, prompting Torrance to raise an eyebrow at the bowl of rice he's started dishing out.

"Tell me, *Lee*." Ezra settles in next to me proprietarily. "The dig, it's out near Holy Ghost Creek, right? Any thoughts about what you've uncovered yet?"

I know what Ezra's thinking. The University just unearthed the site a month ago, and they've already dug up enough bones to fill a graveyard, not to mention a handful of curious altars. The dig is so close to the Pecos pueblo, Ezra's sure they've uncovered a Pecos holy site, a place of worship belonging to his ancestral tribe.

Lee stares at Ezra for an uncomfortably long moment before answering. "It's still open to debate. But it's an amazing find. It's, how do you say . . . a mixed bag? At the moment it looks like numerous indigenous cultures overlapped there. And it's tempting to think we've found Aztlán, the Aztec's fabled ancestral homeland. But it'll take years to confirm, if indeed that's even possible."

Ezra's eyes briefly turn a brighter gold, and I know enough to guess that Lee's managed to rub Ezra just shy of angry. "It's a Pecos site." He sits back and crosses his arms over his chest.

Lee nods. "Perhaps in part. If it is Aztlán, I'd presume to say the Pecos were likely an offshoot from one of its seven original tribes."

Ezra frowns at him. *The site belongs to the Pecos.*

I smile, pretending Ezra's voice isn't as loud as a bell in my head. *Probably.*

He knows I'm right.

More reason for me to take the internship, Ezra. I'll be your eyes.

Ezra nods and asks Liddy to pass the bread. *Maybe. But I don't trust him.*

I laugh, then pretend to choke. The last thing I want is for Lee to think I've lost my marbles and retract his offer.

Torrance slaps my back. "You all right?"

"Yeah. Spicy." I point to my cleared plate. "Sorry."

I eye Ezra. *Jealous, much?*

No. Suspicious.

He squeezes my leg under the table, but I brush it off and shoot him a look.

I worry, Ruby. Don't make a capital case of it. It's not like I don't let you live your life.

LET ME live my life?

Whatever. Jesus.

Ezra is Ezra, which means he isn't always the most sunshiny person to be around. But we almost never fight. And he almost never questions me, even though I know that he knows I haven't been one-hundred percent honest about my visit with Mom 2.0 last winter.

Across the table, Lee scoops up a large portion of paella and dumps it on my plate, even though I didn't ask for seconds. "Eat," he says, "and it's marvelous," he tells Liddy. "I'd love the recipe, if you'd be so kind."

Liddy wipes her mouth daintily, smiling at Lee like a schoolgirl. "Of course." She plops another helping onto her own plate, then giggles. "It is good, isn't it? I don't remember the last time I ate so much."

I can't remember either. Liddy is no bird, but she's already scarfed down four sizable helpings. Come to think of it, I've made a dent in the dish as well; we all have. Liddy's paella has turned us into gluttons, all of us except Lee, who's swallowed each small bite like a delicate socialite.

After cleaning his plate for a final time, Torrance throws his napkin on the table and sits back, clearing his throat. "Don't forget to file that final site permit, Lee. Better find a name for it and come up with an agreeable description soon. I don't want to hassle with the state, about as bad as I don't want your dig to end up a contentious tribal matter."

"The small assortment of bones we've found so far hardly makes the site ripe for tribal interference," Lee informs him. "And most of the bones are that of animals."

"Small?" Ezra snorts.

Lee and Ezra lock eyes. "I understand your concern," Lee says. "And I assure you, the University is going to great lengths to guarantee the safe handling of each artifact it uncovers. At this juncture, however, as I've already made clear, we're as unsure of *what* we've uncovered as we were when we first uncovered it."

Liddy leans toward Lee at the same time Torrance grumbles *load of crap* under his breath. "Tell us everything," she says, her pitched voice near purring. "What have you uncovered?"

Ezra scowls. *Even Torrance sees Lee's full of it.*

At least the University's protecting the site. You've been down there, Ez. You said it yourself, it looks like everything is being handled by the book.

Since the find, Ezra's been down to the site at least a half dozen times. All at night, always in lion form. And the only bad thing he's had to say is that the rope they use to cordon off the area isn't thick enough.

Ezra grimaces, but he rubs my leg under the table again, listening while Lee talks in this slick but convincing way about the artifacts they've uncovered. Unlike Liddy, who's suddenly become a fan of giggling, neither Ezra nor Torrance seem to like Lee much. And I get the whole dig issue. Why the idea—that it might be a Pecos site—has Ezra wound up. But I don't understand why Lee rubs them *both* so raw. Far as I can tell, Lee is a pleasant, if not charming, person.

Lee gesticulates over the table as he continues to describe some of his team's finds. Listening, I'm near mesmerized by his voice and the fluid way he waves his hands around while he speaks, not to mention the graphic tattoo circling his forearm. Beneath his rolled-up black oxford a colorful snake, or maybe a serpent, sheaths his skin, its head and body spiraling from his wrist up his arm like a boa constrictor.

Lee catches me staring, briefly glancing down at his forearm before meeting my eyes. "Spellbinding, isn't it?"

"Yes, actually. Sorry." I blush.

"Never apologize for being curious." His eyes linger on mine. "Do you have any?"

"Me? No." I nod at Ezra. "But he does."

Lee briefly shifts his focus to Ezra, raising an eyebrow as if to dismiss him. Then he turns back to me, smiling mischievously before flipping his arm back-side up, exposing the belly of his forearm. The snake circles a smoother expanse of skin. One of its middle coils bulges where the outline of another distinct animal takes shape, like the snake is digesting a bird. Lee taps it. "Change through conflict."

Off to my side, Ezra sniffs. And I don't blame him. I can't help it. The tattoo is stunning, but it doesn't stop me from rolling my eyes. *Change through conflict. Right.* "It's beautiful," I say politely.

Lee sits back in his chair. "I think so."

Through the kitchen's bay window, the setting sun casts russet light over Lee's head, igniting jet black hair that in turn offsets irises so dark, they almost swallow his pupils. Unlike, Ezra, Lee's face is imperfect, but those imperfections almost make him more interesting to look at. His striking countenance, and refined, almost noble features still probably make plenty of women swoon. *I* feel a little flushed, and I'm not even remotely interested. And *Bingo*! I think I just answered my own question. Ezra and Torrance are both jealous.

Silently, Ezra snickers. *Really*?

Seriously? Stay out of my head unless I invite you, Ezra.

Ezra and I haven't perfected our whole telepathic communication thing, but we made a deal after discovering we can hear each other's thoughts. Something like, 'always knock before entering each other's inner sanctum.'

Ezra shifts toward me. *What's up?*

What's the deal?

What are you talking about?

Digging around in my head without asking?

His dark eyebrows meet over his nose. *I wasn't.*

Across the table, Liddy stares at us inquisitively. "Is there something you'd like to share, Ruby?"

Ezra looks at me. "Is there?"

"No . . . no," I stutter, confused by Ezra's response. "I'm sorry, Liddy. I think I just ate too much."

The air around the table feels thick. Like the taint of at least one of our suddenly foul moods poisoned it. Abruptly, Torrance stands up, almost knocking his chair over. "Ezra why don't you and Ruby take off. Go get some air."

Ezra mumbles his response. "Best idea I've heard all day." He grabs my hand off the table, asserting himself for Lee more than anyone. "You done?"

"Yeah. I could use a cup of coffee," I mumble, shooting Ezra a look. Pulling my hand from his, I shove my plate sideways and stand up, rapidly pushing my chair in to punctuate my answer. After a second, Ezra, then Liddy, follow suit, though Liddy is a hundred times daintier when she stands. She slides her chair against the table quietly, rather than slamming it like Ezra.

While I say my goodbyes, thanking Lee profusely for the internship, Ezra stands back, eyeing us suspiciously. Lee takes my hand, shaking it gently before grazing my knuckles with his lips. When his mouth meets my skin, my chest thrums with an unexpected wave of adrenaline.

Beside me, Ezra shifts restlessly. *What the hell?*

"I'll see you next Saturday," Lee tells me. "Eight a.m., on the dot."

Liddy stands to my other side, gripping Torrance's arm. Before I can say anything, she answers, "She'll be there," almost too enthusiastically.

CHAPTER TWO

SOME PEOPLE WE DESPISE

AS LIDDY, LEE, AND TORRANCE wave goodbye from the porch, Ezra just about throws me into his truck. He speeds down the driveway, taking the back roads into La Luna too fast for comfort. Between the adrenaline still coursing through me and the tension rolling off him, I feel a little uneasy.

"That was weird," he finally says.

"You think?"

"And you're mad at me, *why*?"

"For poking around in my head."

"I wasn't." He makes a face at me.

"I heard you, Ezra."

"Heard what?"

"You snickered and made a comment when I told you to get out of my head."

"Except I didn't," he answers flatly. "I promised you I wouldn't, and I don't. Not unless we're both on board. Or I have something to tell you I don't want to say out loud."

I believe him, but I also know I didn't imagine it. "I heard something."

Ezra frowns, then laughs. "Chalk it up to too much paella?"

"Oh, God, I've never eaten so much." I clutch my stomach, groaning inconsolably.

He grabs my hand off my stomach and twines our fingers, pulling me closer across the bucket seat. "You really want that job?"

What I want is to talk more about why I worried he was snooping. But I also know the discussion is a slippery slope. Ezra will ask me about the ruin and my mom again. He always does. And since I've been avoiding talking about both things since last December for a reason, I have no desire to open that can of worms now. Especially when we're both already sort of crabby.

"Seriously? You have to ask."

"You'll have to work with him all summer."

I shrug. "Lee seems fine. I'm sure I'll manage."

The spindly trees outside sway south with the spring winds as Ezra steers, keeping his eyes glued to the cracked blacktop as if it's prone to suddenly disappearing. He's too silent. And a too-silent Ezra means his wheels are in overdrive.

"You don't like Lee much, do you?"

He looks at me, his right lip following his right eyebrow as it hooks into a wry question mark. "What gave it away?"

"Ezra, he's doing Liddy a favor. I'll bet she pushed to get me the internship. You don't have to like him, just don't be rude, all right?"

Ezra pulls into a parking spot near Margarita's while simultaneously asking, "Margarita's okay?"

"Fine. Did you hear me?"

"Yes, Ruby. I'll be nice."

Inside, we choose a booth near the back of the quiet diner. Ezra drops down on a worn vinyl seat and pulls me in next to him. He throws an arm around my shoulder and kisses my cheek, burying his nose in my hair. "Don't be mad at me."

"I'm not. I just really want that job and I don't want it to be an issue."

"Ruby," he says softly. "Look at me."

I twist on the seat, hitching my chin to meet his stare.

"I don't like him. You're right. But I like you. And I want you to be happy. If you really want the job, then you should take it. I'll get over myself."

It takes a lot to hold back my smile. Ezra is so . . . *Ezra* sometimes. Like he's trying on 'nice' for the first time and still isn't sure how to wear it. "You know you look like you just swallowed a porcupine."

His face is immobile, and I know he's trying hard to bite back a smile. "And?"

"And thanks for trying." I kiss his nose, snuggling into his side. "It means a lot to me."

"You mean a lot to me," he answers quietly.

I order us coffee when Daisy stops by. We settle in, and I ask Ezra about the house he just started restoring over in Villanueva for a client, losing myself in his obvious passion for the project while he talks. Ezra started taking on home restorations this spring, and already, word's gotten out. He's got a gift, and people are beginning to take notice.

While Ezra talks, I stare at his face. He's been working in the sun a lot and his normally dark hair looks gilded. He reminds me of a John Singer Sargent portrait, and even when he stops talking and frowns at me, I feel like singing the freaking "Star-Spangled Banner."

"Hey, what's up?" I hold up a hand, hovering it over my coffee. "You suddenly look like someone just stomped on your puppy."

"I don't have a puppy," he says, subtly motioning across the diner. "I just don't like the way that guy is staring at you."

I turn, ready to ask who. Other than us, with the exception of a few old timers and the man sitting alone at the counter staring pretty seriously at our booth, Margarita's is almost empty.

"Do you know him?" I ask Ezra.

Ezra's frown etches creases into his brow, reminding me of how just months ago, it was scarred and grey, as if scorched by fire. It's been almost six months since Ezra shed the face I first fell in love with, and I'm still getting used to it. I still have to repress an urge to say, 'huh' every time I see him.

"Ruby." He snaps his fingers at me.

"Sorry," I shrug. "But do you?"

Ezra gives me the once-over. His eyes change, turning a golden violet as his jaw softens. "No. But he's been staring at you since you sat down. You're a catch, no arguing it, but there's something off about him. Plus, he's old enough to be your father."

Turning in my seat again, I intentionally hold the man's stare. He's like a darker version of an all-American jock, circa Barbie and Ken, but his bottle-glass green eyes swallow his otherwise handsome face, homing-in on our booth unrelentingly. And Ezra is right, he's definitely staring at me. As I stare back, a sharp pain rips through my head, sending my palm to the bridge of my nose.

Ezra pulls my hand away. "Ruby?"

"My head," I mumble.

Ezra massages my temple and a blur slides into the booth across from us. A pair of cowboy boots meet the seat beside me, one propped on top of the other. I hear a soft plunk and look up just as Angel's hat settles in the space beside him. "Evening." He smiles, lurching forward. "Ruby, you all right?"

Ezra drops back in the booth. "It's her head."

"What a freaking weird night," I sigh.

Angel squints at me, silently waiting for one of us to elaborate.

Ezra makes a face. For months now, he's been making efforts to socialize with Angel, Racine, and Las Gallinas. He's been nothing but his version of 'nice' since the day we swore to stay together despite my mother's warning last winter, and since then, Racine especially has warmed up to him. But persuading other people to give Ezra a chance hasn't been as easy, and until just recently, Angel was the sharpest thorn in Ezra's side.

"We had dinner with Liddy, and Torrance, and some University stooge," Ezra finally explains. "Strange guy."

"That's right. Torrance said you guys had company coming over. Some new professor or something?"

I nod, rubbing my forehead. "He offered me a job at the Holy Ghost dig this summer."

"The new site?" Angel sort of frowns. For a second, he seems far off, like he's mapping out the dig in his mind.

Squinting at him, I shake my head *yes*, tapping Ezra's knee to get his attention. He's still staring at the man across the diner.

"Did you take it?" Angel asks.

"She took it," Ezra mumbles, keeping his eyes trained on the counter.

Angel cocks his head at me as if asking *what's with him*?

I shrug. "That guy over there keeps staring at me."

"I've seen him before." Ezra nods to his left toward the front of Margarita's. "Do you recognize him?"

Angel and I glance toward the counter at the same time. Only, when my eyes meet the man's again, I can't look away. He holds my gaze, somehow piercing my refuge. Seriously, it's like his eyes are parasites burrowing straight to the center of my brain.

"Ruby?" Ezra toggles my arm.

I rip my eyes away. Across the table, Angel is so still I see his pulse throbbing just below his collar. He mashes his lips together, then rubs his mouth, then sucks in his breath. His wide eyes look alarmed. "What the hell is *he* doing here?"

Ezra leans across the table toward Angel. "Who is he?"

Angel drops his boots on the ground and sits up straight, almost defiantly. Nodding at the stranger across the diner, he says, "My father."

CHAPTER THREE

BEDAZZLED

RACINE MOANS AND DROPS HER backpack on the lush meadow floor. Winded from trekking up the steep incline, she throws her arms out and lays down, spread eagle over the ground, crushing a clutter of wildflowers. "How in the hell did I let you talk me into hiking three miles straight uphill in freaking Hell's bells weather?" She throws an arm across her face dramatically.

"I don't know, maybe because you know it's more fun than sitting around the house doing calculus homework." I plunk down, pull a water bottle out of my backpack, and hand it to her. "And because you love me."

Racine half-sits, sucking down water from the bottle. She wipes her mouth with the back of her arm and sighs. "It's so pretty. I can't believe I've never been here before."

A few feet in front of us, heaping piles of crumbling wood dot the small dale, surrounded by skinny aspens, wildflowers, and craggy mountaintops. Formerly a miner's camp off a now defunct dirt road on the way to Mt. Baldy, the site sits in a narrow valley, on a strip of once-cleared land. At its apex, the earth seems to sheer away, dropping where the plane meets the sky.

"That's why you came with me. Because you knew it'd be amazing. That, and to get away from Marta."

"Imagine *her* hiking up here." Racine giggles at the thought of holier-than-thou Marta hiking anywhere. "She was super bent out of shape about Angel's dad showing up out of the blue. I mean, like he's *her* father or something. *Gawd*, she was an absolute monster today. I swear, lunch couldn't end fast enough."

Racine is so on point. The way Marta railed against Angel's dad having the gall to come back to La Luna during lunch earlier, you'd think it was her long-lost son-of-a-bitch-father who suddenly materialized out of the ether.

Racine squints up at a line of spindly birch trees growing in rows out of the verdant but rocky ground. "So, how is Angel doing?"

"I'm not sure. But he literally stood up and walked out of the diner when he saw his father. Like not a word. Nada. How weird is that?"

Racine moves her head against the ground, her long black hair catching on stubby blades of grass. "He was bad news, Ruby. I mean, I don't really remember him, but I heard enough growing up. It probably just freaked Angel out."

"The weird thing is, Angel didn't even recognize him at first. He walked right past him when he came into the diner. Anyway, I don't blame Angel, either. He told me about how his dad took off when he was four. I don't think he's seen him or heard from him since. It's not like there's any love lost between them."

Racine covers her forehead with a hand, blocking out the sun. When she tilts her head, looking at me with those deep blue eyes, I know exactly what she's thinking. Her face is an open book framed by blinking neon. "Wow," she says, raising her eyebrows for effect, "you're really protective. Like it's personal."

"I am protective. And it is personal. I hate seeing Angel look so hurt."

"That's not what I meant."

"I know what you mean, Ray. And there's a big difference between me and Angel. *I* never met my father. No one knows who he is, and as far as I know, he never made my mother any promises. I don't even know if he knows I exist. I have no reason to hate him."

"Uh-huh." She drops her head back and closes her eyes. "Well, if Angel needs anything, or if there's anything I can do, let me know. Marta said he's a mess."

"Marta's full of herself." Angel isn't capable of being a mess. He's just not built that way. A little off his game, maybe, but far as I can tell, he's angry on his mother's behalf more than anything. Not to mention, Liddy told me he wasn't thrilled to have to break the news to Torrance. Torrance hates Angel's father worse than Angel does. "Seriously, Ray, from what Liddy told me, I think Angel's more concerned with keeping the peace. If Torrance had his way, he'd run Angel's father over."

"Why do you think he came back?"

"No clue."

"Does Angel look like him?"

"Not exactly. But I mean, I didn't stare." Talk about an understatement. I couldn't even look at the man without feeling dizzy.

Racine speaks to the sky, shielding her face again with her arm. "Just wondering if Angel got those gorgeous green peepers from his dad."

"Gorgeous?" I raise an eyebrow at her.

"What? I'd jump him in a heartbeat if he somehow managed to tear his eyes away from you for a minute."

"Ray!" I squawk. "Really?"

"Seriously, the boy's still got it so bad. He acts all fine around you, but he's not. Trust me. Don't pretend you don't see it."

"I see it." I sigh and drop back beside her. "But that's not what I meant."

She gives me some side eye, turning her head just slightly to squint at me. "Yes, Ruby. Really."

"How come you never told me?"

She shrugs. "He's been one-hundred percent team Ruby since the day you stepped foot in La Luna. Guess I didn't see the point."

Flustered, I close my eyes and count to five silently. Yes, Angel still likes me. But our friendship is as real as it is important, and ever since that evening in his office just after we discovered that Ezra shifts, we've had this unspoken agreement—it's better for our friendship if we both just pretend that he doesn't.

"He knows I love Ezra. And he respects it. We've talked about it. We really are better friends now. He said it himself."

Racine snorts.

"I'm serious," I say seriously, working on looking as serious as possible.

"Then, maybe drop a few hints that I like him?"

As quickly as it crosses my face, I try masking my frown. "Really? I mean, for real, should I?"

"Yeah, for real. It's worth a try, right?"

Racine and Angel. I love them both fiercely, but their names don't click in my mind smoothly. It's not jealousy—I don't think—but I just can't imagine them together. "I guess. If you really want me to."

"Such enthusiasm," she mutters.

I stare up at the sun, exactly the way Mom always told me not to. The bright light burns my eyes, and they water, but I force them open until it feels like they're melting in my skull. Slowly, I let my head fall sideways, away from Racine, blinking furiously. Off to my left, on the apex of the hill, a blurry plume of feathers races past a ruin that was once the old miner's hotel. From my periphery, the plume, now half obscured by an ancient, abandoned truck rusted from years of inertia, looks like a turkey's tail.

A turkey. Right. Because tons of turkeys roam the Glorieta Pass, Ruby. "Here, birdie, birdie." I gently hold my hand out to my side. "Come out so I can see you better."

Racine half-sits, nudging me with an elbow. "What's up?"

"Over there." I point sideways, up the hill.

She leans over my body, following my finger. "I don't see anything."

As she says it, the bird waddles out from behind the truck. In the open meadow, it stands as still as the woodpile beside it.

I sit up as it unfurls its plume again. "You don't see it?"

"Oh my God." She furrows her brow. "It's huge!"

Under the midday sun, the bird's feathers reflect black so deep and glossy, it's blinding. It waddles forward, looking straight at me as it gets closer.

"Hey, birdie, where'd you come from?" When the turkey waddles closer, dipping its head as if glaring at us for being interlopers, I add, "Didn't your mom teach you any manners?" channeling Ezra.

"Weird," Racine says.

Slowly reaching for my backpack, I unzip the middle compartment and pull out my camera. Adjusting the camera's F-stop so I can snap a picture to sketch from later, I look down at the monitor, trying to focus on the turkey's feathers. On my right, tall, skinny birch trees vanish up into the atmosphere, shooting off the screen. To my left, meadow grass and wildflowers wind up the hillside. But through the viewfinder, at least, the stupid bird has disappeared.

A shrill squawk pierces my eardrums. I look up from my camera in time to see a beak shooting forward, aiming for my cheek. Matching the bird's war call with my own shriek, I flinch, clipping the bird's face with my camera as its beak grazes my skin. "Ouch! What the . . ." I shoot up and jump back, kicking at it.

Dizzy from my abrupt about face, a strange kind of melancholy washes over me. The sun is oppressive; I feel hot and dizzy, and the heat suddenly burns up every ounce of my energy. I swoon and the bird shimmers, flexing like a rippling flag, shifting from opaque to transparent. It stands still as a statue as the hillside wavers around it.

"Stupid bird," I mumble, reaching out to steady my balance.

"Ruby!" Racine jumps up, grabbing me. "What the . . ."

The day shifts, darkening as the turkey's plume swells into an enormous, magnificent fan, blocking out the sun. It looks at me, tilting its head sideways again as if to say, *Stupid girl, look who's talking now,* before the bright sky peters out, fading to a dark stain. After a brief moment of muddy nothingness, an ethereal city made of rough-cut blocks sparkles under a purple sky, as if made of mica, perched high on the mountain above the trail, almost as though suspended.

Blinking furiously, I shove my fists at my eyes, and as quickly as the city appeared, it disappears, leaving a ghostly imprint against the sky. The day burns bright again, the sun grazes my shoulders, and the turkey takes off running toward the horizon.

"Did you . . ." I suck in so hard I wheeze. "Did you see that?"

"It freaking jumped you!"

Beads of sweat cling to my upper lip and cheeks. "I mean, the city?"

She frowns deeply. "What?"

"Oh, Ray, I don't feel so well."

Holding onto my shoulders, Racine sits me down. When she's sure I'm stationary, she scuttles around the meadow, throwing all of our stuff together. She adjusts my backpack on her shoulder, along with her own, then holds her hand out. "Can you stand?"

I take it, standing slowly. Every inch I gain makes my head pound.

When I'm completely upright, Racine touches my chin, gently pushing my head sideways. "Sucker really got you," she says, following it up with a *tsking* sound.

My face stings as she swipes a thumb over my jaw lightly, wiping something away. "Rabid turkey?" I try to joke.

"That's messed up." Her soft voice comes out pitched. She may not have seen the city, but I can tell she's still totally mystified.

Is this what Ezra meant when he said to keep my eye open for strange or unusual things? Freaking rabid turkeys?

Ezra is paranoid. And probably rightfully so. *Stay off the mountain.* It's his motto. But this hunk of forested shale isn't *the* mountain, just *a* mountain, one of many in the Pass. One of the handful I've explored since promising Ezra I'd stop hiking in my own back yard. Until now, it seemed relatively normal. For the last few months life has been relatively normal—at least compared to the Otherworld.

Racine and I walk slowly down the steep dirt trail, winding alongside a ribbon of creek in a tight valley between two mountains. Every twenty minutes or so, we take a break beside the stream, or against a tree, so I can sit and gather my bearings. Near the end of our hike, I stop at a burnt-out truck on the trail, resting against its rusty side. Racine checks my chin as I dig through my backpack for a half-full bag of Cheetos. When in doubt, junk food makes everything better. I munch and Racine putters around me like a mother hen, speculating out loud.

"Maybe it escaped from someone's ranch."

"Mmmm," I answer, licking my fingers.

"Or maybe it's wild." Her eyes light up. "Maybe there's a colony or something up there. I mean, it's pretty far up, who'd bother them, right?"

"Ranch." I frown at the ground. "Stupid thing had a lot of gumption. It wasn't scared of us."

"Probably," she nods.

The rolled up Cheeto bag crunches when I shove it into my backpack, rubbing up against my camera and sketchpad. I grab Racine by the arm, leaning on her the rest of the way to the car, listening to the last of my snacks crackle all the way down the widening trail. The inside of Racine's car is hot, warmer than the air outside, and the stifling heat is almost too much once we climb in. My head hurts, and I'm sticky, and though I know it's probably the heat that had me in a state up the mountain, mirage or not, I can't help wondering about the city on the hill.

On the way back to La Luna, Racine sings in Spanish, occasionally glancing at me sideways. She rolls my window down and my hair slips across my face, making its way outside, where it promptly tangles into a knot near my chin. "Hey," I yelp, pulling it into a ponytail at the top of my head. "A little warning, please."

"You looked overheated." She grins.

I laugh and realize my head isn't pounding anymore, though I still feel a little queasy. When I touch my face, and Racine notices my shaky hand, she holds up my water bottle and points down Main Street as we turn into downtown, gesturing toward the corner market where I first met Ezra. "You need more fluids."

Racine pulls up in front of the market and tells me to sit. She hops out, leaving the car idling. While I wait, I flip the visor down, checking out the thin scrape across my jaw. Of all the strange things that have happened to me since moving to La Luna, I can now add being attacked by a wild turkey to the list. But the strangest thing about it is how I'm not even really surprised. If living in the Pass taught me anything this last year, it's to expect the unexpected.

"So, real wild turkey or evil Otherworld spirit masquerading as a turkey?" I say out loud, chuckling to myself as I rub my forehead lightly. Because both seem equally as plausible.

"What?" Racine opens the door and plunks down in the car. She hands me a bottle of water and a soda.

"Nothing."

"You sure you don't have sunstroke? I could see you talking to yourself through the window."

I shrug, rolling my eyes for effect. "I'm the only one who listens to me."

"*Nice.*" Racine half-frowns half-smiles, then orders me to drink before pulling away from the curb. When she's satisfied that I've drunk enough, she picks up speed and drives me to Ezra's, dropping me off in front of the huge lavender bush near his workshop. "What are you guys up to this weekend?" she asks before I get out. "Want to see a movie tonight? You could invite Angel."

My plans with Ezra tonight involves two things, curling up with him in his room, and watching an old movie. My internship at the dig starts early tomorrow morning, and I want to get a good night's sleep, especially after the whole almost passing out after being attacked by a potentially rabid turkey thing. "Not tonight, Ray. I've got the dig tomorrow. But I can see if Angel's free tomorrow night."

"Yeah?" She smiles. "Okay, call me when you know."

Racine nods and blows me a kiss as I hop out, struggling to pull my backpack along. I wave as she backs down Ezra's long driveway, then tiptoe to his workshop, peeking through the doorframe before walking in. Startling him while he's being friendly with a power tool isn't going to earn me a girlfriend-of-the-week award.

"Hey," he says, with his back turned to me.

"How'd you know I was here?"

He chuckles and turns around, facing me. "I heard Racine's car."

"Right." I smile. "I keep forgetting about all your superpowers."

Ezra wipes his hands off on a dirty rag and walks over to the doorway. He pulls me against his stained jeans and gray tee, and digs his nose into my neck, inhaling deeply. "You've been hiking."

"Bloodhound." I swat at him playfully. "Guess it'll be useful if I ever go missing."

"*Ruby.*"

"I'm just saying."

"How about you don't." He grimaces.

"Go missing? Or say it?"

"Either." Gently, he touches the Band-Aid Racine stuck to my chin. "What happened?"

I shrug, looking just past his left ear at a large, restored mirror hanging on the wall, ready to downplay the truth. But what comes out is, "I bumped into the end cap at the market."

He laughs. "Poor end cap."

Surprised at my own lie, I nod. "Seriously, I took it down."

Ezra kisses my cheek and then my lips, lingering before moving to lock up his studio. He powers his tools down, scrubs his hands with vegetable oil to get the varnish off, and then wraps an arm around my shoulder, turning me toward his house.

"Ready for a movie binge?" he asks, maneuvering me from the studio, through the backyard, into the kitchen. When I shake my head *yes*, he adds, "Let's grab a snack. I made you chocolate chip cookies."

"For real?" As far as I know, Ezra's cooking skills only extend to BLTs, frozen dinners, and oatmeal. "Liddy told you they're my favorite, right?"

Facing away from me, he grabs something from the cupboard above the kitchen sink. Balancing a plate of cookies piled in a haphazard mound, he sets it on the counter, then nudges me to try one. "No." He shrugs, trying to mask a smile. "I've got you figured out."

I grin at him. It's not like I don't know that over the last few months he's been surreptitiously compiling a list of *Ruby's Favorites*. Ezra thinks he's being clever. But I've been on to him since the beginning. He does this thing, like he'll come up with a personal question, act as if it just popped into his head, and then tie it into whatever conversation we're having. Then, if he doesn't get an answer from me, or the answer he wants, he finds some way to finesse it out of Liddy later.

Graduation is in a month, and ever since I announced I'm going to the University of New Mexico this fall for sure, he's been subtly—or, at least, his version of subtle—trying to persuade me to move in with him. So far, Ezra has relied on his ingenious secret plan to learn all my preferences. And I love him for being so bad at being sneaky.

"Try one," he insists, looking at me curiously.

"I'm not very hungry, Ez." I smile and hold my hand out, squeezing his fingers when he wraps his sturdy palm around mine.

"Just one," he purrs, flashing a smile that manages to be both menacing and magnetic.

Maybe hiking in the heat for a couple hours killed my appetite, or maybe it was the stupid bird. Whatever the case, I have zero desire to ingest something sugary. But Ezra's smile, combined with the effort, make it impossible to refuse. I take a cookie, made more of chocolate chips than flour, and talk through a chocolatey bite. "So, out of the blue, you just happened to make my favorite cookies, and for no reason?"

"I had a reason."

"Yeah, what's that?

"They're your favorite."

"Mmmm, they're really good," I admit. "Can't you just suck at something once in a while?"

"It's not my fault that I'm perfect." He grins. "Want to take the plate upstairs?"

As Ezra reaches out to take a cookie, I grab the plate and run for the stairs, holding it tipped against my chest so the pile rests against my shirt. When Ezra realizes I've ditched him, he runs around the counter, chasing me as slowly as he can, so I can at least pretend I have the advantage. Because we both know if he really wanted to catch me, he'd be in front of me, blocking my way before I even left my chair.

At the top of the stairs, he grabs my shirt and snakes his other hand around my waist, pulling me back against him. I hold the plate in a vise grip, stretching my arm out as far as I can in front of me, losing a few cookies to the ground.

"No way. They're mine," I giggle.

"You're not a very nice houseguest," he breathes into my ear.

Ezra sweeps me up, balancing me above the floor in a princess hold while he walks. I screech my response, attempting to keep the cookies from sliding off the plate on the way to his room. When I yell at him to put me down, he laughs, holding on even tighter. Nearer to his bed, he reaches around me and swiftly plucks the plate from my hand, then drops me on the mattress. He holds the plate high over his head and grins down at me, cocking an eyebrow.

"What?" I ask coyly.

"You have the reflexes of a snail."

Simultaneously, Ezra manages to duck the pillow that glides past his head *and* put the cookie plate on his dresser without dumping a crumb. He jumps toward the bed and then he's gone, and I feel the mattress sink behind me. "Boo," he whispers, breathing on my neck before sending me to the ceiling.

"Jeez, Ezra!" I yelp, clutching my chest.

Ezra laughs and drags me back against his body, pulling me down on the bed. His face relaxes, and for a brief second his eyes shimmer, his irises swimming in purple before settling on gold.

I reach out and touch his cheek. "It's so much easier to read you when you let them go."

"And when I don't?"

"You're completely inscrutable."

He meets my stare. "I never hold back when I'm with you. I'm only inscrutable when I don't always know what I'm thinking myself. When I do, you're always the first to know."

I turn sideways, mapping his beautiful face, charting his perfect cheekbones, and nose, and lips.

"I love looking at you," he tells me.

"I was just thinking the same thing about you."

Ezra taps his head. "I know." Winding his fingers through my hair, he smooths it out, strand by strand on the pillowcase. "So, have you thought more about it?"

"About?" But I know. I know he wants me to make up my mind already about moving in with him. Like he somehow worries that the longer I take to decide, the less likely I'll be to commit.

"Waking up in this room. With me. Every morning."

The ceiling is my focal point, and I stare at it and breathe, feeling my muscles tuck around my ribs with each exhale. I want to be with him. Forever. But I don't want him to want me just because he's scared of what might happen if he isn't around to protect me twenty-four-seven. "I said I would when I'm ready, Ezra, and I meant it. I just want to wait a while. Maybe after first semester ends. Or after I finish my first year."

"I don't think I can wait that long."

"Why?"

"I miss you when you're not here." He grabs a pillow and curves his body around it, curling up like a child. "See this? This is me, pretending the pillow is you when I'm alone. She even has a name." He smiles wickedly. "Sapphire." When I burst out laughing, he pulls me close, rolling on top of me. "So, what do you think?" he asks, looking down into my eyes.

"I think I love you."

CHAPTER FOUR

SUGAR AND SPICE AND EVERYTHING NICE

EZRA RUNS A HAND UP my side under my shirt and his eyes change swiftly from amber to deep purple. Carefully avoiding my Band-Aid, he tilts my chin, kissing me so slowly his cashmere lips feel like a silk bubble. They linger and my nerves go haywire. I kiss him back, pressing against him until it feels like I might suffocate us both.

"So?" he asks, pulling away slightly. "Watch a movie, or fool around?"

I giggle, pulling him so close our noses nearly touch. "Watch a movie."

Ezra snakes his hand higher under my shirt, up my mid-back. He kisses my ear and neck, then singlehandedly unhooks my bra, running his other palm over my arm to my shoulders, leaning back as he pulls me upright. He sits up straight, balancing on his knees, and pulls off his shirt. And seriously, I want to die.

Ezra grins, and a swath of sable hair falls over his eyes. I blush, catching fire. Ezra could look like a shriveled-up beanstalk and I'd still be wild for him. But he doesn't look like a beanstalk, and his not looking like a beanstalk drives me crazy.

He kisses my collarbone, toying with the hem of my t-shirt before pulling it over my head. "Still want to watch a movie?"

I swallow and shake my head *yes*.

He leans forward, nestling his face in my hair, whispering in my ear. "Maybe afterwards?"

"Maybe afterwards, what?" I pull back, feeling a little lightheaded.

Ezra's eyes are a flurry of different colors. He runs a finger up my bare arm, stopping at my bra strap to give it a small tug. "If you're ready."

"Are . . . are you serious?" Ezra has been avoiding even talking about sex with me for months. We stalled somewhere around third base last January, and that's as far as we've gone.

He sighs and bites his bottom lip, worrying it with a canine. "You have no idea."

Swiftly, I slide my bra off, afraid he'll chicken out. "This doesn't mean I agree to move in sooner."

"I know," he whispers.

Ezra's eyes blaze a deep gold; he pulls me against his chest, and his skin feels warm and electric. I want him so much I can taste it, but I also sort of want to drop through a hole in the ground. When he was 'Ezra the Tortured,' I felt bashful, but never insecure. But compared to 'Ezra the Beautiful,' I sometimes feel like a freakshow.

"You make me so nervous," I tell him.

He kisses the edge of my chin near my Band-Aid, then my ear. "You're gorgeous," he whispers against my neck. "You know I think so."

Gently, Ezra lays me back against the mattress, leaving a small pocket of space between us. He kisses me slowly, bridging the gap until our bodies become a tangle of limbs. When I feel like my own need might suffocate me, I flip him over, moving to tug at his large, silver belt buckle before shucking off my own jeans. I straddle him, pinning him to the bed with my legs, slowly unlatching his belt. But when I pull at his button fly, a bolt of lightning pierces my head. I let go of him and smack my forehead, squeezing my eyes closed.

Ezra catches me as I push my palms against my eyeballs, tipping forward. He half-sits, balancing us both, holding onto my shoulders. "Hey." Keeping one hand on my arm, he brushes hair off my cheek, craning to see my expression. "Are you okay?"

I try focusing on Ezra's face, but my vision blurs and the room sort of spins. Reaching out, I feel for the mattress, then let my body tip over, falling out flat beside him. With both hands, I cover my face, blocking out the light. "My head . . . I think I might . . ." before I can finish, I lean over the side of the bed, literally projectile vomiting across his wood floor.

Ezra leans over me, pulling my hair back out of my face, holding me so I don't tumble face-first off of the bed. With a steady grip, he holds me until I'm done throwing up, then pulls me against him. "That's probably the most extreme reaction any girl has ever had to me," he says, making light of my sudden barf fest. "If you're not ready, Ruby, you could've just said so."

Keeping my eyes closed, I hold up a hand, trying to shush him. All I know is that I still don't feel very steady. "Maybe it was your cookies."

Ezra hugs me for a few moments, then gets up and disappears before coming back with a wet towel. He wipes my face, props a few pillows under my head, and lays me back gently against the bed, topping me with a blanket. Before I can thank him, he rushes out of the room again, returning with towels he uses to clean the floor.

When he's through, he lays down on the bed beside me, turning on his side to see me better.

"Are you okay?" he asks.

I moan my response.

Ezra strokes my cheek and chin. "Too much sun earlier on your hike?"

"Migraine?" I shake my head, completely flabbergasted. Whatever it was, the bolt came out of nowhere. Speaking through my arms, I mumble, "I'm so humiliated."

He laughs softly. "Stranger things have happened."

"I'm half-naked, Ezra. And I threw up on your floor. Right when . . . you know. So romantic. I'm guessing the next time you touch me will be right around never."

Ezra props himself up and moves my forearms off my face, peeking down at me. "Hey, look at me." When I squint up at him, he says, "You don't feel well. That's not your fault."

"I ruined it."

He sighs, then smiles. "Ruby, I'm at your disposal. You pretty much own me. Besides, I'm male. A little throw-up doesn't change that I'll always want you."

"I'm sorry. I don't know where that came from. But I wasn't feeling well earlier, either. It's sorta come in waves since we left Mt. Baldy."

"As long as you're okay now, I'm good." He wraps an arm around my waist, pulling me closer.

Gently, I push him away. "Sorry, Ez. Do you have another toothbrush I can borrow?"

Ezra gets up and walks to the bathroom, disappearing behind an old oak door for a moment. He returns, waving a green toothbrush, which he hands to me along with a pair of old sweats and a tee. "You should have told me you weren't feeling well. I would have put you to bed and fed you chicken soup while we watched a movie."

"You don't have chicken soup," I say, changing into the clothes he gave me.

"Cookies and bacon, then."

"Ugh," I moan, flopping back down on the bed.

Ezra crawls beneath the covers and bundles himself around my body, resting his head between the crook of my neck and the pillow. He strokes my arm. "Think you'll make it to the Holy Ghost site tomorrow?"

I nod, loving how his hair sweeps my cheek as I do. "I'll drag myself down there, vomit and all if I have to. I really want that job."

He leans over and turns off the bedside lamp. Light from the setting sun colors most of the room, but the bed melts into the shadows. "Try to get some sleep, then."

"It's only like, eight thirty."

Ezra pushes me on my side and starts kneading my neck and shoulders. "Just try. I'll stay with you. I'll read a book or something once you fall asleep. And I'll call Liddy and let her know you're staying the night."

Snuggling back against his chest, I cover my eyes with the corner of his comforter, murmuring *okay* into the sheet. My head still feels fuzzy—extra sleep will probably do it good. But I also know I should probably just tell him about the turkey before I drift off.

"Ez, have you ever shifted into a turkey?"

He chuckles beside me. "No, do you want me to?"

"I saw a turkey on the trail today. For half a second I thought it might be you."

Ezra is quiet for a moment, and I feel him toying with the sheet behind my back, twisting it into knots against my skin.

"You think wild turkeys live in New Mexico?" I ask him.

"I know they do."

Ezra is so quiet. The room is so quiet. And my head is completely full of muck right now. If he wanted to, he could walk right in. *Do not think of that city on the hill, Ruby.*

"But?" I ask hesitantly.

Softly, he presses a finger against my temple. "You're doing something in there. I feel it. Pushing me out for some reason."

"Headache," I mumble, "remember? My brain feels like a pulsar."

He wraps an arm around my chest, pulling me back tighter against him. *Promise me?*

Admitting I hear him means admitting my mind is keener than I just owned up to. What if I say *yes* and spring a leak? What if the strange shimmery city I saw earlier, even if it was just a heatstroke induced hallucination, seeps out with my answer?

"I'm trying to keep you out of my head," I admit, unsure why I'm trying to hide anything from him. Ezra is usually the first person I want to tell everything to. "Or maybe not keep you out, but keep my thoughts in."

Suddenly, it's as if I backed into the arms of a statue. "Why?"

His warm breath tickles my neck, reminding me I am lying in bed with someone I love and not some stranger. I *can* talk to him. "When I saw the turkey, for a second, just a second, I saw like, like this city on the hill. Like a phantom city. One moment it was there, the next it wasn't. But my head was pounding, and it was really hot outside. Racine thought I had sunstroke or something."

"You weren't going to tell me?"

"I wanted to." Slipping farther under the covers, I push a hand against my forehead. "I was going to. I don't know why I waited."

He sighs so quietly I only feel it. "All right."

"That's it?"

"What else do you want me to say? I'm sorry you don't trust me."

"I do trust you."

"Then, why does it seem like you're always working so hard to keep me out?"

My eyes water, betraying my efforts to stay collected. "I don't. Most of the time, unless it's something big, I just don't want to worry you. You're seriously like the Jewish grandma I never had, as it is."

I want him to laugh, but he doesn't. Instead, his grip around me tightens. "If you trusted me, you would have told me outright, and then let me decide for myself how to feel."

"That's not true. Just sometimes, you act like every little thing is a sign. Ezra, occasionally an apple is just an apple." Throwing the cover off my face for emphasis, I turn and squint at him, shielding my eyes with both hands to block the searing light.

He frowns at the ceiling. "It bothers me that you lied to me."

I sit up, holding my head between my palms, squeezing my skull more to fend off tears than to keep the pain at bay. "I didn't lie. I just told you. You're getting worked up about something I didn't do."

He looks up at me with a blank face; even his eyes are static, stuck on amber. "An apple can just be an apple, but if you don't tell me it's an apple to begin with, as far as my mind's concerned, it could be a watermelon."

I touch his arm, hating keeping anything from him. Knowing I haven't been one-hundred percent honest with him about what Mom 2.0 said back at the ruin last winter already makes me feel like a terrible enough person. "Please don't be mad."

"You saw a turkey and a ghost city."

"Yes."

"And *then* you got sick?"

"Well . . . yes."

"And you don't think I should worry?"

I don't think he should worry, but part of me doesn't believe the two are just strange coincidences either. I don't blame Ezra for going somewhere I would if the tables were turned.

Ezra pats the bed beside him curtly. I lay down again and wait quietly for his hand to find mine. "I know you, Ruby. When you tell me not to worry, it's usually because you *are* worrying. When you tell me things are fine instead of good, it's usually because you can't say they're great, which means something's off."

While I argue with myself about how to answer, he faces me again, digging through my every layer with his blazing gold eyes. "You're tired. Let's just talk about it tomorrow."

"Do you still love me?"

He sniffs. "That's the stupidest question you've ever asked me."

Ezra's mouth pulls tight before he closes his eyes. As I lie next to him, watching his jaw flex, I try to drift off, despite the tension rolling over his body. Ezra said I don't trust him, and I denied it. But as he works to hold his anger in, I realize that while I've been trying to persuade Ezra to trust me for months now, somewhere buried deep inside, there's the smallest part of me that isn't sure how to completely trust him.

Despite my efforts to ignore the things Mom 2.0 told me at the ruin last winter, her warning has slowly been nibbling away at me for months. I love Ezra, but when I let myself think about it, I worry that because I'm a True and he's a Watcher, there's a tiny part of him that will always shut me out no matter what he says. And I worry a tiny part of me, because of the Otherworld, and my mother, and all the things I'll never really know, will let him.

CHAPTER FIVE

HOLY GHOST AT FIRST LIGHT

EVEN FROM A DISTANCE, LEE stands out. Though he has a slight limp I hadn't noticed before, his lanky frame glides between the dig's boundaries effortlessly, stopping to gesture wildly at something near Angel's feet.

"I wonder why Angel's here?" I point down at him standing on a berm.

Ezra shifts his truck into neutral. He shrugs but doesn't turn off the engine.

Ezra's been quiet all morning. I feel like I should apologize again for throwing up on his floor, among other things, but being the new kid on the dig is messing with my nerves. Combined with my still-stuffy head, I'm just better off keeping my mouth shut. "Torrance said he'll pick me up later this afternoon. Should I call you when I get home? Maybe Angel and Ray can join us for a movie?"

"Sure." He turns toward me, throwing an arm over his headrest. "How do you feel?"

"Bad."

"I mean your head."

"Yeah, I meant my head too." I sigh.

Ezra's smile is small and tight, but at least it's a start. He shrugs toward an area near a silvery sliver of creek that's cordoned off, where Angel and Lee are now obviously arguing. "Looks like fun."

"Want to come check it out with me?"

"Not really."

My eyes burn, but I'm not sure if it's because I'm tired, or worried Ezra is still angry. "Okay. Well, wish me luck?"

His hand brushes my cheek. Gently, he tugs my chin toward him, avoiding my Band-Aid. This time, when he smiles, his eyes light up. "You'll be great." He leans forward and kisses my temple. "Just keep an eye on Lee, all right?" When I nod, he pulls something out of his glove compartment. "Here." He hands me a small bag of Cheetos. "For later."

Gripping the bag like he just handed me a diamond ring, I grin like a goon. Some people live for fancy dinners and goopy poetry, but I'm the lucky girl who landed a guy who knows enough to console me with my favorite junk food. "You're amazing." I kiss his cheek before opening the passenger door. "Thank you."

He winks. "Call me later."

I nod and hop down from the truck, throwing my treat into my backpack as I make my way over hard-packed clay and glittery dirt through the site, over to Angel and Lee near the babbling creek. Walking up behind Angel, I place a hand on his back. "What's up?"

Lee stops gesticulating and looks at me cheerlessly. "Someone disturbed the site last night. And Mr. Ruiz here isn't taking it seriously."

I bite back a smile, winking at 'Mr. Ruiz' while I wait for him to explain. Angel rubs his chin, looking more than put out. "You've got one broken pot, a ragged hole in the ground, and a set of animal tracks in the mud there." He points to a leveled, slightly terraced area of dirt and wilted flowers. "*Someone* looks more like an animal."

I glance down at the tracks and the patches of dead chickweed surrounding them. "Whoa. A big animal," I add.

Angel shoots me a look. "At any rate," he turns back to Lee, "it's hardly enough reason for us to assign an extra man to the site. The University hasn't put in an official request yet, but even if it had, we just don't have the extra staff to secure the dig every night."

"Mr. Ruiz, the loss of even one artifact is enough; it can hinder years of studies. Do you have any idea what we're doing here?" Lee narrows his eyes, not really expecting an answer. "No, I'm quite certain you don't."

"Freaking intellectuals really piss me off," Angel mutters at the ground. He looks up at Lee, meeting his eyes. "Why don't you enlighten me?"

Lee leans in, intentionally invading Angel's space before speaking, mirroring Angel's arrow-straight, better-than-six-foot frame. "Legend has it, the Aztec came from seven shamanic tribes that in the beginning, lived in seven mystical caves somewhere between what is now Utah and Mexico before forming one council."

"Like the twelve tribes of Israel," I interject without thinking.

Angel and Lee both stare at me, though where Angel looks confused, Lee looks delighted.

"Sorry," I bite my bottom lip and raise my hand, "too many years of Hebrew school."

"Yes, Ruby," Lee says wryly. "And like your twelve tribes in Israel, the mythos here in the West has its seven tribes uniting to rule over Aztlán, the Aztec's homeland prior to what is presumed to be the Aztec migration down to Mexico." He pauses and the rising sun ignites his dark irises, turning them a reflective, almost silvery onyx. "Based on the artifacts we've found buried with some of the bones so far," he sweeps his finger in an arc between a boulder and the rocks littering the ground in front of us, "there's a better than good possibility this is that site."

"*Fantastic.*" Angel spits on the ground.

Gross as it is, I know Angel; he spit to drive his point home. When he's truly angry, all his refinements fall by the wayside. "So, you're what, digging up magic wands and witches? That's just what we need around here, a brand-new set of ghost stories."

Angel glances at me, and I know he's thinking about Ezra.

"Mr. Ruiz," Lee says calmly. "It's a legend. While Aztlán itself may actually exist, it does not mean Aztlán was really enchanted. Townsfolk," he mutters, shaking his head. "I suggest to you, Sheriff, that all that glimmers is not, indeed, gold. Many a culture rose and fell on wives' tales and embellishment."

"Lee," I say, excitedly. "We're so close to the Pecos Pueblo. If this is Aztlán, do you really think the Pecos and Aztec could be connected?"

Lee holds his hand out, motioning me nearer. "Everything is connected, Ruby," he says, almost conspiratorially. "In one way or another. Now, shall we get to it?"

I blush and walk closer, energized by the possibilities. Angel stands up even straighter, almost like he's daring Lee to make a move. He frowns at me and clears his throat. "I'll talk to Torrance. That's about the best you'll get right now, *Mr. Lipoca.*"

Lee dismisses him with a slight wave. "Quite fine. That's all I want."

Angel shakes his head at me when Lee turns away. Smiling sympathetically, I mouth *I'm sorry.* Lee isn't doing a good job of endearing himself to La Luna's male population, but then it took me almost a year to acclimatize to small-town customs.

"Hey, Angel," I pause before following Lee up the hill, "want to catch a movie with me and Ez, and Racine tonight? We can talk more then."

He shakes his head. "I told my mom I'd stop by Rojo later."

"Oh, maybe we could all go together."

Angel looks perturbed, maybe because of Lee, but more likely because I asked him to come out with me and Ezra. Still, he nods *yes*. "Call me when you get home."

As Angel walks off, Lee stops up ahead on the dirt path to the dig's makeshift headquarters, impatiently waving at me to follow. When we reach the main workstation—really just a tent pitched on a brush-speckled berm with a cooler, a metal shelving system, and a few chairs and tables beneath it—he stops again, nodding at me when I catch up. "Do you think I pulled it off?"

"Pulled what off?"

"Árbol que cr*ece torcido jamas su tronco endereza*."

I shake my head and shrug, smiling apologetically. "My Spanish skills don't apply to people who speak faster than I can interpret."

His expression is flat, which makes him hard to read. "It means, *trees which grow bent never straighten out*. From the beginning, always take charge of your site. Do you think that came across to Mr. Ruiz?"

"If you're asking if he thinks you're a jerk, yeah." I quickly cover my mouth, surprising myself. "I mean . . ."

Lee grins, amused by something, possibly me. He fiddles with the pendant around his neck and lifts his chin. "You speak your mind."

"My mind could have been politer. Sorry."

His sudden laugh seems to come from the rolling, cholla-dotted hills around us. It's deep and commanding, and echoes through my ears like a gust, almost like it broke from the wind to reach me. Embarrassed, I look away, fiddling with a set of calipers on the metal foldout table next to us. "Angel's really smart, Lee. You're in charge here, but as long as you act like you think you're superior, you won't get far."

He considers me, taking in my face as if mapping my psyche. After an eloquent nod that conveys absolutely nothing, he steps out of the tent toward a partially dug-up plot, motioning for me to follow. Crouching down, he dusts a flat but fractured plate buried in the reddish-brown dirt with his fingers, then holds up a small, sable-haired paint brush. "Here, start with this. The first step is to gently unearth the top and sides." As he leans forward over the mostly buried dish and patch of shriveled grass surrounding it, the pendant around his neck swings out. It glints like a mirror, like his eyes, reflecting sunlight.

"What is that?" I ask, pointing to it.

"Obsidian."

The black disk, secured by a silver snake twisted around its edges, looks like a smooth, polished rock. It's flat, but its optically disorienting surface makes it appear deeper, like a lagoon, and I can't help staring. Crouching beside him, I reach out, rubbing the pendant between my fingers. I move it back and forth, catching glimpses of the scrubby hillside and brilliant blue sky reflecting off its surface before stopping to look into it, at myself.

"It's like a mirror," I tell him.

Lee wraps his fingers over mine, cupping the pendant and most of my hand in his palm. "Imagine it's a mirror to your soul, Ruby."

His warm hand prickles against mine, transferring heat that spreads up my arm in a rush. I pull my hand away, swallowing a heaping dose of embarrassment. Suddenly, my mind is completely blank. All I know is, even at a distance, it still feels like he's touching me. Mumbling something about having to pee under my breath, I break away, nearly running up the rocky path back to the tent. Lee is a little much. But he oozes this odd charm that seems out of character for someone so young, and the fact I notice is unsettling.

At the tent, after a few deep breaths, I introduce myself to Lee's right-hand techie, Michael. As friendly as Lee is odd, Michael uses a little plot of dirt, in a box on the table, to show me how to use the brush Lee gave me to unearth pottery. Then he sends me to the graded area nearest the tent, site number five. For the next few hours, except for when Lee stops to check on my progress and I basically pretend to ignore him, I brush in circles around the plate, alternating between staring out at the perfect indigo sky and the delicate black and red-banded artifact at my fingertips. I refuse to let myself think much about Lee again until late afternoon, when Torrance drives me home and tries to pick my mind about how my day went.

"You're awfully quiet for a Brooks," he teases as we pull out onto the frontage road.

"Just thinking about the dig."

"Good day?"

"Yeah. Or . . . I think I'll like it, if that's what you mean. Lee's weird, but maybe it's because he hasn't been at it long. Michael told me he's like the youngest professor in the Anthro Department. Anyway, I'm sure I'll get used to him." I smile at Torrance, whom I affectionately dubbed 'Tordy' behind his back after he moved in last month. Honestly, Liddy and Torrance may as well share the same name. Turns out they're like the left and right halves of the same, super-awesome person.

"Angel mentioned they exchanged words this morning."

"Lee was being a jerk. Something went through the dig. An animal. He wants you guys to get someone out to watch the site at night, and I get why he's worried. But he definitely could have been nicer about it. You should really tour the site. Some of the things they've unearthed are amazing. I mean, they're irreplaceable."

Torrance pulls up our driveway and turns the car off. Inside the house, he throws his keys in the bowl near the front door and plops down on the couch, kicking his cowboy boots up on the coffee table. "Don't get mad, kid, but Angel wondered if it might have been Ezra. He says there's tracks around the site that look like a large cat's, and we all know Ezra's been uptight about the dig from the start."

For about a second this morning, the same thought crossed my mind, but Ezra was with me all night. And those tracks are huge. Ezra in cat form is nothing short of spectacular—he's enormous. But these are more like a gigantic bear. "I don't think so. He'd never be careless enough to break something."

Torrance nods. "Angel said that too. You're probably right."

I sit down beside him, dropping back against the cushions. "How is Angel? He won't talk to me about seeing his dad."

"From your lips to my ears. You think he's any chattier when we're together?" Torrance sits forward, resting his elbows on his knees. "I wish I knew why that son-of-a-bitch came back." He sighs and stands up. "Give Angel a little time. When he's ready, he'll talk." He pats my shoulder and walks off toward the stairs, calling back, "and I know he'll appreciate it if you're there for him when he does."

CHAPTER SIX

FALLING UP

AFTER A LONG SHOWER, I dig through my mom's old clothes and pull out a silky, turquoise summer dress. Another high-fashion item that looks better on a mannequin than it ever will on anyone but Mom in real life. Sometimes I don't know why I keep her clothes; it's a constant reminder. Mom is dead. I'll never fill her shoes. And I'll never know what really happened to her, either.

Holding the dress up to my torso, I pull the hem down to make sure it's not too short. On Mom it would have fallen just below her butt cheeks. But comparatively, I'm a shrimp; though, at almost three inches above my knees, the dress is still a little skimpier than I'm used to. Sighing, I pull it over my head. *Life is a catwalk. It's not the length of it, but the impression you make that matters.* That's what she'd tell me. Words to live and die by. Which is exactly what she did—short walk, head-spinning last impression.

Fingering the smooth material, I skip the mirror altogether. Turquoise is Ezra's favorite color. As long as he likes it, I don't need to know what it looks like. When I hear his truck idling in the driveway, I run outside, teetering in strappy brown wedges as I rush to his driver's side door. Opening it, I grab his hand, tugging him out of the cab.

"Whoa." He steps down, gripping my bare arm to steady himself. "What's going . . ."

Swiftly, I snake my arms around his neck, pulling him flat against me. His thin, navy summer sweater smells incredible, like sunbaked cottonwoods. "I don't want to fight. I was wrong last night. I mean, not telling you right away. Please don't break up with me."

Ezra lets go of my arm and steps back. He studies me from head to toe, grinning cockily. "How can I, when you're wearing that?" After a moment, he wraps me up in his arms, pressing his lips against my crown as he sighs into my hair. "Why are you always so convinced I want to leave you?"

"I don't think you *want* to, I'm just worried I'll do something that drives you away."

"Ruby, it'd take the end times to come between us." He walks me around to the passenger door, bows deeply at the waist, and helps me up. As he drives backward down the ponderosa-lined driveway, he glances sideways, grinning. "Also, I accept your apology."

"How gracious of you." I joke.

His eyes glitter, catching the last of the setting sun. "You know you look incredible, right?"

"Thank you."

"I mean it. You're blinding. I won't be able to see anything else tonight." He swerves to the right, pretending to lose sight of the road.

Dropping my head back against the seat rest, I laugh, feeling lighter. "Try," I joke.

In Santa Fe, we cruise down Cerrillos Road toward Viviane's restaurant, Rojo, looking for Racine's car in the front lot. When she sees us pull up, she climbs out of her beat-up yellow Honda, sashaying on stacked sandals like a queen all the way to the front door. "I'm so nervous I got here like twenty minutes early. How do I look?"

Ezra shoots me a sideways glance. Racine and Angel together, *together,* hasn't come up in our conversations yet, but she's so obviously nervous, it's not hard to figure out. "You look fantastic, as usual," I tell her. Actually, she looks better than fantastic. Dressed in a pair of tight black jeans and an off-the-shoulder cream sweater, she may as well own her own runway.

Racine points to Angel's Bronco near the back entrance. "He's inside. But I was too nervous to go in without you guys."

She grabs my hand as I lead us through the wood and adobe entry toward the kitchen. Walking through the main dining room, I head for the back of the café. "Hey." I peek my head past the swinging kitchen door and wave. "We made it."

"Ruby!" Viviane exclaims when she sees us. "Ray! How are my girls?" She rushes over and grabs us at the same time, pulling us into the kitchen for a hug. Racine hugs her back, blushing when she sees Angel at a counter across the room, watching us. He smiles, holding up a large butcher's knife that he waves in the air enthusiastically.

"Come on." Viviane pulls us over to the counter near Angel. "Angel just finished chopping the line for me. We're short tonight." She sneaks behind him and pinches his cheek.

Angel grimaces, swatting her hand away. "Aye, Mama."

"I set a table for the four of you out on the patio."

Angel pulls his apron off and crumples it into a ball, throwing it on the metal counter near the sink. He washes his hands, and we all follow Viviane to the back patio, where she seats us at a lovely Talevera-tiled table. "Chef's choice?" she asks. "Or do you want to order."

Ezra smiles. "Whatever you recommend, ma'am."

Viviane looks down at Ezra, plainly amused by his response. She pats his shoulder playfully. "Such manners. Abagail would be proud. But *Viviane* is just fine."

Angel rolls his eyes. "Go, Ma."

Viviane swats Angel's head and walks off, muttering fondly under her breath. When she's out of earshot, Racine laughs. "I totally love her."

"You and me both." Angel smiles and sits back in his chair, looking at me across the table. "Sorry about this morning, Ruby."

"You mean because you gave me that death stare?"

"No," he laughs. "That I was such a jerk to your boss. He just really rubs me the wrong way."

"You and everyone else who isn't female." I laugh.

Ezra glances at me, knitting his eyebrows together. "That so?"

"I just mean that you, and Angel, and Torrance, and really most of the dudes on the dig this morning, seem to dislike him. But from what I've seen, he gets along famously with women."

Racine bats her eyes. "Whatever. I doubt he holds a candle to you, Angel."

Angel blushes. At least, I think he does. He bites his lip and half-smiles at Racine. "Glad to know you think it."

Ohmigod, they're flirting!

So? Ezra looks at me.

I look down at the colorful ceramic tabletop. *So, nothing.* Mentally redirecting myself, I give Ezra a look, then tell them about my day, happy to ignore Ezra's intense stare while I answer questions.

"So, what was Lee going on about this morning?" Ezra asks, hijacking my pause as I dig into a plate of enchiladas mole. "He looked like he was ready to bust a vein."

"Something rummaged through the site last night." Angel stares at Ezra for a minute, then adds, "I thought it might be you at first, but whatever it was, it dug up a few relics. Lee was red as rocks about it."

"I've gone down there at night," Ezra admits. "But I don't walk through the cordoned-off areas. I'm the one who wants to protect the site, remember?"

"I figured as much. But it is an animal. Tracks look like a cat."

Ezra shrugs, biting back a smile. "El Maldito?"

Angel shoots him a look. "It might *actually* be a mountain lion. They're pretty big tracks, though."

"Maybe a bear?" I suggest.

"I can probably tell you what it is if you want to go down there with me," Ezra volunteers.

Racine looks at Ezra quizzically.

"Smell." He points to his nose.

Angel coughs around his ice, gulping down a drink of water. "Like a bloodhound?"

I laugh. "Just like that."

Angel doesn't hesitate. Setting his glass down hastily, he says, "Let's do it. After dinner," as if he just stumbled upon his own personal K-9 unit.

Ezra shrugs. "All right."

Angel and Ezra engage in this weird boy stand-off, staring at each other across the table. They have an odd sort of like-hate relationship, but I can never really tell the difference between the two with them, so I'm not sure if they're glaring at each other or bonding.

Uncomfortable with whatever it is going on over our plates of cactus salad, tamales and red chile shepherd's pie, I finish telling them about my day, focusing more on what I learned, less on how much Lee hovered while I learned it. "Also, Ray, there'll be another opening this summer," I tell her, excited at the thought of her joining me. "You should apply. I'll put in a good word for you. Assuming I don't blow it myself in the next few weeks."

"I'd love that," she says enthusiastically. "Hurray for nepotism."

"Nepotism has to do with family," Angel tells her. "And don't you already have a job at some chichi gallery on Canyon?"

"First off," Racine shuts Angel down with a fierce scowl, "I'm not stupid. Second, Ruby may as well be my sister. Third, the gallery's shutting down in May for renovations. It'll be closed until mid-June. And I can handle both if I have to."

"Sorry, Ray," Angel grimaces, peering at her across the table. "I didn't mean it like that. I'm a little wound up lately."

Instinctively, I drop my hand over Angel's, squeezing it reassuringly. When Ezra and Racine both shoot me looks, I pull it away. "Um . . ." I stutter, looking around the table at them, "how's it going with the whole dad thing, Angel?"

My cheeks burn as Angel shrugs. I'm not looking at Ezra, but I know he has me in his crosshairs; I feel it just like when he goes crawling around in my head.

Angel tips back in his latticed chair. "He's stayed away from me completely and he hasn't contacted Mom. Which is exactly how I want it. He's a stranger. No reason to pretend otherwise."

"It must be rough, though," Racine says. "I mean, I know it's not my business, but it's not like he gave you any warning. Just popping into town like that? The guy has some serious cojones."

Angel's green eyes glimmer as he dips his head, picking bashfully at the breadbasket on the table. "Don't I know it."

"If you want to talk about it, I'm here," she tells him, stressing the *I'm here* part as if the rest of us aren't.

I open my mouth, about to add that I am, too, but Ezra reaches out and squeezes my hand.

"Thanks." Angel looks at her, genuinely touched. "It's been a rough couple days, honestly. I might take you up on that."

For a moment, it's like the two of them have the table to themselves, and right or not, it makes me prickly. Angel always talks to me, or at least, he used to. And the fact that he seems to be shutting me out, coupled with the fact that he might talk to Racine instead—I just don't know how to be good with that.

CHAPTER SEVEN

NIGHT SHIFT

ANGEL PULLS INTO THE DIRT parking area and kills the Bronco's headlights. For a second, his head disappears beneath the dash, his torso suddenly disembodied.

"What's he doing?" Racine whispers, squinting at me.

Quickly reappearing, Angel fiddles with something on his visor before hopping out of the cab carrying his rifle, Tess. He walks toward us gripping a huge Maglite, which he switches on and shines on us when he sees us standing near the administration tent.

"Hey," he says quietly. "Thanks for waiting. Took me a moment to unlatch Tess." He gives his rifle a slight shake.

"All good?" Ezra asks.

Angel nods and hands me the Maglite, motioning for me to lead the way toward the cordoned-off site. Ahead of us, the mica-flecked hillside, lit by the half-moon shining off the nearby creek, looks radiant. Illuminated by the moon's reflection, exposed pots and bones buried near the creek's bank glow, almost as if the site itself is magic.

"It's peaceful here at night," I say softly, turning my face up toward a sheath of twinkling stars before leading them to the area just above where Lee found tracks. At the berm, I stop and point. "Down there."

Ezra sniffs the air. "It's definitely not a mountain lion."

I shrug. *Then what?*

Out loud he says, "Another feline, probably. Just not sure what kind yet."

Angel scrubs his head, lifting his top lip just enough to look ornery. "Dude's a tool. Raising the roof over a little wildlife. They're digging here in the freaking Pass. What does he expect? An extra man, my ass."

"Give me a minute." Ezra lets go of my hand, stepping back.

"Ezra." I grab him. *You're not going to . . .*

He grins, already predicting Racine and Angel's inevitable reaction. "You don't mind if I commune with nature for a moment, do you?"

Racine's eyes rival Angel's for size. They both shake their heads *no*. "Should . . . should we like, stand back or something?" Racine asks.

Angel glances back and forth between us. Knowing what Ezra can do is one thing, seeing it actually happen another. "Ezra, maybe you should . . ." I point up the hill, to a ledge dotted with pinyon.

"Screw that," he growls.

Angel pulls Racine back as she crosses herself, muttering, "*Nuestro padre dios santo.*"

Ezra snorts. "God has nothing to do with it." Then, he steps backward, grinning shamelessly. At the edge of the bank, he stops and wobbles, blurring for just a second.

"Ohmigod!" Racine shrieks.

"Ray, shush!" I turn to her, covering my own mouth to hide my squeal.

Angel gawks, gripping Tess like he needs to secure himself to something solid. "Jesus, that was fast." He looks Ezra up and down wondrously.

Ezra stands in place, immobile as Racine walks over to his furry form and hesitantly extends her hand. She touches a jowl, then pulls back, then touches him again, moving from jabbing pokes to rubbing his neck. Ezra purrs low in his throat and yawns, exposing a jaw full of razor-sharp teeth.

"Wow," Racine whispers reverently. "I had no idea."

Racine's expression is priceless, like someone gave her a brand-new shiny bicycle after convincing her that bicycles were a figment of her imagination. "It's a little mind-boggling," I agree.

Ezra dips his head, waiting for my okay before taking off up an embankment. Tightly knit bushes swallow him up, and when he's gone, I turn to Angel and Racine, both standing motionless beside each other.

"Hello?" I wave at them.

"In my wildest dreams . . ." Angel mutters. He motions me closer and pulls me against him protectively. Racine clears her throat, and he puts an arm around her shoulder too.

The three of us stand together, silently linked, waiting for Ezra to return. Moonlight shimmers off the creek, connecting little silver blips that rise and fall with the current. Following them as far down the stream as my eyes will allow, I watch as they disappear, swallowed by the dark night. After a few minutes, Racine moves away from us and walks toward an exposed pot, breaking my intense concentration. She crouches beside it and leans over, supporting herself with her hands. Carefully, she crouch-crawls from relic to relic, dipping her head near each little orange marker to get a better view.

"She likes you," I whisper at Angel.

"Oh."

"*Oh*?"

"I've known Ray since she was in diapers," Angel whispers back.

"You don't think she's pretty?"

"I think she's beautiful."

"And smart?"

"That too."

"So?"

"I don't know," he sighs. "It's just . . . weird."

"Because of me?"

"Yeah, a little."

"Do you like her?"

Angel doesn't answer, and since I can't read *his* mind, I have no idea what to make of him. "It's okay if you do, Angel. Really. Not that you need my permission or anything."

"I *don't* need your permission." He frowns at me.

"I didn't mean it that way."

"I know what you meant." Angel drops his arm off my shoulder. He shoves his hands into his pockets and steps back. "I do like Racine. And I'd be lying if I said I don't think she's attractive. But it feels strange. I get that there's zero chance you and I will ever be together. Honestly, Ruby, knowing you as well as I do, I'm not even sure I'd want that. But this thing between us, this *connection*—it's really freaking confusing sometimes."

"I'm sorry," I whisper.

"Yeah, me too."

He says it and my throat constricts. Like, is he sorry we're friends? Or does he feel like he's stuck with me? Is he sorry we ever met? Or am I just being a huge baby over nothing? "Do you want to see what I worked on today?" I gulp, suddenly desperate to change the subject.

Angel nods and sweeps a hand forward, waiting for me to lead the way. We join Racine, stepping carefully over the trail to the plot of dirt I hovered over all morning. "There," I point, bending at the waist to brush the surface of an ancient clay pot.

"Wow," Racine whispers, lightly touching its still-intact banding. "Amazing."

Angel crouches next to her, so close their shoulders touch. As she wonders about the pot's design, I stand up and back away, letting her take the lead. Angel stays fixed beside her, listening, rapt while she describes what she thinks the pot's motif resembles. Racine really knows her stuff, and Angel obviously notices. He touches Racine's shoulder, and Racine pulls a piece of leaf off his jeans, then throws an arm around him when she loses her balance.

Watching them, my heart feels tight in my chest, which makes it hard to swallow. *And oh, Ruby, you are so your mother's daughter.*

Ruminating, I turn to walk back to the tent just as Ezra sails down from the berm. He backs up, corralling me against a root-tangled crumbling shoulder, growling at something up the hill as he blocks my way. When Angel and Racine notice, they shoot up. Angel grabs Racine's hand and tugs her back, closer to me.

Ezra roars, and his deep, agitated rumbling shakes me to the core. He growls low in his throat, warning away whatever it is up the hill that suddenly growls back. Breathing hard, I move closer to him, positioning myself right behind his hindquarters. Angel and Racine follow.

"I really thought Ezra *was* La Luna Maldito," Racine gasps.

Above the terraced hillside the bushes rustle, and a set of wide, round eyes catch the moonlight. Staring out above the tallest sage brush on the hill, they look like glowing red embers.

"Bobcat?" Angel asks, positioning Tess.

"I don't think so. It's way too big," Racine whispers.

"I think it's a jaguar," I tell them.

"In New Mexico?" Racine gasps.

"It's rare to find them this far north," Angel says.

In the moonlight, glassy black spots glisten from the cat's huge, tawny crown. "Maybe but look at those markings."

Ezra backs up a step. *You're partially right.*

Partially?

From the bushes, the jaguar purrs, churning out a low hum like a generator, defiling the otherwise still night. Racine's hand finds my wrist, closing around it in a death grip. "Oh God," she whispers.

"You think Ezra can handle it?" Angel trains Tess on it just as Ezra jumps away from us, toward the brush, growling low in his throat.

Unnerved, I spit out, "Yes, I think so. Just don't move or freak out."

The jaguar slowly creeps down the bank and my heart speeds up, beating so hard I feel it in my throat when I swallow. Racine squeezes my hand, and this time I squeeze back, frozen beside her and Angel. Angel keeps Tess trained on the jaguar's sleek frame, but Ezra's body blocks his line of sight. Until the jaguar meets Ezra face to face, and I realize what a beast it is, towering over him.

"I won't shoot unless you tell me to, Ruby," Angel says through his teeth. "Or it gets too close for comfort."

"It's already *way* too close for my comfort," Racine whispers.

Ezra releases another deep rumble from low in his throat that reverberates through my body. The sound provokes a rash of goosebumps up and down my arms, but it doesn't stop the jaguar from slinking closer. The cat saunters toward us, its muscular haunches rippling as it approaches, backing Ezra into the berm.

If it gets any closer, tell Angel to shoot.

No! What if he hits you instead?

I grip Racine's fingers, nearly snapping them off. The jaguar continues forward, its eyes reflecting silver moonlight as it drops its head and trains them on us. "If you get a clear shot, take it," I choke out.

Angel hesitates and Ezra pounces, sailing straight for the jaguar just as it drops and rolls, turning on its back to grab Ezra in a death lock when he lands on top of it.

"Ezra!" I scream out loud. "Angel, do something!"

Angel retrains Tess on the snarling ball rolling around in front of us, looking down the barrel for a clean shot.

Now, Ruby!

Ezra sinks his teeth into the jaguar's side then swiftly jumps back, mowing the bushes down behind him before skidding to a stop just beside Angel. As he grapples with his footing, Angel takes a shot, tilting Tess up as the cat howls and leaps high in the air, sprinting up the hill too quickly for my human eyes to follow.

Ezra shifts, startling the heck out of Angel. He doubles over, dropping his head toward the dusty ground for a moment. Racine immediately starts talking, asking frantic questions that Ezra shushes. "Stop." He runs a hand through his messy chocolate hair, rubbing his forehead. "Please."

I need a minute, Ruby. My head's a mess.

Worried, I nod, visually examining him for blood and gashes.

"Just wait, all right? I'll answer all your questions about Ezra and shifting later. I swear," I tell them.

"That was a huge freaking cat!" Angel keeps Tess trained up the hill.

And something else.

I look at Ezra.

His eyes widen, warning me to keep quiet. *I'll explain later.*

"It was a huge freaking *pissed* cat," Racine gulps. "Why the hell did it rush us?"

"They're territorial," Ezra answers her. "But they don't hunt for sport. They prefer to scare people off than attack."

"This isn't its territory though, right?" She gulps.

"They're migratory. And I haven't seen it or smelled it before, so I'm guessing it's just passing through. But I'm no expert. They are predatory, though, so if it's hungry, I guess it all depends on what it's got a taste for." Ezra straightens out and pastes on a solid for-show smile, good as always at keeping his cool in tense situations. Still, I feel his mind working, holding something back. "He's a big sucker, though. You're right."

"He?" I ask.

Ezra points to his nose.

"We should get out of here before *he* comes back." Angel grimaces.

Shaken by our surprise visitor, Ezra, and Racine and I quickly tidy up the site, awkwardly maneuvering around each other as we smudge Ezra's and the jaguar's tracks while Angel keeps watch. Then we walk backward up the hill toward the lot, behind Ezra, and Angel, who still has Tess cocked and ready. "I'll have to put a call in to the state. Put flyers up in town warning people to be on the lookout when they hike."

Ezra nods, purposefully looking away from me.

"You want Ruby down here knowing it's skulking around?" Angel asks.

Finally, Ezra meets my stare. "No. I don't."

In the parking lot, Racine places a hand on Ezra's shoulder when he stops walking, looking up at him worriedly. "Are you all right? I mean, you literally sank your teeth into it." Her breath hitches for a second. "And it pawed you."

"I'm fine," he answers quietly.

Angel shakes his head at the moon, miffed by something else. "Ezra," he says softly, "you think you might have shared that with someone growing up. I mean, it explains a lot."

"*That*?" Ezra echoes testily.

"Your . . . that you shift."

Inadvertently, Ezra squeezes my hand. He grits his teeth before saying, "And you would have believed me?"

"No," Angel admits. "Probably not. I just saw it for myself, and I'm still standing here telling myself I'm not crazy. But I wish I'd known. Things might have been different."

Ezra exhales so hard his shoulders slump. "Thanks," he mumbles at the ground.

"I'll post flyers around town tomorrow," Angel says. "But tell me, honestly, is there anything else you think I should worry about?"

I know Angel is really asking whether Ezra is being entirely truthful about what he thought we just saw. And before Ezra even answers, I also know Ezra will lie. Neither Racine nor Angel know about the Otherworld. Ezra and I agreed to keep it secret. It seemed like the safest option at the time. But Angel has this uncanny sixth sense and ever since learning about Ezra's abilities, he's been asking questions.

Maybe we should just tell them about the ruin.

No. Ezra claps Angel on the back as he answers me, pushing him toward his Bronco. "Beyond the obvious, I don't think so. Get those flyers circulated and I'll come down at night over the next few days and keep an eye out."

Angel nods. Apparently, Ezra's word is good enough. Fiddling with his car keys, he opens his car door, then stops. "I have to file a report at the station, Ray. But it'll only take a few minutes. Want to follow me and grab a slice of pie at Margarita's after that?"

"Oh, hell yes." She exhales hard. "And coffee. I don't think I want to close my eyes tonight."

Angel walks Racine to her car and whispers something to her I can't hear. When she moves closer to him, he tilts his head down and grins at her just as she looks up and giggles. And, oh my God, I'm a terrible person. Because it kind of kills me.

"Margarita's," Racine calls out to me as she climbs into her car. "You and me after school Monday, Ruby. You have to tell me how he does it."

"Sure." I shake my head and wave as she shuts her car door. Talking about Ezra shifting will be one-hundred times better than talking about her now super obvious crush.

When they're gone, and it feels like I've waved to Racine until my hand is ready to fall off, Ezra shuffles me to his truck. "I don't want you working here," he tells me outright, turning to unlock the passenger door. "Something's really off."

"It's my job, Ezra."

"You've been at it for a day, Ruby. I'm sure you'll survive the loss."

Ezra's terse response feels insensitive. But I know him better. "You said it's migratory. Do you really think it'll come back? And during the day? Or is there something else?"

"I only picked up its scent on the way back to you. Whatever it is, it came out of nowhere. And when it ran up the hill, that's exactly where it went. Its scent just—disappeared." Ezra jumps into the cab and slides across the seat, starting the engine before I can answer. He grips his gearshift, knocking it around as he backs up and pulls onto the main road like it's pissed him off.

"Are you saying the jaguar disappeared? Like *for real* disappeared."

"Yes."

I don't want to ask the next obvious question, because things these last few months have been really good. But I make myself. If there's one thing I've learned, it's that when it comes to the Otherworld, ignorance does not equal bliss. "What did you mean by *whatever it is*?"

"It's not exactly a jaguar. Whatever it is, it only took the form of a cat." Ezra shakes his head slowly, drawing it out as he shoots me an ominous look.

One of the things I really like about Ezra is how well he weathers drama, even when something is deadly serious. He's not melodramatic. It's not his style. Which is how I know he's currently in doomsday mode.

"Okay . . . so it's not *all* cat." I shiver as the words leave my lips. "But if it's not all cat, then what?"

"Whatever it is, it shifted, Ruby. It wasn't a cat when I first caught up to it."

My voice catches in my throat. "*Another* shifter?"

"That's the problem. It's not exactly a shifter either. It doesn't have a human *or* feline scent. I've never smelled anything like it before."

The truck's tires hum as they spin over the road. The sound reminds me of the hum up at the ruin, which reminds me of Mom and her never-ending arsenal of bad advice. *Coincidence is the real fairytale. Life always has a plan.* It was one of her favorite sayings. But if life really has a plan and Ezra is right, whoever's in charge must be having a hell of a laugh at our expense tonight.

"Do you mind if I take you home?" Ezra asks solemnly, staring between my face and the road. "I do want you to come over, but I should probably check on the gate."

"I mean, no. But can we hang out after work tomorrow so we can talk more? You're freaking me out."

Ezra nods and drives down the backroad quietly, moving between budding aspens and oaks beneath a band of moonlight. From the side his face glows a bluish white, enhancing his steely expression. He looks like an effigy, like something hard carved out of the rocks at the dig site. Feeling shaky, I reach out and squeeze his hand over the steering wheel, taking some small comfort in his strong grip when he squeezes back.

Still silent as we round the bend up my driveway, Ezra parks in front of the porch and walks me up the steps. He stands near my front door and kisses me goodbye, anchoring me to his sturdy body. When he steps back slightly, holding me at bay while he searches my face, I lock my arms around his shoulders.

"You're going up the mountain now, aren't you?"

"I am."

"I wish I knew what it felt like," I say, gazing up at him. "Shifting."

Ezra leans in and kisses me again, and a wave of electrical pulses course through my body. Suddenly, I feel dynamic, and hypersensitive, and alive in this way I can't describe. He touches my face, unleashing a rollercoaster of emotions, and for a moment the sky seems brighter, the moon crisper and more vibrant. The air smells fresh and uncluttered, and each distinct scent holds its own in the atmosphere. I know that to the left of me, lavender bushes sway in the breeze, and that the pines up above in the foothills are starting to bleed sap, and that the fireplace inside needs stoking.

"Incredible."

"That you are," he murmurs, stepping back.

"Please be careful."

"I will."

"I'm sorry," I tell him.

"For what?"

"I don't know? For last night? That it's so hard for us to talk to each other sometimes?"

Ezra cocks his head, looking at me carefully.

"Say something."

He taps his head. *I heard you. I'm listening to you both.*

It takes me a moment, but then I hear it too. The hum is extra loud tonight. "The ruin?"

He frowns. *And something else.*

I tilt my head, mirroring him while I listen. "You think it has to do with the thing at the dig?"

"Maybe? Go inside. I'll text when I'm home," he promises.

Ezra waits on the porch steps until I close the door behind me, still angling his head, still tuned into some unknown frequency. Inside, I watch him from the hallway window, struck by his ability to concentrate on just one thing, to dial everything else out. He stares up the mountain, then in an instant, he's gone, like a flame snuffed in the dark.

CHAPTER EIGHT

FERAL BOYS, WILD HEARTS

"YOUR BOYFRIEND IS AN INTERESTING fellow," Lee says, looking up from the area of the pit we're surveying. He narrows an eye, examining one of the pots I'm cleaning with a soft-bristled toothbrush. "Unusual."

"You don't know the half of it," I say without thinking. Surprised at myself, I jerk my head up, concerned that my filter is so dodgy. "I mean, he's confident."

Lee sniffs. "Obviously." Reaching out, he carefully takes the mostly intact clay pot I'm working on and places it on a wooden stand before brushing his hands together. "You're above him, you know. You're . . . what do they call it . . ." he waves a hand in the air, "ah, right, slumming. It takes confidence to pretend you don't know that."

My laugh is so automatic, it's almost a snort. "That's a shitty thing to say."

"But true. Ezra's hardly a man. He's hot-headed and inexperienced."

"And I'm so sophisticated?"

"You're of different worlds," he says bluntly.

I arch my eyebrows at him. Of different worlds? *Seriously? He doesn't even know how right he is.* "I'm betting 99.5 percent of New Mexico's female population will disagree with you. Ezra may be a little rough around the edges, but he's smart, and talented, and keen as hell."

"Ruby, blink." I do, and he says, "You could have anyone. Just like that."

"I don't want 'anyone.' I want Ezra."

Lee bends back, stretching as he raises his arms over his head toward the sky. As he moves, his pendant shifts, and for a second I glimpse myself across its surface. I look beautiful. *Exactly* like the kind of face that could have anyone it wanted.

Startled, I move away from him abruptly.

Lee flashes a crafty smile. "Are you so easily persuaded by smoke and mirrors, Ruby?"

"Ezra's a lot more than his looks."

"I wasn't talking about Ezra," he answers slyly.

My teeth catch my bottom lip mid-frown, biting down hard. I never look in the mirror. Who is he to judge me? "Really?" I challenge him. "You don't even know me."

Lee raises an ebony eyebrow, turning on me with dark eyes that drill into all the fragile places in my heart. "Do *you* know you?"

"Of course. What a stupid question!"

"If it was stupid, I doubt you'd be so quick to jump down my throat." He holds his hand out, waiting patiently for me to step closer. "You're young, but you'll learn. Relationships built on lies are no better than dust."

"We don't lie to each other. I trust Ezra with my life."

Hand still outstretched, Lee takes a step closer, smiling like a jackass. "If that's true, then you are betting *on* your life," he says, echoing something Mom 2.0 once told me. "But I don't believe you. You *want* to trust him, you want him to trust you. But neither of you have earned it. So you convince yourself otherwise." He dips his head, snaking it sideways at an unnatural angle. "I see you, Ruby."

I squint at him until he's barely more than a fuzzy blur standing in front of me. My head is spinning, as in, I feel like I'm about thirty seconds away from throwing up. But there's no way I'm doing it in front of him. "Thanks for the totally off-base life lesson."

Holding his other hand against his stomach, Lee laughs quietly, restraining what I sense is something like a hurricane inside him. It's in his poise and the way he straightens, swallowing down a storm he hasn't unleashed yet. "You don't like me much."

"Is that a question?" Sighing, I drop my face so he can't see my expression, suddenly afraid I'm going to lose it. "I don't *know* you, Lee. And you're not making it easy to remedy that."

I look up to see Lee's sheepish smile. It softens his face, making him seem boyish. He slumps a little, relaxing a holier-than-thou posture that matches his attitude, still holding his hand out. Looking contrite, he motions for me to come forward. "You're right. I apologize."

Oddly, his apology makes me feel better. My nausea passes and I walk closer, letting him clasp my palm. Softly, he rubs a finger between the freckles on the top of my hand, connecting one to another as if moving between points on a map. He holds it, turning it face up. "This line here," he touches my palm near my thumb, "should be longer. And this one," he slowly drags his finger across the surface, "is broken up."

"Which means?"

He looks down at me with a mesmerizing stare. "You've cheated death. And your path ahead is full of strife."

I pull away. As I swallow, my heart tries thumping its way up my throat. It's been five months and I still haven't stopped thinking about what Mom 2.0 meant when she hinted that my real mom sacrificed herself to save my life.

"Are you an archeologist or an astrologer?" I snort.

He smiles, looking past my head at something that seems farther away than just the hillside behind me. "Everything we do, everything we dig up, it's all best viewed through a multitude of lenses. Not the least of which is cultural construct. Astrology serves a purpose in nearly every culture worldwide. I'm merely culling from many years of research."

I grimace at him before stepping back. "Do I look like someone who should be dead?"

"You look very much alive."

"Well?"

"Curious."

"What?" I frown.

"That my answer so upset you."

Frustrated and a little freaked out, I throw my hands up, attempting to walk off. But two steps into what I hope will dramatically display just how much I'm starting to dislike Lee, he grabs my arm. "Why waste your second chance on a boy with no future?"

Second chance? His words dig deep, uprooting my confidence. "Instead of what, wasting it on someone like you?"

"I'm speaking as a friend, not a suitor."

I bite my lip, dropping my head to hide the blush spreading across my face. Lee undermines my confidence. My heart, mind, and soul are Ezra's, no question, but Lee is strangely prepossessing. I think I hate him. But even the things I've known for years feel new when he speaks. And I despise how I find myself wanting to listen.

Lee does something that might be whistling. The sound is soft, and calming, and comes from his mouth in a singsong web of pitch and melody. He smiles at me and drops to the ground again, where he resumes cleaning the pot. "I'm not in the market, Ruby," he says, looking up at me with enough poise to power a nuclear reactor. "Not yet."

"And if I *were* in the market," I shake my head, thinking about how I met Ezra in a market, "you'd have less than zero chance."

"Is that so?" He looks sideways at me, across his regal nose.

I sigh, fixated on his pendant. "Yes."

Already in pivot mode, I will myself to walk to the site's makeshift bathrooms before Lee can answer. Ezra will be here any minute to pick me up, and I need a few moments to scrub Lee and this conversation from my mind.

At the holding tent, I gather my backpack and camera, stopping for less than a minute before beelining to the parking lot. Ezra is here, and despite the fact that we haven't talked since he left me on my porch last night—or maybe because of it—I'm crazy delirious to see him. Lee is the worst. I don't feel well. And Ezra is the best medicine. Even though I know we're in for a hell of a talk later.

"Hey." He drops an elbow out his open window when I walk up, resting his chin on his wrist.

"Hey," I say, amused by the look on his face. "Thanks for picking me up."

He tilts his head sideways, toward Lee down in one of the pits, frowning. "You ready?"

Ezra swings the passenger door open from the inside. When I'm seat-belted and situated, he flips the radio to some country station and cranks the volume up. Closing my eyes, I twine my fingers in his on the seat beside me and drop my head back against the rest, trying to clear my mind. Minutes tick by as he drives through the Pass, and after he turns into his driveway and leans over me to open my door Ezra-style, I finally give up.

Ezra doesn't wait for me to get out. He hops down and walks to the front door, obviously expecting me to follow. Inside his house, he throws his keys and straw hat on an antique side table in the hall, and then plunks down heavily on an old Victorian sofa he restored, dwarfing its delicate frame with his rock-solid body.

After I dump my backpack in the hall, I walk over to him and curl up in his lap. "You're being kind of weird. What's up?"

Ezra drops his head back, staring up at the wood-beamed ceiling. "Long day."

"That's it?"

He runs a hand over his face and shrugs. "That and I hate you working at the dig."

"Because of last night?"

"Yes. And Lee. And the fact that you're down there screwing with my heritage."

I pull on his chin, tilting his face forward so he's forced to look at me. "That's not fair."

"It's a Pecos site, Ruby. And you're digging it up."

"But what if it's not. You heard Lee at dinner last week. He thinks it could be Aztlán. And they're digging up all kinds of weird artifacts that are different from what archeologists usually find at ancestral pueblo sites."

Ezra's pupils dilate. He stirs restlessly, leaning forward, then blows out hard enough to ruffle my hair.

"What?" I shake his knee.

"Why are you defending him?"

"I'm not defending him. I'm asking you to keep an open mind about the site."

Ezra rubs his face. "Fine."

"Fine?"

"Honestly, at the moment I'm more concerned about the ruin up the mountain than Lee's playground. And I don't want to fight." He pauses and his eyes narrow, pinching with his mouth. "Something definitely tripped it last night. But I wasn't able to track it."

"The not-jaguar?" I breathe out.

"That's what I'm thinking." Ezra leans closer, obviously still on the defense.

My head feels light and I automatically hold my hand out, angling for Ezra's on the couch. "So, you think it's what? A ghost? An escapee from the Otherworld? Something the dig churned up?"

"I don't know, Ruby. But I don't like it. And I don't like you working down there because of it." He smashes his lips together so hard the space around his mouth turns white. "But I also know you're not going to listen to me, so there's that."

"I live down the hill from the Otherworld. How much worse could it get?"

He stands up, pulling me with him. "I don't want to find out."

"I want the job, Ez. And I can't always be running away from everything that goes bump in the night. I mean, that's sort of the nature of *us*, what we are, right? Besides, I'm only there in the day, around lots of people."

He drags a hand through his hair, pulling roughly at the ends. "You got rushed by a wild turkey, then saw some magical city on the mountain. Then the night before you start working down at the dig, something inhuman goes rummaging through the site. That's more than off. That's *way* off. I'm not asking you to hide, I'm asking you to be reasonable."

If only I could nod my head and say, *Yes, Ezra everything you said is righ*t. I want so badly to tell him I agree, but I can't make the words form in my mouth. It's like there's another Ruby inside of me, an evil Ruby who wants to keep arguing. "Look, something weird is going on, obviously, and I agree that we should be vigilant. But until we have some real, concrete reason to worry, I just want things to be normal for a while."

"They're not normal!" he says gruffly, rolling out the word 'not' with a growl. "Do you need me to spell it out for you?"

"Why can't you just trust me?"

"Why can't *you* trust *me*?" His face is hard, and when he looks down at me, his eyes are so purple they're almost black.

"Ezra, it's my job," I whisper miserably.

"It's not your job," he says coolly. "It's your life."

"Right. You're right. It's *my* life." His eyes are like marble, and his laser focus on my face makes me uneasy. Angry, I stare back as intently, steady as possible, even though I want to run back into his arms and hide.

Ezra's shoulders droop. "I don't want to argue with you."

I walk over to the staircase and sit down on a wood step. I don't want to argue either. I don't even really know what we're fighting about. "Ezra, what's wrong with this picture? We don't do this. We don't fight."

"Until now, we never had reason to." He looks up at the ceiling. "Look, just because we don't know what's happening doesn't mean it's not dangerous. Whatever that thing was at the site, it *isn't* human." Ezra sits down beside me on the step and traces a smooth leaf carved into the wood railing lining the staircase, moving his finger slowly, mirroring the deliberation going on inside his head. "For now, can we just agree to trust each other?"

"I'd like that."

"That includes trusting my instincts."

"It also means trusting that I can take care of myself."

He shakes his head at the ground slowly. "I will if you promise to talk to me the next time *anything* feels off."

My conversation with Lee earlier briefly flashes through my head, but I push it away. "I'm not quitting the site, Ezra. But I will be extra careful, and I promise to check in a couple times a day during my shifts. And I'll try to be more . . . open with you." Moving closer, I hold my hand out, offering a truce. "I will quit, if it comes down to it. But not yet. I want to wait. The ruin, and the whole True of Heart thing, and the Otherworld. It's a lot. I mean, I can deal, but it weighs on me sometimes. I need this, Ez. You know, something to take my mind off it all. Will you back me?"

Ezra sighs but takes my hand, standing up as he simultaneously pulls me against his chest. Breathing into my hair, he says, "We need to get out of La Luna for a little bit. Soon. This place is driving us both crazy."

"Is that a yes?"

"Yes. I'll back you. But you'll tell me if anything, and I mean anything, happens, right?"

"If anything seems off base at all, I mean, more than already, I'll tell you immediately. I'll go back to the dig next weekend and keep my eyes open like the world might end at any minute. All right?"

Ezra squeezes me against him so hard I gasp. He picks me up, sweeping me off my feet as he walks up the stairs toward his bedroom.

"So, you're not taking me home?" I ask sweetly.

"No," he purrs, "I'm not."

Upstairs, he drops me on his bed, propping himself on his elbows over me.

"Are we okay?" I ask him.

"I think so," he answers quietly. "But, Ruby, I'm telling you now, I'll put you in my truck and drive you out of town myself if it turns out you're in danger."

Luckily, pessimism is a trait Mom didn't pass down. One thing Liddy and I have always agreed on is that it never hurts to at least look for the light. I want us to be okay, so I nod, then crane my neck to kiss his cheek, scooching closer. "My knight in fur-lined armor."

"You know, it's not a crime to worry," he says bluntly. "You're a True. Ottomundo's your destiny. Which means this, right now, is all you have. If anything happens . . ." He closes his eyes. "There is no bone closet for you, Ruby. There is no next time. I'm pretty sure you don't get another life."

CHAPTER NINE

LIGHT AS A FEATHER, STIFF AS A BOARD

MONDAYS HAVE NEVER BEEN MY favorite, but between Racine's new glow, which I'm sure has to do with Angel, her never-ending story about the jaguar over lunch, and Ashley and Marta's incessant questions about Racine and Angel hooking up, every minute past the one after Ezra drops me off at school feels like an hour. By the end of lunch, I'd kiss an Ancient just to make it stop.

Clearly, a stellar Monday just isn't in the cards for me, because on our way to fifth period, after Las Gallinas break off for other classes, Racine stops me in the hall. "Hey," she grabs my arm, "Can we talk for a sec?"

Racine walks beside me to my locker and pulls out a hairbrush, holding it up toward my head. I block it with an arm, knowing all too well what she intends to do with it. "Why do you always want to brush my hair when you have something serious to say?"

She shrugs and laughs. "Why is your hair always so messy?"

"No fair changing the subject."

Racine takes a deep breath. "He kissed me. When we said goodbye Saturday night."

I don't want to react, but my heart skips anyway. "Angel?"

"Yes, Angel." She knocks my arm. "Are you mad?"

I swallow. "I don't have any reason or right to be."

"Doesn't mean you're not."

"It's okay, Ray. I'm not mad. I swear." And I'm not. I'm just surprisingly unsettled by the image.

"Are you jealous?"

"Yeah. A little bit, I guess."

"Because?" she prods, waiting for me to fill in the blanks.

"Because I'm afraid if you have each other, you'll forget me," I blurt out.

"Ruby! Seriously?"

"It's not about the romance part. Or the *you and Angel* part. I'm seriously happy you hit it off. But . . . I guess I like being someone's first. And I really do love Angel. He's special to me. I don't want to stop being special to him—to be replaced."

Racine purses her lips, giving me an exaggerated once over. Finally, she says, "Ruby, Angel loves you. *I* love you. Nothing's going to change that. But you already are someone's first. Clearly. Liddy? And I mean Ezra would die for you in a heartbeat." She shakes her head when the bell for fifth period rings. "I understand where you're coming from, but it's not fair to hoard Angel when you have no intention of getting with him. I mean, I know you know that, but I have to say it, right?"

"I do know, Ray. And it's not like I want to be with him like that anyway. Even if I wasn't with Ezra. I don't know where it's coming from."

"I like Angel. A lot. And he seems to like me. But if you don't make it clear to him that you're really okay with it—if you don't let him go—he won't give us a chance. He has feelings for you still, obviously. So, if you mean it, you can't leave the door open even a crack."

Ashamed by my bad behavior, I mumble, "I'm sorry. You're right. It's just an adjustment. Give me a few days and I'll talk to him."

"I'll give you a week," Racine says authoritatively. "But then I'm coming for you." She holds her fist in the air and threatens to fake stab me.

"You know, when I moved here, I thought you were the most beautiful thing I'd ever seen. Except for Ezra, I still do. You're nobody's second, Ray. You're wicked smart, and funny, and beautiful in every way, inside *and* out. And I know Angel thinks so too. He told me himself."

"Really?" She blushes.

"Yeah. The other night, while you were crawling around digging stuff up." I smile, happy to see how much knowing it cheers her up. "Even on your hands and knees in the mud, you're all goddess."

Racine grins and links an arm in mine. Late for class, we rush to Media Tech over her hurried chatter. Because just like that, she's happy to move off topic. Racine's like that. She never dwells, and you always know what's on her mind—qualities I envy and admire. Angel is an idiot if he doesn't immediately fall head over heels in love with her.

In Media Tech, Racine grabs a seat across the aisle from me at the back of the room, whispering about the graduation party she and Ashley want to throw in a couple weeks. "We could have it at your house," she says under her breath. "In the backyard."

"That could work," I whisper as I lean under my desk to dig through my backpack, accidentally knocking my ear on the desk's edge.

Racine giggles. "Loser."

"Ms. Brooks!" Someone barks curtly from the front of the classroom. "Would you like to share?"

At the sound of the man's voice, I whip my head up, shocked to find myself looking at Angel's father.

"My name is Mr. Tillin. Mr. Franco had an emergency to attend to out of state. For the next few weeks, I will be your substitute. And had you two been on time, I wouldn't have to repeat myself."

Mr. Tillin. Because of course, Angel must have taken his mother's last name.

I cough, choking on a swallow.

Across the aisle, Racine smacks me on the back. "Smooth," she snickers.

I bat her hand away, whispering, "That's Angel's father."

"What!" she squawks.

Mr. Tillin scans the pool of desks in front of him. "Let's get back to it. Before Mr. Franco left, he had you examining twenty-first century media and internet challenges. We'll go ahead and wrap that discussion up, then move into the wild west of the Internet: cyberlaw."

"You're shitting me," Racine mumbles under her breath.

"No." I shake my head slowly, still shocked.

Mr. Tillin stops talking and looks directly at Racine. "Question, Ms. Vasquez?"

She looks mortified. "No."

"Then, let's get started."

"How does he even know who we are?" she whispers.

I shrug. *Good. Freaking. Question.*

Pacing the aisles, Mr. Tillin asks each of us random media-related questions, drawing his words out slowly. His green eyes are already oddly luminous, but the sunlight coming through the classroom window makes them look atomic. He speaks, but I miss everything he actually says, too lost in the hazy green abyss moving in front of me, as if my brain burst a seam and leaked cotton into my eyes, spreading gossamer across their surface.

Finally, the end-of-class bell breaks the spell and I throw everything into my backpack as fast as humanly possible. Grabbing Racine's arm, I pull her away from her desk, trying to rush out of the classroom.

We make it to the door before Mr. Tillin stops me.

"Ms. Brooks?" he says as we start to trail out behind a group of students. I turn around, and he adds, "Can you pop in for a moment after sixth period?"

Racine snorts, nudging me in the arm with an elbow.

"Umm, okay. Sure."

He nods, "See you then."

"Ohmigod!" Racine exclaims on the way down the hall. "What do you think he wants? Seriously. Angel is going to freak the hell out!"

I nod stiffly. *I'm* freaked out and I'm not even related to Mr. Tillin.

"And how did he know us off the bat?"

"He saw me with Angel at Margarita's. Maybe he figured it out. I hope he doesn't think I'll help him with Angel or something." On principle, I already hate Mr. Tillin. Whatever he wants, I'd never betray Angel.

"I can't believe he's subbing. How did *that* happen?"

"I don't know, Ray, but Angel is going to lose it when he finds out."

At the end of sixth period, I reluctantly throw my books into my backpack and make myself walk down the hall with Racine toward Media Tech. As my inner voice tries to convince me I'm on a fact-finding mission for Angel, I head straight to Mr. Tillin's room, avoiding Ashley and Marta when they stop and wave, leaving them standing open-mouthed in the hall as Racine fills them in.

Inside Media Tech, Mr. Tillin is at the dusty chalkboard, his back to me, and for half a second I contemplate walking out. Until he clears his throat.

"Ms. Brooks," he says, without turning around.

"Uh, yes. Hi."

He claps his palms together, sending milky plumes of chalk above his hands, dirtying the air. Dramatically, he drops down into the thick wooden chair at his desk, letting his body unspool, reminding me of a loose skein of yarn. Without looking up, he taps the desk's surface with a slender finger and motions for me to sit down in a chair across the aisle.

"Mr. Tillin," I pretend to check my cellphone, "I only have a minute."

"Call me Mick."

Angel never told me his father's name. And now that I know it, I hate it. I have no desire to know him whatsoever.

Mick stares at me, training his electric green eyes on my already-warm face, and an uncomfortable, prickly sensation moves through my head, seeping between my ears to my eyes. Sniffling, I rub my temple, wondering if it's possible to be allergic to someone. "I'm worried I'm going to miss the bus," I mumble.

Mick leans forward, eclipsing the desk, focusing his penetrating stare on my face as if constructing a carbon copy of me inside his head. "Your contempt for me is palpable."

"I . . ." How am I supposed to respond to that? "Um. Yes, I guess it probably is."

"I suppose it's fair to assume Angel and you have talked."

His words make me squirm, which makes me frown at him.

Mick smiles knowingly. "I'll take that as confirmation."

I stand up, as convinced as ever that even just talking to Mick is a betrayal. But as I throw my backpack over my shoulder and turn to leave, he says, "Your mother, her name was Seraphine?"

My heart skips, stopping me cold. Nodding, I try asking how he knows, but my throat catches, and I choke the words down before they make their way out.

"You're her spitting image. When I saw you in Margarita's the other night," he drops his head. "Well, let's just say it rattled me."

"Ho . . . how," I stutter, "do you know my mom?"

"We were friends. Years ago. She would have been around your age then."

Suddenly, I'm all kinds of panicky. "W . . . when? How?"

"She used to road trip out here to meet up with friends. I met her through some mutual acquaintances." He smiles and his eyes shift, moving back in time. "I can't get over the resemblance."

"Why'd you come back?" I blurt out.

"Business."

"Business?" I raise an eyebrow. "To teach?"

"No. This is just a side gig."

Honestly, I don't know what to say to him. Other than reconciling with Angel, what could possibly be important enough to bring him back to the Pass? "Business here? In La Luna? What kind of business?"

He smiles. "The family kind."

"Family?" I frown at him. "Like you would even know what that is."

"You're loyal, I respect that." He casually crosses his arms over his chest. "But your judgments limit your sight. If you're not careful, you'll only see what you expect to see until the smoke clears."

"Are you seriously giving me advice?" I step closer to him, leaning toward his desk. This picture is wrong in so many ways I don't know where to start. "Angel and Torrance are pissed as hell you're back. And you obviously don't care. I know you haven't called Angel, or even tried to reach out." I shake my head curtly for emphasis. "I don't know what you want from me, Mr. Tillin, but I have less than zero interest in hearing it or helping out."

"You think poorly of me. I understand. But your mother didn't. And neither did Viviane. I left *for* them, you know. Not *because* of them. Angel has his story, but I wouldn't bet on it being right."

"*Them*?" I spit out. My heartbeat matches the growing thudding in my head. Mick's eyes glow as if charged, briefly igniting a storm of green-hued sparks that swim around his irises. My breath hitches and I reel back, instinctively registering that though I should be scared, I'm not. There's just something so familiar about him it's uncanny.

"I have to go," I gulp, rushing out of the room before I have time to think about what I'm doing. I run down the mostly empty hall, and out the front door into the warm afternoon air. Outside, the day smells like it's been soaked in creosote and pinyon and the sun feels like fire on my skin. The marching band is practicing out on the football field, and it's like I'm stuck in an echo chamber of resounding brass and drums. I sneeze and my head explodes. My senses have gone haywire.

Apparently, I missed the bus, and like three-hundred texts from Racine asking if I'm okay and whether we're still meeting at Margarita's later. Confused, I walk in a daze toward downtown, past gnarled oaks, and a smattering of old adobe homes, and a lot full of rusty pickups propped up on blocks, and don't even realize I've made it all the way past downtown and through the Pass until I find myself walking up my driveway. Completely disoriented, I drop my backpack in the hall and shuffle upstairs to my bed. I can't keep my eyes open, and only know I need to clear my head.

After the longest, most restless nap ever, I roll on my side, dipping into an unexpected indent. My mattress sags, and when I open my eyes, I see Ezra lying beside me.

"Hey." He tucks a piece of hair behind my ear, leaning over me.

I rub my sleep-bleary eyes, sluggishly sitting up. When did Ezra get here? And why is it dark outside?

Ezra hooks a pinky in mine and pulls it toward his chest. "Racine and Angel and Torrance are downstairs with Liddy. She sent me to check on you."

"What? Why?"

Ezra raises an eyebrow. "You tell me."

"I must have fallen asleep."

"Racine called me earlier. She said you stayed after school to talk to Angel's dad, and that she called you over and over and sent like a hundred texts. She must have called Angel, too, because they're both downstairs freaking out. I headed over after I called Liddy and she said you pretty much came home and passed out. That was three hours ago. You're not a napper, Ruby. So . . ." He wriggles my pinky. "Want to come down and tell us what's going on?"

My head is full of cotton. I don't even know where to start. "M'kay."

Ezra holds out a hand and helps me stand up. For a girl who just slept three hours, I still feel exhausted. Kind of like my brain spent the last three hours processing my deepest, darkest thoughts. About Mom and all the secrets she kept.

Grasping onto Ezra, I follow him down the stairs. "Angel is going to kill me."

He looks at me strangely. "He's not."

"He hasn't mentioned his dad since Margarita's. He won't like that I talked to him."

"Probably not. But he'll deal. If he doesn't—" he makes a face.

"You'll what, go all mountain lion on him?" I try to joke.

"If that's what you want."

"That's not what I want," I mumble, pulling him into the kitchen.

Early evening light floods through the kitchen's bay window, illuminating the square room, turning the navy walls violet. We barely all fit around the kitchen table, and crowded around it like we are, the purple cast makes the setting seem like some dream-induced still-life—like some evil painter crossed Michelangelo and Dali.

Everyone stares at me, waiting. "Love," Liddy finally breaks the ice, reaching out to touch my hand across the table, "are you all right?"

"Yeah. I'm just tired."

Angel's pinched lips part, and I cringe when his eyes meet mine. The perpetual playful twinkle that animates his lovely face is gone, replaced by disquiet. "Did Mick tell you why he's here? After eighteen years? I mean, he didn't come back just to teach at Pecos, did he?"

"He said he has family business," I tell the table.

Angel stiffens, leaning back against his chair as if to distance himself from me. When he does, Racine places a hand over his balled fist, squeezing gently.

"What did he want to talk to you about?" Torrance asks.

Tearing my eyes away from Racine's hand, I resist the urge to shrug. "I really don't know. I tried to leave before he could explain, but he said something about my mom."

Liddy frowns. "Sera?"

"He said he knew her. He recognized me. He said I look just like her. He also mentioned Viviane and Angel, but only briefly."

Gritting his teeth, Angel asks, "What'd he say about us?"

"He said he left *for* you, not *because* of you." Slowly, I raise my own hands over the kitchen table, turning my palms face up to stare at the lines Lee traced back at the dig. Being interrogated isn't at all fun. "But I'm the one who brought you up. I mean, I shouldn't have, I get that, but I wasn't thinking straight."

"That's all he said?" Torrance asks.

From my periphery, I'm aware of Ezra's intense gaze. His eyes are like drill bores, and I know he's searching for the truth beneath what he thinks is a lie. I know he thinks I'm lying to protect Angel.

Ezra. Stop. Please. I'll melt if you stare any harder.

Ezra shifts, turning slightly to gaze out the kitchen's bay window. *It's not intentional.*

Sighing deeply, I spit the rest out. "He implied he left for good reasons. To protect them. That Angel's recollection isn't right."

Them. Except Mick meant Viviane and my mother. But how do I tell Angel that?

Torrance stands up and walks to the refrigerator. He grabs a soda from inside and waves it around in the air. "Bastard has no right dragging you into this, Ruby. It's bad enough Angel has to go through the ringer. Selfish prick."

"Tory!" Liddy gasps. "Hush."

Liddy's voice isn't harsh, but it is firm. She's good at calming people down in situations where other people are on the verge of losing it. I admire that about her. On the other hand, the fact that my bomb about Mick knowing Mom barely fazed her is weird. She's almost too calm.

"Maybe Mick's back because he wants to get to know Angel." Racine rubs Angel's arm and smiles, struggling to stay neutral. "People do change."

"Except he ignored me at Margarita's," Angel growls.

Torrance snorts and scratches his chin, which has morphed into all kinds of granite. "I don't trust him. Not to mention, it was totally unprofessional to drag Ruby into his private life."

"Angel dragged Ruby into his private life first," Ezra mumbles.

Angel shoots darts at Ezra across the table. "I don't remember her complaining," he counters.

"I'm not saying you should get to know him, Angel," Racine leans into him, grasping his fist with both hands, this time to redirect his attention, "and either way, it's your choice, not his."

"Ray's right," Ezra tells him. "Just because Mick's blood, doesn't make him family. You're not obligated."

Grateful, I meet Ezra's eyes. Given their history, I know being nice to Angel is still sometimes really hard for him. *God, I love you.*

I'm not saying it for you, Ruby. I've been there. But I'm always glad to hear it.

Appeased by Ezra's concession, Angel backs off. But just as quickly, Racine and Torrance get into it, arguing about whether Torrance should shank Mick, or just civilly ask him to leave town. Already overwhelmed, I move to the alcove, curling up on a pillow against the bay window to get away from their bickering.

"Ezra and Ray are both right, love," Liddy tells Angel. "Don't beat yourself up over it. As for you," she shoots Torrance an exasperated nod, "no one's shanking anyone."

Her voice is stiff, and I stare at her, searching for the something I know she's not saying. When she smiles tightly, turning away from me before I have a chance to really examine her face, Angel cuts in. "You're right. It is my choice. And I made it a long time ago." Looking over at me, he adds, "I'll talk to him, Ruby. I don't want him bothering any of you again, especially not my mom."

"Unless you really *want* to see him again, I swear I'll kill you if you do." Racine twists her mouth into an exaggerated grimace. "You do what's best for *you*, Angel. The rest of us will be fine."

"And if he wants to talk to you next?" he asks her.

"Why would he?"

Angel looks at her shyly. "I mean, you know, if he sees us together."

"Oh," she blushes. "Well, believe me, I'll give that asshole a piece of my mind before I ever tell him anything. He'll never know what hit him." She rests her head on his shoulder, nuzzling it affectionately.

Quite unexpectedly, my stomach drops. Angel's expression—the look he just gave Racine—is emblazoned on my eyeballs. And for the rest of the evening it's all I can do to keep my feelings to myself. That look stays with me during dinner, and after dinner when we try pretending Everything Is Fine while we play Celebrity by the fire. And even after that, when Angel says goodbye and takes Racine home. It bothers me enough even Ezra notices.

"You're seriously quiet," he says when they leave, curled around me on the couch.

"I'm still really tired."

"You want to talk?"

When I shake my head *no*, Ezra grabs my sketchbook off the coffee table, flipping through it absently. Toward the middle, he stops, lingering on a picture I drew of his face after the first time he took me fishing. "I was so damned ugly."

I lean over him, peeking into the book. "Not really. Sometimes I even miss that you."

"Me too."

"Really? Why?"

"You never lied to him."

I stare at him, unsure how to answer. Because he's right; I've been walking around carrying the secret about my mom, not to mention her warning, for months now. And it's wearing on me. "You think I'm lying to you?"

"I know you are."

"I wish you'd trust me."

Ezra strokes my face, sweeping a strand of hair off my cheek that he tangles around his finger. "You mean, you wish I'd trust you have a good reason to lie to me."

"Yeah." I meet his eyes. "I guess that too."

Ezra inhales as though startled by my confirmation. His irises are a kaleidoscope, finally settling on amber. "And I suppose you think you're doing it for me."

"Yes. I do." My eyes tear up and my nose starts to run, garbling the speech I've planned out over and over for just this moment. "You . . . you kept things from me when you thought you had a good reason to, Ezra."

"The difference is that you wouldn't have believed me then if I had told you the truth. Not in the beginning, at least. And I was trying to protect you. Plus, I thought you'd leave me."

"Well?" I sniffle.

"Ruby." His exasperated smile is a small consolation. Half of me is relieved to see it, but the other half is mortified. I *am* keeping things from him. "Look," he says, "I'm not going anywhere. How do you not know that? I've never given you any reason to doubt my feelings."

"It really bothers me that Mick knew Mom," I blurt out. "The way he said it, it's like he implied . . . like they were into each other or something. And honestly, did you see the way Liddy responded? I think she already knew."

Ezra sits up straighter and grabs my sketchbook, tugging at me to follow. "Let's get out of here."

"What? Why?"

He drags a hand through his hair. "Because I'm short on answers, and I think a drive will do us both good."

"You think it's weird he knew her too?"

"Yes," he admits. "I do."

CHAPTER TEN

FAITH, TRUST, AND PIXIE DUST

A CANDY-APPLE HALF-MOON LIGHTS THE night sky, brushing moonlight across the billowy clouds pushing up against each other over the Pass, turning them into ethereal bits of gossamer. I breathe in, looking up at the stars before climbing into Ezra's truck, then exhale, shivering as the fresh night air tucks around my body. It scrubs my lungs, cleansing the suffocating heaviness that threatened to strangle me earlier.

As we drive, Ezra reaches across the cab and squeezes my shoulder. He turns the truck onto a back road and shifts gears, cruising slowly down the blacktop until we reach an empty dirt lot surrounded by trees. He parks and hands me my sketchbook, then reaches for something in his glovebox.

"Here," he hands me a new set of charcoals. "You can draw me."

I stare at him, close to crying. "You bought these for me?"

"You haven't been doing a lot of sketching lately. I was going to give them to you tonight anyway."

Opening the tin, I finger a powdery stick, swallowing down a wave of emotion. "When I was little, my mom made me paint my feelings out whenever I threw a tantrum."

"I remembered you telling me that," he says softly.

In the moonlight, Ezra's beautiful face is a study. He's an emotional Picasso, full of feelings I know he won't outright share with me, but that still shine through his stoic façade. The gesture, these charcoals. It kills me.

"Look straight ahead. The shadows on your face right now . . ." I choke up, "I'll draw your profile."

Ezra looks out at a gnarled thatch of overgrown chamisa and moonlight sweeps his face, dissecting his nose from his cheekbones. Turning on the seat to see him better, I pluck out a charcoal, savoring the way it feels between my fingers.

I sketch, listening to the way the charcoal sounds scraping against the page, filling the silent cab with comforting, familiar noises. Outside, the wind picks up, gusting against his truck, making me feel like we're the only two people left in La Luna, anchored in our own safe harbor.

"You know you can share Angel, right?" Ezra says quietly, breaking the spell.

I look up at him. "I just, I don't want to share—either one of them. I'm afraid they'll forget me." Ezra laughs and I look away, staring out at the night. "You think it's stupid."

"They're not going to forget about you just because they like each other. Especially not Angel. It kills me to say it, but that boy adores you like he made you with his own hands. With good reason, of course," he adds, winking at me when I turn back to him. "You're so preoccupied with people leaving you lately, what's going on?"

"Lately?" I swallow.

Ezra reaches out and rubs the fabric over my left thigh gently, bunching my skirt into an eddy. "Remember when you had to do all the convincing? I think I liked it better when I was the insecure one in this relationship."

I hold the sketch up to stop my hands from shaking. "Here. I'm done."

Ezra tilts his head, examining it. "That's how you see me?"

"That's what you look like."

He bites his bottom lip and starts the truck, pulling out onto the highway. Staring straight ahead at the moonlit center divider, he looks mystified. "You and I, we don't always see the same things," he blows out, disturbing the hair that's fallen over his eye. "But at least when it comes to us, Ruby, I'd like to think we're on the same page. You mean everything to me."

"I feel the same, Ez."

"Then what's really going on?"

"I just . . . I have this feeling. It's like a dark spot in my periphery. I have it so good now, you know? Here. With you. But knowing what I do, after everything that's happened, I don't see how it can last. Especially not after talking to Mick today."

Ezra squeezes my leg and leans sideways a little to brush his lips against my temple, swerving closer to the center of the road. "I know how difficult losing your mom has been. I do. But you have to start trusting people. And not just me. Your friends and family too. Liddy, and Racine, and Angel."

There's that word again. *Trust.* It's not like I'm not a trusting person, because by nature, I am. I'm just not as stellar at keeping my insecurities in check lately. Besides, Angel *is* family, and I'm pretty sure that losing another family member will kill me.

Faking a cough to buy a second, I wipe my smudgy fingers on an old fast-food napkin stuffed in the console and think about how to say so without alienating Ezra.

Finally, I blurt out, "I love him."

Ezra keeps his eyes trained on the road. "I know you do."

"You're not mad?"

"I don't like hearing it, but I also know you're not *in* love with him. You and Angel have a strong bond, I see it. But I believe you when you say that's all it is."

"But do you worry about *him*?"

"Stepping out of line? No." He snorts and shakes his head. "He's way too much of a wuss to try and muscle his way between us." Ezra playfully flicks my earlobe with a finger. "He's a good guy, okay? I know that, but that doesn't mean I have to tell you I know it all the time."

"You're a good guy."

He leans over to kiss me again just as something jumps in front of the truck. It's big, and spotted, and when I see it, I scream, startling both of us. Ezra slams on the brakes, grabbing the steering wheel with both hands to keep the truck steady as it skids across the road. When a scrubby bank of shrubs stops the truck cold, protecting the front end from smacking into an oak growing from the rocky slope of the encroaching foothill, Ezra quickly leans across me and unbuckles my seatbelt.

"Jesus," he says breathlessly, pulling me into him. "Are you okay?"

His heart is pounding, or maybe it's mine. I nod and try to speak, but nothing comes out except wheezing.

Ezra kills the engine, searching out his window. "Close call."

"I think it was the jaguar," I say when I catch my breath.

He unbuckles his own seatbelt. "Stay here for a minute, all right?"

"No!" I grab his arm. "Are you crazy?"

Ezra smiles, working hard to make sure it reaches his eyes. When I don't smile back, he leans in and kisses my nose. "Just give me a minute."

"No, Ezra! Don't leave me here alone."

Already halfway out of the truck, he points to the keys in the ignition. "Lock the door. If I don't come back, go home. I'll be all right. I'll meet you back there."

Even if I could come up with a compelling-enough argument, it wouldn't matter. Ezra wobbles, then shifts so fast my protest is still on my lips as he lopes between a stand of pines up the hill. One second, he's human, the next, a cougar disappearing into the forest.

Under the canopy of thick, leafy oaks lining the road, the street seems like a tunnel. I feel claustrophobic, and too aware of every little rustle. For a few minutes, I keep myself from hyperventilating, but the effort is like using my pinky to slow down a freight train. Minutes feel like hours, and I imagine every bad thing known to man, and then some, happening to Ezra.

The quiet around me is unnerving; it's so still inside the cab I hear my heart throb in my ears and the way my breath catches as I exhale. Sucking in, I embrace a clutch of air, sputtering over a half-choke, half-scream when Ezra lands in front of the truck on all fours, with such a *thwack* the frame rattles.

In an instant, he shifts back and climbs into the truck. As soon as he's in, I smack his chest with both fists. Hard. A couple times.

He grabs my arm as I wrench away. "Hey. Calm down."

"Calm down? You left me!" I sock his shoulder again the way Torrance taught me with my free hand. "And you almost gave me a heart attack."

"Ruby!" He raises his voice and grabs both my hands, sending blips of energy up my arms. "Stop."

Trembling, I turn toward my window, away from him.

"Hey, look at me." When I do, his stiff jaw loosens. "I'd never leave you alone if I thought it was dangerous. You know that."

"It's not about me." My eyes water, and I drop my forehead against his sweater, mad at myself for overreacting. "I just really worry about you sometimes."

"Me?" he asks incredulously.

"Yes. You. Of course."

"Why?"

"What do you mean, why? You guard the gate to a world full of strange creatures. You fought one the size of a bus when it followed me out. That's what I think of when something weird happens, and you tell me to hold on, and then jump out of the truck all of a sudden. Something whipping you around like a chew toy. Especially now, with that thing roaming around."

Even in Ezra's shadowed cab, his eyes shimmer. He pulls me closer, securing me against his body with a strong arm. "We never talked about it. But I should have known. I get it, Ruby."

"I'm sorry I overreacted," I whisper into his shoulder.

"I'm sorry I left you."

I swallow and drop my head back against the seat rest. "So, what was it?"

"The not-jaguar," he says gruffly, adopting my name for it.

"Does that mean we have a problem?"

"Yes," he says quietly. "Probably."

I scoot closer, closing the space between us. Today has been the strangest day all around. Ezra wraps his arms around me, and little blips of electricity bounce between us. He rubs my lower back over my shirt, and his hand burns a trail over the fabric, searing every inch of me that he touches. For a few moments, distinct smells ride the wind as if the air fractured into discreet molecules, from the gas in the truck's tank, to the tar on the street, to the acorns outside buried beneath blankets of drying pine needles.

When Ezra kisses me, I climb onto his lap kind of desperately, smashing myself between his chest and the steering wheel. He pushes my skirt up my legs and drags his fingers over a bare thigh, and every inch of my skin seems to rip away from my muscle and bone, tugging toward his hand as though desperate to wind around his fingers.

Ezra groans into my neck. "We should go," he exhales.

"You're so disciplined," I whisper, kissing one of his perfect cheekbones.

"I'm not. Twenty minutes ago you were freaked out about Mick and Angel. Five minutes ago I was chasing that *thing*. I don't want our first time to be in this truck, *or* while you're upset, *or* while something otherworldly watches us."

I pull back, trying to collect myself, then let my head drop against Ezra's collarbone. Ezra hooks his fingers around my skirt hem, pulling it tight and neat down my leg. He runs his hands down my arms, lingering at my wrists. When I look up at him, and he brushes a long strand of hair off my face, looking at me earnestly, I'm still so wound up it feels like I might explode.

"Let's take a trip. A long weekend. Like when we went to El Morro," he says.

"What about the ruin?"

"I'll get my mom to come out for a few days."

"That doesn't seem like such a good idea right now. Shouldn't you be here to keep an eye out?"

"She'll know what to do," he assures me. "She's had a lot more experience."

I slide off him, plunking down on the seat as I adjust my skirt. Ezra starts the truck, watching me silently as I put myself back together. "I'll invite her over for dinner," he says, backing the truck out of a bunch of shrubs. "She wants to meet you anyway. And she might have something to say about Mick, and the dig, and the ruin." When my eyes bloom at the thought of having dinner with her, he laughs. "Don't worry. She's a pain but she's smart."

"That's not it," I gulp. This isn't the first time Ezra's mentioned introducing me to his mom. I know it's important; he wants her to meet the dumb girl he's sworn to love and protect all his life. Just, what if she hates me? What if she takes one look at me and thinks, *that's all*?

Ezra searches my face. "I'd never let anything hurt you, Ruby. Not even my mother."

CHAPTER ELEVEN

PRETTY UGLY DISTRACTION

MORE THAN SKILLED AT PRETENDING Everything Is Okay, I go to school all week as if I'm not worried about the not-jaguar, or nervous as hell to meet Ezra's mom on Friday, slipping into my seat in Media Tech a couple minutes late every day, then sneaking out a smidge early to avoid Mick. Because even just looking at him gives me a headache.

Over lunch all week, I listen to Marta's stories about how utterly terrible it is to actually have to pretend to be nice to customers at her new job, and Ashley's accounting of her weekend trip to New York to scope out housing at NYU, where she pretty much did nothing but tour the campus and hole up in her hotel room, and Racine's detailed description of her Wednesday night date with Angel. It's enough to distract me, until Friday after school, when I meet Angel at Margarita's for coffee.

"I finally tried to corner my dad," Angel tells me, sprawled out in a booth against the window in the back of the diner. "Yesterday.

And maybe it's a blessing in disguise, but he basically gave me the slip."

"Asshole," Daisy mutters under her breath as she stops to refill our coffee cups.

"Among other things," Angel nods.

"I don't remember him that well." Daisy grips her waist, waving the coffee pot around in her other hand. "But Dad called him a drifter when Racine brought him up at dinner. Said he always seemed to have one foot out the door."

"Makes me wonder what Mom saw in him." Angel drums his fingers on the table. "I've asked, but she doesn't like to talk about it. I don't even really know why he left. Though, it's pretty obvious that whatever the reason, he could give a crap now." He looks down at the table, then up at me again. "When I was little, I made up stories—like he left on a tour and got kidnapped across enemy lines. Or fell in love with lion taming and joined the circus."

Daisy snort-laughs. "You told that lion taming one during sharing time in kindergarten. Remember Missy Tanenbaum?" She looks down at me. "She followed Angel around for days after that. She thought he was so cool."

Angel's brows move in a wave across his forehead. "Did I? I guess I made a lot of excuses for him. It was easier than thinking I drove him away, you know?"

Daisy wrinkles her nose, curtly waving away a regular who motions at her for a coffee refill. "You could drive him off a freaking cliff as far as I'm concerned."

Reaching across the table, I pull his hand closer. "You were four, Angel. It's not even remotely your fault he left. Children don't drive parents away." *Except maybe my mother.* I bite my lip, trying to ignore my own insecurities. "His leaving like that, that's all on him."

Daisy pats his shoulder. "She's right, you know. The bastard."

Angel pulls his hand from mine, sinking back into his seat. "Before he showed up here, I could at least pretend he was a decent guy, that he had his reasons. Now . . . I mean, he won't even talk to me. What the fuck am I supposed to do with that?"

Startled, Daisy meets my eyes, as thrown by Angel's choice proclamation as I am. Angel sometimes talks tough, but he's really more Rick Grimes meets Mayberry. Curse words aren't typically part of his wheelhouse. "You don't do anything. Trust me on this one. Trying to figure it out, especially if he doesn't want you to, it'll drive you crazy."

"It's hard, Ruby, knowing he's here and that you're the only one he's talked to. I mean, why? Why is he so interested in you?"

I grimace out my reply, topping it off with a shrug. Why, indeed? "It's not the same, I know, but it bothers me too. I feel really bad about it. Angel, you know I would never come between you guys or take his side, right?"

He pauses, mulling something over before answering. "I do."

"I've thought about it a lot this week, and the only thing I keep coming up with is maybe he knows you and I are close and somehow thinks he can reconnect with you through me. Though, just so you know, I sneak in and out of class every day before he can corner me."

When Daisy walks off to wait on an annoyed customer, grumbling under her breath, Angel hunches over the table. "You and I both know that's a load of bullshit."

"What is?"

"The idea that he's interested in reconnecting with me through you."

It would be nice to think the best of Mick, because that's what I do. But there's something about him, something about the way he stares at me in class and the way he spoke to me after school, that drives Angel's point home. Whatever Mick's here for, it isn't Angel.

"We can try to give him the benefit, right?"

"Ruby, do me a favor for a moment and just be honest with me."

I bite my lip and count to five, waiting him out. Because it's clear from his tone his appeal is more of an accusation than a request, and I'm not sure how to feel about the pit that just opened up in my stomach.

Angel splays his fingers out on the table's laminate surface, looking at me curiously. "You don't really think I'm this nice all the time just because I'm a pushover, do you?"

"No." My jaw sticks, refusing to cooperate. "I don't. Think you're a pushover, that is."

"I watched my mom pine after him for years. And I've seen more than my fair share of crappy people doing crappier things to each other since becoming a sheriff's deputy. It's always been pretty clear to me that the best way to assure I don't end up like him is to just lay low and be a nice guy unless I'm really pressed otherwise."

It's like Angel just pulled a curtain back, exposing that his happy-go-lucky veneer is more of a pretense than he lets on. And I don't one-hundred percent recognize the man standing behind it. "Are you telling me you're this really great guy by design, because you think it makes you better than your father?"

"I know it makes me better."

"Here's the thing, Angel." Pointedly, I meet his eyes. "There's no way you could keep it up for twenty-two years if it was all just a front. I get it. I get what you're saying. You're not always the happy, easy-going person everyone thinks you are. You have to work at it. But I also know who you are here." I reach over the table and tap his chest over his heart. "And I know it's not a front."

He frowns. "Maybe I'm just not the person you think I am."

"Or maybe Mick being here is messing with your head."

"Or maybe I'm tired of being everyone's go-to boy."

"Angel." I reach out for him again. It kills me that something about Mick being here after so long has steered Angel to this darker place. When he pulls back, I frown, frustrated for him. "Look, if you're asking me to be honest, because that's what you need, I will. But that doesn't mean I padded what I really believe because I think you can't handle the truth. You matter to me. I'm just trying to make a crappy situation a little bit better because I care about how you feel, and I didn't really think it'd help to go all dark side on you."

"I don't need you to coddle me, Ruby. And honestly, I'm a little bit tired of coddling you." He scrubs a hand over his close-cropped hair and briefly glances out the window.

When he turns back to me, I meet his eyes, breathing in to tamp my anger. "Fine, Angel. The truth is, I think Mick's a jerk and a crappy-ass father, and I have no idea if he's here to see you or Viviane. And I do think he asked me to stop in after school specifically to talk about my mother, not you."

Angel narrows his brilliant green eyes. "That so?"

"That's exactly so. And thinking about it is driving me crazy."

"I figured as much."

"Are you happy now?"

"Not really." He grabs his hat off the seat beside him and abruptly stands up. "But at least you told me the truth."

"Wait, where are you going?"

"Back to the station. You've got dinner in an hour and I'm done talking."

Angel looks as conflicted as I feel. "Are we mad at each other?"

"I have less than a clue how I feel right now." He throws a ten on the table and positions his hat on his head, tipping the brim at me. "But how about this. After I get the asshole to talk to me, I'll let you know."

CHAPTER TWELVE

MOMMY DEAREST

"MOM'S COMING OVER AT SIX," Ezra says as I climb into his truck. "You still good with that?"

Until lunch earlier, I was excited about meeting Ezra's mom. Until I mentioned it to Las Gallinas over my salami sandwich, and Marta counted off all the ways I might totally blow it, and I started panicking. My row with Angel didn't help either.

"Yeah. I'm still good."

Ezra turns down Main Street, away from Margarita's, and drives toward my house. "So, how is Angel?" he asks as we turn off into the Pass, almost as if he already knows the answer.

"Mad at me for some reason."

Ezra snakes his hand across the seat, overwhelming my palm with his much larger one. "Tough. But I get it. Maybe cut him a little slack. Mick showing up out of the blue after eighteen years, it's got to be screwing with him."

"I'm not upset that he's mad at me. Just worried about him. Anyway, how are you?"

"Me?" He cocks an eyebrow.

"Yes, you. How are you? How was your day? How are you feeling about dinner tonight?"

Ezra doesn't answer until he pulls up my driveway and shuts the engine off. Finally, he sighs, deflating like a balloon. "Nervous. I've never introduced my mom to anyone I've dated."

"So am I," I say, caught off guard by his candor.

"Comrades," he tries to smile. "Now you know how I felt when I first met Liddy."

"We weren't even dating then."

"Doesn't mean I didn't want to. I know how important she is to you. I wanted her to like me."

Ezra being so open is new to me. And it's a side of him I instantly want to package up and carry around in my heart.

"What? You're making crazy eyes at me."

"Crazy eyes?" I laugh. "I just really love you right now. More than normal."

"Does that mean you want me to come in? Or should I go home and come back when you're ready?"

"Come in while I change?" I ask coyly, batting my eyes at him.

Ezra follows me into the house and up to my room, lingering on the edge of my bed while I sift through outfits. As he watches me with his keen eyes, I rummage through my mother's old boxes, looking for a non-threatening ensemble that says, *I'm a respectful girl who's totally in love with your son*, not screams, *I'm an attention-seeking diva.* Unfortunately, neither my closet nor Mom's boxes have a lot to offer in the way of respectable. Finally, I settle on a clean pair of dark blue skinny jeans and an emerald, slouchy sweater.

Ezra grins as I tug my pants off, grumbling to myself. "She won't even notice, Ruby."

"Notice?" I look up at him.

"Your outfit."

I scan the clothes strewn around my bedroom floor. "I just really want her to like me."

"She'll like you. She knows I love you. Plus, she thinks you're the reason I finally manned up and took responsibility for the ruin. Even if she doesn't like you, she'll fake it."

I hold up the jeans and sweater, and sigh. "I guess that's good because I've decided on casual." When I pull off my t-shirt and replace it with the sweater, his eyes turn a lighter shade of brown tinged with violet. "What?" I blush.

"Well, first, feel free to change in front of me more often." He gazes at me appreciatively. "Second, that color's really nice. It makes your eyes shine."

"Yeah?" Still in just my underwear and a sweater, I shimmy up to him and plant myself in his lap. "When is your mom supposed to be over again?" I ask suggestively.

He kisses me, running a rough hand over my bare thigh. "In about forty minutes, unfortunately. And I still have to get dinner ready."

Shivering from the tension that bounces between us, I untangle myself from his lap, moving to slip on my jeans. When I'm fully dressed, Ezra reaches for my hand, pulling me back into a hug. "Ruby, so you know, as far as I'm concerned you are the smartest, most interesting, most beautiful girl I've ever met. Nothing anyone else says or thinks about you matters. You're what I want. My mother's opinion, good or bad, won't change that."

"Thank you." I push the tip of my nose against the warm cotton t-shirt draping his muscled chest. "I think I needed to hear that. And I feel the same way."

"You think I'm the most beautiful girl you've ever met?"

I snort. Because I think he's the most beautiful everything.

After I'm dressed, I stuff an overnight bag full of clothes in case it gets late and I decide to stay over at Ezra's. Then I leave Liddy a note in the kitchen and walk with Ezra back to his truck. At Ezra's house, Ezra straightens up in the living room while I go about setting out silverware and plates, gussying up his restored cherrywood dinner table. Together, we put the flowers Ezra picked up earlier in a gleaming crystal vase and place them in the middle of the table, between take-out dishes he ordered from Margarita's that he heated up in ceramic bowls to make it look like we cooked everything ourselves.

At six, his mother walks in, calling out in a language I've never heard before. She's shorter than I imagined, and both beautiful and fierce-looking like Ezra. When she sees me, her dark eyes take me in, until Ezra comes out of the kitchen carrying the last reheated bowl, speaking to her in the same language before switching back to English.

"Ruby's here. No more Towa," he tells her.

She drops her purse on the couch. "Of course," she says, addressing me. "It's good to finally meet the woman my bigheaded son won't shut up about."

I blush. "It's good to meet you too."

She smiles almost too sweetly. "He thinks you're perfect."

Stammering, I answer, "Um, thanks, I guess? Though, since he's your son, you probably already know he's full of it."

She laughs and her face breaks, softening the sharp lines around her eyes and mouth. "Well, at least he likes smart women. I'm Abigail." She holds out her hand.

"Ruby." I shake, super aware of her grip. "We have food. From Margarita's," I blurt out.

Ezra shoots me a look. *Thanks.*

Abigail squeezes her lips together, shooting Ezra her own look. "Ezra, we both know you don't cook. Stop giving Ruby the evil eye."

Smiling, I get Abigail a drink, then shuffle her to the table, reminding myself as I sit about what I can and cannot talk about. Abigail knows I know about their 'gifts' and the ruin, and the Otherworld, but for now, Ezra has decided not to tell her about me being True of Heart.

"Ruby agreed to move in with me," he says casually, dumping a mound of rice on his plate as if starting off the conversation like that is perfectly normal.

Abigail snaps her head up at me, and I nearly choke on my food. "Oh. You sure you want to do that?"

I stare at Ezra like a mad person. If I could be sure Abigail wouldn't hear me, I'd give Ezra a serious mental kick in the ass. Because way to put me on the spot.

"Yes?" I answer hesitantly. "But I haven't said when."

She chuckles, blowing softly through her nose. "Good luck to you, then."

Ezra shakes his head. "Mom, why do you do that?"

Abigail answers in a different language, but this time Ezra doesn't tell her to speak in English or translate. "Towa," he explains afterwards. "My grandfather made us learn it."

"It's oral, right? Not written?" I ask softly, trying to show her that I'm interested and paying attention.

Abigail forks a bite of enchilada into her mouth. "Correct. Passed down by word of mouth," she tells me through her bite. "Stops the white man from corrupting it."

"Ma," Ezra sighs.

"Son," she answers curtly.

"My aunt Liddy speaks Yiddish. She made it a point to teach herself after my grandparents died, sort of to honor them. They taught her that in Western Europe, at least, at some point, non-Jews started claiming it was a corrupt dialect, and that because of that, Jews felt pressured to acclimatize to the outside world and learn the local language instead. Because they assimilated, Western Yiddish only survived in close family circles and trade groups."

"Interesting." Abigail sets her fork on her plate, narrowing her eyes as she sizes me up. "But not surprising. Westerners always think they know best."

Ezra shoots his mom an exasperated look. Beyond that, his face is inscrutable, and I can't really tell if he's wishing I'd kept my mouth shut, or happy I shared. And then it hits me, I don't even really know if Abigail knows I'm Jewish. Or if it matters to her either way.

"Good for Liddy." He finally smiles at me, turning to angle his head at Abigail almost defiantly. "Don't you think?"

Abigail and Ezra have a strange relationship; they're tense around each other, like they both have durable walls up. I see now that Ezra comes by his honestly. But underneath that they seem to have a strong underlying affection for each other.

"Yes, son, I do think," she answers testily.

Through the rest of dinner, Abigail talks about life in Jemez, filling Ezra in on all the pueblo gossip. But she doesn't speak to me directly, and I can tell she isn't sure what to make of her son's girlfriend. Ezra brings up the dig, and I talk about how Lee thinks it may be Aztlán, trying to gauge her reaction, which other than to quietly roll her eyes, pretty much equals zero. After dinner, we clear the table and settle in front of a fire in the living room with a couple pints of ice cream. As she leans back into the couch, she asks me how I feel about Ezra—in front of Ezra—almost like she's questioning my intentions.

"I love him. I want to spend my life with him."

"You're too young to make such sweeping decisions."

"Mom," Ezra interrupts, "butt out!"

"Probably," I smile. "But I know what I want."

Abigail frowns. "Let's see if you don't change your mind in a few years. When it really sinks in that you're stuck."

"Mom!" Ezra stands up quickly.

Abigail meets his eyes, challenging him to disagree.

"I know Ezra has to stay for the ruin," I say softly. "It doesn't affect how I feel, Ms. Pena. I want to be here with him. Maybe I'll change my mind one day, but I doubt it."

Abigail raises her sable eyebrows exactly the same way Ezra does when he disagrees with me. "Well, I hope you're right."

I shoot Ezra a look, imploring him to sit down and keep his cool. We still have to ask Abigail about Mick and the ruin, and if Ezra wants her to take over his duties for a weekend, his stony attitude won't do us any favors.

Frowning, Ezra plunks down on the couch. "Why do you have to be so . . ."

Abigail arches an eyebrow again when he trails off. "What?" she asks pointedly.

"Difficult."

I expect her to respond tersely, but instead she laughs. "Look who's calling the kettle black." She sits back, clearly pleased with herself. Her posture is triumphant, and for a second, everything about her reminds me of Ezra. And I kind of love her for it.

Ezra glares at her, but I can tell he's more amused than mad. "I learned from the best."

Abigail digs into her bowl of mint chocolate chip ice cream. "So, you're uptight about the ruin," she says casually, not even pretending it's a question.

"Yeah. How'd you know?" Ezra asks.

"It's off."

Ezra looks between us, moving his head slowly. "You feel it?"

"Since I got here," she says. "Yes."

"Something came through it."

Ezra tells her more about the dig, and our not-jaguar, and how the ruin hummed like a charged transistor the other night, adding how every time he sets out to investigate, he comes up empty.

"Anyone new in town?" she asks.

"Actually, yes," I chime in. "A bunch of people down at the dig. And Angel's father moved back."

"Tory's boy?"

Ezra shifts forward expectantly. "Right. Mick. He's a weird one."

"He always was." Abigail nods her agreement. "Beyond looks, nobody got what Viviane saw in him."

"He's teaching at Pecos. Anyway," Ezra looks off to his side for a moment, "yeah, I guess things have been weird since he got here."

She looks thoughtful. "Any reason to think he may be responsible?"

"For the gate?" I squawk. "He's Angel's father. And . . ." I stare at her, slack-jawed. "I mean, Angel's normal."

Abagail snorts, then covers her mouth, holding back her laugh. "I'm sorry, Ruby, but that means nothing in these parts. *You're* normal."

Ezra whips his head toward her. "And?"

"And you don't think I know what you are?" she asks me.

Ezra's eyes threaten to jump ship, bulging from their sockets before turning a burning ember color. "Do you?"

"I can smell it. The piety." She snorts again, though this time it's not as friendly.

I choke on my knee-jerk reaction, waffling over how to respond. I can't believe she didn't say anything earlier.

Abigail nods toward Ezra. "I figure he's keeping me out of the loop for a reason. Far as I'm concerned, he's a grown man. He can make his own decisions."

I meet her eyes, stare for stare. "But you don't like it."

"Actually, dear, I think you're good for him. And I'm not one-hundred percent convinced by all that Watchers and Trues don't mix bullshit. Seems like more of a convenient story the Ancients conjured up to make sure they kept us at our posts on separate sides—so we'd continue being the Ancients' faithful, clueless soldiers. You're all they have. You decide to do it any differently and they're fucked."

"Mom!" Ezra growls.

"You disagree?" She purses her lips, shooting him a mighty frown. "Since when did you start taking your job so seriously? Ezra, my sweet, you can't be all *that* concerned, or you two wouldn't be together."

Ezra looks between me and Abigail, pulling his bottom lip between his teeth before finally volunteering, "She's been there. To the Otherworld."

"What?" Abigail volleys her head between us. "*Why*?"

I note that she doesn't ask me how, and file that tidbit away for later. It's like she already knows I can open the gate from this side. "I wanted to know what being True of Heart means. To see my mother. To know we'll be okay. To know Ezra will be okay," I let it slip out in a rush.

"They gave us their blessing," Ezra adds.

"The Ancients?" she asks without any hint of surprise.

Ezra looks at me, and I know the ball's in my court; it's up to me whether to tell Abigail about speaking with my mother. Except Ezra still thinks it *is* my mother, not Mom 2.0.

Nervous to bring Abigail into our circle, I tell her about going up there last winter anyway, pausing when Ezra breaks in to pepper my story with his own explanations about why we went up there, and why I crossed over. When we're done, she nods knowingly, but something in her eyes convinces me she's questioning my version.

"So, you've been there." Abigail sounds far away, like she's talking about one thing and thinking something else altogether. "And you understand the stakes."

"Not really," I admit. "That's part of the problem. Beyond guarding the gate one day, neither of us really knows what being True of Heart means."

"You're not supposed to. A True's role begins *after* death. It's unheard of that you'd know of what you are *now*, Ruby. And yet even in human form, you exude the Otherworld. As if you're meant to be there now, not here on Earth."

Abigail's declaration chills me. It reminds me of what Lee said at the dig, not to mention Mom 2.0's last words. *Your mom loved you. It wasn't her intention to hurt you. She traded her life for yours. To keep you safe. So you'd have the opportunity to live out your own life.*

"Way to put it into perspective, Mom." Ezra moves closer to me on the couch and wraps an arm around my shoulders.

"It's okay," I squeeze his hand. But I wonder—am I wearing some Otherworldly sign that says *walking dead girl*? I've heard it three separate times now, except in this case three times isn't a charm. I'm as clueless as ever.

"We'll figure it out," he reassures me.

"Or you won't," Abigail says flatly.

"My mom said I'm just supposed to live my life. Like being True means nothing now as long as I stay away from the ruin. She wouldn't tell me anything else other than I should pretty much forget about it."

"She told you not to worry about it?" Abigail raises a single, dark eyebrow.

"I mean she also told me to stay away from the ruin. That getting too close could be dangerous. But that's all."

"That's all," she echoes.

All she says are those two little words. But it's enough. I know she doesn't believe me.

Abigail leans forward, toward me. "Ruby, *you're* likely the reason for the disturbance. Whatever it is. It's the simplest answer."

"But I haven't been anywhere near it."

"So, you do think something is wrong?" Ezra asks tersely.

"I feel it. Something big came through the gate, right under your nose. Though, to be fair, son, the way the gate's still ringing—whatever that 'something' is, it's much craftier than your typical Otherworld runaway. Unless they gave *you* some kind of guidebook," she looks to me, "not sure what's to be done about it. But let's be real, far as I know, three and three still equals six, right?"

"Mom said Ezra would keep me safe," I say quietly.

"Presumably, it's his job." Abigail speaks between clenched teeth, as though just thinking it hurts her. "I'd keep an eye on Mick for now. Especially around Ruby."

"Mick's not a shifter," Ezra says forcefully. "I'd smell it."

"Oh, son. It's so like you to over-estimate your abilities." She sighs. "You know what your grandfather would say: appearance has no relation to character, especially in the Otherworld."

"All are not hunters that blow the horn," Ezra adds nostalgically.

"There's so much about the Otherworld we don't know," she reminds him.

Ezra sighs long and hard, letting go of me to plunk back against the couch as though he has a beef with it. "So, in other words, we do nothing."

"Reaction doesn't require *action*. Don't do 'nothing.' I'm telling you to keep your eyes open, to be even more vigilant patrolling the ruin. Whatever got out, it's out now. If it turns out there's real danger in the Pass, we'll know soon enough." She sighs again, rolling her eyes at the ceiling. "He always was prone to extremes."

"Maybe I should go back up to the ruin."

"No!" They both answer in unison.

"What about the dig?" Ezra asks her, still staring at me.

"Your Aztlán?" She snorts. "I suppose it's possible. Your grandfather believed the stories his grandfather told him about an ancient city straddling two realms somewhere between Las Vegas and Santa Fe that fell to ruin thousands of years ago. He called it Azcale. He believed it was the original entry to the Pecos Circle before the Ancients shut it down. His grandfather used to take him out hunting through the Pass for some sign of it. I guess your great grandfather believed the city was a shortcut, like somehow he could get to the Circle without dying or brokering with the Ancients over his afterlife."

"I can't believe you never told me that before." Ezra leans forward on his knees, running a hand through his hair. "I've never put the Otherworld and Grandpa's Pecos Circle together—but it makes sense."

"Or maybe the dig's exactly what you think it is, Ezra. An ancient Pecos site."

"Or both," I interject. "I mean, you think it's coincidental that the names are nearly identical?" My voice wavers as I say it. Because the answer suddenly feels right. Like I somehow just know the way I know how to breathe that the two are related. "The Aztec Empire rose three-hundred years *after* the Pecos Pueblo was already here thriving, and the Aztec came back here regularly to trade—there's proof of that."

"Academics," Abigail frowns.

"Gives us more to go on than fairytales," Ezra snorts.

Abigail turns her nose up, as if contemplating something distasteful. After a moment she drops her chin and meets his stare, narrowing her eyes. "Maybe go try digging up that book your grandpa was always going on about."

"Grandpa liked to read," he frowns. "Which one?"

"Some secret tome Old Jimmy claimed to keep locked up in a safe. Supposed to hold all of our peoples' mystical secrets." Abigail stands up and shakes her head disdainfully. "Dad really had a thing for it. But Jimmy's never been all there in the head. Likes his drink." She mimics tipping back a bottle with her hand, throwing her pinky up. "I figure he's full of it, but Dad swore on its existence till the day he died."

"Right." Ezra sits up straighter. "I do remember. Old Jimmy and his archaic book full of secrets and prophecies. You think it really exists?"

She shrugs. "No. But it couldn't hurt to dig around a little."

Ezra frowns, drawing his dark eyebrows into a ball above his nose, pouting more like Leo before reconciling with Ezra. "Will you?"

"Me?" She pulls her head back, squishing her chin into her neck. "I'm in no place to hash out something so pigeon-livered, son. Far as I'm concerned, the Ancients are in charge. Whatever's going on, it is what it is until it's not. We'll find out soon enough.

But you want to ask around about it, be my guest. You come down to the pueblo and you can pay Jimmy a visit." She grabs her empty ice-cream bowl and walks it into the kitchen, speaking to us over her shoulder. "I should probably go. It's a long drive back to Jemez and I'm tired."

Ezra rubs his palm down the sides of his blue jeans, standing up stiffly near the couch. Grabbing her jacket, Abigail walks over to him and pecks his cheek. Then she comes over to me and tries to give me a hug. "You have a lot on your plate. I know he's watching out for you. But take care of my boy where you can. He doesn't do such a good job of it himself."

"I will," I promise her.

Ezra stays glued to the same spot in the living room until Abigail walks out the front door. When it shuts behind her, he deflates, sighing as he drops into a chair. "Well, shit."

I turn to look at him.

"That went swimmingly."

"Sarcasm?"

"No. I mean it. She was *lovely*."

I walk over to him, collapsing in his lap. "I'm glad I met her. She's interesting, Ezra."

"Interesting?" He pulls his eyebrows together.

"I mean, she basically told us we're screwed and to deal with it. But she did tell us about the book and your grandpa's stories. Plus, she at least tried to pretend she doesn't completely detest me."

He pulls me up off the couch, leading me to his room. Moonlight shines through his bedroom window, and though it's mostly still dark, the white hue lights his face, illuminating his striking features. Mesmerized, I let him lay me down on his bed.

Ezra turns the light on and crawls over me, crouching like a lion. He tugs my shirt up and lays a hand on my bare skin, electrifying my stomach like he's drawing currents out of my body. Arching my back, I shiver as he runs a finger between my breastbone and pelvis, freezing when the bedroom lights flicker out.

"Sorry," he whispers in the dark. "Guess I should work on that."

"Don't you dare."

"It'd be nice to just do this all night and forget my mom came over."

"Or that she questions us living together."

With a single finger, Ezra runs slow circles around my belly button. "After what happened between her and my dad, do you blame her?"

I shrug, then shake my head, because he's right. His mom and dad had an awful relationship. And it literally drove his dad off a cliff.

"So, Mick . . ." he says hesitantly.

"Mick," I echo, distracted by his touch and equally cautious about going there.

"I guess the fact Mom didn't freak out about the gate is a good thing. She knows more about the ruin and the Otherworld than I do."

"You think she's right?"

"That Mick's our *something*? Or that he may not be Angel's actual dad but some . . . *imposter*?" He shakes his head. "I don't know."

The thought makes me queasy. Angel's real dad suddenly just showing up after years is bad enough. How in the world would we explain that he's actually a supernatural fraud?

"At least for now I want you to stay away from Mick, Ruby."

"I have a class with him."

"Outside of that."

"Or maybe I should talk to him again."

"*Ruby*," he sighs.

I sit up slightly, balancing on my elbows. "It might help. If he's not really Angel's father, he'll either admit it or deny it. If he admits it, at least we'll know."

"Or he'll lie. And maybe hurt you in the process."

"On school grounds?"

"You asked. My answer is *no*."

"If I don't talk to him, what do we do next? Ezra, we pretty much know nothing. If he really is Angel's father, then it's probably just a coincidence he's back now. But if he's not . . . maybe he'll tell me why he's here and what he wants."

Gently, Ezra pushes me back against the bed. "Or maybe he'll just kill you."

"If he wanted to hurt me, don't you think he would have already?"

"I said *no*."

"What if you stand outside the door so you can hear me if anything goes wrong?"

He palms the back of my neck, drawing his face closer. "I know how tenacious you are. So I'm just going to keep saying it. *No,* Ruby."

"If you know how tenacious I am, why bother? You know I'm going to talk to him."

Ezra rolls over on his back, blowing out hard. "Then, why even ask?"

I stare out his window, wondering whether it's fair to expect him to change his mind just because I say so. "I guess I was hoping you'd back me."

"I'm not okay with putting you in harm's way, Ruby."

"Ezra, you promised you'd let me decide if I'm actually in danger. And as long as we're in public, I don't think I am."

Staring at the ceiling, Ezra reaches out and grabs my hand. "I think we should stop talking about it right now."

"You want me to go home?"

"No, I just don't want to say something I'll regret. Give me some time to think about it, all right?"

Ezra can be hot-headed. And I know he's asking for time to prevent himself from jumping down my throat. It's a huge give on his part. So, though I want to push, I don't. It won't make a difference anyway. I already know I'm going to talk to Mick after school on Monday, whether Ezra wants me to or not.

CHAPTER THIRTEEN

BREAKFAST OF CHAMPIONS

TRACES OF SUNLIGHT PAINT EZRA'S room through a window above his bed. I sit up, disoriented by the fact that I'm still here and still wearing last night's clothes. Normally I might have stayed up late and tried to talk to him again, waiting until Ezra cooled his heels, because I'm not very patient when it comes to knowing what's on his mind. But after the last emotional week, I really was *that* tired.

Bleary-eyed, I throw my legs over the side of his bed and stand up, wondering which Ezra is going to step out of the shower. Since I can hear him in the bathroom, and I'm not sure I actually want to know until I've downed at least one strong cup of coffee, I head downstairs to the kitchen. Using a paper towel for a coffee filter, I jury-rig a pot and a baker's funnel, frowning at the contraption. If he *really* wants to convince me to move in with him, he'd score massive points just by buying a real coffee maker.

"Hey." Ezra sneaks up behind me and kisses my neck. He smells like newly cut peonies and looks even fresher.

"What?" he asks, giving me a lopsided smile.

"Your soap," I tease. "You smell like a girl."

"I got it for you. For when you stay over."

"I know." I reach out and poke him in the ribs. "And I appreciate it. I just never get tired of baiting you. Your face," I bite my lip, "so wounded. It's precious."

Ezra's eyes flare. He moves like lightning, snatching me up in his arms, carrying me straitjacket-style to a barstool at the kitchen counter. "Stay," he demands, pointing at the seat.

"Woof," I answer cheerfully, hoping this means we're good.

He makes a face and shakes his head, muttering something under his breath as he pulls out two bowls, milk, and a box of Cheerios. After filling me a bowl, he unhooks my filter contraption and pours me a cup of coffee, careful to put just the right amount of milk in, the way I like it, before handing it over.

"Thanks." I wrap my hands around the thick mug, inhaling the to-die-for smell. "I'm sorry about last night. Are you still mad at me?"

He hunches over the counter, digging into his cereal. "I was never mad at you. I just hate that I know you're going to talk to Mick whether I agree or not. It's like I can't even pretend I have a chance at convincing you otherwise."

"I'm complicated." I bat my eyes at him.

"You mean stubborn."

"That too. I'd like to think that's one of the things you like about me."

He stares at me intently, as if debating how to answer. "It's one of the things I *love* about you. But it's also a huge thorn in my side."

"I know." And I do. But being 'tenacious'—my preferred term—is how I've made it this far despite everything. "But we promised to trust each other, right?"

"Right. Just do me a favor, don't ask me what I think anymore if you don't care how I'm going to answer."

"I do care." I place my spoon on the counter and reach across it for his hand. "But that doesn't mean we're always going to see eye to eye. And I'd rather ask just in case. Because what you think and how you feel do matter to me. It does have some bearing on what I decide. But I mean, Ezra, you don't always do everything I want either, right?"

He nods and pulls his hand away. "Guess we'll have to work on meeting halfway."

"That's all I'm asking."

I push my empty bowl away. He's not happy with my decision, but I also know how hard it is for him to stretch even a little when it comes to my safety. So, though it's a small thing, I still see our stalemate as more of a happy compromise. "Drive me to the site now?"

Ezra looks me over. "You going to do something with that?" He points at my head and I know he's talking about my wild, unbrushed hair.

Grinning at him, I wrap the elastic on my wrist around it, pulling it into a messy ponytail. "Better?"

His expression makes me laugh. Like *I'm* the anomaly, not him. "I don't get you."

"Well, sometimes that's mutual."

"It's so weird you don't care."

Collecting my stuff in the hall, I say, "I do care. Sometimes way too much. That's mostly why I try and ignore it."

He raises an eyebrow. "You're not your mother, Ruby."

"Just making sure I never will be."

Ezra shoots me a look, but he doesn't follow it up with something snarky. Instead, he opens the front door and trails me to his truck, motioning for me to climb in. On the way to the site he flips the radio on, but he keeps the volume turned down low, still formulating a response. Ezra often needs space to think, and I respect that, but sometimes he's an emotional tortoise.

At the site, he leaves the car on, idling in the dirt lot. "Pick you up at four?"

"Sure. Movie tonight? I think Angel and Racine want to join us. I mean, if he's still talking to me."

Ezra nods slowly.

"Everything still okay?" I ask.

"You know, if it wasn't for your mother, you wouldn't be you. And you wouldn't be here. We wouldn't be together."

He's right. But I'm not ready to forgive her. She *is* the reason I'm here. And sometimes, I can't decide if that's a good or bad thing. Like if she'd just stuck around and been my mom, instead of this object of everyone else's affection, maybe I'd be off at Stanford now, living a mostly normal life. *She's* the reason it all went off the rails. And according to Mom 2.0, she's also the reason I'm connected to the Otherworld.

Turning away from Ezra, I sniff, inhaling the smells baked into the landscape, mesquite and Russian sage, and the lingering scent of desert rain from last night's light rainfall. The moment passes in a second, but the smell also anchors me to the Pass, reminding me that I'm home. I may never forgive my mom. But it's true she brought me here. And it's true that despite the Otherworld, there's no place on the planet I've ever belonged so completely or felt so much like myself. She messed up big time. But in a twisted way, her last act was also the only real gift she ever gave me.

CHAPTER FOURTEEN

ALL THAT GLITTERS

CROUCHED OVER A TEST PIT the diameter of my fist, I wield my trowel as though it were a piece of fragile glass, carefully digging around the artifacts embedded in the hard ground to loosen the dirt around them. As sunlight bakes my bare shoulders, I hold my breath, leaning in when I spot the effigy. Its surface looks intact, like some sort of animal, but more importantly, it's surrounded by small bones.

"Lee!" I stand up and wave him over, pointing excitedly to my find.

Lee ambles toward me, flowing over the earth. He moves like a streamer caught in a light gust, his pendant bouncing against his chest as he advances. When he sees what I'm pointing at, he crouches down, leaning forward on his haunches. He grabs a soft-bristled toothbrush, swiping the outline of what looks like a cat, delicately removing a thin layer of dirt. "It looks like a nagual," he sighs appreciatively. Lee carefully digs the nagual out, holding up the golf ball-sized figurine for me to examine. "Quite a find."

"Is it bronze?" One thing I do know is that bronze isn't a material endemic to the archeology of the southwest.

"I believe it is."

Lee places the heavy figurine in my palm. As I turn it sideways, two tiny rubies flash up at me, offsetting its deep-set eyes. "I think it's a cat." Though dirty, the rubies are still a brilliant blood-red, bumping off glints of light that linger in my vision. "Maybe a jaguar."

"Yes," he breathes out. "And I don't think it's Puebloan." Still crouching, he looks up at me. "See here," he uses the end of the toothbrush to point at the small bones still embedded in the dirt, encircled by a ring of wilted clover, "this one looks like a parrot mandible."

Lee moves the toothbrush between avian bones, flexing his forearm beneath his rolled-up shirtsleeve so that his snake tattoo appears to coil over his skin. Mesmerized by the sight, I barely notice the heavy nagual burning my palm until my head starts to spin. The sun flares, and all the birds in the Pass screech in unison, and I'm like gauze caught up in the gust that abruptly blows over the site. "The bones . . . were . . . were they an offering?" I stutter, throwing my hand out for balance.

"Yes. Likely part of a ritual."

Lee stands up and wraps both of his hands around my palm, encasing it and the nagual completely. "Do you feel it? The power?"

The nagual floats between us as a wild gust whips my hair around my face, blinding me. The space between his palm and mine is a black hole. It pulls everything in the universe toward me, crushing matter into a mass of unrecognizable atoms that take root down my arms, molecularly joining me to Lee, and the hard-packed earth, and the scrubby sage and lavender dotting the hillside.

I watch Lee's mouth move, too removed from myself to understand what he's saying. My body is an empty vessel, a skin suit, like my soul ditched me to sneak off to the fabled city of Azcale untethered. Like I'm stuck inside a void, looking out at the Pass from a dimension the nagual carved out between our still-adjoined hands. Woozy, I have the vaguest sense of Lee catching me as I fall, wrapping me up in his arms before I hit the ground. Then nothing until I come-to under the awning sheltering the site's workstation.

"What the . . . ?" I sit up abruptly, rustling the metal cot I'm lying on.

"Whoa, easy." Michael, the site tech, motions his hand near my face to keep me from standing up. Then he holds out a water bottle. "Drink first."

I try waving the bottle away but stop when I hear Lee's voice. "Heatstroke is serious, Ruby. I'm not going to have you on site if you can't take care of yourself."

"Heatstroke?" I croak, torquing on the cot to see him better. "I don't have heatstroke."

Lee stands off to the side of the long metal workstation, arms crossed over his chest. When I move to stand up again, he walks over. "Stop." He places a hand on my shoulder firmly, looming over me. "Heatstroke or not, you most assuredly overdid it."

"The nagual . . ."

He squeezes my shoulder, flexing the snake over the muscles in his forearm, stopping me mid-sentence. "Has been safely catalogued."

"That's not what I meant." I wriggle his hand off. "You asked if I felt its power. I did."

Lee looks back over his shoulder at Michael. When he turns to me again, his face is a mask, wearing a pretty good approximation of concern. There's worry on its surface, but something darker swims underneath all that disquiet. "I'm not sure I follow."

"You . . ." His eyes jump just as his pendant reflects a glint of light. I catch my reflection in it, my distraught face, totally void of self-possession. Swallowing, I drop my feet on the ground and sit up straighter. "You handed me the nagual. Then you grabbed my hand."

He exhales his concern, shaking his head slowly. "*You* handed me the artifact. Just before fainting."

Lee's voice sounds sincere. It's convincing, and for a moment, I really do wonder if I imagined everything. But my palm still burns, and I can still see the city on the hill that glowed in my periphery just before fainting. The same one I saw up on the mountain with Racine. "I'm sorry. You're right," I lie. "I probably do need to drink more water."

"Never apologize." He frowns. "It's a weakness. Just acknowledge your mistake and move on."

I nod eagerly. Because whether or not I'm hallucinating, or dehydrated, or exactly dead on, I'm certain the nagual has something to do with fainting. Using Lee's shoulder for support, I stand up and lean over him, reaching out to take Michael's water bottle. Voice pitched, I fake excitement, batting my lashes over doe-eyes. "So, what do you think the nagual means? Do you think you're right? That the site could be Aztlán?"

Lee looks pleased. He stands up, eclipsing my comparatively petite body. Looking down at me, he nods. "But let's keep it between us for now." He nods at Michael as well. "Dig personnel only. Yes?"

"Of course." I smile, outright lying as I back away from him. "I should finish up."

"You're done for the day, Ruby." Lee glances down at his watch. "It's nearly three, and I've already called the sheriff to collect you."

The sheriff? "Torrance?"

Thinking about explaining how I fainted to Torrance makes my stomach turn. It means re-explaining it to Liddy, which means enduring a lecture about wearing a wide-brimmed hat and a head-to-toe Kevlar jumpsuit on site, probably.

"The argumentative one," Lee says pointedly. "The boy. Your guardian angel."

As if on cue, Angel pokes his head around a canvas panel. He stops just short of a table full of yet-to-be catalogued relics when he sees me. "Hey, there. Everything okay?"

Angel quickly scans the artifacts, taking inventory as he goes. I've been around him enough to know it's something he just does in any new setting, like an instinctual tick or compulsion. Nothing gets past him. It's partly why he's so good at his job. And why lying to him now is so hard.

"Yep. Totally." I shrug like I'm embarrassed. "I just forgot to drink enough water."

"Gotchya." Angel holds his hand out toward the dirt lot. "Ready then?"

After extricating myself from Lee's intense gaze and assuring him that *yes, I'm really fine* and *yes, I'll be back to dig up old bones and pots again tomorrow*, I grab my backpack and walk with Angel to his Bronco. Out of sorts, I climb in and buckle up, staring toward the plot I worked on earlier. It's still marked, but from here it looks like it's already been backfilled.

We drive off, bumping over the rough dirt road past a stretch of gnarled, dying cholla toward the highway. Angel taps his middle finger against the steering wheel. At this point I know his tells. He's trying to figure out how to talk to me.

"Just say it," I nudge him.

Angel glances sideways. "You reading my mind?"

If only. I lean into him, halting his maniacal finger. "No. You're fidgety."

He raises an eyebrow. "You've hiked all over the Pass. You grew up hiking in the Santa Monica Mountains. It's hot out, yeah. But *you* don't *forget* to drink enough water, Ruby. So you want to tell me what really happened?"

"Why do you think Lee called *you*?" I ask in response, purposely avoiding his question. Because how do I tell him I'm worried his dad might be some kind of shifter, and that I've started seeing phantom cities around the Pass, and that I think all of it might be connected to the dig? Especially after our tiff yesterday. Especially knowing I'm going to talk to Mick Monday, even though I promised him I wouldn't.

"Lee hates Ezra worse than me, and Liddy and Torrance are down in Albuquerque."

"You think he hates Ezra?"

Angel gives me some side eye, shaking his head as though shocked by my apparent naïveté. "Yes."

"Why?"

"Aside from the fact that Ezra's a pain in everyone's behind?" When I frown at him, he adds, "Seriously, have you seen the way Lee stares at you?"

"That's crazy." I flick his thigh playfully. "Lee's like probably almost thirty. And I'm his intern. Gross."

He shrugs. "Whatever. You know I'm right."

"You're projecting," I say absently, covering my mouth the moment I realize it slipped out. "Wait, I didn't mean that, not like the way it sounds."

Angel stays focused on the blacktop, squinting or maybe glaring out the window. "You are so full of yourself sometimes."

The road ahead seems to unfold, stretching all the way toward the northwest end of the Sangre De Christo mountain range, and I know if I don't say the right thing, the rest of our short ride is going to feel like freaking forever. "I really didn't mean it, Angel. It was just a joke." I drop my head back against the seat rest. "Sometimes I'm just really dumb. I don't always think before I speak, especially around you. Maybe because you're the only person I know I'm *never* on my guard around. It's not a good excuse. I know. But it's true."

Angel contemplates this, and while I know it's not the best excuse, it's a real answer. One I guess he decides will do for now. "So what really happened?"

Barely hesitating, I let it all out in one deep, breathy exhale. "We dug up this effigy, a cat, and when I held it, I got dizzy, and I guess I fainted."

"Because of the effigy or because it's hot out?"

"I think the effigy. But I'm not one-hundred percent sure."

He turns up my driveway and shuts off the engine. "That's weird."

"It is. But I'm fine now."

Angel doesn't know what to think, obviously. He has no clue I'm True of Heart, or that the ruin is a gateway to another world. A natural skeptic, his weirdness threshold stops at ghosts and Ezra. "Maybe you should see a doctor."

"I really am fine. I probably just need a nap before we go out tonight. I mean, if you still want to."

"I'd like to see Racine," he answers evenly.

"Alone?"

"She'd like it if it was all four of us."

"What do *you* want, Angel?"

He frowns at the windshield, then shrugs. "If I knew that, I wouldn't be so freaking annoyed right now."

"You mean at me."

"I mean at all of it. The whole situation, you and Ezra, Mick, the way him being here seems to be working up my mom, pretending it all doesn't bother me." After a moment, he pivots on his seat and just stares at me.

"I wish I knew how to help."

"It's not your fault that Mick wanted to talk to you, and I get that you want to know more about how he knew your mom. But I don't want to have to pretend I'm always okay around you. And I don't need you pretending for my sake, either." He scratches his head. "You're my best friend. And I'm here for you. But you can help by hearing me out and just letting me feel what I feel, good or bad, whether it's for you, or Racine, or about Mick, for real. Stop telling me to look on the bright side all the time or rationalizing my feelings."

His eyes are so intense, I feel a little squirmy under his gaze. Plus, I'm speechless. Angel never let on before that my tendency to compartmentalize peoples' feelings bothers him. But maybe he shouldn't have had to. All of a sudden, it's plain as day. When he tells me how he feels, they're *his* feelings. And when I rationalize them away, it's like I'm a thief. Refusing to acknowledge his hurt—all it does is diminish it, really.

"You're right. And I think I'm more like that for me than you. Because *I* don't know how to deal with it when you're not happy. But that's also *on* me. And it's not fair to you. I'm sorry. And from now on, I promise to do my best to just be . . . honest. At least as much as I know how to, because I don't always really know how I'm feeling all the time either. Deal?" I hold out my hand.

He takes it and holds it tight. "It's a good start, Ruby."

Angel's hand covers mine, flexing as he squeezes. In the sunlight shining through the cab's windshield, his tendons and muscles look strong and defined, like the rest of him, and I suddenly want to sketch the golden planes of his hand and arm. "Do you want to come in? I'll make you a grilled cheese sandwich. Nothing says sorry like fried bread and gooey cheese."

"Rain check." His voice is soft, and much gentler than earlier. "I've still got a couple of hours left on my shift. Besides, you should probably call Ezra and tell him what happened before we meet up later. Give him a chance to be here for you. He won't like that I'm the one who picked you up."

I touch his arm, hesitant to admit I don't want to tell Ezra just yet. Especially not after our talk last night. "Angel, can you do me a favor? Please don't say anything to him. I mean, later, when we go to the movies. Or Racine, either."

Angel opens his mouth to answer, but the mic on his epaulet crackles, distracting him. Quickly, he recites his call sign, then waits for a response, shaking his head dismally. "Accident on I-25," he echoes the operator, "got it. I've got to go, Ruby. Look, I won't say anything. But for what it's worth, I really think you should talk to Ezra before then."

"I will tell him. I plan to. But later, after the movies. After I've had time to think about it more. He's got enough on his mind as it is. And it's really not a big deal."

"It is a big deal. People don't just faint for no reason."

"I do," I try to joke. "Remember my birthday?"

"That's my point." Angel looks both suspicious and uneasy. "It's not the first time. And I'm pretty sure that even back then, you knew it wasn't normal."

CHAPTER FIFTEEN

INTRO TO A RECKONING

ANGEL IS TRUE TO HIS word. After we meet Angel and Racine at Margarita's, and Racine asks me how it's going at the dig, Angel acts as if he gave me a ride home earlier because he was in the area putting up warning flyers at all the trailheads.

"Stupid kids keep pulling them down," he grumbles.

"Any more jaguar sightings?" Racine asks him.

"Not that anyone's called in." Angel leans back against the booth, casually draping an arm around the backrest, and by extension, Racine.

I watch them, feeling a little bit left out and maybe the tiniest bit jealous. Especially after our talk this afternoon. But I give myself a speech. I mean, what kind of person resents playing Cupid just because it knocks them from the center to the sideline?

The shitty kind.

Surprised by Ezra's voice, I turn to stare at him. *What?*

You've been projecting all night. I'm trying to ignore it.

Inhaling, I close my eyes for a few seconds, as if the act itself will establish a wall that shuts him out completely. Until I talk to him later, Ezra cannot be in my head at all.

"What are you doing?" Racine asks me.

I open my eyes and stare at her.

Lying to Ezra. Ezra smirks.

"I think I have a headache coming on."

And Racine, apparently.

Still facing Racine, I dig my nails into Ezra's palm under the table. *I don't know why you can hear me. But you're being a jerk about it.*

Really? Well, imagine being in my shoes right now.

The awful thing is, I can imagine it. If I really am projecting, then Ezra obviously already knows why I left the dig earlier. Which means he probably knows Angel's lying, too, which in no world helps anyone ever.

"Maybe I should take you home," he says out loud. "A movie tonight might not be the best idea."

Racine looks sympathetic. She reaches across the table, resting her hand on its surface palm side up. "We'd seriously understand," she says sweetly, wiggling her fingers toward my free hand. "We can catch a different movie tonight. Save this one for when you're feeling better. Right, Angel?"

Ezra gives her his best fake smile. "Sure. Maybe next weekend?"

"Of course," she chirps. If Racine's brain was actual tickertape, it'd be scrolling *I'd rather be alone with Angel, anyway.* Sometimes, she's that obvious.

"Ezra's probably right." I rub my forehead. "It's been getting worse all night"

Ezra throws enough cash on the table to cover our cheeseburgers and shakes. He feigns concern, rubbing my arm as he tugs me up out of the booth and says, "Enjoy the movie."

Racine follows, scooting out of her seat to hug me. "Go home and eat like a pint of ice cream," she says. Because ice cream is Racine's cure-all for everything.

"I will," I reassure her, hugging her back tightly. "Have fun."

"Feel better, Ruby." Angel winks, and I know he's signaling that he's fine being alone with Racine. "And call me later."

As we walk out of Margarita's under washed-out streetlights that form a string of amber halos down Main Street, Ezra stares everywhere but at me. He's quiet as we pull away from the curb onto the mostly empty blacktop, and even quieter as we drive out of La Luna, almost like the cricket songs outside, and the warm night air blowing between our open windows, are just too much to talk over.

"I *was* going to tell you," I say as he turns onto a backroad. "After the movie."

"I know."

"Then why'd we leave?"

"Because I can't wait until after the movie to hear it, and I really don't love feeling like I'm sneaking around your head."

"I just wanted to think on it for a while first."

Ezra doesn't answer, just bites at his bottom lip as he flexes his fingers around the steering wheel.

"I asked Angel not to tell you. Don't be mad at him."

"I know that too."

Ezra glances at me, and I know from the look on his face that even though he probably understands I had good intentions, he's still angry. "I don't like that you can hear what I'm thinking, Ezra."

He snorts.

"You really can't shut it out?"

Ezra sits like a hunk of granite in his seat, tensing his already-brickwork jaw. "Do you really think I want to hear even half of what's going on in your head right now?"

I swallow down my snarky response. He has a right to his anger, and I know it. I just hate that we've been arguing so much lately. Reaching out, I tap his blue-jean-clad knee, moving my finger in circles around his kneecap. "So can we talk? Please?" I drop my voice, asking as sweetly as possible.

When I reach out and try to touch his cheek, he recoils. "Can't you just let me be mad for a few minutes before insisting I get over it?"

My heart squeezes and I pull my hand back. Pitching toward the window, I stick my head outside, loosening my hair from its ponytail to let it fly free. As the warm night air whips it around my face, I inhale, then let it out slowly, breathing through the tendrils lashing my cheeks. He's right. So right. Mom and I always fought, and since she died, I've gone out of my way to avoid conflict with people I love. And I'm equally bad at staying out of other peoples' bubbles. Case in point, my talk with Angel earlier. But it still hurts to hear Ezra say it.

Ezra whistles through his teeth. It's a heavy sound and I know he can still hear me. Which sucks, because right now, I can only imagine what he's thinking. And that makes me feel too vulnerable for words. "Maybe you should just take me home for real."

"Or maybe you should stop shutting me out when you think I won't like what you have to say and finally tell me what you've been keeping from me."

Still hanging out the window, I drop my head, trying to tame my thoughts completely. I don't know why he can hear me, or whether it has anything to do with what happened today—that's a conversation for later. Right now, I just want to set things straight. Sliding back into my seat, I throw my sandals up on his dash, leaning forward to rest my arms on my knees before taking a breath and starting over.

"So, you know what happened earlier today."

Ezra nods, then glances at me.

"I *was* going to tell you about it tonight, but I should have told you before Angel. I didn't call Angel, though. Lee did. I would have called you if I'd had the chance. I'd barely had time to think about it myself when Angel showed up."

Ezra slows the truck to a crawl, moseying down the dark road away from both of our houses, apparently just driving.

"I have no idea what happened, Ezra. Lee handed me this relic he'd just dug up and I went somewhere. I saw that city again. The same one I saw up in Glorieta when I was hiking with Racine." I rub my nose against my jeans. "Pretty sure it's Aztlán. Like an imprint or something." Ezra's laser focus on the road makes me uncomfortable, and I know he's waiting for me to continue. But I wish he'd look at me. "There's more. When I went to the Otherworld last winter, it wasn't my mom who met me. I mean, I thought it was, at first. But it's not. Whatever *it* is, it took her form. So I'd trust it. That's what it told me. Mom 2.0—that's what I've been calling it in my head—said my real mom died buying me time so I could live my life out here, or something like that. Like she sacrificed herself or something. She kind of implied I should be dead."

In a rush, I tell him the rest—what Mom 2.0 really said about staying with him, and the gate, and my place here on Earth and the Otherworld, and then about Lee's ramblings and his strange effect on me. My heart skips beats at a time, reinforcing the rush of crazy

I'm feeling as I speak. Hearing my own thoughts out loud makes everything that's been going on seem so much more serious. Like giving breath to the words makes everything real.

Shaky from rushing it out, I trail off at the end, inhaling until my lungs want to burst. "Say something," I finally gulp, turning to meet his eyes.

"I don't know where to start," he says softly.

CHAPTER SIXTEEN

TRUTH IS NOT A FOUR-LETTER WORD

EZRA PULLS ONTO THE SIDE of the road, stopping on a bluff overlooking Apache Canyon. He turns the engine off and hitches sideways, toward me, draping an arm over his steering wheel. Below us, the rocky canyon looks luminous, partially lit by the moon above. Only faintly outlined, trees meet at angles above the canyon floor, merging into shadowy Rorschach-like clumps that remind me of an ocean, its surface broken by spindly branches and leafy treetops instead of surf and waves, only hinting at what lurks below.

"I can't hear you anymore." Ezra pulls one of my hands off my knee and twines our fingers. "Whatever was going on with you earlier, it's not now."

"Now that you know, do you still want to be with me?"

He waits a beat before answering. "Yes."

"But?"

"I heard everything you said, Ruby. And I understand why you kept it to yourself. *But* it changes how I view the ruin, and the dig, and how I feel about you being there. It changes *us* in a way, you know. Because it's not as cut and dry as you made it seem before."

A stack of boulders across the canyon catches my eye, and I focus on them, looking away from Ezra.

"You made decisions for both of us without me. Without including me so I could decide for myself." He speaks quietly but conclusively.

"Would you have done anything differently?"

"Between us?"

My stomach turns as I nod, burning a queasy trail up my throat.

"Probably not. But I might have approached it differently." Ezra pulls his hand away and drags it through his hair, dropping it with a thump on the seat between us. "I know you, Ruby. I know who you are and what I want, and what you just told me doesn't change that. But that doesn't mean I trust you entirely either. And it's obviously mutual, or you would have told me all of this much earlier. We have some work to do where *us* is concerned."

A tear slips down my cheek. This isn't how I wanted to tell him. Especially not after our conversation last night. "I'm not sure I know *how* to trust you."

"Because of Leo and last winter?"

"I thought so at first . . . " I turn on the seat, mirroring his posture as we face each other. "I really do understand why you did what you did. And as much as I know how to, I do trust you. The rest of it . . . I think it's my mom. You know? My real mom. Dead or not, she's still in my head. I *never* trusted her. And I know I'm *not* her, but I am a lot *like* her." I inhale, suddenly flooded with feelings I've tried hard to shut out over the last year. "When it comes down to it, though, I'm pretty sure it's me I don't trust most of all."

"*Ruby*." He stares off at the canyon beyond my window.

"It's not just you, though. It's the same with Liddy, and Angel, and Racine. There's always a voice in the back of my head, a *what if.* And sometimes it's hard not to listen."

Ezra reaches out, slipping his hand around my balled fist until I uncurl my fingers and let him press our palms together. "We don't have to be like our parents. It isn't inevitable."

I squeeze his hand, pulling it toward me. "Can we start now?"

"Being different?" Ezra's eyes graze my face, swimming with shifting colors. He moves closer on the seat, pressing our thighs together. "I'm bad at this." He exhales. "I thought I was really bad, and that you'd run off screaming as soon as you figured me out. But you're just as terrible. Honestly, I'm a little relieved."

I lean sideways and drop my head on his shoulder. "Want to know my dirty secret?"

"What's that?"

"I'm bad at lots of things that count."

He sniffs, then laughs. "That's not a secret, Ruby."

Ezra's eyes dance and my heart explodes. His banter is like this weird salve. I know when the snark appears, he's forgiven me. "I promise you, I am trying to be better. For both of us. I spent eighteen years living in my mom's shadow. It's just really hard to get over it."

"I know that too. And I have faith in you. In *us.* But we have to be straight with each other. Always. Because we're not exactly a normal couple. And we can't afford to let our guard down."

I hold his gaze, then search his face, mesmerized by the curved bow in his perfect upper lip. "I've read a lot of love stories. They all make it seem so easy. And this is a lot harder than I thought it would be." I lean in and lightly brush my lips against his. "But I have faith in *both* of us, Ezra. And I really want this. You. Us."

Ezra inches closer, pressing against me. He kisses me deeply, with a hunger that makes me want to crawl inside him and wear his skin. It's a reckless feeling, overpowering the doubt I've felt since talking to Mom 2.0 last winter. And like that, I know. Whatever Mick, and the dig, and Lee represent, I can deal with it all as long as Ezra is still in my corner. Together we're like diamonds encased in tungsten.

Ezra laughs against my mouth and it echoes through me. *You think so?*

"I really do," I murmur, glad he only hears me now when I want him too.

He pulls back and maps my face, landing on my eyes. "I need a little time to process the whole Mom 2.0 thing. But the dig and what happened earlier—Lee's a problem, Ruby."

"He's . . . weird," I concede.

"Angel's convinced he has an agenda." When I make a confused *did-he-say-something-to-you* face, he adds, "You were thinking it earlier."

"I guess I was wondering if Angel's right."

"Can you show me what happened?"

"You mean, like . . ." I tap his head.

"It's worth a try."

"Maybe? Close your eyes for a moment?"

He does, and I reach out, palming his cheek as I try to recall in detailed images everything that happened at the dig earlier. I focus on projecting it frame by frame, like something you'd see in a movie theater.

Ezra sucks in his breath. "That's what you saw before you fainted?"

"Yeah. Lee says I imagined everything. He was pretty convincing. But I *know* the things I just showed you actually happened, even if it really did happen differently for him."

"Mick, the not-jaguar, and now the nagual? It's too much to be coincidence. And whatever his game is, *I* don't trust Lee." Ezra's jaw flexes. "Do you?"

Everything about Lee is weird. But I don't hate him and I'm not afraid of him. Not like with Mick. "No. But I mean, it's like I *want* to like Lee, almost like I want to please him. Even when he's annoyingly bossy."

Ezra raises an eyebrow.

"I know, right?"

He plays with my fingers, working something out before speaking. "I already know what you're going to say, but I have to ask."

I sigh, focusing on his elegant, work-worn hands. "You want me to quit."

"You fainted today. That's how it started with the ruin. If it is Aztlán or Azcale, and Azcale really is some portal, being there is as dangerous as being up the mountain."

"If it really is the Azcale from your grandpa's stories, and Mick's here because of it, does it even matter? In this case, I'd rather have boots on the ground than watch from a distance. At least until we know more."

"And Lee?"

"I handled your identity crisis. I think I can handle him."

Ezra pulls me into his arms, resting his chin near my ear. Pressed together in the center of the darkened cab, he points out stars in the crisp sky, weaving pictures out of pinpoints of light. We're both quiet, and I know we're both thinking similar things. That whatever is unfolding in the Pass, it's all too much to be coincidence. And that regardless, we're both useless until we know more.

"If you're not going to quit, do me a favor," Ezra says, breaking the silence. "Don't talk about Azcale or my grandfather's stories with Lee. They don't belong to him, and I'm not in love with how he seems to think he knows everything. Whatever's going on, he doesn't need to be a part of it."

"I'll just stick to his theories about Aztlán, I promise. And I'll keep my ears and eyes open. If anything weird happens, I'll tell *you* first."

"Be careful around him, Ruby." He drops his chin on my shoulder and I feel his gaze on the side of my face. From Ezra's lips, it's not a request as much as a command, but it's one I also happen to agree with. I don't know for sure if Lee is lying about what went down at the dig earlier today, but I definitely don't trust him either.

"I will," I agree softly.

Ezra pulls me tighter against his chest and I lean into him, too aware of all the hard muscle beneath his checkered button-up. He's put together like the things he makes in his woodshop—thoughtfully built, equipped with magnificent, almost indestructible hardware—and feeling him solidly up against my back is comforting. But knowing he's as unsure as I am about where to go from here unsettles me. Pretending Everything Is Fine was easier when Ezra didn't know the truth about Mom 2.0 and our talk last winter, because at least then, I could fantasize he had some control over our futures. Now, though, more than ever, even just the word 'future' feels like a vague, intangible thing.

CHAPTER SEVENTEEN

EVEN ONIONS HAVE LAYERS

FAT DROPS OF RAIN PELT the windshield as I pull into the dig's lot, adding to my melancholy. Out of nowhere, the sky opens up, pouring down hard over the cracked clay ground, quickly forming muddy rivulets that run down the adjacent hillsides toward the overfull creek. It rains all morning, and the rain turns the dig into one hell of a mud-splattered, red-brown swamp.

Near mid-afternoon, drizzle and howling wind replaces the downpour, blowing everything into a jumble. Wrestling with a tarp, I try to re-shield the same large plot we've been attempting to protect all morning, unsuccessfully clutching my jacket's hood at the same time so it doesn't fall down. Across from me, Lee places a large brick on one of the tarp's corners, covering another patch of wilted chickweed, while Michael and I secure the other ends. Quickly, we gather brushes, and picks, and water bottles from around the site, throwing them into large pails we carry back to the main tent.

Under its canvas covering, I shake my wet hair out, running my fingers through tangled ends, spattering an already-damp wall.

Across from me, over at the workstation, Lee washes his muddy hands under a jury-rigged spigot, wiping them on a dirt-stained towel.

"The weather here," Lee mutters. He looks up at the canvas roof, shaking his head. "It's an abomination."

After running around all morning pumping out holes and checking under tarps, I almost agree. When it comes to rain especially, the Southwest is like another dimension. It comes out of nowhere. Not to mention, it could be raining on one sidewalk and bright as day just across the street. Like the Ancient's couldn't all agree on the status quo and staked out sides.

Lee drops the towel on the basin board and turns toward me, resting his lanky frame against the wash bowl. "How long have you known Ezra?"

I look up at him, gauging his expression. It's a harmless question, but it kind of came out of nowhere. "Since last summer. Why?"

His black eyes shimmer down at me, like the pendant around his neck, taking in my face with unnerving intensity. "Perhaps I just want to know my intern better. You do work for me, Ms. Brooks."

I frown. "No, I work for the University."

"In this scenario, I am the University. Not that I begrudge you the difference." He puts his hands up as if to say, *Don't shoot the messenger*. "Your aunt wanted you here. I thought you wanted you here as well. Perhaps I'm wrong."

"You're not wrong, but that doesn't mean we're friends."

"That's a shame," he says sincerely.

"Do you want to be?"

"I want a lot of things, Ruby."

Lee's answer is straightforward, but not flirty. Still, the way he says it—with a kind of aching—stirs something in me. "I'm sorry," I say, banking on honesty to get him to open up. "Yesterday was weird and I'm still feeling it."

"I understand," he says. "No skin."

"Huh?"

"It's a saying, no?"

He looks so confused it makes me laugh. "Off my back."

"What?"

"No skin off my back, that's the saying."

"Yes, of course." Lee makes what seems like a genuine effort to smile.

"So, do you drive up from Albuquerque every weekend?" I ask, too aware I know nothing about his life outside of the dig.

"No. I have a rental in Pecos. Now that classes are out for the summer, there's little reason to stay in Albuquerque when my focus is here."

It's weird knowing I've been working for him for a couple weeks now and had no idea he's living right next door. "It must feel pretty small compared to Albuquerque."

"It'll do," he says dismissively. "And I prefer to be near my work."

"You're from Mexico City originally?"

"Tenochtitlan for a time."

"Tenochtitlan." I try the name out, rolling it around my mouth. "I've never heard of it. Is that like, a suburb?"

He smirks. "You might say that."

Lee collects his satchel and steps out from under the tented station, waiting for me. Grabbing my own backpack, I follow him. There isn't much to be done now but let the site dry. It's still pretty damp out, and the earthy desert smells of wet dirt and dank sage hang in the air as we walk, impregnating the low, misty cloud cover snaking through the Pass.

As usual, Lee moves beside me like a rivulet. I watch him walk, struck by how his movements make it seem like he's emulating his best approximation of a human; like he hasn't quite figured out how to emote, or even just move his muscles correctly beneath his skin. It's like he's put together oddly, tall and lithe in a way that should be gangly, but isn't, sporting a striking face full of angles that clash, offsetting dark eyes, a sharp nose, and a thin-lipped mouth. Handsome but off-putting.

Silently, I walk beside him toward Liddy's car, surreptitiously staring while I try to think of a politic way to avoid talking about yesterday's events should he bring them up. But he doesn't mention the nagual or my fainting episode, and as we reach the lot, a large raptor soars overhead, riding the wind below the cloud bank above us. It circles the area, then drops lower, scooping something off the ground near a row of parked cars. I gape at its enormous wingspan in awe.

"Look." I reach out to stop Lee, pointing up at the limp squiggle hanging from its beak. "It caught a snake."

"What a magnificent eagle," Lee replies.

Glancing away for a moment, I unlock Liddy's car, leaning in to throw my junk into the backseat. As I offload my too-stuffed backpack, Lee places a hand on my side and I follow his outstretched arm, looking up again to catch the end of the eagle's descent maybe twenty feet away. It lands on the thick arm of a giant cholla. Spreading its impressive wings, the eagle drops the snake, which falls limply to the ground.

Lee steps back, delighted. He clasps his hands together several times, almost clapping. Wings still spread, the eagle sits on the cholla, still for a moment while it scans the dig site. Then, it extends its head toward us and a tinge of anticipation grips my chest. The hillside behind it glimmers, and an ancient metropolis appears, superimposed over the desert foothills—a golden mix of ancient architecture.

"Lee!" I stab point in front of me. "Do you see it?"

As quickly as I ask, the city disappears and the eagle swoops down off the cholla. It scoops the snake up, then soars upward, whipping its prey around as it snaps its beak sideways, disappearing into the clouds above us.

Lee's eyes are like fireworks, luminous with energy and momentum. "Like the Aztec prophecy," he says almost breathlessly, staring at me as if I've turned to gold. "An eagle with a snake in its beak perched upon a cactus, denoting the land where the Aztec were meant to build their great city."

"So, you did see it!" I almost screech.

"I've never not seen it. I *knew* this was Aztlán." Lee pauses and looks out at the hillside. "Legend says the prophecy came to fruition in Mexico City. But acumen comes from seeing past appearances." He homes-in on my face, capturing my full attention. "You of all people know that."

I nod, because I didn't just see it, I felt it. Aztlán. *And* what Ezra's grandfather called Azcale. There's so much to say, to tell Lee about Ezra's grandfather's legend. If Aztlán really is Azcale and belonged to the Pecos first, it probably at least half-explains my reaction to the nagual yesterday. But I also promised Ezra I wouldn't talk to Lee. And how in the world do I explain that I know it's a Pecos site *and* an Aztec site without telling Lee everything anyway?

CHAPTER EIGHTEEN

DADDY'S GIRL

ZIGZAGGING THROUGH THE CROWDED HALL on the way back to Mick's classroom after sixth period, I nearly run over Las Gallinas.

"Whoa, where are you going?" Racine grabs my arm. "Are we still meeting at Margarita's?"

"Back to Media Tech." I'm too nervous to come up with a lie. "And I still plan on meeting you guys. I'm just going to be a few minutes late."

Marta raises an eyebrow. "Because?"

"I need to talk to Mick."

"Awesome." Marta purses her lips, squinting at me. "We'll go with. I'd like to give the son-of-a-bitch a piece of my . . ."

"No!" Racine cuts her off. "It's not our business. It's really none of yours either, Ruby." She looks at me sharply.

"Like hell," Marta says. "Angel's my cousin. Mick's an asshole. That gives me two good reasons to get involved. And if Ruby wants to stick up for Angel, more power to her."

I'm not thrilled Racine called me out, especially not in front of Ashley and Marta, but I almost choke when Marta defends me; it's like pigs just flew through the hall. "I'm not going to see him to talk about Angel," I reassure Racine.

"Then, what?" She puts her hands on her waist.

I look between them, studying Marta especially. She's not my favorite person, and I don't trust her, but I also know Racine will keep her in line. I'd bet on the fact that she's as interested in protecting Angel as she is in keeping the peace between us. "I want to know how he knew my mother."

"What?" Ashley screeches before covering her mouth. After a moment, she drops her hand and stares at me. "Wow."

It's clear Racine kept that little bit of information to herself. And I'm grateful for her discretion. "Yeah, wow."

Marta continues to stare at me. "We'll go with you."

"I'd rather talk to him alone."

She grabs my elbow, pivoting me toward Mick's room. "Then we'll wait outside."

On my left, Racine gives me side eye, shrugging. She motions forward, grabbing my other arm so that they flank my sides as Ashley follows us down the hall.

Outside Mick's classroom, Marta lets go of my arm and grabs my hand, squeezing lightly. "My dad used to gossip about how Mick left Viviane for another woman. What if that's how he knew your mother?"

I stare at her, mortified.

"Marta!" Racine gasps. "What's wrong with you?"

"I'm just saying."

Ashley looks down at her shoes, but Marta meets my stare, totally oblivious to the rocket-force willpower I'm exerting to stop myself from clocking her. But her eyes are wide and open, not defiant, like she genuinely feels bad for me. I'm pretty sure her sudden interest isn't a ruse; for some reason, she's actually trying to be supportive.

"We'll be right here," she reassures me.

In a thousand years I doubt I'll figure Marta out, and right now it's the last thing on my list of Things To Do. So I let it go, taking a deep breath as I smile and thank her. Worrying about whether Mick is dangerous is bad enough. I don't need Marta's voice in my head too. Inhaling, I steady myself, pulling my hand away from hers, then walk into the classroom.

Across a sea of desks, it almost seems like Mick is waiting for me. He's just leaning casually against a desk corner, arms crossed over his chest as if he knew I was on my way. Our eyes meet and he grins, his green irises radiant like neon against his skin.

"Forgot something?"

"Uh. Yeah." I purposely left my sketchbook behind, so I had an excuse to come back to talk to him.

Mick walks over to a desk near the window and plunks down. He reaches beneath the seat and produces my sketchbook, holding it out to me. "Come sit for a moment."

Nervous, I walk down the aisle and sit in a desk across from him, holding my backpack on my lap, against my chest protectively.

"I won't bite," he assures me. Mick makes a face, and something about his expression looks almost skeletal. "I'm guessing by your reaction you're not particularly sure if I'm joking."

"Are you?" I breathe, trying to keep my voice from squeaking.

He laughs a loud, booming laugh. "You're just delightful."

"Are you really Angel's dad?" I sputter.

"I am." He tilts his head from side to side, as if weighing my character. "You're close to Angel?"

"He's one of my *best* friends." My hackles raise, quick to go on the defense.

"Then it's not a stretch to assume you'd want what's best for him."

"Do *you*?" I spit out.

"I always have." He says it like there's no question; like he didn't just up and disappear years ago.

I zone in on the flecked floor, counting the linoleum squares leading to the wall. Hearing him say it feels weird. Angel has been waiting for something, even just a peep from Mick for days. "I didn't come here to talk about Angel." It slips out, and Mick catches my unwitting admission—that I purposely came back to talk to him. The knowing flickers across his face as soon as the words leave my mouth.

Mick sits back, straining the desk. "How about we make a deal. Information for information."

"I'm not going to talk about Angel anymore."

"I don't want to talk about Angel. I want to talk about you."

"You want to talk about me?" He nods and I waffle, confused by the turn of events. This was supposed to be a confrontation, not a conversation. And it's definitely not meant to be mutual. "Fine, me first. How did you know my mother?"

"Sera liked to hike the Pass."

"You told me that last time."

"Then maybe you're not asking the right question."

The weight of what I don't know settles over me. It's pervasive and scary, but in a way, it's also my security blanket. Because the reality is, I'm not sure knowing the truth will be any easier.

"Okay," I try again. "How *well* did you know her?"

"Quite well." His eyes glass over for a moment, and I know he's with her, reliving something I can only hope to drag out of him. "My turn. Who are you, Ruby?"

The question catches me off guard. Partly because I wasn't done asking about Mom, partly because I'm not sure what he's asking. "Other than Ruby Brooks, daughter of Seraphine Brooks, formerly from Venice Beach, California, now living in La Luna, New Mexico?"

"Yes, other than that."

Other than that? I sniff. What's he expecting? Ruby Brooks, princess of the Otherworld? "That's really all there is."

He shifts, leaning forward knowingly. "You need to stop underselling yourself."

Taken aback, I struggle to come up with a spirited response, trying to mask the wave of dread that passes through me. "Okay, I'm a gremlin. If you get me wet after midnight, I multiply. Better?"

"Closer, at least." He tips the desk back again, balancing his substantial weight on two measly metal legs. "You pretend to turn a blind eye because you're drawn to ugly things and it scares you. Like Sera. I see it there inside you."

My heart pounds against my rib cage as I command myself to keep it together. "All right. My turn. You say you knew my mom well. How well? Did you spend a lot of time together?"

His toothy smile is both dark and radiant at the same time. "That's two questions."

"It's a compound question. Just freaking answer."

"Yes. We spent a lot of time together. I know that your grandparents died in a car accident when Sera was fourteen. And that Sera barely knew them. I know Liddy raised her, and that it was hard for them. But that Sera adored her. I know her *that* well."

"You said *know*." I gulp, caught up on the word. "You *know* her that well. You know she's dead, right?"

My eyes water thinking about Mom and Liddy together, how they must have been when they were younger. Mom never talked much about her parents, or her relationship with Liddy. But I know from Liddy that they were close before I was born. To hear Liddy tell it, they were more like conjoined twins than siblings separated by almost ten years.

Lee's brilliant green eyes darken. "I do. And that's three questions now. My turn." He fingers the skull pendant around his neck, rubbing the top of its bronze cranium absently. "It's wise to fear the ruin, Ruby. But there's wisdom to be had there too. Can you still hear it?"

My eyes are so wide they actually hurt. Whatever he is or isn't, he's not just here to teach and tie up loose ends, and knowing that for sure scares me. "Yes," I rush out. "I can. How do you know about the ruin?"

"My friendship with Sera blossomed out of her obsession with it. She was so excited to share her discovery with someone. When I realized what she was, I played along because I loved her. I thought I could straddle both worlds, one with Vi in the here and now, and one later, with Sera."

"You . . . you loved her?"

Mick stands up, running his fingers along the long, rectangular windowsill as he walks the length of the room. With his back to me, he says, "I gave it my best shot with Vi for Angel, but Sera . . . *she* made me feel human. I'd always intended for her to go back with me."

"You . . . with both of them?" It's like I can hear myself talking, except I'm not really tethered to my body. I'm weightless. And bewildered. And utterly, inexplicably confused. Nearly tripping over my backpack, I shoot up, out of my seat. "But you're not human."

He turns to me, eyes flaring. "Is that a question?"

My head suddenly splits, severing down the middle. Pushing my palm into my forehead, I squint at him. "Are we . . . are you . . ." Drowning in puzzle pieces I don't want to put together, I can't make myself finish the sentence.

"From Ottomundo?"

"Yes," I breathe out.

He dips his head, locking his eyes on mine as if charting my past at the same time he plots my future. "I'd been here awhile when I met Vi. Hiding in plain sight. I never intended to stay so long but we had Angel, and I met Sera. I know what you think, but I'm not the villain here. When I did go back, I went back for all of them."

"How did my mom know about the ruin?" I whisper, not one-hundred percent sure I want to hear the answer.

"She was drawn to it. Like you. It's your bloodline, Ruby."

"Was she True of Heart?" My voice is calm, masking the turmoil inside me.

"Yes." Mick's directed gaze pierces my exterior, penetrating deeply as if laying blacktop throughout my soul, leaving inroads he can navigate later. The invasion feels physical, almost violent, yet I still can't look away. "But she couldn't open the gate in this world. Not like you. She didn't even know what she was until much, much later."

The room fills with shadows, swallowing every stationary thing until they're nothing but inky silhouettes that pulsate as the space grows darker. A dusky canyon appears in front of me, its maw glimmering like onyx between ancient structures on its far side. My mom materializes, billowing off to the side. She opens her mouth and motions me closer, but then disappears in a blinding flash, leaving my skull crushed between my palms as I press against the pain behind my eyes. Without warning I double over, treating the floor to my half-digested lunch.

"Enough," Mick murmurs. He picks up the receiver from a beige phone still jacked to the wall near his desk and mumbles something about 'janitorial' into it. "Ruby," he turns back to me afterwards, "sit."

Shaky, I drop into a chair, angry at my legs for betraying me. The last thing I want to do is take orders from Mick. But my nervous system seems to be operating from a place beyond my conscious mind. I toggle my ears, plunging them with my fingers. "My mom," I strangle out, wiping saliva off my mouth, "were you . . . *involved*?" My heart speeds up, bashing against my sternum. It's possible I'm about to have a heart attack.

"Ruby!"

I whip toward the sound of Racine's voice, grabbing the edge of the desk to keep from tipping over. Racine's mouth puckers into an 'O.' She rushes over, bumping Mick out of the way, placing a comforting hand on the small of my back when I double over again. "What the hell?" she says under her breath, looking up at him.

Marta and Ashley stand in the doorway eyeing us suspiciously. Marta cocks her head, staring back and forth between the room and the hall. Reeling, I grab my backpack and Racine's arm at the same time, desperate to get out of the building. I'm not done questioning him, but I can't deal with how raw I feel. And I need fresh air.

I rush out of the room and down the hallway, stopping to wilt against a row of lockers when it feels like I might pass out again. Trying to stop the hall from spinning, I swallow down bile. My ears sync to the clock on the hallway wall, ticking in slow motion. The smell of floor wax, and chalk, and mold in the ceiling tiles assaults my senses. Half my mind is mush, but the other is crystal clear, and I don't at all like where it wants to take me.

CHAPTER NINETEEN

IN PLAIN SIGHT

"ARE YOU ALL RIGHT?" RACINE looks really worried. "You were in there forever."

"He's a smug bastard," Marta adds. "What did he say to you, Ruby?"

Before I can answer, Ezra calls my name from down the hall.

"What's he doing here?" I croak.

"I called him." Racine rubs my shoulder. "You were in there with Mick for like an hour. And, Ruby, you should have seen your face when we peeked through the window. We were freaking out."

An hour? How is that possible?

I close my eyes until I feel Ezra's body heat spread up my arm, riding an electric wave across my chest. "You didn't have to come," I murmur, agitated by his worried expression.

"What's going on?" Unease lodges in the creases where his eyes smile. "Ray said you were in there with Mick forever. She said you looked terrified."

"It was nothing," I lie.

"Then why do you look like you might throw up?"

"She already did," Marta offers. "All over the floor. In front of Mick," she adds unhelpfully.

"Marta," Ashley mumbles under her breath, "really?"

"It's my head. Or maybe being around Mick. I'm not sure which."

Ezra pulls me into a tight hug. "Let's get out of here."

Las Gallinas walk us to the parking lot. After Marta and Ashley leave and it's just the three of us standing near Ezra's passenger door, I sputter out, "Mick claims he and my mom were close. He implied they had a thing." The words bore into my skull, daring me to scratch them out.

Ezra and Racine both look like deer caught in headlights; it's obvious neither know how to answer.

"I left before he could explain." Palming my face, I cover my eyes, leaving my hand to shield out the world for a few seconds. "I'm a mess, Ezra."

Don't say anything else. He squeezes my hand. *Not around Racine. Not yet.*

I won't. Out loud I add, "Don't tell Angel, Ray. Let me. Please."

"Of course." She hugs me hard.

As Racine heads to her car, Ezra unlocks his truck and helps me up. He even buckles the seatbelt around me. "Do you think he's dangerous," he asks, driving away from the school toward my house.

"He *is* from the Otherworld."

Ezra grips the steering wheel, white knuckling its worn leather cording. "Did he tell you that?"

"Not in so many words. But he mentioned Ottomundo and he knows about the gate." In a rush, I babble out the rest, removed from my own voice as the words leave my mouth. "When he said he went back, I think he meant he went back . . . there. To the Otherworld."

Ezra's jaw flexes. "You think he's really Angel's father?"

My stomach rebels, clenching like a fist around a sea of fear. "He says he is."

Ezra pulls up my driveway and turns the engine off.

"And you think he and your mom . . ." He trails off.

I cover my face with both hands, breathing into my palms. "The way he said it, yeah. He knew things about her life. Things Mom would have had to tell him."

Ezra turns toward me. Gently, he removes my hand and tucks it into his own. He holds on tightly, meeting my eyes. "All we know for sure is that Mick says he's Angel's dad. It'd be good to figure the rest out before jumping to conclusions. Like *what* he is and why he's here now."

I shake my head, dumbfounded. "Ezra, if Mick's really Angel's dad, what does that make Angel?"

Ezra looks straight ahead, his jaw morphing to steel. "I don't know," he finally answers. "But this affects everyone. If Mick came through the gate, then he's probably our jaguar. And given everything, I doubt he's visiting out of the goodness of his heart."

"If he even has one."

Ezra takes his keys out of the ignition. He doesn't say more, but there's obviously an elephant in the truck with us.

"Should we go inside?" I ask quietly.

Still silent, Ezra trails me into the house. Liddy hears me as I dump my backpack in the hall and calls out, inviting me into the kitchen. Pulling Ezra along with me, I peek around the wall, hoping to catch her alone. I want to pick her brain, to ask her every question I can possibly come up with about Mom, about how often she took off for New Mexico when they were younger. But Liddy is already in the middle of making dinner. Brisket. Which means *she* has something important to share; something she's probably worried I won't take well.

"Hey." She wipes a blazing ginger strand of hair out of her eyes and turns away from a sink full of vegetables, looking over her back at me. "Oh—Ezra. Hi."

"Liddy," Ezra tips his head at her.

"You're back from the U early." I search the kitchen for clues, indexing my mind for any little thing I might have done wrong. "What's up?"

Liddy wipes her hands on a towel and grabs what looks like a corn muffin off the counter, shoving it at me. "New recipe. What do you think?"

She's acting weird, but I play along. "Mmmm," I answer through a bite.

Ezra shoots me a look. *Should I go?*

I'll kill you if you do. Seriously, she's in Martha Stewart mode.

"We're going upstairs," I tell her lightly.

"Dinner's at six." She turns back to the sink and picks up a vegetable scrubber. "Torrance, Angel, and Viviane will all be here just before then. Ezra, you're welcome to stay too."

Torrance, Angel, *and* Viviane*?* I eye her, my heart aflutter. It's not like I haven't picked up on her weirdness or her overly chirpy tone. Judging by her demeanor, she's probably not mad at me. But she is planning an event, not just dinner, which means there's something big brewing beneath her cheery Liddy façade. And Viviane? How am I going to face her?

My bet is on Mick. Maybe Liddy and Torrance have something to tell us about him they've been keeping to themselves. Because why else would Angel and Viviane be joining us for dinner on a Monday night? After today, it almost makes sense. The look Liddy and Torrance gave each other when I first told them Mick knew Mom. And how neither of them acted surprised. Maybe they know a lot more than they're letting on. Maybe I won't have to ambush her.

In my room, Ezra stands at the window, eyeing a canvas I'm working on. Vibrant pinks and blues fill out the left corner, hinting at the palate knife skyline I've started painting above an abstract rendition of the Pass near my house. "Can I see it when it's done?"

I join him, wrapping an arm around his waist. "You're the only person I show them to."

Ezra turns to face me, brushing a hair off my cheek before placing his hands on either side of my waist. "That means a lot to me." He kisses me gently and drops a hand, moving on to find my fingers. As he twines them in his, he says, "Assuming Mick told you the truth about your mom, there's obviously *a lot* more to you ending up in La Luna than just coincidence."

"You believe him . . . the True of Heart part?"

He nods vigorously. "It makes sense, like me and my clan. It's all about lineage."

"Lineage. That's what he said. But he also said she didn't know what she was until much later."

"She wasn't supposed to. *You're* not supposed to."

"But she obviously figured it out." My lungs feel tight, leaving little room for air. "Ezra, what if it *was* really her. Up at the ruin," I rush out. "I need to go back up there." If I could just get to Mom 2.0 again, maybe she'll tell me who Mick is and why he's here.

Ezra places his hands on my shoulders, holding me steady with both his grip and his serious eyes. "You're not going up there. She told you to stay away for a reason."

His face is full of concern, and I can tell by the way he's looking at me that I'm acting crazy. I feel crazy. But I don't know what else to do other than talk to Mick again. And honestly, I really don't want to be anywhere near him alone either.

I break free of Ezra's grip. "She also told me to stay away from *you*."

His nostrils flair beneath his fiery eyes. "Ruby, you're not going *anywhere* near the ruin again until you cross over. Step back," he says calmly. "I'm not asking you to take what Mick said lightly. It's pretty big. But I *am* asking you to keep your head. He could be lying. This could all be part of some really messed-up plan. We don't know yet, and the worst thing either of us could do right now is let our emotions drive us into a tailspin." Ezra's voice is strident. "I can't afford to lose you, Ruby. Liddy can't afford to." He wraps me up tight when I step into his arms. "It can't be coincidental that Mick's here *now* given the dig and Lee's find. Let's concentrate on that; start there, all right?"

I rub my nose against his chest. "I have no idea where to go from here."

"But I do." He holds a finger up and tells me to wait a second before rushing out of my room. When he returns, he walks to my bed, sitting down crossed-legged in the center. "I was just getting back from Jemez when Racine called."

Ezra pats the space beside him with purpose and holds up a tattered book. I settle down next to him and he places it gently on my lap. Its textured, worn cover, stained blue around the embossed word *Tshiquite* emblazoned in faded gold, looks ancient. I run a finger over it, looking at him curiously.

"It's another, much older word for the Pecos pueblo."

"But what is it?"

"Hopefully the book my mom told us about."

"It is real," I say breathlessly.

"Fingers crossed. It was a pain in the ass to dig up."

"I can't believe you found it."

He nods. "I remembered Grandpa joking that one day, when Old Jimmy passed, he'd unearth him and pry the book from his cold, dead hands if that's what it took to finally get a look at it. Far as I know, Gramps never got the chance. But Jimmy's still kicking. Ninety-eight and blind as a bat, and still living in his old adobe. I had time today, and I figured it couldn't hurt to see, so I went and paid him a visit. He thought I was his grandson, and I didn't try to convince him otherwise."

"Ezra!" I sort of squawk. "That's terrible."

"You can give me back the book if you'd like." Ezra holds out a hand. "No?" he snorts, angling his head cockily. "As I was saying, I asked him about it, and he grinned like a jack o' lantern, then talked my ear off about how kids today don't give a squat about tradition, before sending me on a wild goose chase. Believe it or not, I found it at the mission. Strapped under a pew where Jimmy's family sits."

"Really?" I try to imagine Ezra sneaking around, playing detective.

"I'm hoping that means it'll be worth something to us."

I flip open the worn cover, taking care to be gentle with its spine. Inside, rows of tight but fluid handwriting, and crisp sketches, and diagrams fill pages of yellowing paper. But the words are in a foreign language, and I can't read any of it.

"It's Tewa," Ezra tells me. "Tewa and Towa differ, but they're both Tanoan languages. We're forbidden from writing in Towa, but I can probably still translate most of it if you give me a little time. And since it's Tewa, I won't be breaking any rules—not technically."

The worn book shakes in my hand, betraying my excitement. "What if there's actually something in there about the ruin or your Pecos Circle?"

"I'm hoping there is," he says softly. "But I wouldn't bet on it."

CHAPTER TWENTY

THE THINGS WE DO FOR LOVE

TORRANCE AND ANGEL ARE IN extra-good spirits, which makes me wonder what Liddy's up to. I'm in no mood to sit at the table and pretend my world didn't just unravel, but whatever it is Liddy wants to share, there's no getting out of it. As soon as Liddy yells for us to come down, and we walk into the warm sunset-lit kitchen, she starts assigning us seats and barking out orders about where to put her piping hot corn muffins and fancy honey butter, and what expensive bottles of wine to open, and generally just being kind of manic.

Ezra sits down at the neatly set oak table beside me, and I'm grateful he agreed to stay. He'd rather go home and get cracking on *Tshiquite*, no doubt, and I don't blame him. I'd give my painting arm for an hour or two alone to sort through everything Mick told me earlier.

When every bit of food is out of the oven and lined perfectly down the colorful runner splitting the sides of the table, Liddy lights the candles she set out in the middle of the display before sitting down beside Torrance. She pours herself a glass a wine and wraps a slender hand around the bulb of her delicate glass before lifting it to take a sip. And that's when I see it. The gigantic sparkler on her right index finger.

I almost choke on my water, covering my mouth so I don't spit it out.

"So," she starts, winking at Torrance. "We wanted everyone together tonight so we could share our news."

Liddy said *we*. It's a *we* thing. And judging by the diamond on her finger, I know what's coming. Under the table, I search for Ezra's hand. My heart fills with even more love for Liddy than I thought possible, and it's such a weird moment, momentarily masking all my anxiety. My life may be fraying, but she's getting a brand-new start. After all these years of taking care of everyone else, Liddy, more than anyone I can think of, deserves to be happy.

"Lydia!" Viviane shrieks, jumping up from her chair. She stands at the table and clasps her hands together, holding them up near her mouth like she's praying while she waits for Liddy to say it.

Liddy holds her hand out over the table, moving it around over a basket of French bread. As her ring catches the light, bumping off a whole lot of sparkle, Torrance grins, looking mighty pleased with himself.

"I guess Tory loves me," Liddy says mischievously.

"A little bit." Torrance laughs.

Ezra rubs his thumb across my palm as if reassuring me. Viviane squeals in delight, and Angel's face is one, big, thousand-watt smile. And before I know it, I'm crying.

"Ruby?" Liddy turns to look at me with wide, suddenly concerned eyes.

I'm out of my chair before she says another word, ambushing her seat. I don't remember the last time I hugged her so hard, but it feels amazing. "I'm so happy for you," I laugh-sob. "So, so happy!"

She looks up at me teary-eyed, her face glowing. "Thank you, love."

Torrance stands up beside her, ready for me when I throw myself at him. He gives me a bear hug, whispering, "Thanks, kid," as I squeeze the life out of him. "I was aiming for a 'that's great.' Talk about exceeding expectations." He chuckles and lets me go, turning the other way to embrace Angel, then Viviane.

After everyone has hugged, and cried, and *oohed* and *ahhed* at Liddy's gorgeous ring, we settle at the table, passing Liddy's cornucopia of food to each other. Liddy tells us about how Torrance proposed at the historic St. James Hotel up in Cimarron over the weekend, and Ezra squeezes my hand or rubs my palm here and there under the table. It's all so surreal, and though I'm absolutely thrilled for Liddy and Torrance, it's hard to reconcile all the love in the room with the things Mick revealed earlier. Like a romantic fairytale on the heels of an H.P. Lovecraft story.

Across a platter of scalloped potatoes, Angel looks ecstatic. Torrance is more like his father than an uncle, and I know Angel's feeling the same way I am about Liddy finally meeting The One. Seeing his face, it's heartbreaking even just thinking about the secrets I'm keeping from him right now.

As I stare at him, Angel winks at me. He wiggles his eyebrows playfully. "So, best man and maid of honor?"

Torrance claps him on the back. "I wouldn't have it any other way."

"I'm just in it for the partying," Angel laughs. "Let's see, there's the engagement party, the stag party, the bachelorette party, the night-before party, the night-after party." He scratches his chin. "Between us," he looks at me, "we have some serious planning to do."

I put on my best fake smile and nod like there's nothing I'd rather do than plan a bunch of celebrations. In another world it would be true. In another world I'd be brimming with enough excitement to power all of La Luna.

Liddy motions at me. "You all right, love?"

"I ate too much." I grasp my stomach. There's no way I'm raining on her parade. "I think maybe I could use a little fresh air. Do you mind?"

"Of course not."

Ezra throws his napkin on the table. "I'll go with."

He grabs my hand and walks beside me out of the kitchen. At the front door, he makes a beeline for the porch, stepping outside as I grab my sweater off the coat tree in the hall. My home is Ezra's home. And he comes over often. But he still has the hardest time being in a room alone with Torrance and Liddy. I hate to even think about it, but I can only imagine what it was like for him all the years his face was scarred, because he already has a hard-enough time talking to people.

"What are you thinking about?" he asks on the porch steps outside.

"You."

"Me?"

I nod back at the house. "Sometimes you're so awkward around them."

He shrugs. "I'm much happier when I'm not around other people."

"I'm 'other people.'"

"You don't count." As soon as he says it, he smiles. "That's not what I meant. But you know what I'm saying."

Nodding, I wind my arm around his. "Thanks for making an exception for me."

"I didn't exactly make an exception. You carved your way in and left an indelible mark on my heart. Case closed."

My face flushes. Ezra is the only person I know who can unwittingly lob a left-handed compliment and make it sound like a love-sick poem. He's such a contradiction. A mess of senseless paradoxes that make perfect sense to me.

"Want to walk?" I pull him closer.

"Sure. Let's go that way." He points away from the ruin.

We walk west, toward Apache Canyon. When we're far enough away from the house that we can't see it from the path, he stops, gently pushing me up against a boulder under a juniper bough. "So, *that* happened."

I look down at my toes. "It did, didn't it."

"How do you feel?"

"I'm *really* happy for them. It was just weird. I wanted to ask her about Mick and Mom, but there's no way I'm bringing it up now. I mean, you saw her, she's so excited."

"Maybe give it a day or two." Ezra runs a finger from my forehead, along the side of my face to my chin, hooking it when he leans in to kiss me.

"Ezra, I really think they might have been together, *together*," I say as I lean into him. He's ungodly quiet for a moment. So quiet I hear my own heartbeat, thumping as if confirming the awful truth. It takes a few moments to swallow back tears before I can speak again; I'm so ashamed to say it out loud. "What if he's my . . ." I trail off, unable to finish.

Ezra's gaze is locked on mine, still as a rock. "It would explain a lot," he says softly. Wind bellows between the high canyon walls, and Ezra brushes at the tendrils of hair that flail around my eyes, tucking them behind my ear. "Mick's our missing puzzle piece. I hate the idea, but we probably should try to get him to talk more about your mom, and Angel, and the ruin."

Moonlight touches Ezra's eyes. I try focusing on his nose, unsettled by how his searching feels more like he's excavating my soul. "I'm not sure I want to know more."

"Would knowing change anything?"

"It'd change everything."

"If it's true, it would make you and Angel family, though."

"We already are." I smear an escapee tear off my cheek. "I don't want him to be part of some grand design. Something has to be mine just because it is."

"You mean unlike me," he says quietly.

My head feels like it's housing a huge ball of wet cotton. If thinking so hard about something so speculative is a headache in the making, Ezra questioning *us* is an imminent stroke. I shake my head brusquely, about to say, "*you* are all choice," when something flashes behind him—a wisp of black smoke sliding across the open valley.

"Ezra!" I grab his arm.

Ezra spins in a circle, suddenly pawing at his ears. He bends at the waist, spasming as if I just punched him, and in an instant, he shifts. It's fast, but he wobbles slightly. I actually see it, which means something is wrong. Usually, the change is imperceptible.

On all fours, Ezra backs me into the boulder, blocking me with his large, furry body. He growls at something I can't see, disturbing the space around us with a deep, shattering rumble. He's all fierce muscle and girth, but as he walks backwards, herding me from the boulder back to the path, his gait seems off.

Across a craggy mesa that drops away into Apache Canyon, a horse runs past—or what looks like a horse, if horses were transparent. It carries an equally translucent rider, shimmering like a rainbow as it moves across the mesa top. The horse lopes across the expanse, followed by a something I can't explain. A something malevolent I feel in my gut. Ezra leaps, roaring as he bounds after it, leaving me standing on a patch of dusty red ground broken by burgeoning wildflowers. I shout after him, but my throat closes around his name.

Go, Ruby. Now. Run home

I . . . I can't. Even in my mind, I stutter.

Ezra stops short between me and the something standing off in the distance, inert on a hill, looking back at us. I can't see it exactly, what it is, but I feel its eyes taking me in. Ezra wavers, swaying back and forth, deciding whether to run back to me or to go after the sudden stream of ghostly spirits making their way across the mesa. Spirits—that's what they are—I'm sure of it.

I'll be okay, I promise, though I know he can probably hear me wondering otherwise. *Go to the gate. Or whatever you have to do.*

Ezra doesn't answer, but I hear his thoughts anyway, eavesdropping, though I know I shouldn't. His loyalties are divided; he doesn't want to leave me alone, but he's equally alarmed by the stream of shadows coming down from the foothills.

Go, Ezra! I'll run home. Come back to me when you're done.

"Please, God," I add, saying it out loud.

Forcing myself to move, I torque at the waist, willing my body down the path home. As Ezra takes off toward the shadows, I move, motivated by raw fear, and trip over something hard and twisted. It catches my shoe, rotating my leg at an unnatural angle as I fall to the ground.

The impact jars my skull, and my head pounds in protest. Disoriented, I stare up at what should be a bright night sky. But instead of the moon and crisp pinpoints of light, my eyes meet blackness. Frightened, I scramble upward, keeping my distance from the root that tripped me. Either thick clouds, or something more sinister, obscures the moon and stars. My path is cloaked. It's nearly impossible to see past my hand, and the sheer darkness is terrifying.

Surrounded by a pool of black, I listen for Ezra's voice, his thoughts, anything, but except for the wind, the Pass is dead silent. After a moment, the black turns to haze, allowing me to scan the canyon's mesas. The stream of shadows moving across the mesa top is gone. Ezra is gone. There's just me, and the insidious feeling that though Ezra ran for the ruin, I'm not alone.

Motivated by dread, I hop-skip toward my house, babying my twisted ankle, stopping only briefly to catch my breath. I hop until I hear hissing to my left, until something generating heat like a bonfire slides from between a tall stand of ponderosas, physically blocking my path. Whatever it is, its amorphous body seems unable to stick to a shape, spilling out into the night before pulling back into a dark, filmy vapor. It hovers above the trail before me, dispersing in all directions like a weeping stain.

As I veer off the path, trying to find a way around the mass, a warm gust whips my hair into a nest around my face. Hair obscures my vision, and I suddenly feel the thing's breath. It smarts like a sunburn against my skin.

Wispy tendrils slip around my shoulders and down my arms as the creature drapes its volume around my body, wrapping it up like a cocoon. The night goes completely black. My head is quiet, but not in a good way. I feel way too calm and know in my gut it means I have to fight.

Even with my eyes open wide, everything is dark. Dark like layers and layers of charcoal on paper. It suffocates me, plugging my mouth and nose. In my head, I scream as loud as I can. I scream and then fall, flailing as the creature lets me go, its shape snapping back into a blob tendril by tendril.

Above it, an oversized peacock materializes, screeching between the pecks it takes at the creature's head, pulling out threads of smoke that dissipate into the night. The peacock jabs at it, and the creature's body moves erratically, spilling out at odd angles then snapping back, churning in a maddening rush.

When the blob pulls into itself directly above the path, the peacock squawks at me. It continues to claw at the creature, pulling it into taffy-like threads, but its luminous eyes fall on my face. The peacock's gaze makes my head swim. It spreads its plume, stunning me with colors so brilliant I feel blindsided. Swiftly, the bird tucks its plume around the mass, compacting the blob into a golf-ball-sized bubble it promptly swallows. The blob disappears, and a shimmering structure appears on the mesa. Only I don't see a city. Instead, I sense a vast, incomprehensible space, like an indecipherable negative. A terminal place where things that don't belong anywhere else go to die.

An unwelcome emptiness hollows me to my core, and I know that wherever the bird came from, it's somewhere I never want to go. And knowing that is enough. Enough to jumpstart the part of me that stalled. Enough to send me scrambling back on the path home.

Moving like the gates of hell just opened beneath me, I hop-limp the rest of the way back, ignoring my screaming ankle. I face forward, eyes focused on the path; I can't bear the thought of looking back and seeing the peacock or the creature again, strange bedfellows that seem of the same ilk, despite the fact that the peacock saved me.

Yards from my house, Ezra bounds out of the trees, startling me to a halt. He runs like the wind until he's right in front of me, morphing back in a blur before grabbing my shoulders. "Ruby," he sucks in his breath, "are you okay?"

His shirt is ripped, and angry scratches crisscross his chin, matching the bruises blooming on his arms. "Oh my God!" I move to touch his chest, then pull back, horrified when he winces. "Ezra, you need a hospital!"

"No hospital," he says resolutely. "Let's just get inside."

Before I can protest, he sweeps me off my feet, carrying me like a baby up the front steps. Luckily, Viviane and Angel have gone home, and Liddy and Torrance are upstairs in their room, probably still celebrating. They don't hear us when we sneak in, and they don't stop us on the way upstairs.

In my room, Ezra sets me on the bed, collapsing next to me in a way that stops my heart. I hover over him, pulling his shirt off, expecting to find bruises the size of Texas. But the damage is already healing; the scratches on his chin are almost gone, and most of his bruises have already faded.

He reaches out to touch my knee, wincing as he moves his arm. "You hurt your leg."

"I ran. Then tripped. On the way back, something . . . something stopped me."

"Something?" He sits up, reaching out to me abruptly.

"It was like, like if the Blob and a ghost had a love child." I try to laugh but can't make myself do it. Really, there's nothing funny about being cornered by a phantom—if that's even what it was. "Ezra, what happened tonight?"

"I don't know. But something tripped the gate."

"Something else attacked the blob. A bird." I bite my lip. "A giant peacock."

"Jesus." He runs a hand through his hair, lingering at his crown. "I shouldn't have left you for so long."

"Hey," I touch his knee, "it's okay. It's your job to guard the gate. You had to check."

Ezra looks up at me with a kind of anguish on his face I haven't seen before. "Shifting, it's never been automatic for me like that. I didn't even think about it. Something set me off before I had a chance to react." His eyes blaze. "Ruby, I'm not completely in control right now. The best I can do is stay by your side until we figure this out. I don't want you going anywhere alone, or anywhere near the mountain or the canyon until then."

I don't respond, but my answer hangs in the air between us anyway. *What if we never figure it out? What if this . . . this unknowable, constant drama is our future.*

"We'll talk to Mick again. Tomorrow after school. I'll meet you and we'll go see him together." He breathes out, obviously unhappy with his own temporary Band-Aid.

Ezra pushes me back against the mattress gently. When I'm laying out flat, I stretch my leg, checking my ankle. It cracks when I rotate it, but the pain doesn't send me into hysterics. I sigh and Ezra leans over me, dirty and disheveled and still entirely stunning. He places a hand on my thigh and gently feels down my leg, probing at my ankle. "It's swollen. But I think you'll live."

"Will *you*?" I frown, struck by how despondent he looks.

He meets my eyes. "I don't know."

Ezra lays down on his side, facing me, and tucks my balled fists against his chest. He wipes a tear off my cheek, then leans in and kisses my nose. Illuminated only by my bedside light, he looks exhausted.

"Sleep," I tell him.

Ezra is still for a long time. His eyes close and his breathing steadies, and I sense he's not asleep as much as ruminating. But I don't bother him. Needing distance from the world, even if only for an hour, is something I understand.

Around midnight, he mumbles, "I should go."

"Stay," I say softly.

"Liddy won't like it."

"She won't even know."

He nods against the pillow and reaches his arm out, signaling for me to flip and snuggle up to his chest. When I'm flush against him, my back against his warm body, and still aware of the slightest buzz running the length of him, he whispers, "Can you hear it?"

I don't want to answer. Answering will confirm what we both already know. That the ruin has amped up and is calling out. It always calls to him, but now it's calling to me as well. Whatever's happening, Ezra's mom is right, I'm a part of it.

"We'll figure it out tomorrow," he mumbles unconvincingly.

Tomorrow. I'll be seeing Mick tomorrow, and the day after that, and the day after that. In a heartbeat, Angel's dad split himself down the middle and became multiple problems. *My friendship with Sera blossomed out of her obsession with the ruin. She was so excited to share her discovery with someone. When I realized what she was, I played along because I loved her.*

He loved her.

What the hell kind of explanation is that?

CHAPTER TWENTY-ONE

LEAKY FAUCET

THE FACT THAT MICK DOESN'T show up to school the rest of the week foils my lofty plan to confront him. Instead of Mick, another sub named Mr. Flambeau gives us a three-day lecture about the dangers lurking on the darknet and the immorality of internet pornography. He's clearly uncomfortable with the lecture topic, and it's seriously all I can do to stop my eyes from rolling out of my head—especially when I glance across the aisle at Racine's face, which is a priceless parody of faux shame and humiliation.

After Monday's debacle, not talking to Mick makes me super anxious. Being in limbo when I already don't understand an iota of what's going on gnaws at my sanity. By Thursday at lunch, when Marta goes off about Angel and how I wouldn't understand how he feels about Mick being around because I'm not family, I'm pretty sure I'm about to lose my mind. And by dinnertime I'm a mess, which means I'm content to just pull into myself while Ezra and I grab a bite with Liddy, Torrance, and Angel at Margarita's. At least with them, I can get away with just nodding and staring blankly.

"So, anyone have a problem with a July eleventh wedding?" Liddy asks, leaning into Torrance's arm.

I frown at her.

"Problem?" she asks pointedly.

"That's only two months away."

"Your point?" She raises a burnished eyebrow, simultaneously squinting and homing-in on me like some kind of demented pirate.

"Didn't you get engaged like six days ago?"

Torrance reclines into his seatback, smiling slyly. "I've waited four decades, Ruby. That's plenty long enough."

Liddy blushes, and it's so weird to see. When it comes to love, she's always been more of a stale cookie. Now that Torrance knocked her wall down, I find myself smitten with the woman standing behind it, not that I feel like sharing that with her just now.

"You guys still thinking beach wedding?" Angel asks her.

Torrance nods. "Malibu."

"You're getting married in L.A.?" I shoot Angel a look. "Why do you know everything?"

I think it's fair to say you've been preoccupied this week. Ezra squints at me.

Angel holds up an empty coffee cup, motioning toward Daisy. "I'm special that way," he says as he waves it around.

"Try nosy." Torrance chuckles.

"Let's split the difference and call it persistent," Angel counters.

Daisy, who just started her shift, comes over and fills all five of our coffee cups slowly, acting like she wants to say something but isn't sure she should. Like maybe she overheard and wants to add her two cents. She makes a particularly funny face at Angel.

"What, Day?" Angel asks. "You've been staring me down since we walked in."

"You really dating my sister?"

Angel looks surprised but recovers quickly. "I'm sorry. Was I supposed to ask your permission first?"

She looks me over next, frowning. "This is your fault."

"My fault?"

"You set them up, didn't you?"

"Jealous much?" Angel snickers.

Daisy looks both amused and mortified. "Are you serious?"

"Daisy, *you* turned me down in high school." Angel laughs.

"Yeah, because you're not a girl."

"Ray and I went on a few dates. But we're not *dating*." He makes air quotes around the word 'dating,' exaggerating the motion just in case one of us fails to miss his very obvious point. "We might even go on more. If that's okay with your Highness."

Daisy shakes her head and swats his shoulder with the menus she grabbed off the table next to us, before refilling our coffee cups. "Idiot."

When she walks away, I whisper, "You asked her out in high school?"

"A couple times." He smiles, almost like he's proud. "She always turned me down."

Ezra snorts. "It's pretty clear you're not her type."

"I'm everybody's type," Angel says innocently.

"Ladies and gentlemen, meet the deputy of wishful thinking." Torrance tips his head at Angel. "Me and Vi, we sure did fuel that pride. Too bad hindsight's twenty-twenty."

"You knocking my big britches?" Angel's eyes twinkle, and I know he's egging Torrance on. They both love sparring in front of an audience. I'm pretty sure it's one of the ways they express their love for each other.

"From small beginnings come great things," I murmur.

"What?" Liddy wrinkles her nose at me.

"Something Mom once said. About beginnings. Just thinking out loud. About you and Racine, I guess." I glance at Angel.

"Failure is the opportunity to begin again, only more intelligently," Liddy volunteers.

"Buddha?" I ask her.

She laughs. "Henry Ford."

"He who chooses where the road starts, chooses the ultimate destination. It's the means that determine the end." We all look up, startled to see Mick walking toward the table. "Some preacher I can't remember," he adds when he reaches us.

My heart kicks into overdrive while Angel stiffens across the table, as hard on the outside as he probably feels seeing Mick walk over. He starts to stand up, but Mick places a hand on his shoulder, which doesn't sit well with Torrance.

Angel eases back into his seat, just as Torrance stands. "You're not welcome here," he tells Mick pointedly. "And next time you put a hand on him," he nods at Angel, "I'll break it. Now get the hell out of here before I arrest you for harassment."

Angel shoots Torrance a look just as Mick removes his hand from Angel's shoulder and grabs a metal chair from the four-top next to us, turning it backwards against the end of the table next to Angel. He sits down, crossing his forearms over the backrest. "I don't intend to stay long."

"Just let him say what he has to say." Angel looks up at a still-standing Torrance. "Tory, please, sit down. He's not worth even a minute of the time it'll take to cuff him and drag him to the station."

Torrance sits down on the edge of his chair begrudgingly, looming toward Mick. Beside me, Ezra bristles. His arm is pressed up against my arm, and I feel the electrical storm that courses through his body. Amped up and ready to shift in a heartbeat, he nods at Angel, silently letting him know he has his back if need be. Under the table he grips my hand, pulling me closer to his side.

Angel presses his fingers against his left temple, shaking his head woefully. "I gave you multiple chances to come talk to me, *Mick*. But I'm done. No one wants you here. Why the hell even bother?"

Mick almost looks wounded, or maybe he just looks unnatural. Staring at him so close up under Margarita's low-wattage lighting, I notice his taut face is like a mask that's a size too small, shiny and pulling at his cheekbones and forehead.

"This will be easy, then." With little fanfare, Mick reaches into his jeans' pocket and pulls out a trinket, dangling it in the air. A small, silver charm hangs from a silver chain that he drops on the table. "It belonged to Sera." He turns to me. "I would have given it to you Monday after you came by to talk, but you rushed out in a hurry."

Angel shoots me a look that breaks my heart, and Liddy chokes on her water, spitting tiny droplets over everything. "Sera?"

Mick pushes the charm toward me, motioning for me to pick it up. But my shaky hand stops me from grabbing it. Instead, I stare at the shiny object like it's the devil incarnate while Liddy and Angel stare at *me*, obviously mortified I didn't tell them I met with Mick again.

Liddy grabs the charm off the table herself and dangles it in the air accusingly. "How the hell did you get this?"

"She left it last time we were together," Mick answers calmly. "I figured Ruby should have it."

"Last time you were *together*?" Liddy repeats, oozing venom.

I grab the chain from Liddy's hand, nearly ripping it from her fingers. The silver charm glistens in my palm, radiating heat.

Torrance stares between me, Mick, and Angel, his eyes narrowing with each swoop over our faces. Finally, his gaze comes to rest on me. He's mad, frowning so deeply his brow pulls down in a wave of fine lines above his nose.

"You need to leave. Now," Torrance growls at Mick.

Mick stands up, exerting zero fight. "I'll be seeing you soon, Ruby." And just like that, he walks off, leaving us all slack-jawed and fuming.

"You want to explain that?" Liddy snaps at me.

I open my hand and stare down at the charm—a tiny, silver peacock with an open plume. My breath hitches looking at it, and I flash back to the bird that saved me in Apache Canyon. I believe in coincidence, but I also know this isn't one.

Beside me, Ezra shifts in his seat. *A peacock?*

My hand trembles, dropping the charm on the table. *Yes.*

As I stare at it, Daisy runs over. "Did he seriously just try and play family with you all?"

Torrance is united with Liddy and Angel in staring me down, but he glances up when Daisy asks. "Not now, Day," he says softly.

They're all pissed, and I want to explain, but I feel lightheaded. Nauseous, I grab my purse, jump up and run for the door, making it to the curb before dry heaving. I sit down on the cement and the still-radiant sidewalk warms my bare legs, heating my thighs as I move away from the small mess at my feet. Seconds later, Margarita's doorbells jangle and Angel appears. He sits down quietly beside me on the curb.

"That you?" He points to my sorry little trickle of throw up.

Anxious, I grab his shoulder, bunching his shirtsleeve into a knot in my hand. "Please, Angel, please don't be mad at me. I know I promised to be straight with you. I should have told you. I'm so sorry I didn't."

"Tell me what?" Angel turns his head sideways, aligning his face with mine, staring unwaveringly.

"That I stayed after school this last Monday to talk to him. I wanted to tell you, but then you all showed up for dinner that night, and Liddy and Torrance sprung the news, and you were all so happy," I rush out. "I didn't want to ruin it."

I scoot down the curb more, away from my regurgitated dinner. Angel follows me down the wayside. "Maybe now would be a good time to tell me whatever it is you talked about."

"Liddy's mad at me?"

"I'd say so. Though, I think she's probably more worried about you than mad." He sits quietly beside me, picking at an errant weed peeking up from a crack in the cement. "Ruby, why did you go talk to him again?"

"He knew my mom." I sob. "I wanted to know how. And I couldn't let it go."

"Did he tell you?"

"Not exactly. He said their friendship had something to do with the ruin." I stop there, unsure how to explain without telling him about the Otherworld and being True of Heart.

Confused, he asks, "Up the mountain?"

"Ruby." Ezra interrupts whatever Angel is about to say, squatting down on the curb behind me. "You okay?"

He looks concerned, and I can tell he's wavering between dragging me caveman-style to his truck and letting me stay and talk to Angel. "I'm okay, yes. I just reacted to the pendant on a stomach full of green chili and fries. Bad mix."

Mick makes you physically ill.

Is that a question?

No. It's a fact. One I really don't like.

I'll be fine. I just need a moment to pull myself together.

Talk to Angel. "I'm heading home," he says out loud, turning to Angel. "Can you give her a ride back?"

And say what?

The truth, I guess.

Do you know what the truth is, Ezra? Because I don't.

"Okay," Angel answers hesitantly.

Ezra leans forward and kisses my cheek. *Trust your instincts. And call me afterwards.*

He stands and tips his straw cowboy hat at Angel, sauntering off toward his truck. A pit grows in my stomach as I watch him go. And for a moment, I avoid Angel's stare altogether, entirely unsure where to start my story.

"What's going on?" Angel eyes me skeptically.

"He wants me to stay and talk to you."

"Why?"

I look at him pathetically.

Angel's nostrils flare as his jaw flexes. "I thought you trusted me."

"I do." Meeting his stare, I force myself to wear a brave face. "I went back to talk to Mick after school on Monday because he said he knew Mom. But I wasn't prepared for what he told me. And I wasn't sure how to tell you all the things he said either. I don't even know what most of it means or where to start."

"You know this is about more than just you, right?"

My stomach tanks at his suggestion. That I'm only thinking about myself. Or that I don't understand how much this all hurts him. "I do know. I know it doesn't seem like I do. But it's just . . . Angel, there's so much more to this story you don't know. And it complicates everything."

"Then you better tell me," he says colorlessly.

The lack of feeling in Angel's voice speaks volumes. If I don't tell him now, I'll lose him. I know it as acutely as I know I'm sitting beside him near a trickle of barf on a dimly lit curb in front of Margarita's.

Frozen on my little patch of cement, I start talking. I tell Angel everything. Every little detail about the ruin being a gate, and the Otherworld, and seeing Mom 2.0, and being True of Heart, and everything that's happened between me and Ezra since then, including Mom's warning about us being together. I include the dig, and Lee, and learning about Aztlán, and almost all of my meeting with Mick—minus the part where he hinted that we might be related. I should have spilled my guts months ago; after all Angel's been through with me, after everything he's done *for* me, he deserves the truth.

When I'm done, Angel stares off into the burgeoning night. He seems calm and is quiet for so long, I have to resist the urge to ask if he heard me. Finally, he says, "Wow" and stands up, looking down at me.

"Wow?" I stand up beside him, searching his face for an answer.

"I don't know what else to say."

The night suddenly feels like it's turned against me. Like it's darker now, and the seeping, indigo twilight suddenly seems sinister, and the stars above intent on reminding me that I'm just a blip in an endless universe. That none of this, not me or Angel, or even the Otherworld, ultimately matter. "Say you're still my friend."

He shrugs. "Okay, I'm still your friend."

I wrap my arms around my shoulders, steadying myself. "Do you want to take me home now?"

He shrugs again. "Yeah."

"Let me go in really quick and tell Liddy."

Angel shakes his head. "Maybe just leave them be. They're both a little upset right now. Give Liddy the time it takes me to get you home to sort it out. I'll text them that you're with me."

Bewildered, I trail Angel to his Bronco, staring at the sidewalk as I walk, counting the squares. Eighteen from Margarita's to his passenger door. Not enough squares for him to think things through and forgive me.

The drive back to my house is quiet and filled with tension, but I don't try to diffuse it. In the past, no matter how mad Angel's been at me, he's never been distant. Between his detachment now and the way he's glaring at the road, I know I'm in serious trouble.

Facing the gutter, I drop my forehead against the passenger window and watch a row of German elms blend together as we speed past, trying to pick distinct trees out from the mass. People say the elms are interlopers, planted by Western European settlers who don't belong, on land that never was theirs to begin with. Right now it's too easy to relate. I am a trespasser. And yet like them, I'm here now. Even if I wanted to, I'm rooted to La Luna, and there's no turning back.

Nearer to my house, I twist toward Angel and stare at his profile, willing him to look in my direction. Even just a smile from me might help blunt his anger. When we turn up my driveway, Angel glances to his right. He tips his head back when I half-smile and laughs softly. "This is so ridiculous."

"Me? Or what I told you?"

"All of it." He sighs. "After everything, why aren't you off to Stanford? Why are you even still here, Ruby? It doesn't make sense that you'd stay."

Before answering, I focus on the sage brush growing in unwieldy bunches off the side of the driveway, staring at their branches so hard, their tiny, mossy leaves form a web. A catch-all for my thoughts, pulling the bad ones out of me, away from him. "You know why."

"Ezra?"

When I nod, he sniffs. "I guess it doesn't matter either way. You *are* here. And the world is in play around you. Like it or not, I'm part of that."

I bite my lip, slowing my breathing. "And you don't want to be?"

He turns fully sideways on the seat and meets my eyes. "I'm so mad at you right now. But it doesn't change how I feel. I just need time to let it all sink in."

"So we're still friends?"

"Friends, Ruby?" He cracks a small smile. "It's deeper than that, and you know it."

Looking at him, I see a little bit of the Angel I love behind the barricade he's erected to keep me out. And that's enough for me to jump on. "I think you're right." My voice is low and shaky, and I hate how it sounds. But I know I need to tell him the truth about everything. "And I want to talk to you about it. But I need some time to figure it out for myself first." I reach out for his hand, pulling it off his thigh while I wrap my fingers around his limp, square palm. "Angel, you're everything to me. And you're right, you are part of my world—I honestly wouldn't know how to live in it without you. I *need* you. I'll always need you. I am *in* love with Ezra, but I love you every bit as much." I tug at his hand, wriggling it when he looks away. "I've told you everything I know. Except for one thing. And I will tell you that too. I promise. You just have to let me sort it out first."

Angel gently extracts his hand from mine and starts the Bronco again, letting it idle. "Assuming everything you told me tonight is true, do you think Mick's my real father? Or, err . . ." He scratches his head. "That he's really Mick?"

A tidal wave of relief washes over me. He's back to asking questions, which means he's reengaged, which means there's a good chance he'll forgive me sooner than later. "It's kind of weird that you believe me."

"Ezra being a shifter, that sort of broke the mold."

I try to smile, to force myself to answer him honestly. "I think he's your dad. And the real Mick. But I'm not sure *what* he is."

Angel extends his hand. When I take it, he pulls me close and hugs me. "I'm not a mad-for-a-minute-and-done-with-it person. And there's a lot here to wrap my head around. It'll take me awhile. But I'm going to give you the benefit." He sits back, wrinkling his nose at me. "Whatever that other something is you haven't told me yet, we'll talk again *soon*?"

Pretending to search for my purse on the floor while I gather all my scattered emotions, I nod my head and say, "Maybe just give me the weekend?"

He nods *yes* as I open the door and step out. "Just don't make me regret it, Ruby."

CHAPTER TWENTY-TWO

A PICTURE IS WORTH A THOUSAND WORDS

INSIDE, THROUGH THE WINDOW IN our front hall, I watch Angel sit in his cab, waving his arms as if talking to himself before turning around and heading down the driveway. The house is empty, like an echo chamber for my thoughts, and as soon as his taillights disappear, I start crying. Lying down on the couch, I smash my face into a scratchy pillow, trying to remember every single detail from the first time I saw Mick in Margarita's a couple weeks ago, to his surprise visit earlier tonight. My mind wanders, full of uncomfortable thoughts that grate in my brain the way I imagine white noise would if my head suddenly became a radio tower. After a while it *is* white noise; I hear an actual static crackle, and realize the ruin is calling me.

In my pocket, the peacock charm radiates warmth, like a tiny ember burning through my jeans. Pulling it out, I hold it up, then instinctively put it on, letting it fall against my chest. And oddly enough, the humming subsides. My mind stills, and I turn over and bury my face in the couch back, holding the charm against my chest in my palm as I sob into Liddy's fancy throw pillows.

After what feels like forever, I finally hear voices and get up, groggily shuffling to the oddly bright kitchen. "Love," Liddy says when she sees me. Her eyes move over my hand, glued to my chest, playing with the charm. "How are you?"

"Okay." I shrug, looking over at Torrance for some sign she isn't about to disown me. "You?"

"About the same," she smiles.

I trudge over to the kitchen alcove and sit down, leaning against the warm, paned window while I squeeze a pillow between my chest and arms. It's light outside now, which is weird, because didn't I just lie down?

"Did I fall asleep?"

"Sorry, love. We thought it'd be good for you if we just left you alone when we got home last night. For both of us."

Torrance hands me a cup of coffee. When I take it gratefully, he gives me a small smile and sits down next to Liddy, quietly waiting for one of us to speak again.

"I'm sorry I didn't tell you guys about talking to Mick. It was the same day you announced your engagement. And I honestly didn't want to ruin your high." I make a sourpuss face at Torrance, biting the inside of my cheek while I wait for him to admonish me. When he doesn't, I go on. "I know you didn't want me talking to him again, but you said it before, Liddy, there was so much more going on in Mom's head than we ever knew. And I thought . . . I don't know, that maybe he'd tell me something that made sense, you know? That somehow, it'd help me better understand what happened to her."

Liddy looks down at a slender hand, examining her sienna-hued fingernails. "Did it?"

"No. It just made things worse. I mean, I think they had a thing. Like a *thing*," I stress.

"Apparently, there was a lot about Sera I didn't know." When her voice quivers, Torrance gets up and stands behind her, rubbing her shoulders. "Sweetheart, I have to show you something," she says softly.

Liddy looks up at the ceiling and bites her bottom lip before dropping her chin and nodding at Torrance. Torrance nods as well, then walks out of the kitchen. A few seconds later he comes back, holding what looks like a worn picture. He hands it to Liddy, who hands it to me.

"It was in a box of photos Vi gave me last summer," Torrance says. "The first time I saw you, Ruby, I was sure we'd met before. You looked so familiar. It finally all clicked when Mick sat down next to you last night."

I grip the washed-out photo in my shaking hand, staring at a group of people standing next to a pueblo ruin I don't recognize. Outfitted in hiking gear, my mother, who may as well be me, stands to Mick's left, along with two other people, a young man and woman hamming it up between them. To Mick's right, an attractive woman attached to his hip is making a seriously funny pig face at the camera.

Torrance sits down beside me, pointing to her. "That's Vi. They went out to Mesa Verde for a week on a back-country trip. I watched Angel while they were gone. He must have been almost two then. Mick left Vi about a year later."

"Mick wasn't lying," I whisper.

"No, love, I don't think he was." Liddy sighs.

"Do you think . . ." my breath hitches and I stop cold, unsure how to finish.

Liddy gives me a sad smile. "We drove into Santa Fe after we left Margarita's last night and met Vi. Tory showed her the picture. Vi only remembers meeting Sera that one time," she pauses, looking to Torrance for guidance. "But Vi also mentioned that when she first met you, she felt like she'd seen you before. She figured she'd probably run into you around Pecos, but when she saw the picture, she made the connection too."

I swallow, waiting to hear the horrible something they both seem so hesitant to tell me.

"Vi never met Sera before that hike, but she remembered it was pretty obvious then that Mick knew her well." Torrance stands up and walks over to the sink. Gripping its ledge with both hands, he leans in, staring out the window overlooking the full creek. "Vi has always been pretty adamant Mick left her for another woman."

"Mom?" I whisper.

He stills and I watch the back of his head. "Vi says she can't be sure. Until last night she didn't really know who Sera was. But given everything you told us, and Mick's behavior, we suspect as much."

Torrance turns back to me and exchanges glances with Liddy. They both look sick, and suddenly, all I want from life is a dark room, a straitjacket, and a heavy dose of tranquilizers. My eyes blur, sending tears down my cheeks. "Please don't say what I think you're about to," I plead with him.

"You don't look much alike, Ruby. But you have the same eyes. Seeing you all together last night, it was really something. You, and Mick, and Angel."

I ball my fists at my side to squeeze the pain in, and my stomach tugs at my throat, threatening to mutiny if I so much as move. Everything in the room creeps closer and closer, the walls especially, stealing my already-labored breaths. One more word out of Torrance, and I'm pretty sure I'll shatter.

"Obviously, I don't know for sure," he says softly.

"I'm . . . I'm going now." I stand up abruptly.

"Stay, Ruby," Liddy pleads.

"I can't." I shake my head violently.

Galvanized by the sudden fear that wraps like an iron fist around my heart, I rush out of the kitchen and dart up the stairs, heading for the bathroom. I love Angel. But knowing so concretely that he could be my half-brother makes what little contents I have left in my stomach after last night's barf fest come hurling up my throat.

Sitting on the cool bathroom floor, I hang my head over the toilet, waiting to expel all the poison inside me. But it never comes. My stomach just roils until my shock fades to numbness. I can't feel a thing. Like my heart finally got fed up with all my drama and jumped ship for fairer shores.

I moan into the toilet, wishing I could pass out and wake up in another dimension. Then, suddenly, it hits me; I know exactly what to do. Moving quickly but quietly, I change into a pair of rumpled jeans shorts and an old NASA tee that I pull off my bedroom floor, twisting my hair into a self-contained knot on my head before tiptoeing back downstairs, moving through the hall toward the door like a mouse.

School starts in an hour, but I really don't care. Instead, I grab my pocket-knife and a bottle of water, then dash out the kitchen door to the trail leading up the mountain, sneaking out before Liddy or Torrance can catch me. Starting from the creek, I jog uphill, ignoring my smarting lungs. When I've gone about half a mile, my head starts to pound, but I'm making headway, so I ignore it, too, focusing instead on the forest's eerie quiet. I'd forgotten how unsettling the silence is.

Overhead, above the trees, the sky is a cornflower blue, full of high-definition clouds with flat bottoms that languish just over the Pass, as if barricading all the little enclaves between Pecos and Glorieta from the truth. It makes me feel isolated but reminds me that life is made up of so much more than what we see with just our eyes, and I wonder at how most of the world is so clueless.

Higher up, I stop on the path, rubbing out the goosebumps that appear up my arms. For a moment, I feel disconnected from myself. The fact that I disobeyed Mom 2.0 has been bubbling somewhere just below my surface for months. I've never been able to shake her warning. But if Ezra taught me anything, it's that even when things are out of control, I still have free will. I can at least try and change my trajectory. Mom 2.0 said it best, *You're free to do what you want as long as you take responsibility for it and accept the consequences.* And I do. Which is why when I reach the plateau, I head straight for the ruin. Maybe, somehow, Mom 2.0 can make sense of everything Mick told me.

CHAPTER TWENTY-THREE

CAT FIGHT

BY THE TIME I REACH the ruin, my ears hum furiously. I'm nervous and run the last few yards past rows of newly greened trees and scattered logs, into the center of the clearing. I run straight toward the sparkling altar, stopping cold when something grabs my arm.

"What the hell are you doing up here?" Ezra shouts, obviously surprised to see me.

"Let me go." I try wrenching my arm from his hand, twisting my shoulder in the process. But he grasps on tighter, dragging me to the perimeter of the pine-needle-blanketed clearing. "Let me go! Ezra, please."

Ezra's eyes are so big I could swim in them. "Don't. Don't you dare go in there."

My arm throbs. "You're hurting me."

"I'll break your arm if it keeps you out."

Ezra's voice wavers, and I know holding me back is killing him. And I want to cave; I want to break down and tell him everything I just learned about Mom and Mick. But I also need to see Mom 2.0. "Break it, then," I yelp.

"You promised me, Ruby."

My words come out heavy, though I'm barely whispering. "I need to talk to her."

When I start sobbing, Ezra pulls me into his arms, holding me so tightly against his chest, I feel the strength of his love move through my body. "I'm sorry," he whispers into my hair. "I can't. I can't let you go back there."

Squeezing my eyes shut, I try to think of the most hurtful thing I can say. Something so terrible, he'll release me and let me run into the ruin. "I hate you, Ezra. I hate you, and your stupid face, and everything about La Luna. All I want is to go . . . away from you, and this town. I'm not stuck here, like you. I don't want to be here in La Luna anymore. And I don't want to be with you either."

Ezra's face twitches. For a moment it blurs, then suddenly I'm on the ground, and there's a lion on top of me. He pins me down, growling low in his throat, leaving me paralyzed on a bed of sharp pine needles.

You're not going to the Otherworld.

Ezra may present as lion, but his expressive eyes are completely human, and what I see in them destroys me. Shaking, I try pushing him off. But he holds me down, pinning me to the earth. My lungs feel like collapsing under his weight, and as I struggle, a part of me understands a part of him actually believes my word vomit.

I didn't mean it, Ezra. I'm sorry.

Ezra stands over me, rumbling low in his throat. He looks down at my face, one paw still planted firmly on my sternum.

Please, I can't breathe.

When I wheeze, he steps off me, moving back toward the ruin, guarding it protectively. *Go home, Ruby.*

Still prone on the forest floor, I gasp for air, trying to catch my breath. The ruin continues to hum, and the force of it moves around me through the ground, reverberating like an idling freight train. Its draw is so strong I half worry it'll suck both of us into the Otherworld.

Early morning sun creeps across the open plateau, igniting Ezra's golden fur and the ruin. The space surrounding us starts to pulsate. Turning my head sideways against the scratchy ground, I watch the ruin throb, palpating as if gathering up enough energy to finally detonate.

Without warning, Ezra hooks my t-shirt collar in his teeth and drag-rushes me out of the circle, far enough away from the ruin that I no longer feel the force of it beneath me. I grab for his neck, holding on tightly until he stops in a cluster of closely knit aspens.

What just happened?

Ezra's peach nose drops, nearly meeting mine, so close I'm lost in the miasma of color swimming in his eyes. *You tripped the gate.*

It wasn't like that before.

It's unstable right now. His words are gruff and definitely angry. *Something's wrong. If you ever needed more reason to stay away from it . . .*

Ezra. I plead when he lets me go. *Read my mind. All of it. To the end.*

Another low rumble rips from his throat, and I concentrate on reliving every single moment from last night on the curb with Angel to just moments ago, scrolling through mental images that spark waves of emotion. I feel dizzy and broken, and reach out to him as I sit up, desperate to apologize, or explain, or grovel if I have to—anything to make it better.

Ezra is a blur. He shifts back, standing over me for a moment, wavering. Then he sits down, crisscrossing his long legs, resting his elbows on his knees as he leans into me. "Angel knows everything now?"

I nod despondently. "Except . . . *that.*"

Ezra reaches out and picks a pine needle from my hair. He twirls it back and forth between his fingers, tapping at his chin while he fidgets, bumping off static. Minutes pass and he sits, quiet as the mountainside around him now, ruminating.

"You know I didn't mean it," I say weakly. "Right?"

"You still said it."

"I am not all right, Ezra. Not even remotely. All I could think about was getting past you to my mother."

"Doesn't mean it didn't hurt." He sighs hard. "I may be an asshole, Ruby, but I never fight dirty like that. Not with you."

I reach out and touch his knee tentatively before resting both my hands on his jean-clad thighs, leaning toward him. "I suck at relationships. I know that. I wasn't thinking straight. I'm sorry."

Ezra scoots forward, closer to me. He drops his clasped hands and rests them on my thighs, mirroring my position. "You also know me so well. Too well. All my buttons. You can't do that again."

The sun rises in the east above the treetops, surrounding us in a ring of shadowed light. Cutting through a canopy of knit branches, it casts striated shadows over the ground, segmenting the clearing. Farther away, in the center of the clearing, the ruin glows, glittering where rays randomly brush the rock and adobe. It looks like the ruin is alive, as if it's calling to me through glittery Morse code instead of static. And all I can think about is how much I want to touch it, to go back to the Otherworld and see my mother, even if she is just a carbon copy.

"Ruby." He touches my cheek, recapturing my attention. "Did you hear me?"

"I won't fight dirty." I drag my eyes away from the ruin and meet his gaze. "But it's so hard to ignore the hum lately. I try. I do. But knowing it's up here, that I could just go through and see her—knowing what I know now, I'm not sure what else to do."

"I don't have a better answer for you. I just know you can't go back. It's too dangerous. You've seen it for yourself now. You have to trust me on this one."

"And Angel?" I whisper.

Ezra's eyes soften, turning a bright shade of lilac that blazes like the rising sun. His jaw relaxes as he leans forward, aligning our faces forehead to forehead. "Other than what I saw, I can't imagine how it all feels. But I've got your back. Tell Angel or don't tell him. I'm behind you no matter what you decide."

"You don't seem that surprised."

"That you and Angel might share the same father?" Gripping my thighs, he presses his forehead more firmly against mine and kisses me, lingering for a moment as little electric blips pass between us before pulling back. "We were both thinking it before. Torrance just confirmed it's really possible. I've gone over it a lot since Monday. It makes sense. I've known Angel all my life; he's loyal and persistent, but I've never seen him take to someone quite like he's taken to you."

"He'd probably say the same about you." I try to smile over the grief I'm feeling. It's like I've lost something, though I couldn't for the life of me say what. I never really had a mother, much less a father or brother to begin with.

Ezra returns my smile with a crooked upturn of his bowed top lip, but he doesn't say anything.

"I kissed him. You know, like for real." When I shudder, he reaches his hand out and pulls me up off the ground, tugging me against his body. Latching on to him, I wrap my arms around his waist and press my face into his chest, rubbing my nose against his checkered flannel. "If it's true, it's just really . . . gross," I mumble into his chest.

Ezra steps back, inches away so he can look down at me. "It was gross anyway. But if it is true, at least you can put that part of your friendship to rest. I know you're not in love with him, but I also know you've questioned *why* if you're not in love with him, you have such a strong connection. In my clan, blood ties are inseverable. It doesn't matter that *you* didn't know they were there. The universe doesn't forget."

Still reeling, I stare off at the ruin. Maybe. But if the universe doesn't forget, then it knows I'm True of Heart and can open the gate, despite the fact that I'm still alive, and human, and residing on Earth. It knows who Mick is—*what* Mick is—and what that means for Angel and me. And if that's true, the Universe is a dick. If it can't be bothered to guide me through this mess, I have no reason to believe it's any more reasonable than say, our Media Tech sub or my mother. I have no reason to believe anything will ever get better.

CHAPTER TWENTY-FOUR

VITAL PIECE OF INFORMATION

I SKIP SCHOOL ALTOGETHER, OPTING to go to the library. This morning's drama has already eaten up two periods, and I'm not exactly in a sunny mood. Besides, when in doubt, the library has always been my place of refuge.

After stopping back at home to reassure Liddy and Torrance I haven't drowned myself in the Pecos River, Ezra drives me into town. As we maneuver through the sun-drenched Pass, he glances over at me repeatedly, searching my face as intently as he watches the black-topped road. He's worried, I'm sure, that as soon as he releases me to the wilds of downtown La Luna, I'm going to turn around and find my way up the mountain again despite his warning.

"I already know there's no way I'm getting past you," I tell the windshield. "And after this morning, I'm not sure I even want to."

"Smart girl."

"How are we supposed to figure it out, though, if I don't?"

"Isn't that why you're going to the library?"

"Right, because I'm sure I'm going to find a totally illuminating book there on magic portals, lost cities of New Mexico, and the current shapeshifting population in the Glorieta Pass."

"If anyone can, it's you, Ruby," he answers wryly.

Downtown, big planters full of blooming succulents line Main Street, lingering under old-fashioned light posts sporting banners highlighting La Luna's upcoming Memorial Day roundup. I lower my window, and the scents of pine sap and mesquite roll in with the wind; it smells like renewal and makes my eyes water. Ezra passes the sheriff's station, headed toward the town's boxy adobe library, abutted against the scrubby foothills. People walk La Luna's broken sidewalks, smiling and tipping their hats at us as we drive by, totally unaware they're living in a magic southwest vortex of otherworldly weirdness. Partly I want to laugh—on the surface, La Luna looks so easy. It's all so normal.

"Something funny?" Ezra raises an eyebrow.

"Life is funny. Humans like to think they're in control. But that's bull. I don't even know why any of this matters. We can't stop whatever's happening, so why not just give up? If it's true there's a plan, then there's nothing we can do to change it, right? And if it's not true, and this is all random and pointless, then I can't think of any reason to care, because it'll never make sense—whatever is happening is going to happen whether I like it or not."

Ezra pushes his hat off the seat so there's nothing dividing us. He snakes his hand across the vinyl, finding mine near my thigh, balled tight. "You still have free will."

"Do I, though?"

He squeezes my hand and pulls into a parking spot in front of the library's entrance. "First, you can choose to see it differently. That's something you're really good at. Second, *you* don't give up. It's not in your DNA."

I sniff for effect. Maybe, but I'm tired of always fighting.

Ezra leans across my lap and unbuckles my seatbelt. "You don't wear wounded wallflower well. Especially not after months of essentially telling me to stop complaining about fate and suck it up. Especially not when you were right. I'm not saying you don't have every right to be miserable, or that the things you've learned aren't devastating, just the answer isn't to sit back and let it swallow you whole."

"That's pretty much what you just said you're doing for now."

"That's not what I said. Not even close. I said all I can do for *now* is keep my eye on you, and the ruin, and the dig, and hope for the freaking best until we sort it out. I don't *accept* it. And I'm not giving up. But I'm not going to fight it tooth and nail until I know how. Otherwise, I'm just railing for the sake of it. That's wasted energy I could be conserving to help you, or protect you, or figure this whole Aztlán-Azcale mystery out. Besides, we don't even know if Mick is dangerous. He hasn't exactly tried to hurt you or Angel. And he sought you out for a reason. If he really is your father, he could be . . ."

I hold a hand up, stopping him. "I'm not ready to go there yet."

Ezra wraps his own hand around my upright fingers, encasing them in his large palm. "Look, if you want to cry on my shoulder, it's right here." He taps his right shoulder with his free hand. "But I'm not going to sit here and shake my head docilely while you tell me you're giving up."

He's right. I just sometimes wish he was a little more traditional, doting boyfriend and a little less tough love. Though, I guess then he wouldn't be *my* Ezra. "Fine. I'm going to go in there," I nod at the library, "and research the crap out of the problem. Better?"

He chuckles and lets go of my hand, leaning over me again to open the passenger door. An Ezra move if there ever was one.

"Hey," he brushes my chin with a finger on his way back to his seat. "I've almost cracked *Tshiquite*. It's kind of a Tewa cypher, and if I'm translating right, I should be able to get through it soon and read it all in a couple sittings. I'll work on more of it today. And I'm hoping to finish by the end of the weekend. We are getting closer." I smile and he drops his hand, sitting back. "I love you. You know that."

I nod, because I do know it. And notwithstanding his sometimes harsher than I'd like way of approaching things, I know I'm stronger with him than without. And vice versa.

Ezra salutes me as he drives away from the curb, leaving me dallying in front of the library. His black truck reflects the early noon sun and I shield my eyes, squinting anyway. For a moment he's a blur, and even the thought of him disappearing for real makes my lungs burn. He's right that I have a choice. And despite all my complaining, I know I've already made mine. I spent half my life wishing on stars and throwing pennies in fountains longing for a 'real' family. No matter what happens, as long as he's here, as long as Liddy and Torrance, and Angel, and Racine are still here—my people—I'm not leaving the Pass.

Resolute, I walk inside toward the back of the library. After staking out a desk and dropping my backpack on the tabletop, I head to the stacks. Though, truthfully, I have no idea what to look for. I browse through the history, archeology, anthropology, and culture sections, pulling out everything I can find on Pecos and native folklore, mythology, and culture. When I'm done, I dump a pile of books on my desk and expand my search, looking at every region from the greater Southwest, all the way down to Central America, keeping an eye out specifically for books about the Aztec. It's overwhelming, and I make a book mound off to the side of an aisle in one of the stacks, taking two trips back to my desk to assemble them all together.

After what feels like hours, but is, according to the clock on the wall, only two, my favorite librarian, Mrs. Gutierrez stops by to chat. "Girlie," she smiles crookedly at me, "whatcha up to reading today?" She gazes over my pile. "Moving on from the Pecos?"

"I'm working on a paper about Mesoamerican culture," I tell her.

She holds up a knotty finger, nodding knowingly. "I got one for you. But it's old and in the back." With that she disappears, shuffling off to my right toward a door plastered with a sign that reads 'Library Staff Only.'

I'm not exactly close to Mrs. Gutierrez, and sometimes I have no idea what to say to her. But since I started coming in last summer, and she started ordering books for me from Albuquerque, we've struck up a kind of special library friendship. Like she seems to respect my need to obsessively research everything from New Mexico's fossil geology, to how homing pigeons operate, and I respect how she always knows just the exact right book to recommend. She's seriously a library whisperer.

"Here you go." Mrs. Gutierrez plops a heavy hardbound book on the desk, right in front of me. "We pulled it years back once folks started calling it bunk. But if you ask me, there's some vital information in there."

I look down at the worn book cover. Skimming the title, my heart skips, fluttering wildly. *The Pecos-Aztec Cross Reference.*

She sniffs. "Based on some high falutin' study in the early seventies that got all the academic folk stirred up. Claimed they were related or some such nonsense. For a while it was all the rage, but then other academic folk got involved and called it a hoax. Thought it might be helpful, though, given your, erm . . . school paper."

"Thanks." I smile brightly, pretending I'm not on the verge of hyperventilating.

Mrs. Gutierrez nods proudly and walks off, waving over her shoulder. "You feel like talking about it, you know where to find me."

Moving my pile of books to read *now* off to my right, I flip open *The Pecos-Aztec Cross Reference,* conscious of its cracked inner spine. It's been well read, and a number of passages throughout the book are underlined. Skimming through the table of contents, I can tell from the chapter titles alone that the author premised the book on the idea that the Aztec and the Pecos were related. Flipping to chapter three, I stop at a passage arguing how the Pecos and Aztec all lived together as one people in an ancestral homeland called Azcan, later translated to Aztlán in what is now the Glorieta Pass. According to the book, after fragmenting over religious practices and politics, they parted ways, and the dissenters migrated from what is now modern New Mexico, down to the Mexico region and became the Aztec, while the people who stayed behind formed the Pecos Pueblo.

Chapter four contends that the Aztec all descended from Pecos bloodlines. It also makes the case that the two groups never actually entirely separated, and that the Aztec frequently traveled back to the Pecos Pueblo to visit, trade, and perform shamanistic rituals, as evidenced by artifacts found in both the Pass and on trade routes.

The book is full of mostly anecdotal evidence peppered by science and hard facts that support both Lee and Ezra's stories. And I can't put it down. But it's chapter ten that stops me cold. Panicky, I jump up, grab my backpack, and dig my phone out, frantically misdialing Angel's number until my fumbling fingers get it right. My heart is thumping, and my hands are shaking, and when Angel answers I babble into the phone until he says, "All right, Ruby. Stay put. I'll be there in a moment."

Less than ten minutes later, Angel finds me in the back of the library. As he moves to hug me hello, I shove the book at him. "Look!"

Angel, dressed in his crisp khaki uniform, pulls his brown campaign hat off his head and drops it on a pile of books, running a hand over his closely cropped hair. He tugs a chair out and settles down before finally taking a look at the page I've marked.

Nodding back and forth slowly as I stare down over his shoulder, he examines it. After a minute, he looks up at me. "What the hell?"

"Right?"

Chapter ten describes the first Aztec empire in Mexico and its leader Moctezuma, more commonly known as Montezuma, whom the author argues the Puebloan people in New Mexico, at least at the time of the book's publishing, still claimed as their own. The book plays Montezuma up as an almost mythical mystic, who supposedly made regular pilgrimages to the Pass for mysterious reasons the Aztec were forbidden to talk about. Montezuma, who in the artist's rendition in the middle of the chapter—a conceptual illustration of the Aztec city Tenochtitlan, and beside that, Moctezuma—is also the spitting image of Mick Tillin, down to his piercing eyes and skull pendant.

"Montezuma ruled in," Angel stares at the picture, scanning the caption beneath it, "1398?"

"But it really looks like him." I bite my lip. "Plus, the book supports that the dig site *is* Aztlán. There's no way it's a coincidence, or that the picture's some lucky rendition."

He stands up abruptly and grabs my hand. "Come on."

Angel drags me to the computer bank lining the south library wall. Dropping into a chair, he starts pecking at the keyboard in front of him, typing in 'Mick Tillin.' When a page pops up, he scrolls it, shaking his head grimly. He points to a heading above his search results, where it says: *Showing Results for Mictlān. Search instead for Mick Tillin?*

Staring at it, I wilt into the chair next to him. Below the suggested search result, a slew of articles about Aztec gods and the Aztec Underworld pop up.

"Mictlān is the Aztec Underworld. Mictlantecuhtli is the god of the Aztec Underworld." Angel turns and gives me a totally freaked out, *are you kidding me* look before clicking on a page and spitting out facts. "Mictlantecuhtli wore a skeleton pendant. He ate the stars every morning. Associated with spiders, owls, and bats. Similar in the Spanish codex to Lucifer." He deflates, leaning back in the wood chair. "Jesus."

"Mick can't seriously be a god. Or Montezuma. Can he?"

Angel's nostrils flare. "You explain it, then, Ruby. Because I sure as hell can't."

"Bright side," I giggle. "That would make you a demi-god, right?"

Angel just stares at me. My stomach rumbles and I can feel the hysteria bubbling smack in the middle of my sternum. Either that or I'm having a heart attack. We sit in a face-off for a moment, until Angel's face cracks and he starts laughing. It rips from his chest, deep and genuine, nearly surprising me off my chair. "Lot of good it's done me."

I move closer, fingering the peacock charm against my chest.

"If he's really the god of the freaking Underworld . . . I know you were joking, Ruby. But for real, if he is, and he's really my father, what does that make me?"

I shrug, leaning forward to throw my arms over his shoulders. "My best friend."

Angel wipes a tear off my cheek, then kisses it. Holding my chin, he leans in and kisses my lips, lingering until I abruptly pull away.

"What the hell, Angel!"

"I don't . . . I don't know why I did that." He shakes his head, looking completely mystified. "I didn't mean to. I'm so sorry."

Horrified, I try answering him, but my throat constricts.

"Ruby, I'm *so* sorry. I *really* didn't mean to. I don't know what came over me."

"I should go," I whisper, gathering up the books I want to take home.

"God, are you completely pissed at me?"

"No. I'm not. I'm just really confused right now."

"That makes two of us." He stands up and holds out his hand, waiting for me to take it. When I hesitantly lay my palm on top of his, he grasps it tightly. "I'd never take advantage of you. Or try to come between you and Ezra. You know that."

"I do know that."

He steps back, wrinkling his nose. "Maybe don't tell Ezra?"

I snort, looking down at my pile of books. "Understatement." The kiss came out of nowhere, and I can't for the life of me wrap my head around it, but Angel looks even more dumbfounded than I am. I *believe* he surprised himself.

Angel checks his wristwatch. "I have to get back." He sounds a little bit stricken. "But we'll figure this out. Are you working the dig tomorrow?"

"And Sunday. Yes."

"Last night you said to give you the weekend. And I will, but we have to talk soon. Will you meet me after school Monday? We'll find Mick and talk to him together."

I say *yes*, but I have no idea if I can tell him the truth about Mick and my mom now. If Mick really is a god, what *does* that make him? And if Mick is my father, what does that make me? And damn, after everything, especially that last out-of-left-field kiss, what in the heck does it make us?

CHAPTER TWENTY-FIVE

CAMPFIRE STORIES

SOMETHING IS OFF. IT FEELS like everything in the Pass is just a fraction out of place. *Everyone* is just a fraction to the left of normal, like Angel when he kissed me, or how Ezra and I bicker so often lately, or the way my usually cautious and methodical aunt suddenly wants to rush to get married, or how Marta's suddenly being so friendly. The disruption in the air is palpable, but I feel it most strongly at the dig.

Today the sky is an ocean of blue, dotted by cauliflower-like blooms of snowy clouds and air that smells like creosote and juniper. It's cooler than normal outside, but the sunbaked plateau is still radiating the heat it stored up over the last week, warming my bare legs. Summer is off to an early start, and outwardly, the day appears to be perfect; it looks perfect, smells perfect, feels perfect. But everyone at the dig site is uncharacteristically edgy, as if with each new item we uncover we release something else with it. The way people are acting, you'd think *everyone* just found out they may have an evil supernatural dad and a half-brother they made out with.

I sigh, standing up with the bowl I just spent hours digging out, taking more care than normal because it was buried face down. The vessel is a sleek, beautiful, burnished sienna, covered with elaborate glyph-like designs that line up in a single row at the lip, spiraling in a tight coil to the very bottom. Amazingly, the paint has mostly survived being buried for so long, and except for a deep chip at the lip, the bowl is perfect. It almost reminds me of the ancient Jewish spell bowls I used to read about in Liddy's biblical archeology magazines.

Standing on a treeless hill under the brilliant sun, I turn the bowl in my hands, losing myself in the intricate motif decorating its clay surface. The coil is like a web, lulling me to the center of a universe I feel but can't see. Until suddenly I do; my magical city shimmering like gold across the plateau.

"What are you holding?"

Lee's voice startles me, and I jump, dropping the bowl. It hits the dirt and shatters into shards as I plunge to the ground, too late to save it from annihilation. "Oh my God." I look up at him, devastated. "Lee, I'm so sorry."

He crouches down beside me, fingering the broken pieces apart over a patch of flaccid deerweed. "Such a pity."

I reach out to touch a burnished fragment and our fingers accidentally meet, sending prickly pulses up my arm. He's been offsite all morning, but the way I feel when our fingers touch, it's like we've known each other on some fundamental level all my life. Confused, I pull my shaking hand back, standing up to look down at him. It's been a strange week, and on top of everything, the voltage Lee seems to be shedding is outright disconcerting.

He cocks his head and stares, his eyes moving from my eyes, down my face, to my chest, where they land on my mother's peacock charm. "Peacock," he almost sneers, "the embodiment of immortality and renewal. Gifted with the power of resurrection, like the phoenix."

I shrug, unsettled by his voice. "I'm . . . sorry about the pot," I stutter.

"Guardians of the gates to paradise," he continues, almost as though reciting from an encyclopedia. "All seeing. Harbingers of benevolence, patience, kindness, compassion, good luck, and kind-heartedness. Believed to aid humanity in their spiritual evolution. They hate snakes," he frowns.

Lee's voice is heavy with disgust, but for some reason, I still feel drawn to him. It's like there's a sheave between us, tugging us together.

"Where did you get it?" he asks suspiciously.

"It belonged to my mother."

He smiles as he sizes me up, too outwardly calm for the turmoil in his eyes. "How lovely."

"Do you want to see it?" I pick it up off my chest, holding it out on its chain.

"I've work to do, Ruby." He shakes his head and takes a step back.

Despite his weirdness, the pull between us is inescapable. I want to be closer to him, to talk to him more about my mom, but I have no idea why. "So, the bowl?" I ask, clumsily changing the subject.

"Leave it." His fine lips purse together. "I'm in no mood to deal with it now."

"Uh, okay. . . so, I wanted to ask you about a book I found at the library yesterday," I tell him, trying to disrupt the stare-off we're caught up in. Lee's normal gaze is intense enough; right now, it's unnerving. "It's in my backpack. It kind of supports your theory."

He clasps his hands together and finally looks up, off at the tawny foothills to his right. "All right, let's go."

Blinking, I turn and head for the workstation. I can still see a shadow of the city in front of me like it's emblazoned on my retinas. And though I can't see Lee, I still *feel* him; his eyes on me, like they're boring into my back as I walk. At the workstation, I rummage through my backpack, crouching in the corner as I dig between two sketchpads and another library book I haven't read yet. Lee stands over me quietly. As I search, he touches my hair, pulling something from it. When I look up at him, he holds out a twig.

"Thanks." I give him a small smile, pulling out *The Pecos-Aztec Cross Reference*. "Here," I hand it over. "The librarian says it was debunked in the seventies. But I read it and I think the author's right."

"You think?" He slants an eye at me. "Or you *know*."

"I know," I admit, staring at the pendant around his neck. Its dark center is spellbinding, and I stand up, reaching out to touch it without thinking. This time, when I walk toward him, Lee moves close enough to look straight down at me. His pendant is shimmery and vexing, and as my fingers touch its surface, I hear Ezra call my name.

The floor heaves for a moment. Ezra is here. Why is Ezra here?

Dizzy, I whip around.

Ezra looks perplexed. He taps his watch. "We said two."

I look between them, unsure what it was I wanted from Lee to begin with. He was standing so close. I was so close. But I have no idea why. "Right," I chirp, staring at the book in Lee's right hand. "Right." I move to grab my backpack. "Seriously, read the book," I tell Lee, walking backwards toward Ezra. "We can talk about it next weekend."

Lee's expression is inscrutable. He nods, watching me unflinchingly until I wave goodbye. When I turn around, breaking eye contact with him, it's like a boulder suddenly rolled off my shoulders. I feel light as I climb into Ezra's truck, and a little confused about what had me in such a tizzy.

"What was that all about?" Ezra asks as he drives out of the lot.

I bite my cheek, chewing on it for a minute. Then, I shrug. "I don't know. I think he was excited about the book."

"Which book?"

"*The Aztec-Pecos Cross Reference*. Our smoking gun."

"You gave it to him?"

"I . . . I guess I did."

Ezra's face is a serious study in incredulity. "I thought we decided you weren't going to talk to him about Azcale. Or my grandfather's stories."

"I'm not. I just . . . he thinks the site is Aztlán, and the book supports that."

"Didn't you want it for when we talk to Mick?"

Mick. Right. Last night, after I spent dinner pretending to be A-OK while I tried to make peace with Liddy and Torrance for running out, Angel and Ezra and I spent hours poring over it, hatching a plan to confront Mick next week. I insisted on meeting Mick with Angel. And Ezra agreed. There wasn't much else to say or do about it. "Shoot. I forgot. I'll get it back tomorrow or Monday. He's on site almost all through the week. Especially now. Their last seismograph found something big and solid buried about two-hundred feet from the primary test pit. The team followed up with a round of sonic detection, and they think there may be a hidden chamber down there. Lee is super excited about it."

Ezra looks at me askew. "Are you all right?"

"Me? Totally. Why?"

"Other than that you're being weirder than your normal weird?"

"Am I? I think I'm still in shock. Yesterday was kind of brutal. Post-traumatic stress?" I joke.

He snakes his hand across the seat and rests it on my thigh. "That's why I talked you into leaving early today. I've got a surprise."

"A surprise?" I kind of want to go home and just sleep for a week, but I'm really trying to adopt a good game face while I work on being *normal* through this mess. I don't want to repeat last year's failure; to get so caught up in grief and uncertainty I stop functioning. "Where are we headed?" I ask as he turns onto Interstate 25 just past La Luna.

Ezra hands me a brown paper bag. He nods down at it. "Look."

Intrigued, I open the bag and peek inside. At the bottom, there's a single plastic container full of wondrous fluffy marshmallows. "Is this a hint?"

Ezra rubs the skin on my knee with a thumb, smiling like he's pleased with himself. Humming, he pulls his hat off and rolls the window down, letting warmish, slightly damp air rush through the cab. Ahead on the road, the blacktop glistens. It must have rained here earlier.

"Are you going to tell me?" I pester him.

"No." He smiles again, still staring at the road ahead. "That would defeat the surprise."

Just past Santa Fe, to the west out my window, a vibrant rainbow hangs in the sky. I watch it shimmer beneath the dark clouds that hover over the Jemez mountains as we head down the interstate toward Albuquerque. After a few minutes, the rainbow splits into a double rainbow, spanning the mountain range bordering the Rio

Grande river, arching over a stretch of scrubby golden land marked by newly green salt bush and jagged rocks.

"Look," I point out the window.

Ezra glances to his right, but more at me. "Beautiful."

Fifteen minutes later, Ezra turns off the highway past a collection of crimson sandstone formations toward Tent Rocks National Monument. Bursting with curiosity, I tug at his sleeve. "Ezra, where are we going?"

We drive down a lonely stretch of empty highway past Cochiti Pueblo, turning right at a sign directing us toward Cochiti Lake. We drive around a bend over a hill and come face to face with a huge mountain of black tuff and rock piled so high it forms a massive wall that Ezra tells me is a dam. Then we dip down into a picturesque basin housing a wind-tossed lake.

Ezra cruises around a section of it, pulling into a parking lot at the water's edge near a campground. When we park, I catch Angel and Racine standing near Angel's Bronco a couple spots over. Racine waves at me excitedly. She runs up to Ezra's truck, leaning into my open window.

"Hiya," she says breathlessly. "Ezra, this is awesome. I haven't been out here since I was like ten."

Ezra gives me a sideways look, smiling slyly. "Surprise."

"You set this up?"

He nods, turning the engine off. "Liddy finagled you a day off tomorrow. Come on. There's gear in the back."

"Gear?"

"Camping gear. I stopped at your house first. Talked to Liddy and grabbed a few things."

Angel walks up behind Racine, leaning into her before dropping his chin on her shoulder. "Hey, Ruby," he says affably, as if our big discovery yesterday never happened.

I swallow down my surprise, attempting to smile. "Hey," I breathe out, "I can't believe you all planned this behind my back. Racine's right, this is awesome."

Angel stands up straighter. "Wish I could say it was my idea. But Ezra was pretty clear you need a break." He winks at me. "Can't say I disagree. We all do."

It's more than a sweet gesture on Ezra's part, and I should be giddy. But I'm worried I might actually need a lobotomy to turn my mind off. I can't stop thinking about Mick, and Lee, and Aztlán, and the fact that Angel could be my brother.

Don't. Ezra nods at me.

Don't what?

Just for a night. Let it go. It'll be good for you. That's all I'm asking.

Angel shakes his head, perplexed by our silent interaction. He raps his knuckles on the side of the truck, then tugs Racine toward the flatbed, waiting for Ezra to hop out and help him pull bags from under the tarp. While Ezra and Angel unload both the truck and Angel's Bronco, dropping everything in a clearing feet from a fire ring near the shore, Racine stands next to me, squealing in delight.

"I love last-minute outings! I can't believe Angel agreed. Ruby, I think he actually likes me."

"Ezra called you guys?"

She shakes her head enthusiastically. "Angel did. Late last night."

Ezra and Angel must have snuck off and planned it between our laborious talk with Liddy and Torrance over dinner, and later, coffee at Margarita's. "It's almost shocking," I say out loud, a nod to both Ezra's plan *and* the conversation we had around the dinner table last night.

After Angel and Ezra finish unloading, we help set up the site. Angel and Racine build a tent on one side of the fire ring. When

Ezra throws two sleeping bags and a soft pad on the beige sand out in the open, across the fire ring from their tent, Angel shrugs inquisitively.

"Ask, Ruby," Ezra laughs.

"I'm tent challenged," I giggle, recalling the first time we camped together in El Morro. I smile, remembering the trip like it was yesterday. The first time I told Ezra how I felt about him. The first time Ezra kissed me. "Remind Ezra to show you the Pecos Circle later."

Ezra wraps an arm around my shoulders, pulling me against him. "I did bring a tent, though," he says quietly, looking down into my eyes, "for later, if you want."

His eyes are a soft, yellow-ringed lavender full of silent longing. "Maybe you should set it up, then," I answer, flushing at the heat that burns up my throat.

Ezra doesn't miss a beat. He grabs a bag from the now much-smaller pile of supplies off to the side, dumps it out on the sand, and has the tent up in minutes flat. When he's done, he grins like he just figured out how to defy gravity.

The late afternoon sun turns the sky around it golden, and we decide to swim before it gets too cold out. Cochiti Lake, along with the craggy mountains hovering behind it to the south, looks surreal; small white caps break on its emerald surface, and it's like the entire valley is preening for us, reminding us of how beautiful the world is when we look past our own lives.

Angel and Ezra change into swim trunks in the men's room serving the campsite, while Racine and I change in my tent. Racine is ecstatic, and her infectious mood chips away at my disquiet. Ezra not only whooshed me away for a night on a whim to ease my angst, but also invited my two best friends. I'm grateful. But it's impossible not to think about dark things looming on the horizon.

"So, you and Angel." I elbow her knee. "Two sleeping bags. One tent."

I've never seen Racine truly blush before, but she does, turning a deep scarlet. "I noticed."

"You're the one who told me way back when that he's a gentleman. Don't worry."

"*Worry*?" She grins. "That's not quite the emotion I'd use to explain it."

"Oh." I bite my lip. *Two sleeping bags, one tent.* Right. Racine is *happy* about it.

"Anyway, you should talk. I saw Ezra's face when you told him to set this up." She points to a tent wall.

I giggle. "You mean how he looked like he just won the lottery?"

"Yeah, that," she laughs.

"We haven't yet."

Confused, she shrugs. "Haven't . . . oh. For real?"

"Not for lack of trying. Nerves. Bad timing. Bad luck. You name it. Something always gets in the way. I actually even threw up once."

"Oh. Oh God." Racine rolls her eyes at me, giggling. "That's awful." She grabs my arm and pulls me out of the tent. "I totally thought, you know . . ." She stops when she catches Ezra walking bare chested down from the lot toward the site, rocking a body that makes both of us sputter. "Well, damn," she mumbles under her breath.

"Yeah. Ditto."

Angel follows Ezra close behind, and it's almost funny. He's just as glorious, and I'm even more nervous for Racine now than I am for me. And also a little weirded out. Angel, my super-hot . . . *brother*? Especially after Angel's slip up in the library yesterday, it feels wrong on so many levels.

"Man," Racine licks her lips. "Remind me to send Ezra a gilded *thank-you* card." She high fives me. "We are seriously the shit, Ruby. Own it, girl."

Ezra waves me over, heading down to the calm shore beside Angel. Racine follows me to the lake, tittering as we trail them.

"Lord," Racine whispers. "I can't believe you never jumped him."

I assume she means Angel, but when I look at her, it's obvious she's still staring at Ezra. "It's not like you're missing out."

"I'm not complaining," she giggles. "Angel's a freaking god!"

At the shore, she runs up to him, laughing when he scoops her up. If our discussion yesterday is on Angel's mind, he isn't showing it. Angel is unbound. He grabs Racine by the waist and drags her screaming into the calm lake. As they go down, laughing over a barrage of water, a pang rips through me. But it feels more like loss than envy.

"Jealous?" Ezra whispers in my ear when I reach him, nuzzling my bare neck.

"He does look good." I wiggle my eyebrows.

"Maybe." He grins knowingly. "But we both know what you're really thinking."

I turn toward him, wrapping my arms around his waist. "That you have an enormous ego?"

"A well-deserved, enormous ego."

I almost laugh out loud but cover my mouth, holding back a squeak. This may be one of those rare times he's right.

Holding hands, Ezra and I dunk under the water, swimming farther toward the center of the contained lake. When we come up, he grabs me and pulls me against him. "Thanks for this," I tell him. I wrap my arms around his neck and lever up, twisting my legs around his muscled back so he has to support me. "I'm just going to pretend we're all fine for a few hours if that's okay."

"You are fine." He smirks.

I run a hand through his wet hair, slicking it back off his forehead. His face glows under the late afternoon sun, as alive as his burning eyes while I search them. I know he's putting on a happy face for me; there's no way the picture I showed him of Mick isn't eating away at his sharp mind.

"None of that," he tells me.

"Are you poking around my head?"

"No. You're radiating anxiety."

"You have a better idea?" I tease.

He lifts a single eyebrow, and damn, anxious or otherwise, it's all I can do to keep my hands off him.

"I do." Ezra's arms tighten around my waist. He splays his hands out flat against my lower back and pulls me in, locking our bodies together. When I gulp, he grins. Tilting his forehead forward, he finds my mouth, pressing his lips against mine, inciting anarchy inside my heart.

"Better?" he whispers against my mouth.

"*So* much better."

Spinning in slow circles while I embrace him, Ezra gives me a panoramic tour of the Cochiti Basin, pointing out the different mountain ranges that spread in an arc from the west to the south around the bowl-shaped basin the lake carved out when the state dammed the Rio Grande. He points out extinct volcanos off in the distance nearer to the Jemez mountains to the north, and gorgeous gold and russet hoodoos perched on the mesa tops encircling the lake. We're surrounded by a fairytale backdrop of desert plants, and errant, majestic trees and unreal geology, and it makes it hard to reconcile the fact that there's a whole other world I don't understand waiting for me back in La Luna. It makes me wonder if that's how Ezra feels whenever he leaves—knowing he can never leave for good.

"You know what I do when I can't stop thinking about something?" he asks, when we come full circle.

"What?"

"I run into the wilderness and yell. Loud as I freaking can. Until my throat hurts."

"Really?" I suppress a smile. Trying to imagine Ezra out in the middle of nowhere yelling at the sky sort of trashes the usually stoic picture I have of him.

"Try it."

"Here?" I look around the mostly empty lake and shoreline.

"Why not?"

He looks amused, like he's sure I won't do it. Which is probably why I tilt my head back and let loose an ear-shattering scream. I hold onto him tightly, digging my nails into his strong shoulders until every last bit of breath in my lungs leaves my body. After a few seconds I deflate, finishing with a whistling sigh as I let my chin drop against my chest. "You're right, that was amazing."

He grins like a mad person. "It's like throwing up. It's all so much better once you force the crap out."

Racine and Angel, up to their necks nearer to the center of the lake, quickly make their way toward us. Angel can obviously swim, and Racine is close behind, doing a half breaststroke, half dog paddle.

"What the hell was that?" Angel asks as he reaches us. His feet touch ground, and he stands in murky green water up to his chest, wiping droplets of lake out of his eyes.

"Therapy." I smile at him. "The Ezra kind."

Angel's eyes sweep over me, taking in the way I'm clinging to Ezra. It bothers him, I can tell, and that bothers me. It's weird enough knowing we may be related. But after yesterday especially, it's unsettling knowing there might still be some lingering attraction.

Racine catches up and we play chicken for a while. As I balance on Ezra's shoulders, wrestling Racine for Supreme Leader and ultimate domination of Cochiti Lake, I savor the way the sun feels on my wet skin, drying it down to a casing that holds everything in tight. We have a handstand competition and a tsunami contest, bombarding each other with waves of water. Unbridled for the first time in weeks, we play until the sun dips below the mountains to the west, turning the surface of the lake a glittering scarlet, until the wind picks up, raising goosebumps all over my body.

Back at camp, Ezra piles a mound of mesquite logs into a teepee shape in the fire ring and builds a fire. Almost giddy, I watch his lithe body move around the pit as Racine and I set out folding chairs around the fire ring, stacking the packages of hot dogs we plan to roast on a small folding table. Angel breaks out a cooler full of soda and beer, then shrugs when he catches Racine eyeballing it.

"I'm off duty and out of my jurisdiction, Ray." He holds his hands up as if to surrender. "I don't care what you do outside of La Luna."

Racine grabs a beer and cracks it open, followed by Angel. Once the fire is blazing, Ezra sits down next to me. He grabs a Dr. Pepper and a blanket and wraps it around our two chairs.

When we're all settled in, Angel rips open a package of hot dogs, stabs long, metal stakes through them, and starts handing them out. I take one, looking up at the luminous sky. Overhead, the first hint of night glows above the fat fuchsia clouds crowding out the last of the sun's waning rays. The air has morphed from early summer to late fall in a matter of minutes, and the chill feels crisp against my fire-warmed cheeks. The air is cool, but my body feels warm beside Ezra, and the wafting smell of mesquite and pinyon from the campfire is like a placebo, heating me from within.

Pulling my damp hair off my neck, I twist it into a high, top knot. "I think I'll be glad for that tent after all," I tell Ezra, pressing up closer against his side.

Ezra looks at me and just barely smiles, biting his bottom lip with a single incisor. His eyes spark and my stomach does somersaults, totally wrecked by the perfect curve of his mouth in the shadowed light of the campfire.

"Let's tell ghost stories," Racine chirps, breaking Ezra's spell over me.

The firelight highlights Racine's heart-shaped face, and snuggled against Angel like she is, she looks lovely. Angel looks content. He seems to genuinely like being with Racine, but he also seems just the slightest bit uncomfortable whenever I catch his eye, which I strenuously try to avoid. He shakes his head. "The Pass is a freak show. We live in a giant ghost story. Now that we're away, can't we talk about stocks and retirement funds and stuff like that?"

Racine knocks his side. "Before you were all like, 'none of that stuff is real.' Now you're all like, 'oh no, the Pass is so haunted, boohoo.'" She laughs.

Angel holds a finger in the air, as if checking the wind. "People who grow up together should never test each other's limits. I have way too much dirt on you, Ray. It won't be a fair fight," he laughs.

"I'll second that. Sorry, Ray." Ezra grins guiltily at Racine.

Watching them, for a brief second, I feel like an outsider. They've known each other far longer than I've known all of them put together. The only one of us I'm positive I know even close to *that* well is Ezra, and even then, I'm only like 94.2% certain I have him down.

Angel nuzzles Racine's head affectionately. "All right, Ruby starts."

"Me?"

Ezra squeezes my knee beneath the blanket. "Go for it."

I wrack my brain for something other than *The Hook Man* or *Bloody Mary*. Scary stories have never really been my strong suit—scary life maybe, but still.

"Well," I take a bite of hot dog, chewing thoughtfully, "Lee told me a good story last week. He is absolutely convinced that these chalice fragments we found are from a cup used for sacrifices to the Aztec god, Titlcauan." I stake my hot dog stick in the ground and pull the blanket up tighter under my chin, mesmerized, staring at the flames flickering in the fire ring. After yesterday's revelation, Lee's story seems like less of a story and more of a real-life detail when you factor in the whole Mick may actually be an Aztec god thing. "When you hear it, you'll totally freak out."

Angel narrows an eye at me, obviously thinking the same thing.

"So, Titlcauan," I continue, "was associated with the night sky, the night winds, hurricanes, the north, the Earth, discord, rulership, temptation, jaguars, sorcery, beauty, war, strife, you name it. His nagual was also a jaguar."

"Nagual?" Racine asks.

"Animal counterpart," Ezra volunteers.

"Yikes," Racine whispers.

"Anyway, Quetzalcoatl was one of Titlcauan's brothers. They were enemies but joined forces to create Earth. *Before* they joined forces, only the sea and a crocodilian monster called Cipactli existed. Titlcauan used his foot as bait to capture Cipactli, then cut her into pieces and spread her body around to create land. After that they created people, and made those people offer Cipactli sacrifices for her sufferings. Later, Titlcauan turned himself into the sun. He ruled Earth and the Universe, but was so power hungry, Quetzalcoatl eventually knocked him out of the sky. That pissed Titlcauan off. He turned into a jaguar and destroyed the world they'd created together, sparking a huge battle that raged for years until Quetzalcoatl eventually won. Quetzalcoatl banished Titlcauan to the Underworld and started a new world here on Earth without him."

"*Groovy*," Angel titters sarcastically.

"According to Lee, the Aztec formed a cult that built temples all over the Americas to worship Titlcauan. Every temple had a few dedicated priests, plus a recruit designated to serve in Titlacuan's image. Usually a sick kid offered up by his parents. The priests would paint and adorn the kid with quail feathers in Titlcauan's name, then treat him like royalty until Titlcauan's yearly feast. Throughout the year leading up to it, the kid would live like a god. Lee said he'd have like eight attendants and four young wives. He'd spend the week before the feast singing, eating, and dancing, then during the feast, climb the temple stairs to meet the priests at the top, where they sacrificed him. After they killed the kid, the priests saved his body to eat later." I shudder thinking about it. "And then they'd choose a new victim for the next year's feast during the ceremony."

"That's disgusting." Racine wrinkles her nose.

"Let me guess, Lee thinks there's a shrine to Titlcauan at the dig," Ezra grumbles.

"Yes! He already had this theory that the temple was overseen by the group that broke off from the Pecos and left for the Americas. Finding the chalice sealed it for him."

"And Titlcauan's nagual is a jaguar?" Angel asks.

"Right."

"There's a jaguar roaming the pass," Racine whispers.

"That's the point. I told you it was a ghost story!" I gloat, elbowing Ezra.

"So what, the University unearthed some sort of angry jaguar spirit?" Racine titters.

I open my eyes as wide as I can, leaning in over the fire. "Maybe it unearthed Titlcauan himself."

Racine laughs, but Ezra and Angel aren't as tickled.

What if you're right?

I turn to look at Ezra. *Seriously?*

Something to think about. He scratches his chin.

I reach for my neck without thinking, searching for my peacock pendant.

What are the chances that Azcale and the gate being so close together is coincidental? Ezra pauses and cocks his head. *You okay?*

My hand circles my neck absently, searching for a chain that isn't there. My mother's peacock charm is gone. *I don't remember taking it off. Maybe it fell off in the lake.*

Ezra examines my chest, then meets my eyes. *I don't think you were wearing it earlier. You sure you put it on this morning?*

I shake my head. I could swear I had it on all day. Actually, I don't remember taking the charm off once since Mick gave it to me. *Maybe it's in the truck*, I shrug. I hope it is. My inexplicable attachment to it only explains half my fear. Without it, I realize I feel naked and a little bit lost.

Ezra manages to raise his eyebrows and squint at the same time. *We'll find it, Ruby.*

"You guys just going to stare at each other?" Angel snickers.

"Just thinking about Ruby's story," Ezra says out loud.

Angel looks at me. I can tell he's thinking pretty much what Ezra was before I interrupted him. That the ruin up the mountain and the ruin we're digging up have to be connected; that if Mick really is Mictlantecuhtli entertaining the idea that the dig might really have unleashed Titlcauan isn't all that far-fetched. Doubly so when you consider the visions I keep having.

Racine shakes her head. "Eh, what's another ghost?" She turns to me. "I always knew the Pass was haunted for real. No one ever believed me."

"I believed you," I tell her, still fingering the space on my chest where my pendant used to lay.

"No, you didn't."

"Well, once Ezra went and lioned out on me, I did."

Racine laughs as Ezra sighs. *Lioned out?*

Yes, you're an animal. I smile at him, pressing my hand against my chest. *More suited to the wilds than anything. Isn't that what* you *told me?*

Ezra's eyes shimmer in the firelight. He licks his lips and looks off at the moon rising over the lake. When he turns back, he smiles vacantly. "Your turn," he tells Angel.

Angel scratches his chin. After a few moments of quiet contemplation, he tells us a story about a headless Civil War soldier who supposedly roams Villanueva. The disembodied ghost is news to me, but Ezra and Racine act like it's old hat, apparently unimpressed by dead soldiers after living with them for so long in the Pass.

Racine goes next, telling us a story about her aunt's house up in Lincoln County—how the ghost of one of Billy the Kid's Regulators supposedly haunts an outhouse her aunt converted into a shed.

When it gets to Ezra, he tells us a story about the Otherworld, pretending for Racine's sake like it's all made up. It's a pretty scary recounting of what my librarian friend, Mrs. Gutierrez, calls the Bone Closet, or what Ezra's grandfather called Apanohuaia, the ninth level of Ottomundo's spine. Near midnight, after another few storytelling rounds that get sillier and sillier, Angel and Racine call it a night, heading back to their tent at the same time.

"He really is a skeptic," Ezra says when they disappear behind the tent flap.

"You wanted Racine to think you were making it up, right? He's just playing along."

Ezra shakes his head. "He knows everything now and still questions it. I wouldn't call that particularly broad-minded."

"Angel's just . . . well, levelheaded."

Ezra covers his mouth, pretending to choke into his shirtsleeve. When I pull his arm off his face, he grabs me, pulling me onto his lap. "You always come to his rescue."

"Yep."

"Does he know how lucky he is?"

I shrug.

"I know how lucky *I* am."

Burying my head in his chest, I run my hands under his shirt over his fire-warmed skin. "It's mutual. You're amazing. Thank you for bringing me here. For inviting my friends. For bringing that tent." I wiggle my eyebrows, then rub my nose against his.

He grins. "Want to see the inside?"

"Yes, please."

I stand up and let Ezra take my hand. He pulls me in for a hug, pausing for a few seconds to stand in front of the warm fire, then leads me to the tent, holding the flap open like a gentleman before crawling in after me.

As we settle in, snuggling up together beneath the blankets he spreads out over our sleeping bags, a light wind brushes the tent's nylon walls, carrying the scent of water and campfire, bringing the wilds inside with us. Ezra reaches up and pulls a Velcro panel from the sloped roof, exposing a mesh pane that opens up the star-saturated sky. Mesmerized by a palette of sparkling pinpoints, I snuggle into him, gazing up in wonder.

"How are you faring?" He turns on his side to look at me.

I touch my neck absently, still not used to the chain being gone.

"We'll find it, Ruby." He strokes the space on my chest I've been touching.

"I know we will," I sigh, hoping he's right. I have a ton of my mom's stuff, but something about the pendant was special. "You know what? I don't want to think about the ruin, or the site, or Mick, or *anything* Otherworldly right now. I just want you, Ez. Nothing else matters."

"Yeah?" he asks softly.

Gently, Ezra pushes me back against the sleeping bag. Putting inches between our faces, his clear eyes take in my cheeks and chin, dart over my nose, then stop for a moment at my mouth before grazing up and down my body.

Despite all the time we've spent together, Ezra still makes me nervous. When he's this close, it feels like my insides are on fire, like I might spontaneously combust. And when I get like this, nothing else, not the dig, or the ruin, or being True of Heart, exists. All I want to do is disappear into his body.

Ezra blows out hard, eyes churning as he runs his hand down my arm. "I hear you," he whispers gruffly.

His voice is like a lit fuse. In the cool tent, nestled against his scorching skin, I feel explosive. One more word and I'll detonate under his touch.

"Take my clothes off," I murmur.

Ezra's eyes are a color wheel, changing faster than I can keep track. Silently, he sits up and pulls off my shirt and jeans. Hovering over me, he pulls off his own shirt and tugs at his button fly, exposing expanses of taut muscle wrapped in supple, bronzed skin. His eyes are wild, hungrily exploring my body as he removes my underwear, then his. When we're both bare, he meets my eyes again, angling forward as he runs a single finger down my neck to my sternum, all the way down to my belly button. Balanced on a single arm, he moves closer, and his chocolate hair falls around his face, forming a curtain that blocks out everything except the space separating our bodies.

"Is this okay?" he asks softly.

I hold his stare, knowing he won't look away. *Read my mind.*

Like my own hitched breath, I feel him inside me, probing my thoughts, hesitant but eager. *I love you too.* He breathes out against my neck. *Always, Ruby.*

Ezra's warm chest presses against mine until our bodies are indivisible. Being so close to him exposes me in ways I can't imagine sharing with anyone else. And this feeling, knowing that the only person on Earth I want to be intimate this way with feels the same, is better than anything I ever imagined. Ezra crafts my body into an ember; makes it ache in a way that burns. He moves against me and I can't think. I only care that his hands are on me exploring. That his body, finally, is my body.

CHAPTER TWENTY-SIX

DOWN THE FOX HOLE

MY PHONE RINGS A MILLION times before I finally grab it, because *hello*, it's past ten on a Sunday evening. After a near-perfect weekend, I'm reserving even the potential for bad news for Monday. Monday already has a bad rap. Might as well let it be my scapegoat.

"Ezra," I breathe into the phone after his name flashes across the screen. "Hey, what's up?"

"I'm outside," he says quickly.

I bite my lip, knowing there's no way Ezra came over this late without calling unless it was so important, he barely took the time to think about it himself. "I'll be down in a sec."

Excited and a little bit nervous to see him, even though it's only been a few hours since we got back from the lake, I throw on a hoodie and tiptoe downstairs, trying to avoid alerting Liddy or Torrance that we have a guest. "Hi," I murmur as I open the door.

Ezra kisses my lips, deep and lingering before stepping into the foyer. "I finished it." He holds up *Tshiquite*.

My first thought is, *awesome, finally.* But the fact that his face suddenly looks like it's wrapped around an extra-sour lemon, speaks for itself—he's not here to tell me it's all chocolate and roses. I tap my head and nod up the stairs. *They're still awake. Just be quiet. Otherwise we'll have to make something up, and you and I both know Liddy can see right through me.*

Ezra nods and follows behind me to my room. Not like I'd know he was even there if I didn't let him in myself. He's in stealth mode, and I'm almost jealous.

As I close my bedroom door, he plunks down on the bed. I settle in beside him and he flips the book open, then places it on my lap, turned to a sketch. To a pencil-scratched image resembling Mick. He taps the picture. *Montezuma. Just like in* The Pecos-Aztec Cross Reference. *According to this, he's an Ancient—sent up through the Pass to the city of Azcale before it split into factions and the Pecos moved farther down the river to where the Pueblo is now. Montezuma ruled Ottomundo's Underworld, but was sent up from Mictlān to rule over the Ancients' original clans on Earth after Azcale grew too powerful for the Ancients' liking. The book claims Montezuma, aka Mictlantecuhtli, led a group of Pecos away from Azcale and its evils, and then shooed another faction down into the Southern world before returning to Ottomundo to weigh the souls of those he deemed unworthy of either. Also, Ruby, before the gate up the mountain existed, Azcale was supposedly the only way to travel between their world and ours. The Pecos built the gate for the Ancients after the Ancients banished Azcale from this realm and called Mick home.* He looks away, pausing for a moment before sitting up straighter. *Are you okay? You look like you want to throw up.*

I meet his eyes. *Depends.*

On what?

Whether the book is right or not.

Ezra makes a face, exaggerating his already deep-set frown. *There's a story in here about two warring brothers, both originals responsible for creating Earth. One brother eventually overcame the other and banished the loser to Apanohuaia . . . just like from my grandfather's stories.*

I'm on tenterhooks, and when he stops, my breath catches. *There's more, right?* Because there always is.

Ezra nods. *The book recounts how Tezcatlipoca, one of four sons of Ometeotl the original creator, was revered by his people but hated by the Council. It explains how humans worshiped him, and how in return, he charged the Pecos with guarding his city, Azcale, despite the Ancients' objections. I'll just read it to you straight from the book.* He clears his throat as though he might actually speak. *Tezcatlipoca, a great warrior, Council member, princely god, and a patron of nobility governs the fates of mortals, rewarding and punishing his followers as he sees fit. A magician and shape shifter, Tezcatlipoca uses sorcery and cunning to exact his will, and will appear as a tempter, urging humans to wrong-doing, testing them through temptation rather than leading them astray directly. He glories in war and human sacrifice, and punishes sinners and cheats, but he himself cannot be trusted. Beware his mirror, which he uses to look into the minds and hearts of humans.* Ezra pauses for a moment, searching my eyes. *The book goes on to prophesize that the banished brother will reemerge in the Pass at the first sign of Azcale's return, to unite Azcale and Earth again, before re-conquering the Southwest and unleashing Apanohuaia on Earth.*

I make a face at him. *Mick?*

He frowns. *Mictlantecuhtli and Tezcatlipoca, they're different gods in the folklore. But they both presided over the Underworld, and both had a falling out with Quetzalcoatl and ended up banished by him.*

Plus, it's all been passed down orally. I don't know much about the mythology, but there seems to be a lot of crossover. So, I guess it's possible.

Mick might actually be here because of the dig. Because of Azcale.

Ezra sighs, then shrugs.

What do we do now?

I guess we find Mick.

And if he doesn't want to be found, or he's here to take over the world . . . I pause and rub my eyes. *Bleh. Seriously, Ezra, I'm even more confused now than before you came over.*

He wraps an arm around my waist and gently drops us back against the mattress. *I'm right there with you. I've never not known what to do when it comes to watching the gate. Part of me,* he turns on his side and hovers over me, balanced on an elbow, *part of me thinks I should just destroy it.*

Can you?

Aside from being riddled with cautionary tales about people who've tried to trick the Ancients, and prophecies about gods and the future, the book's a little bit of a how-to manual for normal people. He makes air quotes around the word 'normal.' *It's full of incantations related to manipulating the gate and crossing over. But it's also full of stories that make it pretty clear no one's ever actually managed to work the gate and cross over successfully. Or I guess if they have, they haven't made it back here to share the details around a campfire. If the book's even for real, the Ancients sound pretty freaking wrathful.*

I reach up and stroke his cheek, remembering how scarred it was before he got his face back. All the damage. *You know they are. You have firsthand experience.*

He stares down at me, but it's more like he's somewhere back in his past, remembering his other face and the lessons the Ancients taught him. *Maybe. But whatever the cost, it might be worth it. No more gate, no more gods showing up in La Luna to mess with us.*

And no more watching.

Ezra gazes down at me with a set mouth that breaks my heart. He wants to be free of the gate as much for him as anyone, and I don't blame him. Getting away this weekend reminded both of us I think, in this really concrete way, that for Ezra, anything more than a life in the Pass will always be a pipe dream.

"It's not worth it," I whisper. "I'm not willing to risk it. You."

"*You* don't have to risk it," he responds quietly.

Stretching out long beside me, Ezra finds my hand on my comforter and weaves our fingers together between our hips. His broad chest rises and falls in sync with my own, and I wonder if he's timing it. Sometimes, he feels like such an extension of me. So indivisible.

What's going on in there? He taps my temple.

Just thinking about Mick and the dig. Just thinking about how I can't bear to even contemplate losing you. *I signed up for an extra shift tomorrow after school so I could get* The Pecos-Aztec Cross Reference *back. I guess we should try to find Mick afterwards like we planned.*

I don't want you at the dig anymore, Ruby. Not if it really is Azcale.

I know you don't. It'll be my last shift. I promise. Afterwards, you, me, and Angel can sit down and talk, decide how to confront Mick together.

Or Angel and I could go without you.

I swallow, gulping down the pressure in my throat. *No. I'm going too.*

He stills and I turn to him, eyeing his strong jaw down to where his neck meets his t-shirt just below the pulse in his carotid artery. Ezra is so vibrant when he smiles, so beautiful, it's almost painful to see him frown.

Want to play a game? I pull him closer.

What's that?

Strip United Nations.

He turns sideways in my arms and looks at me, pulling his eyebrows together.

It's where I tell you what I want in exchange for a piece of clothing and vice versa. When we're done negotiating, we'll move on to the contract part.

Swim in the River Nile?

Huh?

You know, denial. Like De Nile. The Nile.

Groaning loudly, I throw an arm around his waist and push him on his back, climbing on top of him. *Nope. No puns for you. You and puns . . . that's a total fail.*

Ezra snakes an arm around my back and pulls me down, squashing me tighter up against him. *Can I be the envoy for the Pecos Pueblo?*

Envoy?

Model UN three years straight. He grins.

Yeah, I say sheepishly, reveling in his muscular, now crackling body. *I like that idea.*

Ezra pulls my chin closer and brushes his lips against mine, letting it evolve into a toe-curling kiss. Leaving me breathless, he pulls away for just a second to tug his shirt off.

Denial it is.

CHAPTER TWENTY-SEVEN

BUT THERE IS NO BOTTOM

AT THE BASE OF A scrubby hill near the overfull creek, Lee motions excitedly, calling me over to a new, mostly unexcavated plot. Leaving Michael back at the workstation, I walk to him and stop near a newish-looking pit, staring down at another upside-down bowl gleaming from the dirt, its tapered underside poking up at the overcast sky.

Intact clay bowls with intricate spiraling designs like the one I uncovered last week seem to be the find of the day. The moment I got here after school, Michael waylaid me to show me the trove they've been digging up since morning. We've been going through them for the last hour, and it looks like Lee just uncovered another one.

When Lee has my full attention, he leans down and runs his finger around a small lump in the dirt. His forearm flexes as he works, animating the snake tattoo populating his arm. It twitches as he pulls up a long strand of golden bells. Holding them up, he jingles them near his face.

"Twelve bells," he says. "Perfect."

"Twelve? Does that mean something?"

Lee's face ignites, etching out a smile so wicked it's criminal. "Everything means something."

He holds the strand out, waiting for me to come closer. I take it from him, dangling it over the pit while I double count the bells. They're caked in dirt, but they tinkle like wind chimes as I touch them. The sound is almost hypnotizing.

"Ringing in a new era," Lee says coyly.

It's somewhere between a question and a statement, and I half-nod, half-shake my head at him, confused by how light I suddenly feel. He takes the strand from me, swinging it in front of my face. As the cord sways, I watch it blur into lumpy drops of gold, feeling dizzy.

Lee moves closer. He reaches out and grabs my hand, wrapping the find around my wrist like a bracelet, tying the ends into a knot. "I'm quite certain they belong to you."

The bells are cool against my wrist, and feel especially welcoming under the hot sun. They seem right on my arm, like fingers or skin. Smirking, Lee steps back, toying with the pendant around his neck, moving it side to side in the sunlight. The pendant sways, rippling the air around it as if emitting ghostly smoke signals.

"Now." He takes my hand again. "We belong together."

Feeling fuzzy, I nod. "We do," I whisper, aware of an inertness washing over me.

"You and Ezra, you were never meant to be."

I nod again, swallowing hard, confused by what he's saying.

"That's a good girl."

Lee takes my hand and places it against his heart, or at least where his heart is *supposed* to be. His chest feels hollow, and when he leans over to kiss me, I feel a tugging inside my own chest, like my soul is being ripped from my body, jumping ship to fill the cavity where his heart should be.

He wraps his arms around my back, pulling me closer, and not one part of me fights despite how wrong it is. Suddenly, his lips are feathers against mine. I kiss him like nothing else in the world exists. Like he's the air I breathe. Like I've turned to smoke and need him to contain me. When he finally lets go, I step back, astonished and breathless. My head reels, and as I turn away, mortified, I catch Ezra standing on the hill above us, holding a big bag of Cheetos as he gapes down at me.

Seeing Ezra breaks the spell, and I push away from Lee completely, running up the hill. "Ezra!" I call after him.

Ezra takes off before I reach the top. At the crest of the hill I catch a glimpse of him, shifting the minute he's out of the public eye. He bounds into the forested hillside above, leaving me standing beside a trampled bag of Cheetos.

In shock, I stand on the hill looking up at the path he took, trying to think him back. I barely remember anything before kissing Lee. But I know that the kiss was voluntary, and that when our lips touched, it felt like even the Ancients couldn't tear me away. Despite how much I love Ezra.

Completely numb, I plop down on a nearby rock, praying that Lee stays away, waiting for Ezra to return. But Ezra doesn't come back, and after a while, I stumble to the main area of camp, jump into Liddy's car, and drive straight into town to Angel. The car is barely in park before I'm out of my seat and inside the sheriff's station, banging on the glass partition dividing the lobby and intake. The station is always quietest on Mondays, but on top of that, it's almost dinner time. Except for Angel and Chuck, it's deader inside than La Luna's library.

Angel stands up, obviously confused when he sees me. "What's going on?" he asks as he unlocks the lobby door and lets me in. "I thought we were meeting at Margarita's in an hour."

My eyes are raw from crying, and I can't bring myself to look at him directly. "Can I . . . sit . . . sit with you, please?"

Angel maneuvers me to his desk. "What happened?"

"I . . . I kissed Lee."

He stares, obviously unsure if he just heard what I said correctly. "How so?"

"Like I kissed him. Tongues and all. Ezra was there watching. But I didn't know. He saw everything."

Angel's eyes narrow. He grips his waist and shoots the ceiling a surly frown. "Why?"

"I honestly don't know what happened."

"You like Lee?"

"No!"

"Then what, Ruby?" he asks curtly.

"Why are you so mad?" I snap at him, surprising myself.

"I don't know. Why did you kiss Lee?"

"Angel, listen to me. I don't know what happened. He dug up this bracelet." I hold up my arm and show it to him, jangling the bells still affixed to my wrist, suddenly dizzy again as they tinkle against each other. "He put it on me, and next thing I knew we were lip-locked."

"You're attracted to him?"

"No. I . . . I don't know. When I'm around him, everything gets a little fuzzy. I love Ezra. I don't doubt us." I stop. It's clear that Angel's compassion meter is about to dip below tolerable. "I have no idea what's happening."

He walks around the desk to his seat. "You slay me, Ruby."

I frown at him, angry he'd even question my feelings for Ezra. "Do you really think I'd jeopardize what Ezra and I have for a stupid kiss?"

"I don't know. Being around you has been like riding a rollercoaster lately. Now that you've got Ezra wrapped around your finger, and you've pushed me at Ray, maybe you need someone new to fawn over you."

"I didn't push you at Ray!" I shout, angry at him for being so angry. "You like her. You said so yourself." My heartbeat speeds up, egged on by a burst of adrenaline. "Or maybe you want to have *your* cake and eat it too. Leave the door open a little? Just in case I change my mind about Ezra?"

His face turns red. I've never seen him so mad, and as I stand across the desk from him, fueling a totally unnecessary fire, most of me wonders just why the heck we're even arguing. I know neither of us mean anything we're saying.

"Angel." I rub my forehead, confused by my own anger. "That was low. I'm sorry."

Angel stares, barely blinking, entertaining some unspoken dialogue in his head.

"Something's wrong. For real. Things haven't been right since Mick *or* Lee came to La Luna. Think about it."

Angel's jaw quivers as he looks away, staring off at Torrance's office. "Sit down," he tells me. I do and he sits down at his desk across from me, laying his hands flat on the desktop. "You're right. I've been thinking the same thing. Everyone is off lately."

"Listen to me, please. First, I just really need you to know that if Racine makes you happy, I really am okay. And what you just said about needing attention, it's not true. I *was* jealous at first, but not for the reason you think. Angel, you being happy makes me happy."

"I do like her." He just barely meets my eyes. "A lot, actually. But the way I feel about you, I don't know. I can't make sense of it. I'm sorry I kissed you Friday. That was totally wrong. But it was like, for a brief moment, I didn't care and couldn't control myself even if I did. I didn't even think about doing it, it just happened."

"That's exactly what happened with Lee! I didn't want to kiss him but couldn't control myself. I love Ezra so much. I swear, Angel, I'd never do something so stupid."

"There's no part of you that likes him?"

"No. At least, not when I'm away from him." I touch the place on my chest where my peacock charm used to be. Despite hours of searching yesterday I still can't find it.

Angel leans back in his wooden swivel chair. "Have you told Ezra?"

"He ran off before I could."

"Ruby, you should have gone over to his place. Not here. You have to tell him. Now. Before things get any crazier."

"I'm scared he won't listen. You didn't see his face, Angel."

I reach for the peacock again, balling my fist at my chest when it finds air.

"Your mother's charm?" He nods at my fist questioningly.

"It's missing."

Angel sits back farther, his bulk audibly distressing his chair. It creaks and the sound echoes through the too-quiet workstation. "I thought more about Mick and why he'd have that charm in the first place. I figure, Ruby, he wouldn't have given it to you unless they were really close, like *really* close. Or he had some kind of connection to you."

"Or both," I say softly.

"You do believe he's my father," he says, not really asking.

"Yes."

His eyes settle on me. "And yours too."

I bite my lip, holding his stare. "Torrance showed me a picture last week after the Margarita's incident. Of Mick and your mom and my mom. He and Liddy—they seem to think there's a good chance we're related."

Angel exhales so hard it's almost a sputter. "That was the 'something' you wanted to think more about before talking to me."

"I always wanted a brother," I nod, trying to smile.

"Damn." He runs a hand down his face, pulling at his chin as he speaks.

It's just one word, but I feel it in my gut anyway. "Are you mad at me?"

"Mad at you?" He shakes his head. "More like wrecked." He leans forward, almost conspiratorially. Peeking over at Chuck, he whispers, "If it's true, it's all just freaking wrong."

It's not like I don't feel the same way. And I know Angel specifically means the kissing part. For me, finding out we might be related was kind of like flipping on an *obsess now* switch. Like as soon as it became a possibility, kissing him was *all* I could think about. And not in a good way. But the truest thing I know is that I can't change the past, no matter how much I rail against it. "Maybe that's *why* you feel the way you do."

He stares at me. "Are you joking?"

"No. I mean, maybe you really do love me as much as you think. But more like a sister."

"I can't imagine looking at my sister and thinking the things I've thought about you."

My face flushes, turning a shade of scarlet rivaling the best New Mexico sunset.

Angel scrubs his chin again slowly. "It's the truth. I'm sorry."

"Angel, I'm really confused about everything. But you're family to me either way. I don't need a blood test to confirm it. And whatever happened in the past, it doesn't have to matter now. The only thing this changes, if it's true, and Mick is who we think he is, is who *we* are."

"It's almost easier to believe he's a freaking god than . . ." he points back and forth between us, then drops his head. When he looks up again, he attempts a small smile. "All right, Ruby, we're in this together." I nod and he says, "Maybe you're right, maybe whatever this is has always been familial and I just totally misread it."

"Ezra says blood ties run deep, even when you're not aware of them. I know I'd go to the ends of the Earth for you without question, so on my end, it's always been a *lot* more than a crush on you, Angel. But I also know I'm completely in love with Ezra. So *this*," I point between us, "this makes more sense."

Angel clasps my hands, engulfing them with his own, forming a bridge over the desk between us. "Promise me it won't change anything."

"Other than that I adore you even more now?"

His eyes glimmer. "Yeah. Other than that."

"I promise. But, Angel, there's something else I need to tell you." Mustering a breath so deep it hurts my lungs, I exhale slowly, then tell him about *Tshiquite* and its prophecy, and how it matches up with *The Pecos-Aztec Cross Reference*. "We were going to tell you about it tonight."

Angel looks at me like I'm crazy, but I know he's turning what I just said over in his head. He looks the way I felt last night when Ezra told me. "We need to talk to Mick ASAP. And you need to talk to Ezra now."

"And if he won't listen?"

"Then I'll talk to him."

"Right," I snort. "Because you and I both know that'll go over well."

Angel shrugs, shooting me a small smile at the same time. "One thing I might actually love about being related to you, is that Ezra no longer gets to claim this all-consuming right to monopolize your time and affection. But even if you're not technically *my people*, Ruby, I'm not taking a backseat where you're concerned."

"You're saying Ezra's not the only boss of me?" I joke.

"No one's the boss of you, except you. Now," he holds out his phone, "call him."

CHAPTER TWENTY-EIGHT

MESSAGE RECEIVED

AFTER CALLING EZRA TWENTY-SEVEN MILLION times and continually getting his voicemail, Angel drives me over to his house. On the way there, I close my eyes, focusing on reaching out to Ezra telepathically. *Ezra, I'm on my way to you. I just want to talk.* I cross my fingers and think it on loop mode until we pull up to the weedy edge of Ezra's driveway. As we crest the top of it, driving past bushels of salt-bush and blooming jasmine, I see Ezra on his porch, sitting hunched on a wooden step. He looks up at us and frowns.

Angel shuts off his engine. "I'll stay. Until you tell me to go."

Nervous, I nod and step down, walking toward Ezra over pebbly gravel. I relate to it; little bits of jagged rock that once belonged to something bigger and stronger. Moving stridently, Ezra meets me between Angel's truck and his porch, stopping me on the driveway. "I don't want you here," he says coolly. "Not now."

"Ez." I try reaching out, but he steps back. "Please. Just let me explain."

"I have eyes, Ruby. You don't need to *explain* anything."

"I'm not interested in Lee. You know that. I love *you*. And there's no world where I'd jeopardize what we have. I don't know what happened. I didn't mean to. Lee did something. I think he . . . he compelled me or something."

"To kiss him?" he asks incredulously.

"Yes."

Ezra's face goes blank. He's quiet as he stares up at the treetops swaying in the evening breeze, his eyes churning with different shades of brown. Finally, he looks at me again.

I believe you. But you can't make someone do something they don't want to unless there's already a seed.

That's not true.

It's called free will, Ruby.

It's called magic, Ezra. You know that every atom of every inch of me adores you. If I didn't, I wouldn't have agreed to move in with you. And we just . . . I mean, it's not like I faked this weekend.

His sharp stare stays locked on my face, cutting me down. *Maybe not, but it was easier pretending things were perfect than facing the truth, wasn't it?*

What truth? This weekend was *perfect! And I wasn't pretending. How could you even think that?*

I don't think, Ruby. I saw! He stares at me like I'm a specimen. *Look, I know you love me. But I also think you've convinced yourself that you and me, that staying here in the Pass, all of it— that it's the 'right' decision.* "But secretly," he says out loud, "especially now, I think you wonder. Sometimes I really do think you'd rather just live in a state of denial. I mean, you barely wanted to talk about *Tshiquite* last night. Like it was just easier to fool around and pretend you didn't hear everything I'd just told you."

First off, I don't remember you complaining last night. And I haven't convinced myself. I don't have to. I know we're right.

Really? Then tell me why you're even still at the dig. If any of this mattered, you would have quit when I asked you to the first time.

Quickly, I look back at Angel, who probably thinks we're crazy standing in the middle of the driveway in a silent stare-off, gesticulating at each other. *Are you saying that since I didn't OBEY you, it means I'm not serious?*

I'm telling you Lee was enough of an interesting distraction to convince you to stay onsite. If you didn't have questions about us in the first place, leaving wouldn't have been an issue.

Ezra, do you hear yourself? That's ridiculous!

"If it was ridiculous, you wouldn't have kissed him!" he shouts.

"You're completely glossing over the fact that something strange is happening! With the gate, and Lee, and Mick, and the dig! I think the book . . . that everything you read . . . that it's all right!"

"You know, Ruby," he crosses his arms over his chest, "I'm keenly aware right now that anytime anything goes wrong, it's *always* somebody or something else's fault. Mick, Lee, the dig, Marta, Angel . . . maybe take a good look at yourself once in a while."

"Are you kidding?" My eyes fill with tears. "You really don't trust me?"

"You don't trust yourself. And you don't trust me, either. It's obviously an ongoing problem."

Crying makes it hard to glare, but I manage a serious scowl while I try to stop myself from hurtling something at him. "Ezra, this isn't right. We don't do this. We don't fight like this. Think about it. Everything's been upside down lately. Something, or someone, is trying to drive a wedge between us."

"I promised I'd protect you, Ruby. And I will. But right now, I don't know about the rest," he says flatly, as if the book, and all our research, and everything we've learned means nothing. As if *we* suddenly mean nothing.

I step back, reeling. "Are you breaking up with me?"

"I don't know. Maybe."

My limbs turn to stone. And all the air leaves the Pass. *Ezra, please. Just think about it.*

My heart stopped up on that ridge. He hugs himself. *I honestly didn't know it was possible to feel that way.*

"But it wasn't real."

"It was real enough," he says gruffly.

"You promised me this weekend you'd always be here. Now you want to walk away? Just like that?" I'm too furious to think straight and can't shut my mouth. "I'm starting to think that the real reason you asked me to move in with you is because you want everything *your* way. Because you're jealous. And controlling. Because you think I can't protect myself. From the moment I met you, Ezra, you've needed me to tell you how great you are, and now that you're doubting it, you can't stand it. You think you've changed?" I shake my head disgustedly. "You haven't."

Even as the words leave my mouth, I know I'm wrong, that what I'm saying is wrong. Ezra *has* changed. And he's all the more amazing for it. But I can't stop myself. It's like evil Ruby entered my body and hijacked my brain. Like there's venom in my blood that's seeping through my lungs up my throat, tainting each breath. Every word that slips out breaks my heart, and the feeling, splintering so completely in front of someone who means so much to me, pushes me over the edge. Ezra falls with me. His face crumbles as his eyes water.

"I want you to go," he says quietly.

"No." I strike a pose, Liddy-style, standing up straighter. I'm not giving in to what I know *has to be* some strange Otherworldly effect on us.

"You're on my property."

"Doesn't mean I *am* your property."

Ezra steps closer and grabs my arm. Before I have a moment to register what he's doing, he walk-drags me to Angel's Bronco. As Angel hops out, looking mighty alarmed by Ezra's behavior, Ezra barks, "I don't want her here right now."

The three of us engage in a stare-off, except I know Angel is on my side. He looks between us incredulously before pulling his hat off and scrubbing his head. "Let her go, Ezra. This isn't right."

"Maybe so." Ezra drops his hand from my arm. "But I'd like you both to leave now."

Angel sizes Ezra up, concluding something he doesn't share with me. "All right."

I want to argue. But whatever Angel decided, he decided it for good reason; I trust this about him. So I nod at Ezra through tears and let Angel maneuver me to the Bronco's passenger door.

Angel takes me back to the station. As he drives, he holds his right arm out, beckoning me to use it for comfort. I scoot closer and wrap it around my shoulders, leaning into him over the console.

"He's really pissed," Angel murmurs.

"You think?" I sniffle. From my perspective, Ezra is more like atomic.

Angel exhales so loudly, I worry he's about to say, *because he's right.* "It's not like him. Not where you're concerned. I mean, I get him being mad. But . . ." he shakes his head. "What was all that stare-off crap."

"Remember how I said we can hear each other?"

"Shit. Right." He exhales, then snorts. "Mental telepathy fight. Good thing ya'll can't *move* things with your mind." He pats his dashboard. "Babe would be toast."

My laugh bursts out of me, startling me into covering my mouth. Angel always knows just the right way to spin things. "We probably looked a little mental."

"Understatement." He pulls up to the station and kills the engine. "Everything's a mess right now. I get that. But, Ruby, given everything, I can't help wondering, what if your mom or whoever is right? You know, that you're not supposed to be together."

"None of this is right. That wasn't us back there. I trust that, even though it feels so fatal right now. It has to be Mick. As far as my mom . . ." I shrug woefully. "It's always been a chance I'm willing to take. A million times over." My eyes burn, and just like that I'm crying again. "I mean, I *was* willing to take. Oh, God, I feel like I'm going to die."

"You won't, though, you'll get through it." He shakes my shoulders.

I wipe my nose, totally wrecked. "Want to meet me at Margarita's when you're off?"

Angel drums his fingers against the steering wheel slowly. "I'm not mad at you, Ruby, I promise. But you dumped a load on me that I still haven't processed. I'm here for you, just maybe not tonight. There's a lot to think about."

I bite my cheek, reeling all my emotions into a tangled but contained ball. "I understand. I hope I can be here for you the same way you've been here for me when you're ready to talk again."

"You're gonna have to be." Angel tips his head back and rolls his eyes. "Because this is pretty freaking bananas." He shoots me a small smile. “I’m heading in now. But I’ll leave my phone on. Call me if you need to. For any reason. And I’ll do the same, all right?”

“Do you still want to go with me to see Mick tomorrow?”

He drops his head sideways and looks at me wearily. “Yeah, I do. After school?”

I nod.

“Pick you up at three?”

When I nod again, he opens his door. “It’s a date, then. You, me, and Tess.”

“You think Tess will make any difference if Mick really is a god?”

His expression says it all. *Duh, Ruby.* “Maybe not, but it’ll make me feel better.”

Lurching out this simultaneous eye roll, head nod, eyebrow lift, I kiss Angel on the cheek and hop down, waving awkwardly as I close the passenger door. There’s so much on my plate right now it’s like a pyramid, adding up to a sharp, pain-in-my-ass tip at the top. I don’t even know anymore, if I’ll ever be able to sort out the important things I know, from everything I don’t. Other than Mick, I don’t even know where to start.

CHAPTER TWENTY-NINE

ABSENTEE PARENTS ARE THE BEST

THE HOUSE IS EMPTY. AFTER I stuff my face with enough ice cream to make a hippopotamus sick, I leave Liddy a note saying I have a migraine, then drag myself upstairs and crawl into bed. Around midnight, when I hear her bedroom door close and know they've gone to sleep, I sneak downstairs, snag a new pack of Cheetos and a handful of Oreos from the kitchen and trudge back upstairs, turning to my easel for comfort. Because really, it's the only thing I know to do to purge the knot of hysteria growing in my stomach. I paint all night, skipping sleep for the colors weeping across my canvas.

After the sun finally breaks and I finish out my painting with a few swipes of tear-spattered paint from my almost dry palate, I manage to shower and get dressed. Downstairs, I eat scrambled eggs in the bright kitchen alcove, shaking my head in all the right places while Liddy talks, fawning over me because she thinks my sour-puss frown is a remnant from last night's fake killer headache. I even go to school, but only because I figure it's good punishment. Marta is absolutely going to tell me what an idiot I am, and I want to hear every little mean-spirited remark. My penalty for the day—a heavy dose of emotional thrashing.

During lunch, I break the news. It's only been fifteen hours, and the only witness to my argument with Ezra was Angel. I'm operating under the theory that we've avoided the rumor mill. Though, Lord only knows how many other people saw me kissing Lee at the site.

"I'm going to start you a freaking fan club online, Ruby," Marta sneers after I spill everything. "I'll charge a dollar per perv and make a fortune."

"Whatever you say, Marta, I deserve it."

She shakes her head. "What a loser."

Ashley looks stricken. Over the last several months, she's not only come to forgive Ezra for dumping her sister Cassie back in the day, but I think she's also started to like him. Plus, she hates confrontation. "I don't understand? I thought you guys were like this forever couple."

Telling them Lee worked some kind of strange mojo on me isn't going to fly. Racine obviously knows Ezra shifts, and some about the ruin, but not the Otherworld, or being True of Heart.

"It just happened. I was being stupid. I'd take it all back," I moan. "Grovel at his feet, quit the site, all of it, like that," I snap my fingers, "if I could."

"He'll get over it," Racine says supportively. "He loves you. And he knows you. Once he cools off, he'll think it through."

"You didn't see him, Ray. He was furious."

Racine grimaces. "I know. Angel told me everything last night."

I drop my head on the warm, wooden table, scratching my forehead against its splintered surface. "He dragged me to the car when I said I wouldn't leave. So humiliating."

Marta laughs. "And to think I used to dislike him."

Frowning at Marta, Ashley pats my back. "Just give him time, Ruby. Ray's right."

"What's the big whoop anyway? So you kissed another guy? I don't see the sky falling." Marta rolls her eyes at me.

"Marta, give her a freaking break." Ashley gives her a weird look. "You and I both know how you'd feel if you were in Ruby's shoes."

Surprisingly, Marta backs off, and after lunch Ashley walks Racine and me to class, shooing Marta off down the hall on her own, which is kind of surprising. Usually, Ashley is more like Switzerland, except for the occasional jab at Marta, she never takes sides. Far as I can tell, it's just not in her nature to be contentious. But the way she just blew Marta off, I could hug her. It's bad enough that I can barely wait for school to end so I can hunt down Mick, who has now been permanently replaced by a substitute, substitute teacher.

When the last bell rings, I mimic an out-of-control tornado and throw my stuff in a haphazard heap in my bag. Ignoring Racine's looks, I sprint for the hall and hurry out to the front quad. Angel is parked across the street, but as I step off the sidewalk, he gets out of his Bronco and struts toward me.

"What's wrong?" I ask when he reaches the quad.

"I searched all the city databases. Then I took it statewide. The address Mick gave the school when they hired him on is bogus. I searched the sales and rental records from Las Vegas to Albuquerque for the last few months, and it turned up nada. I don't think we're going to find him."

Standing on the quad dejectedly, I stare down at the new sprigs of grass jutting up in a manicured patch, offset by desert landscaping. Until Racine shouts Angel's name, and the next thing I know, she and Ashley are beside me, determined to grab shakes at Margarita's.

Too tired to argue, I give in and follow Racine to her car, focusing on the tail end of Angel's Bronco as we trail him to Main Street. In the few minutes it takes to get to Margarita's, Racine gushes about Angel like she might run out of air if she doesn't expel every little detail fast as the speed of light. And I agree with everything she says. But there's so much in there, and I'm in such a lousy mood, I half worry I might choke on all her enthusiasm.

Almost every booth in Margarita's is full, and as we walk in, jangling the bells on the door loud enough to make Daisy stop near the pie station and shoot Racine the evil eye, Angel scopes out a booth in Daisy's section.

"Still haven't heard from Ezra yet?" Angel drops his hat on the seat and sits back in the booth casually, throwing an arm around Racine's shoulder. He looks a little paternal, which makes me feel all kinds of itchy.

"You mean since you dropped me off last night?" I ask testily. "No."

He looks at me, smiling wearily. "He'll call, Ruby. I'd bet my life on it."

Daisy comes over and takes our order, rolling her eyes at Racine. Since Angel and Racine started coming in together, her favorite thing to do seems to be giving them a hard time. "Angel's right," she tells me. "He's the king of cold shoulders. Remember high school?" she asks Angel. "He'd just straight ghost people, especially after one of his weekly girlfriends pissed him off. It's kind of his thing."

"Daisy knows too?" I grumble, dropping my face in my palms.

"Day," Angel sighs, rubbing his forehead. "That was a long time ago. And Ruby isn't one of his *weekly girlfriends*."

"I'm just saying." She throws her hands in the air.

"Well, don't," Racine frowns at her. "It's not helping."

"He obviously had other girlfriends before me, Daisy, I know that. And I get that he was a player. *Was* being the operative word. But I don't think he's ghosting me."

"He just needs time," Angel agrees. "He's a muller. Pretty rare his heart takes the lead first. You know that."

Dropping my head on Ashley's shoulder, I sigh dramatically. "You're right. He's said before I don't give him enough time to think when he's angry. I just . . . it's just . . . I mean, last week we were talking about moving in together. That's kind of big, right? Plus, it was his idea. Why would his go-to be breaking up?"

"Especially after what happened this weekend," Racine adds, nodding knowingly.

"Wait. What happened this weekend?" Ashley chirps.

Angel sort of frowns. He checks his watch and flips his hand at me. "You know, I completely forgot we have to get back to the station."

"I thought you had until four thirty." Racine's bottom lip plumps out below her top, which bows into a perfect little valentine above it.

"Torrance wants me to bring Ruby by. Something he wanted to ask her about the wedding when Liddy's not around. But he's off at four. We'll have to get those shakes to go."

"Wait!" Ashley grabs my forearm, still stuck on Racine's big revelation. "You don't mean . . ." Her eyes bloom. "I can't believe you didn't tell me. You and Ezra? *Like you and Ezra*, you and Ezra?" Her mouth drops open. "Ohmigod, you kissed Lee after . . ."

Racine shoots up. "I should get home too, Ash. I'll tell Daisy to make all our orders to go." She gives me a *God, I'm so sorry* look. "And I'll give you a ride."

Ashley stands up, letting me out of the booth without further interrogation. "Let's go to the movies tomorrow night. That'll cheer you up." She kisses my cheek and tries to smile, and not for the first time I appreciate how easy it is to distract her. Ashley hugs me goodbye, and Angel waits for the three of us to go through our standard departure routine—yes, I promise to call later. Sure, let's see a movie. Yes, I promise I'm fine—then nudges me toward the door.

"What about our shakes?" I mumble under my breath.

"We'll come back for them." Outside, he walks me to the station as if we're about to go inside, then stops me near his Bronco. "You could have told me."

"About this weekend?"

He cringes. "No, Ruby. I already figured that. I mean, about moving in with him."

I shrug.

"Cat got your tongue?"

"It just never came up before. I'm sorry."

He stands on the corner, staring at me.

"Is that why you dragged me out here? To give me a lecture?"

"I dragged you out here to save you from an uncomfortable conversation." He snorts. "You're welcome, Princess."

"Ugh. *Princess.*" I hold out my hand, waiting for him to take it. "How about from now on, I promise to share all my life-changing events with you."

"I know it's not exactly my business. But moving in with him, it just feels like something big, you know?" Angel slouches a little, shoving his hands in his khaki trouser pockets instead of taking mine. "Anyway, if that's what you were planning, I doubly doubt he really wants to break up with you."

"You don't think it's *more* likely because of that?"

Angel shakes his head. "No matter how pissed he is about Lee, I'm pretty sure he'd cut you deep and stick around to watch you bleed before he outright left you. That's way more his style. It's probably what he's doing now. Letting you suffer a little before manning up."

"That's kind of terrible."

"You knew who he was when you decided to get serious with him."

"I'm starting to wonder." But I'm not, not really. I may question Ezra sometimes, but I also know like I know my own face that he'd never purposely do anything to hurt me.

Angel looks down at the sidewalk. "Do you really think moving in with him is such a good idea if what your mom, or whoever said, is even remotely true?"

"It's not true."

"You think she'd tell you to stay away from him for no reason? He's volatile, Ruby. Obviously."

"Angel, you're the one who said he'd never hurt me. Just because you and I might be related doesn't mean you get to give me a lecture."

"Blood or not, you're family. And dating him isn't the same as living together. That's a game changer. I'd be lying if I said it doesn't worry me."

"I get it." I sniff. "But you'll have to trust me on this one. Besides, it's sort of a moot point right now anyway, you know? He's not here, and he's made it pretty clear he wants me to stay away from him."

"And *I'm* saying he'll be back. Likely sooner than later. And when that happens, you should know what you're getting into."

"I do know."

"Do you?" he asks pointedly.

Clenching my jaw hard enough it feels like my teeth might snap, I close my eyes and count to five. Sage fills my sinuses, mingling with the smell of fried food wafting from Margarita's, and I focus on that for a few seconds before looking at him again.

I've been asking myself the same kinds of questions for weeks. It isn't fair to be angry with Angel for voicing them. But Ezra's *my* stupid boyfriend, and Angel knows maybe a fraction of everything we've gone through together. Ezra may be volatile, but he's also always supported me—hasn't he?

"It's something I just trust, okay? The way I know I can trust you."

"Then do you trust the Ancients? Because if you're really not supposed to be together, or if even parts of that book are true, do you seriously think they're just going to sit around sniffing roses ignoring you?"

"I don't know," I say too quickly.

Shaking his head, Angel looks off toward the station. "I think you do."

CHAPTER THIRTY

PORT IN A STORM, COMPASS IN THE PITCH OF NIGHT

"LET US IN!" RACINE AND Ashley stand outside on the porch, banging on the front door. "Ruby, you can't miss the last week of school."

Reluctantly, I open it, shielding my eyes from the glaring sun. "Go away."

Racine and Ashley march into the hallway, past me. Grabbing my hand, Racine drags me upstairs to my bedroom, pulling clothes out of my closet that she throws at Ashley. "Take her in the bathroom and make her wash her face." She points at me. "Ruby, you're a mess. Go."

I let Ashley maneuver me into the bathroom. She sits me down on the toilet and shakes her head, *tsking* sympathetically.

"Why don't you all just let me die in peace?" I moan.

"You've been moping for almost a week. We all know you're not sick. Come on, don't let the fact that Ezra's being a jerk ruin your last three days of school."

The fact that Ezra's being a jerk. And that Angel may be my brother. And that Mick may be an evil god slash shifter slash my father. And Lee, some . . . something. I cough, stalling. What in the world am I supposed to tell Racine and Ashley? They both know me too well; when it comes to Racine especially, I'm a horrible liar.

"Okay."

Ashley puts her hands on her hips. "Okay? That's it?"

"Yeah."

She grins goofily. "So you'll come with us to school?"

I already missed first period. They missed it, too, to come here and drag me out with them. "Yes." I wash my face and brush my teeth, then shuffle into the bedroom and let Racine nitpick while I dress. Ashley sits me down and pulls a bunch of junk out of her purse. She does my makeup, squealing something about the most off-the-hook shade of pink EVER as she assaults my lips, smiling at her handiwork gleefully after she finishes. When she steps away, Racine does my hair. Then they haul me off to third period.

When fourth period ends, I prepare myself to face Marta at lunch, knowing that Racine and Ashley's quest to get me out and functioning again likely didn't include her. Racine meets me in front of class, rightfully worried I'll try to sneak off somewhere alone. She links an arm in mine, walks me out to the lunch quad, and pushes me down on a bench at a table already occupied by the rest of Las Gallinas.

Marta smirks when I sit down. "I didn't think they'd be able to drag you out of the house."

"Hello to you too," I mutter.

"Three days, Ruby." Ashley's eager eyes glimmer. "Three more days and you'll be rid of her for good."

Marta pouts. "Bet she misses me."

"We'll all mis you," Ashley says, without a hint of sarcasm. She turns back to me. "Ray said you quit the dig. Any other summer plans?"

"Fall through a hole in the ground?"

"She got me a job there before the whole Lee thing," Racine tells Ashley, ignoring me. "I'm not working without her, so she's coming back."

I shake my head, thinking about Lee and how I've gone out of my way to avoid him. "Not a chance in hell."

Lee hasn't bothered me since his lips attacked mine last week. But the bracelet he wrapped around my wrist before I kissed him is still sitting on my dresser; it has to go back to the dig. I just can't stand the thought of facing him.

"Come on," Racine insists, pressing her lips together commandingly. "Are you really going to let some a-hole guy ruin something so important to you?"

"You're not changing my mind, Ray."

She raises an eyebrow. "Really? Just watch me."

"You still going to work at the mall this summer?" I ask Ashley, not so deftly changing the subject. "When are you taking off for New York?"

"Not until July," she says excitedly. "After I throw a hell of a going-away party."

Ashley moons over her party plans, describing the local band she plans to hire, and the copious amounts of alcohol she plans to drink. The way she describes her last weekend in La Luna, she may as well be recounting an over-the-top scene out of a cheesy coming-of-age eighties movie. And honestly, it sounds freaking wonderful.

"That reminds me," Racine cuts in. "What about our graduation party, Ruby? If you don't want to have it at your house anymore, we'll spread the word it's at my place instead. But we should figure it out like ASAP."

I nod. "Next Wednesday, the night after graduation, right?"

The year I started junior high, I fantasized about senior year, conjuring up dreamy boyfriends and memorable senior get-togethers—drama of all kinds. But even my wildest play-by-plays weren't as sensational as reality. Creativity may come naturally to me, but my imagination isn't elastic enough to include shape shifters, gods, and alternate dimensions. A party, however, fits in perfectly with my childhood dreams. Assuming I don't get sucked into a black hole or go supernova over the next few days, at least I can say one thing went right this year.

"I still want to host it," I tell them.

"Really?" Racine squeaks.

They all start talking at once, finalizing things like who should bring food, and what kind of music to play, and who's in charge of beer, presuming we can sneak it past Liddy. All *I* have to do is offer up my house and be there, which all things considered, doesn't seem like too much to ask for. The conversation keeps them occupied; no one talks about Ezra or the dig anymore, and I'm grateful.

The end-of-lunch bell rings and Racine pulls me up off the bench, tugging at me to walk with her to fifth period. After what feels like the longest march ever down locker row, I take a seat in Media Tech, painfully aware Mick is gone and that I may never have the answers I so desperately need.

Presenting a totally different Ruby on the surface than how I feel, I make it to every last day of my remaining three-day high school tenure. I take care of loose graduation ends, staying after school to help plan our graduation procession, and fill out paperwork I procrastinated completing. I even help Racine plan a bunch of last-minute party details. But afterwards, I make up a lame excuse to go straight home, then hide in my room until the next day, when I do it all over again.

I'm the world's most pathetic mess, until Sunday morning, when I come downstairs and find Angel, Liddy, and Torrance sitting in the kitchen. At first glance, everything seems normal. Angel lounges in the alcove with a book, staring absently out the window while he drinks a cup of coffee across from Liddy and Torrance, who are at the table reading the Sunday *Santa Fe New Mexican*. But when they notice me walk in, time seems to stop. They all turn to stare at me for a beat too long, like I've materialized out of thin air.

"Uh, hello?" I mutter tentatively, quickly running through all the things I might have accidentally done in the last few days to tick them off.

"Ruby." Liddy smiles. "There's coffee, and Tory made eggs."

Since Torrance moved in, it's like I have a surrogate father. He's warm, and protective, and treats me like family in the best ways, but after learning he might actually be like my step-uncle or whatever, I've felt kind of awkward around him.

"Thanks." I drop my head and walk to the fridge, grabbing a glass of orange juice. When no one says anything after another few minutes, I place my glass down on the tabletop loudly. "All right, what's the deal?"

Angel stands up, looking to Torrance for affirmation. When Torrance nods, Angel bows his head at me. "I have something for you. I want to give it to you before graduation." He motions toward the backdoor. "Think we can talk outside?"

I look down at the clothes I slept in, a pair of old yoga pants and a tank top, and shrug. "Okay, I guess."

Angel and I walk outside, into the bright sun. I follow him barefoot through the backyard down to the creek and sit on a small rock, dipping my toes into the still-icy water.

Angel takes his shoes off and tests the water, then sits at my side, shielding his eyes as he looks up the mountain before speaking. "You've avoided me the last few days."

"Yep."

"Why?"

"If I had it my way, I'd avoid everyone."

"Lame."

I turn my head sideways, sizing him up. I don't know how I didn't see it before, but Angel really does act like an older brother sometimes. "Now that Mick's gone, I can't answer any of your questions, Angel, *our* questions. I don't know who I am, or if Ezra's stupid book is folklore or reality, or if Lee is . . . I don't even know. And I feel lousy about it all. And then there's Ezra. I feel like an awful human being when I let myself think about what happened. If I even am human," I grumble.

"Ruby, you aren't responsible for me or my feelings. As for the rest, isn't that exactly when you're supposed to call me?" He taps his shoulder. "To cry on my shoulder. To commiserate. I don't have anyone else to talk about it with either."

"You said you needed time. I didn't want to bug you."

"I meant like a day or two." He moves to grab a stem from a nearby bush but then straightens, back to his confident self. "Look, I'm here for you no matter what. No matter what *we* are. But, Ruby, does it really matter?"

A warm breeze ruffles my hair. When he reaches out, pulling a strand off my lips, I know that in most ways it probably doesn't. He may as well be my brother, I love him that much either way. "Just don't kiss me again." I wrinkle my nose at him.

"I don't plan to." Grimacing, Angel runs a palm over his face, scrubbing at his dusky, five o'clock shadow. "Now, give me your hand." He motions at me, waiting for me to place my hand in his. When I do, he tilts sideways, and with his other hand, reaches into his pocket and pulls something out. Straightening, he unfolds my fist, placing an antique-looking ring sporting a single, gorgeous, faceted topaz in my palm. "It was my grandmother's. She gave it to me when I turned eighteen to give to someone special. It's a family heirloom."

I look at him, confused.

"I want you to have it—a graduation present."

"Angel, she probably meant like for your fiancée or something."

"Maybe, but this means more to me."

I'm shaking, floored by both my love for him and my uncertainty about accepting it.

"Topaz is a protection and healing stone. My grandma was superstitious. Her grandmother had it made to ward off the spirits in the Pass here and then passed it down. Ruby, I know you. And I know part of the reason you've been avoiding me is because deep down, you still worry I might be mad at you because of Mick and your mom. And I want you to know that I'm not. You aren't her. And whatever she did or didn't do isn't your fault."

"Even if that's true, I don't deserve this ring Angel."

"I disagree. This belongs to you—you're the someone special she wanted me to give it to, and I'd be really honored if you'd just accept it. You don't have to wear it. Just keep it, and know that however things turn out, I love you."

I start crying and hand him back the ring. When he frowns, I shake my head and hold my right hand out, stuttering, "I just . . . will . . . will you put it on me?" He exhales, then smiles before I add, "Lawfully bonded siblings, no matter what any stupid test says."

Angel slips the ring onto my right index finger, then pulls me into a hug. "Just remember I'm older. I'm not exactly sure how sibling law works, but I think it means I'll always be in charge."

I let go of him and wipe my eyes, smiling despite my mood. "We're good, then?"

"It'll take some time. The whole attraction part, you know . . . now it's just weird. *Really, really*, weird. But yeah, we're good. That's my thing, not yours."

Angel throws an arm around my shoulder and walks me inside. Liddy drops her paper on the kitchen table, breathing an audible sigh of relief. "You guys okay now?"

"Yes." I hold my hand out. "Look what Angel gave me for graduation."

Torrance smiles almost nostalgically. "Abuela would be happy you gave it to Ruby."

A little more comfortable in my own skin than when I first came downstairs, I sit down with Angel and join them for breakfast. Over Torrance's to-die-for coffee and scrambled eggs we talk about graduation on Tuesday, and Angel's pending promotion to under-chief. We talk about Liddy and Torrance's upcoming wedding, and how awesome it'll be to spend a week frolicking on the beach. We talk about everything but the dig, though I know Liddy's dying to ask me about it again. She doesn't know the truth about why I quit, and she's been pushing me to rethink my decision.

Later, Angel and I spend the day together, perusing Main Street on the hunt for a new pair of sunglasses for graduation and other trinkets, and afterwards floats at Margarita's. Huddled in a booth nearer to the front door, we talk for hours, until our conversation turns to Mick. Angel and I each take a shot at coming up with worst-case scenarios, brainstorming how we might handle them.

When Liddy and Torrance finally join us again for dinner, settling down in the now-crowded diner, I'm glad for the breather. After all that talking, my throat feels like industrial sandpaper.

As twilight breaks, I gaze out the window, zoning on the vehicles passing by. The setting sun paints the sky above the Pass in shades of turquoise and beryl. From my seat, I can see just over the foothills; it's an endless panorama, marked by the fluid crest of the Sangre De Christos in the distance, and the expanse reminds me there's a whole other reality outside of the tiny bubble that is La Luna.

"So, I talked to Lee," Liddy tells me after Daisy takes her order. "He says he's happy to have you back at the site, and that's he's sorry if there was any misunderstanding."

"Misunderstanding?" I choke out.

"All he would say is that you two had words and that he got a little heated. He apologized for being so strident, Ruby. He said he'd apologize again in person if you give him a chance. And since you haven't told us what happened . . ."

"Liddy," I cut her off, "why would you even talk to him? I told you I don't want to work there anymore, and I meant it." Aside from Lee, knowing Mick might be waiting in the shadows to conquer Azcale and unleash hell on Earth makes even the thought of working at the dig a thousand times less appetizing than the least appealing thing I can think of.

Liddy taps a scarlet fingernail on the table and glances sideways at Torrance before shrugging. "He called me. And he sounded genuine. And I know how excited you were to be onsite at the beginning. I just want what's best for you, love."

"What's best for me is if you stay out of my business where Lee is concerned," I say curtly. "I love you, Liddy, but I am eighteen. I don't need you fighting my battles."

She looks a little taken aback, and I feel bad. I didn't mean to come off like such a brat.

Smashing her lips into a flat line, Liddy holds her hands up in surrender. "Message received."

"I'm sorry. I just, it has to do with Ezra, all right? And I don't want to talk about it. But trust me when I tell you Lee was more than strident."

Liddy looks concerned, but she doesn't pursue it. "All right, love."

"Have you heard from Ezra yet?" Torrance asks. When I shake my head, he mirrors the motion, obviously disappointed. "He's had a week now to screw his thick head on. That's more than enough time in my book."

I want to snort but don't. Torrance might be more sensitive about my maybe-breakup than Liddy. For one, he adores Angel, and anything that bothers Angel bothers him. Second, as far as he's concerned, if Ezra was dumb enough to actually break up with me, he had whatever I did—*Not that I'm saying you've done anything, Ruby* he emphasized—coming.

"I guess we're still taking a break," I tell him, swallowing my indignation.

Ezra hasn't returned a single call. Despite the fact that I've called him every day and told his voicemail why I think Mick's somehow involved in what happened and how I at least deserve a hearing. I called him Wednesday, twice, muttering about trust and magic. I called him Thursday and Friday crying, and yesterday I lost my temper. Talk about giving someone's voicemail a piece of my mind.

Looking between them in our booth, at Liddy's sympathetic face, and Torrance's twinkling eyes, not to mention the rock-solid guy slash probably-my-brother across the table, I know that no matter how it plays out with Ezra, I'm lucky to have them on my side. Angel and Torrance are the clan I never had, rounding Liddy and me out. And as sad as I feel about Ezra, finally being part of a family is no consolation prize.

"I'm all right though," I try to smile. "I have you guys."

Liddy's eyelashes flutter over her soft grey eyes, turning down just a little as if observing a moment of respectful silence. "Give him a few more days. That kid loves you."

I squeeze her hand again. "Thanks, Lid."

"You *do* have us," Torrance says. "And you definitely don't need that blockhead."

Angel snorts his agreement, smiling at me across the table.

After a couple more coffee refills, and a nauseating story from Daisy—who doesn't know about my run-in with Lee—about how every woman who comes into Margarita's gossips about how gorgeous the new professor at the dig is, we finally pack it up and head back to the house. On the way home, Angel takes county roads, driving the long way around La Luna on purpose, traveling a winding, dark stretch of juniper-dotted blacktop between the mountains. The night is practically moonless, and the road ahead of us is pitch black, meandering through the deepest cut between two rocky escarpments just before the turn-off for my house.

I'm exhausted, and when Angel turns down a dim stretch of road that leads to my driveway, I start babbling about graduation and my grad party. Angel seems excited about it, but he's apparently even more enthusiastic about showing up with Racine on his arm. Their first official function as a couple. He explains this nonchalantly, to the windshield, and I pivot on my seat, amused by the way he just let it slip out so casually.

"Seriously? That's how you're going to play it?"

"What?" He shrugs.

"Way to slide that into the convo."

"Sly, right?" He grins sheepishly. "After everything else this week, it just seemed easier to drop it on you without actually dropping it on you." He glances at me. "So yeah, we made it official."

"Wow," I breathe out, toying with the ring he gave me. Because I'm genuinely happy for them, but also at a total loss for words. Angel and Racine. As in an actual, joined-at-the-hip couple.

"Yeah. Wow. But in a good way."

"You really like her."

He shoots me another sideways look and nods. "I've known Ray all my life. But I never really saw her before, you know?" He grins and taps the steering wheel. "Thanks for bringing it to my attention."

"Sure," I smile back, biting my lip as it trembles.

"Hey, you okay?"

I look down at my hand. "I just . . . the ring. . . "

"Is yours. Ruby, Ray and I, we're still getting to know each other. I *really* like her. But it's not the same. You and I—we're bound by something else. And the ring represents that."

"When I set you guys up, I imagined us all as a foursome, not a couple plus their third wheel," I try to joke.

"Ezra figured it out once before, right?" Angel pulls into my driveway, parks, and walks me to the door. "He'll come around. Just give him more time."

"You keep saying that. But I know you're just humoring me." My shoulders drop. "What if what you said about my mom's warning, what if you're right?"

"Ruby, it doesn't matter what *I* think. You *don't*. You said it yourself a couple days ago, you know better."

"When did you stop hating him?" I wave my hands in the air. "You're supposed to hate him."

I unlock the front door, and Angel opens it around me, gently pushing me inside. "Fine, I hate him. Now go inside and stop obsessing. You have one day to get it together before graduation. And you're going to own it."

CHAPTER THIRTY-ONE

BEGINNING OF THE END

AT ONE O'CLOCK, I THROW on a blue, strappy sundress and brush my hair, twisting it into a top knot. We'll be out on the football field this afternoon, standing in the sun for at least an hour, and it's been wicked hot out lately—wilted cornflower has never been my best look.

Dressed and ready, I linger on the edge of my bed for a few moments, staring at the painting of the Pass I finished last week, wishing Mom were here to see me accept my diploma. Despite all our problems, I know she'd be proud, especially because I'm wearing one of the dresses she wore on the runway, her favorite, actually. My way of honoring her.

At two, after nervously barking out orders to Liddy and Torrance about when to arrive at school, where to sit in the stands, and where to find me afterwards, Racine picks me up in her mother's new Rubicon and drives us over to the high school, where we meet up with Marta and Ashley. Linking arms, we join our class in the auditorium, donning caps and gowns along with everyone else.

"How come you get a purple sash?" Marta grouses as I straighten it over my shoulders.

"Because she's graduating summa cum laude," Racine answers bluntly.

"Guess I'm good at being smart." I shoot Marta a look.

Marta raises a manicured eyebrow, flipping her long, blown-out hair at me. "At least you're good at something."

Ignoring her, I hug Racine, then Ashley, and even Marta in succession before stepping into my place in line. "Good luck," I tell them. "I'll see you afterwards."

When the music starts, I walk with everyone in an orderly procession out to the field. I'm actually kind of giddy, and quickly find Angel, Liddy, Torrance, and Viviane in the stands, waving at them playfully, though I don't see Ezra. My last name starts with B, so I'm at the beginning of the ceremony, and when the principal calls my name, I walk to the podium in kind of a cloud, riding a rollercoaster of euphoria, sadness, fear, and glee. Holding back tears, I climb the stage and accept my diploma over a wave of hoots and clapping, then walk back to my seat. Caught up in the class-wide groundswell of excitement, I clap for my friends, and laugh at the valedictorian speech, and throw my hat in the air on cue. Despite Ezra's absence, for a little while I feel normal, like the same Ruby Brooks I used to be before my mother jumped off the pier.

After every last name is called, and every last teacher takes the stage to sing our praises, we converge on the green in a mass of hats, and hugs, and tears. Racine runs up to me first, followed by the rest of Las Gallinas, laughing and crying at the same time. Liddy and Torrance find me. Torrance picks me up off the ground, spinning me grandiosely. Then Angel pulls me into a bear hug and whispers, "I'm so proud of you, Ruby." Liddy is next, wrapping her slender arms around my waist. "What a road," she says, her eyes shining. "I hope you're proud of yourself, love. I know I am. You've always been the most amazing young woman. And I never, ever doubted you." She pulls me closer and hugs the daylights out of me, and I cry like a stupid preschooler. Then we all hug, then Liddy and all the other parents take a gazillion pictures. It's the worst, perfect moment ever, because I am both elated and also keenly aware of my mother and Ezra's absence.

After the field clears, Torrance treats us to a fancy graduation dinner at a swanky restaurant in Santa Fe. Angel and Viviane join us, and Racine and her parents show up, along with Ashley and her parents, who are as easygoing as she is, and her brother, who made it back from Iraq in time for graduation. Everyone is elated—genuinely, blissfully overjoyed. Everyone but me. I am *happy*, but at least half of my emotional legroom is filled by Ezra's absence and what it does to my heart.

By the time we finish dinner, and then dessert, and then walk it all off alongside the still-full Santa Fe River, it's late, and so many stars blanket the sky it looks like someone draped an entire warehouse of Christmas lights across the firmament. High desert winds make them twinkle, blinking in what seems like Morse Code, and I imagine it's the Otherworld trying to message me. Laying breadcrumbs to my path back to Ezra.

We head home and pull up in our driveway just after eleven, and seriously I'm ready to sleep for a week. But as we park beside an overgrown lavender bush, Torrance points at someone standing on the porch, killing my dreams. "Looks like Abbey."

"I didn't see another car." Liddy looks back at me.

I shrug and I see it dawn on her. If Ezra can shift, maybe Abigail can too.

"Abbey?" she asks without finishing the sentence.

"Ezra says it's genetic," I answer cautiously.

Why is Abigail here?

I'm halfway out the truck before Torrance even turns the engine off. Worried about Ezra, I rush toward the steps, followed by Torrance and Liddy. Abigail meets me at the top, looking nervous and a little bit impatient.

"Abbey!" Torrance gives her an enormous hug. "What are you doing here?"

Abigail smiles at Torrance, but holds her hand out at Liddy stiffly. "I'm Abigail, Ezra's mother."

Liddy shakes Abigail's hand, then gives me a sideways look. When I shrug, as unsure of what Abigail wants as Liddy is, she invites Abigail inside.

Abigail shakes her head *no*. "I just wanted to check on Ezra."

Confused, I ask what she means.

"He hasn't returned any of my calls for nearly a week. I got into town a couple hours ago—figured I'd have a word with him after your graduation ceremony. His truck is gone, so when he didn't come home, I assumed he was still out with you." She looks at me.

I swallow down the lump that swells in my throat. "We haven't talked since last week either." It comes out strangled. "And he didn't come to graduation."

She looks disappointed, concerned, and angry all at the same time.

"Maybe he's up at the ruin?"

"I've already been all over the mountain." She sighs deeply. "I guess he decided to take off after all."

"*After all?*"

`She purses her lips into a chilling frown. "He's been rambling on about leaving town for good since your fight last week. I told him to go see you before deciding."

"What? No. Why would he do that?"

She motions to her side. "Can I talk to you alone for a minute, Ruby?"

Liddy makes a funny face at me, squishing her lips together while she scrunches her brow. I shoot her a *just give me a sec* look, and her face relaxes only slightly, but she nods in Abigail's direction.

I follow Abigail nearer to the bushes lining the gravel driveway.

"I'm not sure what happened between you two, or just what the hell went through that boy's head, but whatever it was, he was pretty bent out of shape about it. It's a damn poor excuse though; he could have at least shown up for your graduation. I'm sorry for that." She flares her nostrils and tucks a long strand of ebony hair behind her ear, staring at me with the same intense look Ezra takes on whenever he's super uptight about something. "When he took off for college, he left everything behind. Just like that. Leaving, running away, it's his MO, Ruby." She glares at the ground. "We both know he never wanted to guard the goddamned ruin. You were his only reason for staying. And he flat out told me he wasn't sure if you were still together."

It hurts to hear her say it, but most of me still trusts Ezra. If he wanted to break up, he wouldn't have snuck out of town in the middle of the night without a word. And he'd never just leave the ruin. Not now. Especially not with everything going on. "Ezra's temperamental. Sometimes he says things he doesn't mean." I stare at her, angry that she seems to have zero faith in her own son. "But I know him. Even if we were over, he'd never abandon the ruin."

"No? He's done it before."

"But he knows better now. It's too important to him."

She looks off down the driveway. "You're important to him. And yet he missed your graduation."

I grit my teeth, suddenly overwhelmed with anxiety. "Exactly. And now that I know he's not at home sulking, I'm really worried." I was worried before, but unless Abigail's right, now that he's actually missing, not just off somewhere ruminating, my concern is in overdrive. Either way, I feel like a balloon that just got dragged over a cattle guard.

"That kid's good at pretending, like his father. He took off for days at a time when he was younger too. Never cared much about who he left behind, or how it affected us."

"Abigail, I *know* he cares about you and the ruin. I see it in his eyes whenever we talk about it. If he did leave, he'll come back," I promise her. "He wouldn't just leave you here stuck with all his duties."

She looks me over. "I was right about you."

A tear escapes my eye, and I wipe it away, determined to stay strong regardless of what she thinks of me. "I love him. And I have faith in him. I'm not perfect, but I never pretended to be or misled him. I'm sorry if you think differently."

Abigail's face softens. She places a hand on my shoulder, squeezing reassuringly. "I'm sorry for you. I don't *blame* you, Ruby. Ezra's difficult. That boy always was a paper tiger. You seem like a good girl. I was right when I told him you'd be good for him if he managed to get his act together. I'm just sorry he didn't listen."

I hate that her go-to is that Ezra ran away. She's his mother; she's supposed to defend him. But I especially don't like the seed she just planted. Last winter, when Ezra realized the Ancients gave him his face back, he disappeared for nearly a month, afraid to tell me. But that was the old Ezra. He's changed since then. Hasn't he?

"What about the gate?" I whisper, leaning in closer. "You know it was tripped and that he chased *something* through the Pass a couple times. He found that book you told us about, Abigail." I inhale, feeling dizzy. "You know him. You know how he is. Like you said, so stubborn. What if he didn't run off? What if he knows more than he told us and took matters into his own hands? What if something bad happened to him?" My heart speeds up with my speech, hammering in my chest.

"We've always been connected by the ruin." Abigail taps her temple dismally. "I'm sorry, Ruby, but if he was still anywhere in the Pass, I'd know. If he was hurt, I'd know. If the gate went off tonight, I'd know. Same way he'd know if something happened to you."

"But what if you're wrong?"

"I want to believe in him too, Ruby." She looks off at the pines. "But he's half his father and half feral beast."

Abigail says it seriously, and I'm caught between loathing and laughter. Angry, I step back. Ezra once told me his mother is a skeptic, that despite watching the ruin, she really never believed her father's stories. I witnessed that firsthand over dinner when I met her. And I know he hasn't told her everything we know about Azcale, or Lee, or Mick. But knowing even just the little she does about the gate and the Otherworld, I don't understand why she's not worried.

"He wouldn't just leave. And if he did, it's not for good." One thing I know for sure is that Ezra isn't a coward.

Abigail shoots me a small, sad smile. "I hope you're right."

She turns to leave, but I stop her. "Please tell him to call me when he gets home? And if he comes here, I'll tell him to call you."

"You mean *if* he comes home?"

"*When* he comes home," I repeat.

Abigail nods coolly, wavering before walking off down the driveway, disappearing into the forest between thatches of shadowed trees. My legs are shaking, but not because it's cold out. Maybe Ezra ran off, but I doubt it. I'm a thousand times more worried something terrible happened to him. That he's hurt or stuck somewhere in the Pass no matter what Abigail believes.

"So that's Abigail Pena," Liddy exhales as Torrance shuts the door in the hallway behind me. "She's intense."

"What did she want?" Torrance asks.

"She thinks Ezra took off."

"Took off? Like, for good?" Liddy looks puzzled.

"It's what Abigail thinks. Like he ran away or something."

Torrance makes a seriously solemn face. He doesn't know about the Otherworld, and to the outside world, Ezra had little incentive to stay in La Luna outside of me. "Are you kidding?" He snorts. "I've just about had it to here with that boy and his bullshit attitude."

"Torrance! I don't think she's right. I think he's probably just running wild somewhere, blowing off steam. That's how he thinks things through." It's not even a half-truth. Part of me knows Ezra would never just ditch his mother unless he was hurt. But the other half knows Abigail wasn't lying about their connection.

"Oh, Ruby." Liddy comes at me with open arms.

"I'm fine, Lid. Really. I know he wouldn't leave without talking to me first. He just needs a little more time alone. He'll figure it out. I'm sure. I bet he's even here for the party tomorrow night." I fake-smile to seal the deal. "It's been a long day. A really *good* long day. But if you don't mind, I think I'm going to go upstairs and call it a night."

Standing on my toes, I kiss Torrance's cheek before mauling Liddy with a bear hug, pretending to have everything together. But in my room, after I've changed into pjs and turned off the light, my face meets my pillow in a faceplant. In the dark, I breathe into it, suffocating myself as I mull over what Abigail said—that Ezra is a paper tiger.

CHAPTER THIRTY-TWO

SUBTERFUGE

THE BACKYARD IS A GRADUATION party wonderland. Colored lights and paper lanterns hang on wires strung from the trees, draping the yard with bright southwestern color. Racine used pinwheels to stake out the yard's rectangular perimeter, and as we stand on the periphery admiring our handiwork, they twirl frenetically in the breeze.

"Angel will be here in a few to hook up the sound system," Racine tells me. "And Ash's brother has an old karaoke machine. Said he'll bring it over."

"Ugh. Do we have to?"

"Don't be a spoilsport," Ashley says. "Karaoke's the bee's knees. Who doesn't like to sing?"

I raise my hand. "Me."

Nervous, I look around. We've set up outdoor speakers, built drink and food stations all over the backyard, and stoked the grill. The creek looks magenta beneath the waning sun, and the warm air smells like baked mesquite. Everything is in place, including the beautiful new morning glory and globe mallow blooms dotting the tall grass growing along the banks of the creek. But my anxiety has been eating away at my stomach all day. I still haven't been able to get hold of Ezra, and if he doesn't show up tonight, I know I'm going up to the ruin.

By eight o'clock, at least half of Pecos High is squeezed into my backyard, generating more noise than downtown Los Angeles during rush hour. Racine invited *everyone*, and Angel expected at least half of Pecos High's younger alumni to show up and help celebrate. Everywhere I look, people gorge on hot dogs, and shout over the music, and dance on the grass, generally elated to be done with high school. I want to be one of them, but Ezra's continued absence is like this piranha swimming around inside my body.

"Hey, Ruby!" Racine yells at me from the back porch. "Come on over here. You've been pouting in the corner for way too long!"

Obviously, my attempt to blend with the trees has been unsuccessful.

Racine walks over, grabs my hand, and pulls me to the middle of the lawn, where everyone is dancing. "Move it!" she commands, pushing me at Angel.

I obey, lifting my feet, trying to scrub the scowl off my face while I move like an under-oiled tinman. I never was very good at dancing to begin with, but dancing next to Angel and Racine, especially while they dirty dance, is torturous.

After a couple songs, Racine stops and shakes her head. "You're killing me with that face. Let's go find Ashley. I haven't seen her since we changed just before the party."

Racine kisses Angel's cheek, then drags me away toward the grill. Marta joins us when we pass her near the back door, handing me a small bottle of tequila as we search the perimeter for Ashley. By the time we find her on my driveway out front, flirting with some hot alumnus guy I don't know, the bottle has made a couple rounds, at least.

"Way to go, Ruby," Ashley giggles, sizing up my outfit. "You wore the dress!"

The dress, another designer number I pulled from the box of clothes I inherited from Mom, is plum-colored, short, and clingy. It kind of makes me feel like a bloated grape, but I was hoping once Ezra saw it, it would persuade him to forgive me. "No, way to go *you*. Way to go, Ashley." I grin at her stupidly, feeling the tequila. "Look at you. You're so . . . so beautiful."

"She is, isn't she?" Marta says without a stitch of antipathy.

Ashley giggles again, swishing her blue-and-white striped frock, shaking her bob while she bats her eyes shamelessly at both Marta and the boy standing next to her.

"You're all so beautiful!" I proclaim, looking back and forth between Las Gallinas.

Racine smacks her forehead, then grabs my free hand and squeezes.

"Enough tequila for you," Ashley laughs, standing up to take the bottle away from me. "Next thing you know, you'll be running off into the bushes with some stranger."

"Rebound sex!" Marta's eyes lit up. "That's a good idea."

"It's a good idea if you're you." Racine *tsks* at her.

"She wouldn't." Ashley's wide eyes search mine for confirmation.

"You're right," Marta snorts, striking a pose in a tight black dress that looks ungodly good on her—not that I'd admit it. "Ruby would *never*. In her head she's forever married to her ideal asshole. Which reminds me, where is he, Ruby?"

I look her up and down, debating whether to slug her the way Torrance taught me. That dress would probably look twice as good on her if she had a black eye to match it.

"Hey, you guys remember that guy Leo, the one Ruby met up in the forest last year?" Marta snickers. "You totally won *that* bet, Ashley."

Ashley angles her head like she has no idea what Marta is talking about and is a smidgen too shy of tipsy to care. "I did?"

"All right, Marta." Racine rolls her eyes and grabs my arm, holding on firmly, obviously reading my mind. "Enough."

Marta sniffs. "Anyway, Ruby, I'm pretty sure one of your *other* fan club members is looking for you." She nods over her shoulder toward the backyard. "I almost get why you played Ezra. Lee's not as hot, but he's pretty damn sexy. I'd do him."

Racine squeezes my arm. "Lee?" she asks.

"Who the hell invited him?" I sputter.

Marta flares her nostrils, raising an eyebrow dismissively. "I did."

"You what?" Racine yelps. "Why?"

"I ran into him in town, at the gas station. He asked what we were up to tonight and I told him about the party. I mean, like all of La Luna's here, right? I didn't want to be rude, so I invited him."

Marta enjoys antagonizing people. I know this. But most of the time, my reasonable self mostly manages to ignore her. Unfortunately for her, right now, my tequila-enhanced bad attitude stole the reins from my reasonable self and isn't about to relinquish them. "Of course, you'd sleep with him." I smirk, reaching out with a finger to boop the tip of Marta's nose. "You'll sleep with anyone. Because clearly, you're bereft of choices. But the truth is, and we *all* know this, Lee wouldn't. None of them would. That's why you're so angry, right? Because in a million years you know you'll never hold a candle to me." My grin spreads across my face, and it's such a terrible feeling. "The fact that people notice me drives you crazy, doesn't it? You can't win."

Marta stands up straighter, ready to rip into me. She starts to speak, but Lee walks up behind her. "Such vanity," he interrupts, rolling it out smoothly.

Marta shuts her mouth and smiles. She even blushes, I think.

Oblivious to Marta's gawking, Lee introduces himself to the rest of Las Gallinas, smiling like a charlatan while they wobble around him like hungry pigeons. Ashley bats her eyes so rapidly she looks as if she might be having a fit. Racine just stares, like she secretly thinks he's hot as hell but feels guilty about it.

Finally, after Lee endures a sufficient amount of fawning, he takes Marta's hand and kisses it. He says something to her in Spanish, and her genuine laugh surprises me. Marta never sounds anything but phony. After a moment, she smiles at me, waving at the rest of the group to follow her back to the yard. "Ruby and Lee have business," she tells them. "Let's give them their privacy."

"What? No!" I turn to Racine, mouthing *don't leave me.*

"I'm harmless," Lee grins at Racine, dialing up his wattage to infinity. "She'll be fine. Besides, Ruby *wants* to talk to me."

Racine blushes. "Oh, of course, she does," she winks. "We'll be in back dancing when you're done. Come find us. Both of you."

I stare at her incredulously, but it's like she doesn't even register how much I don't want to be alone with him. "I really don't want to talk to him," I tell her. "Please, don't leave."

She giggles. "You'll be fine, silly. See you in a few."

My blood boils as Las Gallinas walk away, totally oblivious to the fact that they've just been bewitched. "Nice trick." I glare at him. "But I'm on to you."

"On to me?"

"You and your magic," I hiccup.

"*Magic*," he repeats, squinting at me.

"Mojo. Sorcery. Witchcraft. Whatever."

He smirks. "Perhaps you've had a few too many."

"Damn right. It's my graduation party. But that doesn't mean I'm not paying attention. I see you, Lee." I point two fingers back and forth between our eyes dramatically.

Shadows move across Lee's face. His irises swallow his pupils as he pulls his top lip to the right over a very sharp incisor. "You have a wonderful sense of humor," he titters. "How refreshing."

Lee's smooth voice puts me at ease, but I know it's a false feeling, fabricated, part of the mind games he plays. "What do you want?"

"My bracelet."

"*Your* bracelet?"

"*My* bracelet," he repeats, still smirking.

"I'll give you back the bracelet if you tell me why I kissed you."

He looks down his nose at me. "Lust is self-generating. All I did was look at you."

"You *said* something."

"I can't plant a suggestion in your head that isn't already there, Ruby."

"I don't believe you."

Lee shrugs. Reaching out, he brushes my bare shoulder with the backs of his fingers, running them slowly down to my wrist. "It's not of any consequence now whether you believe me or not."

Shivering, I yank away and step back. "I'd like you to leave."

His eyebrows raise with his forehead, stretching his skin taut against his skull. "I'll consider it when you give me back my bracelet."

"I'm not negotiating."

"Oh, but you are. Especially if you'd like to see Ezra alive again."

Tendrils of inky ebony seep from his dark irises, engulfing his sclera until I'm staring into blackness. My breath catches and my heart plummets to my feet, and for a half-second I'm incapacitated. Lee crooks his arm and holds it out as if offering up a gentlemanly stroll. My hands are shaking, and I can't move, but his eyes are like coal, and my gut tells me he isn't bluffing. He's dangerous, and I need to get him away from my friends and family.

I swallow and make myself take his arm, leading him through the front door, away from everyone, toward my room. As we walk, Lee emanates strength. But it's less physical power and more this all-encompassing force. Like he's loomed the universe's wisdom and energy around a spool and woven it into an invisible cape around him.

Lee laughs and it sweeps through me as we climb the stairs, tugging at me like a riptide. "You're so beholden to him. I wonder, Ruby, if you'll ever love me so passionately."

I stare at him, dumbfounded. "I'll *never* love you, Lee."

His small, dismissive grunt feels like a bellow, knocking against me. Placing a hand on each of my shoulders, he turns me around and walks me into my bedroom, bowing politely when I stop near the dresser. Locating the bracelet on its top, he plucks it up, dangling it out near my face. "Hold out your wrist."

Turning to stare past him down at the brightly lit backyard out my bedroom window, I trace patterns on the windowpane, watching my friends move around below, aware something unfamiliar has taken hold of my body. My wrist raises out to my side on its own, and I'm mad at it for disobeying me. "You . . . you're doing something."

Lee steps behind me and runs a finger down my outstretched arm, stopping at my right wrist, chanting in a sing-song voice in an unfamiliar language. If I could scream and dash out of the room, I would. But my limbs have stopped heeding my brain, and I stand glued to the ground, powerless to do more than sniffle.

Over my shoulder, he whispers in my ear, moving my hair with his cold, cold breath. "Now, I want you to do something for me."

"What?" I struggle out.

"Take a walk with me up the mountain."

I don't want to. But even just pretending to agree will get Lee away from the house; plus, if there's a chance I can talk to Mom 2.0, I might be able to figure out how to help Ezra.

"What do you want from me, Lee?"

"We're a proper fit, Ruby."

"Proper?" I bite my lip. "I doubt we're even the same species."

The light inside my room blinks off. I startle and he turns me around to face him. Under the backyard glow illuminating his profile, a hundred different countenances flash in and out of focus before blending into one, solid, mesmerizing veneer. Spellbound, I reach out to touch his face, but he grabs my hand, holding on tightly.

"I'm not a 'species.' Moreover, I am the only reason you'll still have a place here when the time comes."

"What . . . what are you, then?"

"I'm many things." He grins slyly. "Creator. Man. Divinity. Spirit. Primordial Son."

A bell rings in my head, growing in pitch as I absorb what Lee is telling me. "Like from Ezra's book. Oh my God, *you're* one of the brothers."

"It's natural to doubt, Ruby. Liars twist truths. They wouldn't be good at what they do if their lies weren't effective. Ezra's a prime example. He isn't Ancient and he isn't True. He's a worker bee. And yet you still believe everything he tells you."

"Did they send you?" I ask breathlessly. "The Ancients?"

"No. Your mother sent Mick. To protect you from me." Lee looks down into my eyes. His intense stare consumes me, and the room, and the house, crushing everything into a tiny ball that he slips like a useless sidenote into his pocket. "The Ancients are bound by rules I never subscribed to. Not before I created you, not after."

"My mother?" I feel sick.

His black eyes shine in the saturated room, partially illuminated by the party lights outside. But his face darkens as he steps back, into shadows.

Trembling, I touch my chest where my peacock should be, finding nothing but skin. "*You're* Tezcatlipoca. Mr. Tezca T. Lipoca." My eyes bloom when it hits me.

"Humans have so many different names for their Ancients. You adapt us to suit your cultures and narratives, but it's all the same. I am Tezcatlipoca. And Titlcauan. But I'm also Apedemak, Camulus, Mars, Maahes, Resheph." He flicks his fingers impatiently. "There's more. But it bores me. Now," his eyes swallow his face, "It's time to take that walk up the mountain."

"Tell me how Mick knows my mom!" I demand, choking on my surprise.

Lee motions at the bracelet snaking tightly around my wrist, constricting in bone-crushing bursts. Gasping, I throw my arm out, trying to shake it off, but it's like a fanged parasite.

"Ruby, if you want to protect Ezra and your family, you'll do as I say."

"Then tell me where Ezra is!"

Lee tilts his head in such a blasé way it's almost menacing in its mediocrity. He looks amused. "Ezra ran at the first sign of adversity. He's a boy. You're a True. You belong to different worlds."

"I don't believe you. He'd never leave the ruin." I swallow hard, fighting back tears. "You did something to him."

"I merely made a suggestion." His words flow smoothly, but contaminate the air, rotting and insidious. "Defiance involves loss, Ruby. But then, I always enjoyed a measurable sacrifice. Still, perhaps if you're good and do what I say, I'll spare him." He stands very still, watching me curiously. Not like prey, but like a specimen. When he speaks again, I hear him in my head like I do with Ezra, though his lips never move. *My only compromise is what I offer you now—a place beside me. The rest is in your hands. You'll bear whatever consequences come your way no matter your decision.*

My head spins at a crazy speed, blurring Lee's face as I try to focus. He speaks in riddles, yet his intent is crystal clear. My heart knows he's going to get his way no matter what I decide.

"I'll take that walk with you," I spit out, praying Mom 2.0 will be there to guide me. "Whatever you want. Just promise me you won't hurt Ezra, or my friends, or family. Promise me that, and I'll do whatever you ask me to."

Lee shimmers, giving off a hypnotizing aura. When I'm more automaton than Ruby, he walks me to the doorway and stands very close, looking down at me from what feels like a temple-high perch. "Lovely decision."

CHAPTER THIRTY-THREE

CROSSROAD SUPERNOVA

I PLANT MY HEELS IN the ground, trying to drag Lee to a stop as we pass the first ring of conifers on the plateau. Exerting more force than I have strength, Lee pulls me past moss-flecked boulders and gnarled logs toward the ruin. We reach its boundary, and I stop and stare at its glittering, mica-imbued bones while I paw at my buzzing ears. The ruin is alive, humming with energy.

Standing before it, currents travel over my body like a magnetic second skin. The ruin's pull is irresistible, and I move toward it, but Lee holds me back, latching onto my arm tightly.

"*Tsk-tsk.* You don't really think you're going anywhere without me?"

Turning to face him, I examine his imperious eyes, and exacting expression, and that stupid, sparkling pendant. The obsidian mirror. Lee looks royal. And dangerous. And completely supernatural. How did I ever miss it?

Frightened, I try twisting out of his grip.

Lee's eyes narrow. "Save your energy, Ruby."

In a nervous rush I blurt out, "Tell me how Mick knows my mother." I cover my mouth again, biting my lip hard enough behind my hand to make it throb.

"Is that a demand?"

My answer sticks in my throat, because I suddenly can't exhale.

Lee tugs at my arm again, dragging me closer to the center of the ruin.

"Wait," I say breathlessly. "I need to know Ezra's all right."

Lee looks down his nose at me, but he doesn't answer.

"You made me a promise."

"And I don't intend to break it." He pulls me by the elbow. "I'm many things. But liar isn't one of them."

Early summer is in bloom. All along the ruin's sparkling periphery, scrubby bushes and wildflowers grow from the dirt between mossy rocks and trees. They're bright and beautiful and a stark contrast to Lee's dark aura, which wilts everything we step over, leaving behind a trail of dead things.

Lee tugs, and I pull in the other direction, slowing him down.

"Tell me!" I insist.

A gust of wind blows over the plateau as Lee sizes me up, concluding something that makes him chuckle. "I created Mick." He says it as if Mick's name feels foreign on his tongue. "My—how do you say—*ace up my sleeve*? I charged him with Mictlān. He ruled the Underworld beside me for a time before the Council banished me. Aztlán was a border town then, the only bridge between our worlds Ancients could pass through, and by the time I found myself back there, they'd already sent Mick up on my heels to oversee it. When the Council caught whisper that I'd taken over, he was ordered to destroy the city. Sealing the bridge between our worlds was a calculated risk—to keep me out of the Otherworld, I presume. But they didn't know, like I did, that Mick would develop a taste for humans. I'd already been here millenniums by then, puppeteering my return. So I waited another few hundred years for Mick to slip up. I watched in the shadows, orchestrating his encounters. But none of them produced you. Not until Sera."

Lee's eyes lock on mine, and his stare makes me quiver.

"I've watched you for years, Ruby. Biding my time until you turned eighteen. Sera was next in line to work the gate, but then somehow the Ancients got wind of you. Humans and Ancients . . . it's against our rules, but because of your bloodlines, the Council settled on bringing you back early to preside over the gate instead of her. Of course, that doesn't work for me. I needed you here. So I whispered in Mick's ear. I knew he'd try to warn Sera. Just like I knew she'd fight for you."

I stare at him, speechless and frozen in this terrible moment when it dawns on me that my entire existence has been orchestrated. "She went there instead of me?"

"The gate's not designed to seat more than one True at a time, and I knew he'd convince her to sacrifice her life for yours." Lee grins wickedly. "I imagine the Council was livid when Mick brought her home in your stead. But then, what else does one expect from the god of the Underworld?"

"But why? Why me?"

"You're my key, Ruby," he says, as if genuinely surprised by my question. "I need you to get home. And later, to help me unleash Apanohuaia in the Pass and merge the Underworld's nine realms with Earth. I've grown fond of it here, but I miss a number of what you might call creature comforts, and I never intended to abandon the Otherworld for good." He lets me go and walks closer to the center of the ruin.

"And Angel?" My voice sounds strangled. "He's Mick's son too."

"You, descendant of the matriarch Rachel, mother of the tribe, Naphtali, are True by virtue of both bloodlines and Kalachakra, the wheel of history. And Angel is a half-breed." Lee pats the altar with one hand, and gestures with the other, motioning me closer with his pointer finger. On the altar, one of the ancient spell bowls we dug up sits beside the jaguar nagual. "Now, come here."

I try to run, but my wrist burns as the ruin amps up. And suddenly, it's like I'm drowning in glue. The bells chime, rattling against my skin as Lee starts chanting in what almost sounds like Hebrew, holding up the spell bowl over the altar.

"Ezra," I choke out.

Lee lowers the bowl and stops chanting, placing the nagual in its center. "Is a pain in my side and the reason the Ancients have paid such close attention to you lately." He *tsks* and shakes his head. "Sera plotted your move here to keep an eye on you. And I let it happen because it suited both of us, until you adopted Ezra. Now imagine, Ruby, orchestrating your grand opus, only to be set back by a rag-sorter. Watchers are the Council's little soldiers. They have no autonomy. In order to get you up here, I had to remove him."

I double over, falling to my knees. Reaching for the ground, my hand sinks into a pile of pine needles. Their sharp tips sting, and smell like sap, and the combination makes me retch convulsively.

Lee's bells cut into my wrist. He's still looming over the altar, but his presence drapes me like a heavy blanket; it's physical, stifling and weighty, smothering so much of what makes me a walking, breathing, animated human being.

In an instant, the air congeals, pulling into small clumps of matter I actually see. It hovers between us before pulling into globules that disappear, gouging holes in the atmosphere that gobble up all of the light in the universe. All the oxygen on the plateau goes with it, and I'm suddenly, very seriously, suffocating.

"Lee," I gasp, scratching at my throat. "I . . . I can't breathe."

Lee crouches down next to me, placing a hand on the nape of my neck. "After all the millennia I've spent waiting for you, I don't intend to let death separate us. Whatever your human fate, on this side or the other, you'll stand beside me."

The bracelet pulls at my wrist as I flail, struggling against it. I understand now. I can crossover at will. Lee can't. The bracelet has bound us, and I'm his forever travel buddy.

"Stop fighting," he tells me.

My lungs collapse and the sky fades, overcome by blotchy masses of empty space that quickly spill into each other. Prisms explode in my head, melting my eyes in their sockets. It's too bright to keep them open, or maybe my lungs lack the air to supply my brain well enough to see. Either way, it doesn't matter. The weight of Lee's palm feels like an anvil, crushing me into a puddle against the burning earth.

The world explodes. Everything evaporates before a soft purple light spills over the plateau, illuminating the once again visible ruin. It brings air back to the mountain, and I sputter, gasping before dropping face first into a pile of pine needles. My ears are an echo chamber, clogged with unfamiliar feedback. Bursts of howling wind, and crackling static, and creaks that don't seem connected to anything come and go, rushing over me. My head pounds, but I push myself up on my elbows, balancing on my hands and knees. Scanning the violet sky, my eyes land on three enormous nearby planets, confirming I'm in the Otherworld.

In a panic, I scurry up, searching for Lee. But he's not on the plateau—at least, not that I can see. Frantic, I try willing myself back to Earth. When that doesn't work, I rip my feet up and circle the ruin, touching each adobe block, making up chants I mumble out loud, but nothing happens.

After a few minutes of frozen terror, I wander toward the trail that winds downhill to my house, knowing that it's not actually where it will take me. Heading through the forest toward the edge of the plateau, I reach the trail's beginning, but where the path down the mountain *should* be, the land shears away, plunging into bottomless canyon. Across the gorge, faint structures shimmer on the edge of a precipice, hovering over the abyss.

"Lee!" I yell as loud as I can, but his name echoes off steep canyon walls, losing steam as it makes its way back to me. "Don't leave me here alone," I beg the trees. I'm not sure which is worse, being stuck here with Lee, or being here alone without him.

Hoping to attract Mom 2.0, I walk the canyon's endless perimeter, calling out for her. When nothing happens, my path takes me back to the center of the plateau, past the ruin, farther out into the forest, through strange plants that cling to everything. As I walk, I snap limbs off of alien foliage, and assemble piles of rainbow-colored rocks that feel like coral against my palms, marking my route.

Tall trees that look like melted candle tapers topped with razor-sharp palm fronds cluster in tight pockets, stretching on as far as I can see. Beneath the trees, tiny bat creatures slither along over exposed radixes, slapping their wings against the ground as they scurry behind me. The slapping generates a hollow patter, like fingers tapping against an empty milk carton.

The air around me sparkles, charged with energy. White hot flashes of light glint off the tree trunks, and occasionally, bubbles rise from the ground, growing in circumference until they pop high above, sending fireworks showering over the forest. When bunches of them rise at the same time and the sky explodes, the creatures at my feet thrash their wings against the ground furiously. The Otherworld is already noisy, but the pummeling sounds like gunfire in a tin can, and the sound is overwhelming.

Traversing what feels like miles of forest, I count out loud, trying to keep track of time, as well as steady my mind. At one hundred, I bite the stick I'm carrying, marking its bark to keep tally. I walk, counting under my breath until the trees finally give way to a sweeping amber prairie.

Up ahead, an enormous body of liquid too thick to be water blankets the plain. Its glassy, purple surface reflects the orb-filled sky, pooling around rocky monoliths at its center that rise toward the heavens, casting shadows over both liquid and land as far as I can see. Huge avian creatures flutter up from a stumpy swath of needle-sharp plants growing at angles from the shore. They screech, and the bat creatures beside me begin to sing, scattering into the ropey underbrush.

Near the lagoon's edge, a patch of soaring, parchment-dry grass rattles as it undulates. Something big moves through the thatch, cutting a trail through the prairie, crushing the grassland as it moves closer to me. Breathless, I drop to my haunches, hiding in the tall blades at the edge of the field. But beneath the grass line, whatever it is in there has an advantage. I can't see it, but somehow know it sees me.

Terrified, I mark another three notches on my stick before finally standing up again, scanning the empty field. The sky changes colors, from sapphire to violet, shifting around the chain of orbs that begin their descent below the skyline, and after another long count, I step out into the clearing, moving closer to the lagoon.

Something rustles, stopping me cold. Behind me, at the boundary where the forest meets prairie, a gangly, pale mannequin with piercing silver eyes in its otherwise empty face hunches awkwardly between two trees. When it catches me staring, it drops to all fours, shedding pieces of papery skin as it moves, slowly gliding on its palms and feet into the grass like a serpent. It slithers toward me and I run, churning up pops of color that explode around my feet, generating wispy trails of blue, and red, and yellow.

Parchment-dry grass crunches beneath my sandals as I rush into the lagoon, out of breath, terrified of being the creature's dinner. I wade farther, making my way through warm, viscous fluid into a razor-sharp patch of spiky plants. They scratch my bare arms, but hide me from the shoreline.

Through a crop of eely stems, I see the creature stop on the shore. It snakes its head side to side, growing taller as its torso elongates, stretching to accommodate its now towering height. The creature's blank face scans the surface of the lagoon, but it doesn't seem willing to wade in. After a moment, its body starts to shake, blurring like Ezra does before shifting. It shimmies, softening at the edges until it's nothing but a smudge that evaporates.

Lightheaded, I huddle low in the reeds, submersed to my chin, gagging as liquid pools around my mouth and nose. The liquid smells like sulfur, and its slimy contents sticks to my body, itching like crazy where air dries it against my skin. Its opaque surface reminds me of obsidian, of Lee's pendant; I can't see beneath its shiny top, and not being able to see below fuels a thousand fears about what might live at the bottom. Queasy, I pick my feet up and the liquid holds me, suspended in my hidden pocket.

Stay still, Ruby!

At the sound of Ezra's voice, I whip my head around. On the shore, a mountain lion paces back and forth. Then it soars into the air, sailing into the muck beside me, displaying a huge set of murderous teeth. Roaring, the lion comes down near my face, and the lagoon explodes. Gloppy liquid flies everywhere, and before I can scream, sharp teeth graze my shoulder, dragging me to the shore.

The lion drops me on the bank, then leaps away, launching at what might be a giant, toothed seahorse rising from a nearby cove off the lagoon. The seahorse whips backwards just as the lion's fangs sink into its neon-blue skin, tearing a gash down its sludgy, ribbed side. The creature's high-pitched squeal shakes the night; it bends to peck at the lion's back, reeling as the lion tears away chunks of mucus-covered flesh that drop with a sickening plop into the liquid below it. Finally, it stops fighting and teeters sideways, hitting the lagoon's surface with a slap before sinking beneath it for good.

The lion paddles to shore, weighed down by the lagoon's quicksand-like contents. On the bank, it tosses its head around, shedding glops of black fluid from its fur. Then it moves toward me, and I scurry backward, almost tripping over my feet.

"Ezra!" I shriek as he shifts. Without thinking I run and throw my arms around his neck, pressing up against him.

Ezra hugs me back, but he's stiff, like there's a bubble between us. He places a finger to his lips and looks down at my face as he motions toward the forest.

What are you doing here? I hug him tighter, afraid to let go. *How did you find me?*

I was here when you came through. I've been tracking you.

Still damp, I anchor myself to him, my buoy in a stormy sea. *How did you get here?*

Lee's necklace . . . it's some kind of portal . . . or . . . he shakes his head, *prison. I trailed him to the ruin. Confronted him. But I caught my reflection in his pendant. It's been a long time since I've seen myself in lion form. Next thing I knew, I was here.*

His expression scares me, but there's also humor in his tone, as though actually saying it confirms he really crossed over to the Otherworld. *He just . . . sent you here?*

Ezra's eyes flare, turning amber. *No, he godsplained first. About his pendant and Azcale, and who he is, about the freaking jaguar—it was* all *Lee, Ruby. The whole time.*

Lee giving Ezra a speech before banishing him to the Otherworld doesn't surprise me. He may be a god, but he sure likes to hear himself speak.

Ezra looks down at his boots. He looms over me, but deflates a little when he sighs, throwing his spine into a C. *You're all dressed up.* He nods down at my damp dress.

Lee showed up at my graduation party tonight. He did something. Like magic or something. He did this. I hold up my bell-draped wrist, jutting it at him. *He dug this up, and I can't . . . I can't get the stupid thing off for the life of me.*

Ezra stares at the bracelet. *Your party was tonight?*

My breath hitches and I inhale, waiting out the shakes gripping my body. *Yes.*

I missed your graduation.

It's all right. I knew it had to be more than just our fight. I knew you wouldn't just ghost me. I mean, not like that. I was going to go up to the ruin anyway, to try and find you. But then Lee implied he hurt you, or . . . I don't know, did something terrible. He promised me you'd be safe, that you'd all be safe if I went up to the ruin with him.

Ezra looks conflicted, like he's elated, angry, anxious, and apprehensive and can't settle on any one emotion for more than a second or two. *I'm so sorry I missed everything.*

I am too.

Ezra nods and his eyes flare again, shifting from rusty amber to deep violet. He scans the prairie. *Where is he?*

I don't know. I couldn't find him anywhere after I came through.

Let me see your wrist again. He takes my arm when I shove it at him and starts tugging at the bracelet. When that doesn't work, he pulls out a pocketknife. *Damn.* His normally steady voice borders on dread. *I can't cut through it.*

Because it's magic. In a rush, I explain everything Lee told me before sending me here. Everything he did, from the spell bowl to the way he seemed to glamor everyone at my party.

Ezra shakes his head briskly. *I can't believe I didn't see it coming.*

He fooled all of us, Ezra.

Ezra's eyes flare a brilliant lavender, glowing yellow at the edges as the last sparkling orb over the prairie dips beneath the trees. Speechless, I stand near the bank of the glassine lagoon, staring slack-jawed at him. The sky is empty now, void of stars or planets, or any kind of sun or moon, and yet it glows diffusely at the edges, as if someone plugged it in. Like the Lite-Brite Mom bought me for my sixth birthday.

Ezra's here, standing at my side; my heart is swelling with this unbridled love for him. He's alive and well, and with me in the Otherworld. But my brain is still tangled in the web of horrible things Lee told me. Now I know. I know why Mom left, and where she went, and who my father is—who *I* am, at least in theory. But it's like telling me the kitchen sink is broken, and that I need to take out all the pipes and rewire the garbage disposal, then put everything back together afterwards without teaching me how to do it. I know now, but the knowing doesn't help me one bit.

CHAPTER THIRTY-FOUR

OF ALL THE DIMENSIONS IN ALL OF THE UNIVERSE

ONE OF LIDDY'S FAVORITE SAYINGS has always been *be careful what you wish for.* For the first time, I feel like I truly understand why she's so attached to it. My truth is laid bare at my feet, and most of me wishes I still knew nothing.

Do you think Mom knew what Mick was when they hooked up? I chew on a thumbnail as we walk across the prairie back toward the ruin.

Ezra slows, turning his head to train his intense eyes on me, but he doesn't stop walking. *Not until Mick went looking for her a couple of years ago.*

Huh. I hurry closer to his side. *Wait. How do you know?*

Ezra bites his lip, looking almost as crazy as I feel. *She told me.*

What? I swallow hard, trying to steady my already too-quick breathing. *You talked to her?*

He makes a funny face. As if discussing something so absurd so casually leaves a terrible taste in his mouth. *She was at the gate when*

I crossed over. But she couldn't send me back—something about the way Lee banished me.

What else did she tell you?

That she watches the gate and sits on a throne beside Mick in the Underworld. She said being with him and knowing you were safe was enough once she knew the truth about what she is. That things were good here until . . .

I search his face, fixed on his rock-solid jaw. *Until?*

Until you met me. Ezra rubs his chin, inhaling deeply.

So, what Mom 2.0 said about us being together. . .

Is all true. He looks down at his feet. *I guess the only reason the Council never separated us is because Sera convinced Mick I could protect you, and Mick convinced the Council I'd be more of a danger to you and the gate than I am already if the Council tried to intervene.* He raises his eyebrows, biting back a small, almost proud smile. *It's partly why I got my face back. Also, Ruby, your Mom 2.0, she is Sera.*

Wait? I pull him to a stop. *What?*

Ezra takes both my hands, squeezing them in a vise grip before softening his hold. *She needed you to believe it wasn't her to keep you safe. So you wouldn't keep coming back here.*

I wince. *Where is she now?*

She was trying to send me back when she disappeared. But before that, she said if Lee ever did cross with you, he'd have to come through the gate using some sort of binding spell, that you'd both probably be cloaked, invisible to the rest of Ottomundo. I'm guessing she doesn't know you're here yet. Or, if she does, that she's searching for Lee before he hurts you or wreaks havoc on Ottomundo.

I grip his button-up into a big, fisted ball and shove my face into his chest to steady myself. Speaking into his shirt, I'm about to ask how, since I can't seem to open the gate either, he plans to get back home without her. But then someone calls my name and we both turn toward the voice simultaneously.

Four figures emerge from the forest. They hurry over, huddled together. Stunned, I gape at them. Racine and Ashley are like extra appendages hanging off Angel's torso. But Marta is a brick boxing glove, ready to smash someone's face in.

"What," I gawk, stumbling over my words, "are you doing here?"

Racine gazes up at the sky, batting her astonished eyes. "Where the hell is *here*?"

Marta stares me down. "It all makes sense now. Daughter of the freaking Underworld?"

My head whips toward Angel.

"We were on your heels at the ruin . . . they had no idea. But then," he sucks in and sweeps his arm out in front of him, "this happened."

"Shh!" Ezra admonishes us. "Keep it to a whisper."

Wriggling from Racine and Ashley's grip, Angel steps closer, reaching out for me. But when his fingers touch my shoulders, he flinches. "What's wrong with you?"

"You mean, other than that you're all here?" I gape at them, unnerved by the way they're all staring at me. "How did you cross over?"

"When Racine told me Lee was at your party, and that she left you with him, I went looking for you. Ezra's book, Lee, everything that happened at the dig . . . it just suddenly clicked. When I couldn't find you, I somehow knew you'd gone up to the ruin. They caught me as I started up," he cocks his head back at Las Gallinas, "and insisted on coming with me. I didn't have time to argue."

"You *all* followed me?"

"Yes," Angel nods. "And when we got to the ruin, it was humming. But we didn't see you or Lee anywhere. Next thing you know, we were here."

"Because of course you'd open a magical vortex," Marta snorts, rolling her eyes.

And damn. Even in the Otherworld she's cheeky.

Angel shakes his head incredulously. "I had no idea how to get back. And it seemed like a good time to tell them the truth."

"Now that we found you, how about you tell us how to get home," Marta snaps at me.

"Back through the ruin. But I already tried, and nothing happened."

Ezra runs a hand down his face. His expression is so dire it's unnerving. *I think Lee destroyed the gate. I was about to tell you.*

What? No. Why would he do that?

To trap you here with him?

"The gate doesn't work," I say flatly, echoing Ezra. I know I should be surprised, shocked even, but after everything, I'm just numb inside. "I think Lee destroyed it after we came through."

"What?!" Ashley shrieks.

"Ashley, hush!" Ezra snaps at her.

I close my eyes, thinking about Lee's story and *Tshiquite's* prophecy. "But I think there's another one. Through, Azcale."

"Azcale?" Racine arches an eyebrow.

"Long story. But I'm pretty sure it's across the canyon from the ruin."

Las Gallinas and Angel stare at us. Angel's stare especially stays glued on me, tracking my every little tic like a radar. "Where did Lee go?"

"I don't know. He left me at the ruin, and I haven't seen him since."

Overhead, a huge swarm of turquoise insects with birdlike wings fly in formation through a swatch of now shimmering green sky. They buzz like a swarm of bees, only louder, and the basso undertone makes my bones vibrate. Everyone looks up at them, pressing their hands against their ears, enthralled.

"But he's out there," I say quietly. "And I have to get to Azcale before he does."

"You?" Angel squints at me.

"He wants to unleash Azcale on Earth."

Ezra reaches out and grabs my wrist, grimacing as he shakes it. *My guess is the only reason Lee isn't here with you now is because he can track you.* "You're still bound to him," he says out loud. "It's how he came through the gate. And it's how he'll know where to find you when the time comes unless we can get this thing off you." He exhales and turns to Angel. "Ruby's right. Lee wants to bridge Aztlán and Earth through the Otherworld." His eyes explode, a cyclone of color. "We have to find that portal." He points at Angel and Las Gallinas. "They have to cross back and destroy the gate on Earth before Lee gets to it."

"They?" Ezra said *they*, not we, and I know it's not a mistake. Ezra may talk in riddles sometimes, but he's always precise. He'd never say *they* unless he meant to leave *us* out of the equation.

"Ruby!" Racine gasps.

Angel pivots toward Ezra. "What's wrong with her?"

"Me?" I look down at my hands, at the way they seem to be shimmering and shifting. "What the . . ."

Ezra is so quiet for a moment I have time to shoot Angel a questioning look. He frowns and Racine moves closer to my side. It's like they all sense the storm brewing inside Ezra.

"Just tell me!" I demand. "What's wrong with me?"

"I think you're in flux," Ezra says quietly. "That your spirit's in flux."

It's not at all funny. But his ultra-serious tone seems so out of place given we're all standing in some weird Otherworld prairie. *Spirit flux? What the hell?*

"Like I have some superhero power?" I ask sarcastically.

"No, Ruby, like your corporal body doesn't exist anymore."

Angel steps closer. "You don't mean . . ."

Ezra and I lock eyes. His pupils contract and I hear his heartbeat in my head, in sync with my own. *I don't know for sure.*

But you think so.

He looks up at the treetops, at Angel, at the ground. Everywhere but at me. He's silent for way too long, and his inability to meet my eyes says more than words ever could.

What does that even mean? I choke out silently.

Finally, he says, "I think you may have actually died when you crossed over."

CHAPTER THIRTY-FIVE

NO ONE GETS OUT OF JAIL FREE

THE SKY LOOKS LIKE WATERED-DOWN ink, uneven and translucent. It's a moonless night, but streams of shooting stars pass by overhead, scattering light particles like confetti over the prairie. Ezra stares at me, searching for something. And for just a moment, I see how fragile he is beneath his bravado.

Angel and Las Gallinas also look pretty tragic huddled in a half-circle, arced around me. They all stare, waiting for me to say I feel fine. That my incorporeal state is just a temporary aftereffect of traveling through the gate bound to Lee or something. But I don't feel fine. I feel undone. If Ezra is right, it means I'm never going home.

"It's probably just this place." Angel flicks his fingers at the sky, but his strained voice betrays him.

"Or because you're still bound to Lee," Racine adds. "Like he's tapping your lifeforce or something."

"Sure," I say. "That makes sense." And it does. It's just Ezra's expression makes it plain he doesn't believe it. I've never seen him look so genuinely horrified. Turning away from him, I add, "Or maybe it's because I'm part . . ." I bite my lip and shrug. Part what?

"Fae? Half immortal? Otherworld demi-god?" Angel tries to laugh.

Except Angel seems okay, Ezra reminds me.

"I *feel* fine," I tell them, doing my best to ignore him. Because he's also right. Crossing over hasn't affected Angel in any discernible way; he looks one-hundred percent normal. "Whatever it is, right now we need to find our way back and . . ." I trail off, unsure how to finish.

Blow up the portal? Bury it? I don't freaking know. Ezra shrugs. *How about we tackle one thing at a time. Let's just figure out how to get them there, first. Before the Ancients find out we're all here.*

I cringe at Ezra's use of the word *them* again.

Ezra's forehead creases, drawing his dark eyebrows down over his wild eyes. *So you know, I'm not going back without you, Ruby. I won't leave you here. Not with Lee and not alone. Wherever you go, I go.*

I hold my hands out, staring at my pale, translucent fingers. *I'm going home after we stop Lee, Ezra,* I insist, as much for myself as anyone.

"What are you guys doing?" Marta squints at us, tipping her head curiously. "Having some kind of mental telepathy fight? That's what all that staring's about, isn't it? Look at them. You never noticed it before? They do it all the time. I just thought they were," she pokes a finger down her throat, pretending to gag, "making eyes at each other."

Racine looks at me sternly, waiting for me to shoot Marta down.

"Marta's right." I bite my lip. "We can . . . communicate telepathically."

"Jesus." Racine crosses herself as Ashley's eyes bloom.

"And I was telling Ezra I think we should head back toward the ruin. Maybe follow the rim of the canyon until we find a way across."

Ashley looks stricken. She folds her arms over her chest and squeezes her shoulders tightly. "What if we don't?"

"Ash," Angel wraps an arm around her shoulder, "we'll be all right."

"But how do you know?" Ashley's voice is dangerously close to hysterical.

"I know, Ash," I tell her. "Listen to me. I've been here before, and Ezra knows tons about the Otherworld, and I'm telling you that as long as we stick together, we'll be fine. We've all got each other's backs, all right?"

"Oh . . . okay," she whispers.

I want to mean what I just promised for real, but the truth is I have less than zero clue whether we're even remotely safe even just standing in this huddle.

Can I die here if I'm already dead?

Ezra looks like I just stabbed him. *I don't know the rules, Ruby, but spirit death is a thing. So yeah, probably. Though, there's no way I'll let it happen.*

"Dudes. You just said we're all in this together." Marta trains her finger on Ezra and moves it in a half circle over the rest of them. "From now on, say it out loud."

"Ruby's right. We should head for the ruin," Ezra says quietly. "And keep your voices down. We're not alone out here."

"Stick together and keep your eyes open," I add firmly, nodding toward the stand of trees off to my left.

Quickly, we walk in a huddle away from the lake, deep into the forest. Ezra and I take the lead, and Angel and Racine head up the back, sandwiching Ashley and Marta. As we move through stands of trees, Ezra walks alongside me silently. Behind us, the bat-like creatures that followed me before come and go, but none of them stick around like they did earlier. We walk for what feels like hours, until gnarly tree branches twine above us into a canopy, knitting a spotty awning as we move even deeper into the forest.

"What the hell?" Angel says quietly, stopping to look up.

"Nothing makes sense here," I whisper. Wind whistles in spurts through holes in the canopy, rattling the trees like hollow bones, and our voices take on the slightest echo.

"It's so creepy," Ashley says miserably.

"And kind of beautiful," Marta murmurs.

And in a dark kind of way it is. I'm just surprised Marta of all people noticed.

"I can't believe you never told us about the Otherworld." Ashley looks up at a bunch of slithering tree branches, shaking her head.

"I can," Racine says softly, moving closer into Angel's side.

"Ezra and I, we didn't think we should. It just seemed too big. Like somehow knowing would change everything."

"Has it for you?" Racine asks.

My mouth opens to say *yes*, because that feels like the right answer. But something stops me. Even before discovering the Otherworld, I knew better than to rely on the surface of anything. My social contract has always been with the people I live with on Earth just *because*.

"I don't know."

"Except now you know you're going to hell." Ashley looks startled, like it just slipped out. She meets my eyes. "I mean, like afterwards," she adds.

Ezra starts moving again, pulling me along through a tree limb tunnel. "Your spirit is weighed here in the Underworld, but mostly so the Ancients know where to send you next. The Otherworld isn't hell. Not the way you see it. And only one of the Underworld's nine realms is its *underbelly.* That's where souls go that have no path back."

"You mean people like Marta," I snicker.

"You're the expert, Daughter of the Underworld." Marta flips me off for good measure.

Ezra holds his hand out to me. I slip my fingers through his and squeeze, and the feeling makes my stomach turn. My palm is like a sponge. Either oblivious, or unwilling to acknowledge it, Ezra clutches me tighter, holding my hand like I might drift away. He pulls me closer and slides an arm around my shoulder, propelling me farther up the path we're on.

I have to tell you something, I say as we move through the forest. *I bet on you last winter and I've never regretted it. I need you to know that. I don't care what the Ancients think or want. If they want me, ever, in this world or on Earth, they'll have to accept 'us.' I love you. I will always love you. No matter what happens.*

Ezra looks away. *I'm a mutt, Ruby. And you're more than just a True. Here in Ottomundo, you're like . . . like if Jesus had a baby with Mother Theresa.*

I laugh out loud, then palm my mouth, fending off the hysterical giggles crawling up my throat. *Are you saying the Ancients are elitist?* I bite my lip. *Anyway, Jesus, really? I'm Jewish, Ezra. And Mick is, like, god of the UNDERWORLD. Doesn't that make me more like Satan's daughter?*

His beautiful eyes narrow. *It's not funny.*

But it is. It's sooooo funny. It's like you're saying the Otherworld is classist or racist or something. How am I even supposed to care about my 'place' or 'station' or stupid arbitrary rules when everything is so freaking absurd?

Ezra's body is wound so tight I see the tremor that moves through him. *I worry it's not in the cards for us.*

Do you love me?

You know I do.

Then I don't care what the 'cards' say. Because there's also this little thing you keep telling me about called 'free will.'

He shoves a hand in his pocket, smiling forlornly as his posture dips with his mood. His eyes trace my face, searching for something, and I see his truth in the set of his mouth; he really doesn't believe I'm going home.

CHAPTER THIRTY-SIX

THE ONLY CERTAIN THING

UP AHEAD THROUGH THE TREES, the plateau comes into view. My plateau, but not really. The rings of logs and boulders that surround the ruin are much tighter here, and they look molten, shining like gems in the now very dark night.

"Where's the light coming from?" Angel asks, looking up at the black sky.

"It looks like the ruin is actually glowing," Racine whispers.

Ashley stops short, tilting her head sideways like a puppy. "So pretty."

Ezra waves us into the clearing. In the center, I drop against a wall, standing limply. Every part of me aches, especially my feet. If I'd known we were going to walk a thousand miles, I would have worn tennis shoes to my party. "Why is the ruin still here on this side?" I look up at him. "I mean, if Lee destroyed it on the other side."

Ezra shrugs. "My guess is the gate's gone, not the ruin."

Closing my eyes, I sit down on the altar, sensitive to my surroundings, waiting for the ruin to hum, or somehow magnetize me. Just in case, I hold my breath and concentrate, thinking about the bag of Cheetos I left on the counter in the kitchen, digging my ragged fingernails into my palms. The altar feels cold against my bare calves, and the cold seeps over my skin, spreading down my thighs to my ankles. I feel like a weed, like I'm all stems rooted to the earth. And for a moment, I'm just another adobe block speckled with micaceous clay, eroding but still shiny. I *am* the ruin. And I don't want to leave it, even if it means staying here in the Otherworld.

"Ruby," Ezra says softly, snapping his fingers near my face, "stay with me."

I open my eyes and smile at him, groggily taking in my friends' worried faces.

"Ruby!" he says more forcefully. "Look at me."

I just want to sit here.

Baby, we can't. We have to get to Azcale.

"Come on," he says out loud, holding his hand out.

I stand and take it, and he walks me off toward the ruin's periphery, peeking through the trees. "Azcale's that way down the mountain but on the other side, right?"

"I think so."

We walk back to the group, and Ezra drops his hands on my shoulders, turning me to stare into my eyes. But he addresses Angel, asking him to watch over us while Ezra treks out to the precipice. Asking him to keep an eye on *me* especially. I hear him, but it's like he's talking on the other side of a wall. Like I'm not really a person, but a drum bouncing sound off its surface.

Angel nods and Ezra becomes a blur, shifting in less than the time between my next few heartbeats. Marta gasps, plunking down wordlessly on the ground near a ruin wall. She shakes her head just as Ashley squeaks, "This is the weirdest freaking day ever."

Angel sits down on a boulder beside me. He leans into my shoulder. "He'll be okay. We'll all be okay," he says as I stare off after Ezra.

"I am not okay." I shake my head slowly.

"But you will be," he promises. Angel holds his hands out, palms up. They're cupped, and somehow, glowing. "Let me be your light."

The glow is mesmerizing, and I stare at him wide-eyed, unsure if the ruin is playing tricks on me. "How?"

"Otherworld perks of being half-immortal?" He shrugs. "It's like the air is charged and I somehow just knew to draw on it. Can't you feel it?"

I do, actually, like static traveling over my unsure skin. "I thought it was just me, because," I hold out my shimmering arms, "this. Angel, how are you so okay with everything?"

"You, Ezra, Mick—you all broke the mold. This only seems weird relative to a world that's normal. And nothing's really normal anymore, is it?"

Racine walks over. She wraps an arm around Angel's free shoulder and tilts closer, tucking us all into a private little hemisphere. "You show her your hands?"

"Yup."

"I'm dating a superhero."

I look to Angel, biting back a genuine laugh. Racine is always *everything* I need. "You told her about us?"

"Before graduation."

"He asked me not to say anything," she smiles apologetically.

"Marta and Ashley?"

"After we got here."

I nod, feeling weird Marta knows he's my brother. Especially because she hasn't said anything. "Ezra and I can communicate telepathically. I guess it makes sense you can mind light the Otherworld."

"Mind light," Angel snorts.

"So not fair I'm all human right now," Racine titters.

Angel stares at me for a beat. His gaze is steady and calm, but I know he's thinking about what Ezra said back on the prairie. That I'm in spirit flux. I can't read his mind, but there's something about our connection, that here, at least, has fine-honed my intuition where he's concerned.

"Live for today, hope for tomorrow," he says, as if he feels it too. "Hope is a powerful thing. And it's stopped you from giving up for as long as I've known you."

My smile is genuine, and it comes from my heart. But my brain is such an ass. Angel mentions hope, and I can't help thinking about how hope feels like an irrational attempt to justify ignoring the obvious. That if you strip it away, underneath are cold facts; I'm probably dead. Lee is in charge. This place is my life now.

"Have faith, Ruby." Racine closes our little circle with her other arm, pulling us into a loose hug. She wipes a tear off my cheek. "You believed in this place, and Ezra, and that you were communicating with your mom when no one else believed you. This can't be real, right? But it is. You were spot on." She shakes her head. "None of us really know squat right now. But we have each other. And we believe in you and Ezra. Trust us, and we'll trust you. We'll stay together until we *all* find a way out. No one's leaving *anyone* behind."

"Except Marta," I murmur.

"*All* of us," she says firmly.

As she pulls us into a tighter hug, Ezra bounds out of the trees, shifting when he comes to a skidding halt. He's electrically charged, and the air around him bumps off sparks that make Ashley jump. Drawn by her movement, a slew of bluish-white flecks swirl over to her, and around her, weaving around her arms and shoulders.

"Whoa!" She twirls around, trying to flap them away.

"Hitchhikers. I noticed them everywhere when I shifted to track Ruby. They're drawn to the charge. I think they're pixies," Ezra tells her.

Ashley's eyebrows meet her hairline. "Like sprites, or fairies?"

"I don't know. More like sprites?" He shakes his head. "I think they're pretty benign."

Ezra is full of electrical energy I literally feel bouncing off of my skin. He takes a moment, bending at the waist, resting his hands on his thighs. "I ran the perimeter of the canyon," he exhales. "Far as I can tell it just doesn't end."

"So there's no way across?"

"No. There's more," he says, standing up straighter. "It's a mirage."

"The city?" I ask.

"The canyon. The precipice. I threw a rock out over the ledge. The canyon disappeared when the rock hit ground. Like a layer over another layer. Like a mirage. It didn't last long, but I took a chance and walked out. It's solid ground across the canyon. And it stayed solid, like a bubble around me."

"Wow." Marta narrows an eye at him. "So, like camouflage."

"Exactly."

"Like even here in the Otherworld someone is trying to hide Azcale," Angel says.

Ezra eyes me. *He has a point.* "I guess, think of the Otherworld like another layer, draped over Earth, hidden from our eyes. The gate doesn't send you to a different place exactly, it's just more of a crossing point between our two worlds. It's probably why this," he points out at the plateau, "looks a bit like our mountain. My guess is, Lee and Mick could see it, both worlds at the same time, all worlds, really. No reason to think it'd be any different here. Maybe I just caught a glimpse of it because . . ." He shakes his head.

"Because you're a Watcher," I finish for him. "You see what's hidden."

"I didn't on our side," he nods toward the center of the ruin.

"That's not true. You see everything that comes through the gate. Maybe you're wired to see the Otherworld."

"I didn't catch Mick," he says pointedly.

"Yeah, but he's a god," I remind him.

Ezra looks thoughtful. "You trust me enough to cross it?"

"I trust you enough to anything." I bite my lip, looking around at my friends' still-astonished faces. They look the way I feel. Like they're about to buckle under the same giant wave of fatigue. "But can we rest first? Just for a little bit. Maybe huddle up here for an hour before we head out?"

"An hour?" Marta pulls her phone out and shakes her head at the dead screen. "I have no idea how long ago we came through, but it feels like we've been here for days already."

Ezra taps his watch face. "It's still ticking. Best I can tell, it's on track. It's been about three hours since we ran into you. And Ruby's right, you all look like you could use it. I'll keep an eye out while you hunker down."

Not long though. He looks at me. *We need to keep moving.*

"This place," Racine swallows, searching for a patch of ground that isn't covered by what looks like barbed-wire moss to stretch out over, "it makes no sense. How can *this* be where everything goes after we die?"

"It doesn't make sense to *you*," Ezra answers.

Marta raises her hand. "Um, me neither," she frowns, settling down over a patch of glittery dirt against a wall.

"Think of it like a train station," Ezra tells them. "Only the Council and monarchs of the Upper and Underworlds live here permanently. But everyone . . . *everything* in the universe starts and ends here. The Council just decides where to place us in the universe and in what form."

If I only had a camera. Racine's jaw nearly hits the ground. Even Marta, for once, looks baffled. "An alternate universe," she hums.

"That's one way to put it."

Angel cocks his head thoughtfully. "I'll bet it's more that *we* don't make sense here."

Marta shoots him a look. "Story of my life."

Hearing her say it surprises me. Marta is normally overly confident. But right now, she almost sounds sad. And for the first time ever, she looks a little vulnerable. Not that I blame her. A psychopath would probably still question her own existence here in the Otherworld.

"What?" She snaps at me. "You think you're the only one here who feels alienated, or like you don't fit in?" She rolls her eyes. "It's not like I don't know ya'll wish I'd disappear sometimes."

Racine shakes her head vehemently. "I don't want you to disappear. We've been friends since kindergarten. I just wish you'd be nicer."

Marta looks straight at me. "She does."

"Actually, I always wished we got along," I admit. "And I hate that you think I'm trying to one-up you. I mean, I get it, but I'm not. I'm sorry if I come off that way."

Marta frowns before looking out at the plateau. "You know my dad had an accident a couple months before you moved here,

Ruby." She says it and everyone nods. "He was in the hospital for a few weeks. Mom and Dad told everyone a semi ran him off the road, but the truth is, he was drunk—like really freaking drunk. He ran into the truck coming back from a bar in Santa Fe, and in the process, forced a car full of kids off the road. Two of them were in the hospital for a month."

Racine's jaw drops. She stares at Marta, bewildered. Ashley looks down at the dirt, and something about the way she bites her lip, worrying it back and forth under an incisor, tells me she already knows the real story. But Angel especially looks mortified. "That's why Torrance won't talk to me about it. *El debe saber. Jesus, Marta, lo siento mucho.*"

She nods. "Thanks. Dad's a mess. When he left afterwards, Mom told everyone he went to go visit Cousin Roberto in Juárez, but that wasn't true. He served sixty days in the Sandoval County Jail. Mom made me promise not to tell anyone. Which was fine at the time, because I was so flipping ashamed of him." She shakes her head at Angel. "Mom doesn't want you to know, so please don't say I told you. And Dad's been a real flipping gem since getting out. She can't get him to go to rehab, even though he clearly needs it." Marta chews on her left cheek, frowning at the ground before looking at me. "And then you showed up, with your stupid face, acting like you're somehow too enlightened to care about things like how you look, or dudes, or whatever, and all your shitloads of problems, and it's like you're *all* anyone cared about anymore. And you just drank it up. So self-centered. You really piss me off, Ruby."

Instinctively, I clench my fists, stopping myself from touching my cheek to check for the tears I know are about to fall. My feelings toward Marta have never been positive; I just always assumed she came out of the womb bitching at people. But I never tried to be better, better *around* her, better friends *with* her, to understand her at all. In that way, I totally proved her right. *She* was the rotten egg, but I'm just as bad.

"I'm so sorry," I say softly. And I really am.

"Well, I don't accept your apology," she answers brusquely. "But," she nods to the ruin, "at least I get it now."

Everyone is way too quiet for way too long. It's uncomfortable, and I know we're all thinking the same thing. How did we miss all that pain? And I know we're all thinking the same answer. Because it's easier than anyone wants to admit to get too wrapped up in our own lives. Case in point. Here I am.

Racine and Angel move closer to Marta, huddling around her on the ground. Racine looks over her shoulder at me, cocking her head to let me know we're also invited. But I don't move away from the wall; instead, I nod at her and try to smile, hoping she gets that as bad as I feel, and as much as I'd like to be there for Marta right now, I know Marta doesn't feel the same way. And I totally understand that. She doesn't want my sympathy. *I* broke up her moral support circle. I am part of the reason she felt so hurt for so long, and not for any of the reasons I thought. She needs Las Gallinas right now, not someone she considers an outsider. I know this because if I were in her shoes, I'd feel the exact same way.

"Ash?" I say, when Ashley doesn't make a move to join Marta's circle.

Ashley groans, staring between her arms. A few remaining blue sparks hover around her like fireflies, intermittently lighting the night. "They're freaking me out."

"Come here," Marta demands.

Stiffly, Ashley shuffles over to their half-circle. Marta reaches up, pulling Ashley by the wrist down beside her. As Ashley sits,

Marta swats at the tiny lights, scooting up to Ashley's side when they scatter. "Assholes."

"They're kind of pretty, though, right?"

Marta simultaneously shakes her head and rolls her eyes. "Yeah, Ash. Super pretty."

I bite my tongue. Marta has good reasons for being so prickly, but I'm guessing that even before her dad's accident, she wasn't all sunshine and flowers. Even knowing what I know now, no doubt we're going to have to work to find some middle ground. But it's a small price to pay for going home and starting over.

Sticking by me, Ezra drops down at my side, sprawling his legs out lengthwise. His warm body radiates heat, and I tuck into it gratefully. "I'll keep watch." *Rest, Ruby. You're safe for now.*

Angel turns sideways, positioning himself so he can see both Las Gallinas and the edge of the ruin. He looks over his shoulder at Ezra. "Me too. There's no way I'm sleeping right now."

"Suit yourself." Ezra shrugs.

He props his head back against the ruin and gazes up at the sky, mesmerized by a shooting purple star that suddenly lights the night. I watch his eyes change colors, and his mouth twitch as I drift off. Then I close my eyes. His heartbeat is forceful and commanding, and I feel it thumping through his t-shirt, and feeling it both soothes and unnerves me. It reminds me that he's built like a tank, but also, like all of us, that he's fragile on the inside.

CHAPTER THIRTY-SEVEN

QUE SERA, SERA

RUBY, WAKE UP!

Ezra nudges my shoulder, rousing me from his lap where my head has apparently nested. Sticks cling to the clumps of hair that roosted next to his hip on the ground, grazing my face as I sit up quickly. I pry my eyelids open, pulling my dry lips apart at the same time. "I'm really thirsty."

Ruby. His voice is authoritative, but his tone is urgent. *Get up!*

The crisp scent of apples waft with the breeze through the forest, mixing with the charged smell of electricity. Overhead, the now-brilliant, orange-streaked sky radiates heat, hovering over the forest like a coiled burner. Disoriented, both my skin and eyes sting. "It smells like apple pie," I mumble. "My stomach's growling."

Ezra wraps an arm around my waist, yanking me up. When I shriek, he backs me against the ruin wall, sheltering me with his body. I grab at his shirt, steadying my balance.

Look!

Rubbing my eyes, I try to clear the dust that's settled in my lashes, smearing away sleep and grime. Across the clearing, near a stand of trees, Lee comes into focus. Except it isn't Lee, exactly. Next to an outcropping of sparkling boulders, an enormous jaguar stands on all fours. He whips his tail from side to side, his irradiant eyes fixed on us, patiently immobile.

It's Lee's nagual. I tell Ezra. *He's only half here. I feel it; his attention is divided.*

Fidgeting with the bells at my wrist, I wiggle a finger under the strand and yank, trying again to pry the stupid thing off me. I look down at my hand, and in the few seconds my eyes leave Lee, he flies across the clearing.

"What the . . ." Angel shoots up just as Ezra shifts and runs toward Lee.

They meet in the middle, hitting the ground in a tangle, snarling loud enough to hurt my ears. Physically, Lee may only be half here, but it clearly doesn't matter how materially he's grounded to the space around us, because he's also all over Ezra.

Ashley shrieks, and Angel quickly strides toward me. I stare between him and Ezra and catch Marta and Racine in my periphery. They nearly simultaneously cross themselves, each muttering, "*En el nombre del padre, el hijo, y el espiritu santo*" in unison.

Ezra struggles with Lee, kicking up dust that hovers on the outskirts of the clearing like a curtain dividing the ruin and the rest of the plateau. Dirty, confetti-like particles hang in the air, forming miniature dirt devils that dance about frenetically, sullying any clear view we might have of the forest. Their growling skirmish takes them from one side of the clearing to the other, and while I stand near the ruin wall, frozen and wracked with fear, the dust turns to rust, mixing with the orange sky. Until I lose sight of them completely.

Ezra! Instinctively dashing toward the rusty cloud, I grab a softball-sized rock, prepared to chuck it at Lee. I'm maybe two seconds from reaching the middle of the clearing when someone grabs my shoulder, stopping me mid-stride.

Run for the canyon!

I jerk sideways, astonished to see an amorphous figure at my back, fading in and out of focus.

Run! Now! And don't stop until you've crossed over into the divide.

I stare at my mom, startled and a little bit disoriented. "Not without Ezra!"

Go! I'll make sure he follows! Mom roars, and the cloud in front of me dissipates, reintroducing me to Lee and Ezra, still locked in battle.

Mom's eyes blaze as Lee catches sight of her and breaks free from Ezra, dashing directly for us. Ezra follows, jumping on Lee's back, swiping at him with an enormous paw that rips a bloody gouge down Lee's side. As they tussle, Mom grabs my wrist and yanks; I feel a snap and hear the delicate sound of tiny bells hitting the dirt. Quicker than lightning, she swoops the bracelet up off the ground, fading to nothing as Lee starts to shimmer.

"Run!" I yell at Angel and Las Gallinas. I don't have to shout twice. They're already at my side as I pitch to my left, pointing forward. "Go. That way. Head straight and keep running until it looks like you can't anymore." I have to trust that Lee is more apparition than solid entity, and that without the bracelet he can't track me. I have to trust Ezra *will* follow.

Angel takes the lead, and I run until my lungs and eyes burn, barely seeing the oddities we pass along the way. But I do notice the sky. The sky is like a melted scoop of rainbow sherbet, and the forest blends with a green-hued layer of air in the lower atmosphere, distorting the path ahead. The trees around us morph into a greenish brown blob, and when the forest gets too thick, we stop, stymied by what looks like one gigantic, never-ending wall.

Angel stops beside me, turning in a full circle. "Keep going?"

"I think so."

"Into that?" Ashley asks with a shudder, pointing forward.

The forest looked different earlier, but I see a cairn I built up ahead, so I know we're still going in the right direction. "It's an illusion. Just a trick of light. Look," I point to the cairn, "I've been through here already."

Marta bends over, resting her crossed arms on her knees as she looks up at me. "I don't think I can run anymore." She points down at her shoes, grimacing. "Heels."

"We're close," I reassure her, looking behind us for some sign Lee followed. "But let's fast walk the rest. Because I'm totally with you."

Angel holds out a hand toward Marta. "Give me your shoes. You too, Ashley."

Marta shrugs inquiringly, but she slips them off without argument and hands them over, followed by Ashley.

"Freaking pumps," Angel mutters as he snaps the heels off of each of them.

Ashley looks crestfallen when Angel hands her back her now heel-less sandals, but Marta actually thanks him. Together, we walk hurriedly in a close huddle, heading into the space where the forest morphs into a wall of tree and sky. The border is physical, yet lucent, and as soon as we walk through it, everything changes. Cool air permeates the space between trees that seem strung together, as if many parts of a whole. Everything in the forest looks like it's connected by ethereal threads. They snap apart when we walk through them, joining again behind us. It's blurry and defined all at the same time, and feels like walking through cobwebs.

We move silently, too freaked out to do more than look at each other. I don't even let myself think about my mother, and how she just helped us. I can't even go there without feeling like someone threw me over a boat tied to an anvil.

Angel stops again, throwing his hand out in the direction we're heading. Suddenly, the air in front of us melts into a translucent tube, as though dissolving. A pathway forms, shimmering at its sculpted edges; like a reality tunnel through an enchanted forest.

"You?" I turn to stare at Angel. At his hand.

"I don't even know how I'm doing it," he marvels.

"Angel," I exhale, "you're magic."

He shoots me a lopsided grin. "Yeah, but we already knew that, right?"

"Baby," Racine says breathily. She glances between us. "You really are siblings, aren't you?" She steps closer to him, pressing up against him as she stands on her tiptoes to kiss him. "Amazing."

Angel drops his hand and winds it around Racine along with his other, pulling her into a hug. And the tunnel stays open. He kisses her quickly, looking down into her eyes for seconds before breaking away. When I nod toward the tunnel, he taps his head. The same way Ezra did when we first discovered we could talk to each other without speaking.

Seeing Angel so smitten with Racine makes me happy. But it also makes me sad. Because here we are again, the five of us together, without Ezra.

CHAPTER THIRTY-EIGHT

MAGIC BEANS AND PIXIE DUST

UP AHEAD, A LIGHT SHINES through a stand of thick tree trunks, blurring the edge of the forest into a prism that sparkles like diamonds. We rush toward it, quickening the pace until we're running again, until we rush out onto a plateau on the other side. Everyone comes to a sudden stop behind me on a thin strip of rocky land. There isn't a whole lot of topography separating the forest and the edge of the mountain, which is littered with aquamarine lichen. It emits thin wisps of smoke that shrouds the plateau, surrounding us in a diaphanous but shadowy teal cloud.

We cut a pathway across the mesa, following each other in a snaking line through gaps in the mist. At the canyon's edge, a thunderous roar shakes the ground, and I stop short, breathlessly waiting for more. Mick blinks into existence near the tree line, as tall as the oddly shaped conifers surrounding the cliff. Behind him, Ezra lopes out from the forest. He runs straight for us as he shifts, pulling me into a desperate hug. "Sera used the bracelet to lure Lee's nagual away. But it won't last long. We have to keep moving."

Holding on to Ezra, I stare up at Mick. He looms over the plateau along with wispy licks of smoke, spreading out like a sail with each windy gust that passes through.

Ezra's right. Mick lifts an arm and points at the canyon. *Physically, Lee's still in Mictlān's bowels, rallying allies. Sera only bound his nagual. If you don't hurry, he'll find you. The other gates are too far. You must cross over to Azcale before Lee or Awonawilona discover where you are.* His voice resonates clear as a bell, echoing over the plateau, but his mouth is static.

"Awonawilona . . . the creator?" Ezra asks uneasily.

"Other gates?" I gasp. Of course. One little gate couldn't possibly traffic all of Earth's people. "Are there other Trues?"

Twelve. But you are the only master key the universe possesses. Mick focuses his intense gaze on Ezra. *The journey across is longer than it looks. But at the end you'll find the entrance to your Pecos Circle. Azcale. The thirteenth realm. And your clan's final kingdom. Only once you cross, you'll need to destroy the bridge for good. Lee cannot be allowed to merge our two realms on Earth.*

Ezra locks my hand in a vise grip, inhaling to steady his breath. Outwardly, he looks calm, but pressed up against me I feel the air leave his chest in jerky spurts. He stands up straighter, grappling with Mick's revelation.

"Azcale belongs to Shiankya?"

Shiankya have always guarded the bridge that separates Earth and Ottomundo. It's the thirteenth of your Pecos Circle's twenty-three worlds. The only permanent settlement outside of the Council and the Underworld here in Ottomundo. Mick's gaze moves over all the faces in our circle, coming back full stop to land on me and Ezra. *Until you, Ruby, Azcale lacked a key to unite our worlds. I obviously understand forbidden love. But you must see why liaisons between*

Watchers and Trues are forbidden. United, you have the potential to unleash Mictlān on Earth.

"Why can't you destroy the bridge?" I ask him.

Azcale is a forbidden city. The only way in or out from this realm is with a key. You.

"Did, did you love her?" I whisper. "My mom?"

I was reckless. Mick says quietly. *I didn't know Sera was a True until it was too late.*

"But did you love her?"

Yes, Ruby. I still do.

"Then why are Ezra and I any different?"

This, right now—this potential for catastrophe. It's why the Council closed Earth to all gods eons ago. And it's why Trues and Watchers have always been forbidden.

I stare out at the canyon, almost afraid to look up at him again. No matter what he says, no matter how it all plays out, I already know I'll never leave Ezra—not in Ottomundo or on Earth. "And what do we do when we get there?"

I'll do what I can from Mictlān to fend Lee off. But know that the canyon isn't stable. It changes by the hour; a device devised by the Council meant to keep all but Shiankya out of Azcale. You'll have to follow your intuition. Once you've reached Azcale, I've appointed an emissary. Someone who understands the gate and its mechanisms. He knows you're coming. He knows to look for you. Mick nods down at us. *Stick together. You must get them back and destroy the bridge before Lee finds you.*

Beside me, Ezra is so still. But I know his mind, and I know what he's thinking about without digging around for confirmation. Mick said *them*. Just like Ezra did earlier.

I take a deep breath and meet Mick's eyes. "Am I dead?"

Mick's stare is like a dagger through my heart. *Lee bound you and Ezra both. You crossed over corporally. Because of that I can't judge you here. And your mother can't bind you and take you back to Mictlān to be weighed as bidden. Your souls are in flux. But your soul especially, Ruby, because you're mine—it's drawn to the Underworld. It will have to decide where it belongs, ultimately.*

"And me?" Angel asks, too calm to be as composed as he appears.

Mick turns to him and my heart aches. It's the first time Mick's addressed him directly. *You,* he says carefully, *are formidable. You'll have a place here, one day. In my kingdom. When you're of this world permanently. But I cannot acknowledge you until then, except to promise you that you are exceptional. The Ancients only know Ruby because of Sera. They do not know of you. A halfling. And I won't risk it.*

"So, it's true," Angel exhales. "We're the devil's spawn."

Mick's surprising laugh rumbles the forest, shaking the ground. I grasp Ezra's arm, reeling as Mick speaks again. *I'm many things. Massau, Yama, Hades, Whiro, Satan. On Earth, as on all planes, I am to you what your people make of me.* His intense eyes blaze again, washing the plateau in emerald light. *Now, you must go.*

In a heartbeat, Mick sputters out like a quenched flame, leaving us standing on the plateau, grappling with half-answers and an unfamiliar reality. Cross the canyon. The path to the Pecos Circle. To Azcale. Aztlán. Without any clue as to what lies ahead in the divide.

I look out at it and shudder.

Ezra squeezes my hand, and together we step closer to the edge, looking over what appears to be a drop off. Angel and Racine step up beside me, waiting for my lead, and the rest of Las Gallinas follow.

We have to go first. To show them. But I promise you, Ruby, I'll never leave your side.

After a moment, I turn to face him. “I won’t either.”

My heart contracts, refusing to beat for a moment before skipping back into a frenzied rhythm. Scanning my friends’ worried faces, I am terrified. But I’m also hopeful. I’m with my family. And from Racine’s own mouth, no one is leaving anyone’s ass behind.

Looking at them all, I nod. Then, take another step forward.

ACKNOWLEDGEMENTS

I had a lot of fun writing this second book in the Wild and Ruin trilogy; Ruby really guided me throughout and we're both looking forward to the upcoming last installment in her journey. But that wouldn't be true if I didn't know ya'll were out there reading. Readers are everything, so I'm thanking you first and foremost, because without all of you this book wouldn't exist. I am eternally grateful for your support, reviews, shout-outs, and interest.

Many thanks also to everyone who helped make *Wild Open Faces* possible. Greg Wagner, whose faith in my writing and never-ending love and backing mean everything to me. Alexandra O'Connell, who once again helped me turn a bunch of messy pages into a polished, more cohesive, kick-ass story. Estella Vukovic, for her incredible, artistic eye and beautiful book covers. Susan and Carolyn Huber, the finest beta-readers/armchair proofreaders/ friends on the planet. My beloved writing group, especially Patrick Lee and Susan Bryant, whose friendship, feedback, and support is incalculable and even more appreciated. Melissa Mendonca and Stef Willen, who listen to me bitch and groan ad nauseum and still give me thoughtful feedback, never walk out on coffee, and still want to be my friends (lucky me). Margaret Marinoff, Shoshanna Bettencourt, Dondra Bowden, and Maria Virobik-Lee, whose friendships and faces make me smile on the regular. And Marty Kinrose, whose advocacy, support, and love have kind of floored me—I aspire to be you, cuzzie!

Elijah and Gabriel, you are the best of the best and a big part of the magic that inspires me to keep writing. Tamar and Abe, aka Mom and Dad, though thank you is not a strong enough set of words to show my appreciation for encouraging me to stick with it, and for supporting all my varied creative whims and 'good ideas', thank you, thank you, thank you. Tamar especially, for reading Every. Single. Draft. Of everything I've ever written. And for spending countless hours letting me run ideas by you. Libby Edelson, for all the everythings that have made my life what it is—there's not enough space here to list them without writing another book—and of course, for Wilder and Lake, whose very existences have brought joy to my life while I finished up the last of *Wild Open Faces* through some pretty dark moments (because, 2020).

Thank you also to my internet writing groups and peeps, and all the other writers out there who've passed *Between Wild and Ruin* along and/or helped me out with kind suggestions, posts, reviews, and comments. Writers are the best people. It never escapes me that you've taken unbidden time out of your own busy writing schedules to help a fellow writer.

ABOUT THE AUTHOR

Jennifer G. Edelson is a writer, trained artist, former attorney, pizza lover, and hard-core Bollywood fan. She has a B.A. in Fine Arts and a J.D. in law and has taught both creative writing and legal research and writing at several fine institutions, including the University of Minnesota. Originally a California native, she currently resides in Santa Fe, New Mexico, with her husband, kids, and dog, Hubble after surviving twenty-plus years in the Minnesota tundra. Other than writing, Jennifer loves hiking, traveling, Albert Camus, Dr. Seuss, dark chocolate, coffee, and meeting new people—if you're human (or otherwise), odds are she'll probably love you.

For more information, please visit Jennifer at www.
JenniferGEdelson.com

All comments, mail and inquiries, including book-club requests,
speaking engagements, and book signing inquiries maybe
addressed to Badapplebooksinfo@gmail.com.

Made in the USA
Middletown, DE
29 January 2021

32537423R00208